DRAIGON WEATHER

DRAIGON WEATHER

PAIGE L. CHRISTIE

PROSPECTIVE PRESS
Winston-Salem

7/10/17
To Jillian—
Enjoy Hang w/ the Draigon.
the journey

PROSPECTIVE PRESS LLC

1959 Peace Haven Rd, #246, Winston-Salem, NC 27106 U.S.A.
www.prospectivepress.com

Published in the United States of America by PROSPECTIVE PRESS LLC

↑ TRADEMARK

DRAIGON WEATHER

Library of Congress Control Number: 2017934695

ISBN 978-1-943419-42-5

First PROSPECTIVE PRESS hardcover edition

Printed in the United States of America
Second printing, May, 2017

3 5 7 9 10 8 6 4 2

The text of this book is typeset in Athelas
Accent text is typeset in Scurlock

Thanks are Given to The Following Amazing People

Patti K. Christie: World's Greatest Mama: For books, and stories, and laughter, and dance. For loving life, and making the most of all the little things. For good food, and good cries. For hugs, and bad jokes. For history, and ancestry, and never minding that your eldest daughter was completely nutty.

Larry Norman: Partner and Friend for the last 18 years: For putting up with me pounding out words every night for weeks on end. (It actually turned into something!) For red wine, good eating, bicycles, and road trips. For loving Kittehs and Hunds as much as me. For never telling me I was crazy for doing this.

Heidi Broomhall: My Oldest Partner in Literary Crime: For 30 years of trading wax, lawn mowers, and epic angst. The story never ends.

Michelle & David Larsen: Old Friends, Big Hearts and fellow Hard Working Dreamers: For smart conversation, good food and wine, couches to crash on, and endless support.

Ellen Morrissey: Dance Partner, Writing Partner and Dear Friend: For dragging me kicking and screaming onto this journey with you, and never doubting that I could do it. My story is better for your thoughts, love and patience. (I'm so not sorry about your fingernails.)

Rebecca Sanchez Hefner: Writing Buddy, Fellow Eater of Chocolate, and Skilled Wordsmith. For always encouraging me, and being there at all hours. It's good to have 'writing peeps'.

Jennifer "Clyde" Webster: Supreme Benevolent Dictator of the Universe, fellow Keeper of The Green Ford Beast Memories: For not going to Kansas without me. For bringing the choe hoe. For telling me when the words were crap. For late nights with Oreos and The Chocolate Society.

Lucia Owen: High School English Teacher Extraordinaire: For teaching me the true power of the written word. And for using Wordsworth and Star Wars in the same lesson.

Robin McKinley: a Heroine in My Personal Story: For coming to visit Gould Academy and planting an image in my mind of a fun and funky writer, doing things her own way.

Deborah Shea: College Adviser and Mentor: For teaching me critical assessment skills and never giving up on my writing, even when my genre choices made your head spin.

Raquel Moore: My Puerto Rican Goddess: For more misadventures than numbers can count. For loving sparkly paint, loud music and long bike rides.

Mahsati Janan: Dance Yoda and Friend: For keeping my creativity flowing on many levels, and never saying it can't be done.

To My Mother—Patti K. Christie

DRAIGON
WEATHER

How should we be able to forget
those ancient myths that
are at the beginning of all peoples,
the myths about dragons that
at the last moment
turn into princesses...
So you must not be frightened if
a sadness rises up before you
larger than any you have ever seen;
if a restiveness,
like light and cloudshadows,
passes over your hands and over all you do...
For after all,
you do not know what work
these conditions are doing inside you.

~Rainer Marie Rilke

The man who fights
too long against dragons
becomes a dragon himself.

~Friedrich Nietzsche

1

Cleod – 38 years – Autumn, 1195

C LEOD TIPPED HIS HEAD, LETTING THE SLOPED BRIM OF HIS HAT BLOCK THE WIND gusting over the cracked ground. The big, grey gelding shifted beneath him. Sand and debris swirled, twisting into towers that rocked and buffeted, before collapsing back into the earth.

Narrowing his eyes against the blowing grit, Cleod pushed the brekko covering his nose and mouth tighter against his cheeks, glad that the tight-woven cloth of the desert traders made an effective filter against the worst of the sand. Still, dust pushed into the fine lines around his eyes. He pressed the back of his hand against them, seeking a moment of respite, but the gesture brought little relief. His gloves, like the rest of his canvas clothing, were coated in the gold-brown silt so thick that their color was lost under it.

When the gust passed, he dismounted, gave the gelding a pat on the shoulder, and crouched to examine the ground. "Well, Kicce," he said to the horse, "this changes things." The grass around them rustled harsh in the wind. It crumbled at his touch; so, too, did the soil he bent to pick up. The whisper of the sand falling through his gloved fingers echoed in his mind, brushed at memories he had long tried to contain.

He squinted into the once lush river valley. Many years ago, he had arrived at this spot for the first time. Then, he had been so stunned by the beauty before him—the staggering push of the great river, the shadow-like rise of mountains in the distance—that had all the wealth of the court at Sibora been laid at his feet, even it would not have inspired the awe of the view before him. That had remained true on every subsequent trip on this trail. But now, the change before him made it hard to draw full breath. Where the great valley usually offered grand welcome—the river-carved plain spreading like arms opened to offer an embrace to a new-crowned King—lay now, instead, only devastation. The Seebo, mightiest waterway in the eastern regions, had been reduced from its normal triple-bow-shot width, to a slender glint of silver in a deep gully of dark mud. Trees stood half-dead, canted by wind and smeared with dust along the crumbling edge of the riverbank.

Blackened and burned, the ruins of the ferryman's house stood on what had been the riverside. Not far from it, the ferry itself tilted on end, down the steep bank into the mudflat that had replaced the riverbed. Many an evening had he and Kilras and the rest of the caravan scouts spent dining with the ferryman, Semmio, and Ejor, his wife. Where had they gone? West to Melbis perhaps? Let them be safe.

Cleod's heart tightened in his chest and he took a breath, trying to ease it. In all his years of criss-crossing Arnan, he had rarely witnessed such a change in a familiar landscape that did not involve a mudslide or an earth-shift. Even the wreckage of terrible floods, wrought by a Wing Wave along the northwest coast, had not unnerved him as much as the sight before him. He shook his head, not wanting to acknowledge the truth that had been creeping up on him for days.

Though two days ride west the farmlands were lush with crops awaiting the coming harvest, he had seen signs of drought for weeks. The memorial gardens that bordered the Inns of Sibora were ill-tended or dead. The meats served in the taverns were gristly and tasteless. Baths were hard to come by. Livestock herds were small in number and thin on the hoof. And the price of a night's lodging was double last year's stay, even for a bunk-house, or pasture for the caravan's herd. But the fields—the vital fields that supplied grain to half of all Arnan—those were lush and green. Irrigation, he thought. And here before him was the price of those healthy stalks. So, there would be food this year. Food for the winter. But next year...? What would the summer bring? Unless something was done to force a change in the weather... Cleod let the thought drift into nothingness and he shook himself a little.

He rose from his crouch, shrugging his shoulders to resettle the sword harness slung across them. "Kilras won't be pleased." he said to Kicce. Kilras was the best Dorn in Arnan, but the trail lead would need all his cleverness to get the caravan through the wasteland below. Cleod shook his head. "Or prepared, any more than we were for this sight. So much for the difficulties of a water crossing. We're not so skilled at negotiating inland mudflats or steep drops into dry river beds." Cleod twisted the reins until the leather straps creased his hand even through the glove. "One problem vanished and four more arisen. Should we mourn the change?"

Kicce shook his head and blew hard, all the answer Cleod could expect. "No. I suppose not," he said. So much to mourn, in weather like this. "Hard times ahead, Kicce. Another day I am glad we live on the trail and not in one place. We'll leave this disaster behind soon enough. Once we find a way through it." He forced lightness into the words, as though speaking with easy conviction would change what lay before him. The tightness in his chest remained. He turned away, swung into the saddle, and reined Kicce around, away from the devastation.

"Running a bit low?" Kilras asked without looking up from the map spread on the tailgate of the lead wagon. "We're fine to cross at the north ferry?"

"I am not certain where we'll cross," Cleod replied, keeping his tone even for the sake of the young scout standing beside the Dorn. Best for he and Kilras to sort the worst of the problem before too many others learned of the situation. At best, the sight of the river would raise fear for the day's crossing. At worst, the true scope for the future horrors presented by the state of the Seebo would send members of the caravan into a panic. Livelihoods and lives would be at stake, now and in the months to come. The most the Dorn could do to hold that trouble at bay would be to plan well for tomorrow and prepare for the fear certain to be roused. "The terrain has...seen some changes."

Kilras looked up, tipped his head the slightest bit, and eyed Cleod for a long moment. He nodded. "Then we had best put this map to use." He turned to the young scout standing beside him. "Rimm—take Cleod's horse while I see if he remembers how to read a map."

Rimm chuckled and came around the wagon to take charge of Kicce. "Well, old man, seems your powers of observation are lacking if you can't figure the best spot to cross a river."

Cleod allowed himself a raised eyebrow as he handed over the gelding's reins. "When your powers are half of mine, you can comment further. Curry him extra. He's had a rough few days."

"Well on my way," Rimm said as he led Kicce away.

Kilras waited until the pair rounded the front of the wagon before turning back to Cleod. "What's wrong?"

Cleod stepped up beside him, took off his hat and set it beside the map. He leaned his hips against the edge of the tailgate, looked along his shoulder at his mentor. "The Seebo's all but dry."

"You mean she's running more than a little low."

"I mean she's all but gone, Kil." Cleod watched the recognition register in Kilras's eyes that the statement was not one made lightly.

"I've never seen anything like it," Cleod spoke low. "The valley is barren. The ferry house has been burned to the foundations. There's no sign of Semmio—looks like they have been gone a while. We could step across what's left of that river. The ferry is sitting on what was the near bank at an angle I doubt a Spur goat could descend. Even once we get the wagons down to the river bottom, I don't know what a two-hundred-year accumulation of half-mud silt will mean for getting anything across."

Kilras pushed his shoulder length hair back with one hand. The grey was more abundant among the dark locks than it had been sixteen years ago when he had pulled Cleod from the bowels of the foulest tavern in the Spur. But the man who wore them was, if anything, tougher and more determined than he had been even then. Cleod shook his head at the memory. Of all the Dorns in Arnan, only Kilras commanded the respect of even the Farlan soldiers. His meticulous planning, and knowledge of every trail in every region throughout the land, would alone have cemented his reputation for competence. His ability to either negotiate or intimidate clear passage for his caravans through even the worst bandit areas had made him famous. He preferred, always, the word to the sword, but his skill in arms was formidable. And when more than formidable was needed... Cleod smiled. That's why he was here.

Kilras tapped the map with a blunt finger. "How close did you get?"

Cleod turned to examine the map. He traced the line of the river and backed away to the low hill that had been his vantage point. "Here. There was no need to get closer. I was afraid Kicce's shoes would spark on a rock and set the whole valley alight. It's brutal out there. There's no ferry left and we're not prepared for what is there. We can't take long making our way through or staying around filling water barrels."

"Make an early run for Melbis?" Kilras shook his head. "That brings its own problems. But, if it's as bad as you say, we'll have no choice." He paused and Cleod could almost feel the turn of the older man's thoughts. "Gather the scouts and go through the animals in the traces. Pick the strongest and most rested. Shift loads for even weight. I don't care who moans about cramped space or property. And confiscate the floor boards from the known smugglers. We'll need them if the mud lies too deep."

"There'll be questions."

"I'll tell the traders. Set the others to work and meet me back here. You'll have to explain what you saw."

"Wern will get ugly," Cleod said. The glass trader had started off reasonable enough, but as the weeks rolled on, he had become more annoying with each passing day. Even good-natured Eurel Woolman had begun to speak snidely behind the other merchant's back.

"We'll be lucky to survive his eruption."

"We can leave him stuck in the mud," Cleod said.

"Him and his fancy boots. We'll take his wagon on to Melbis. Nothing wrong with the man's wares if you leave him out of the mix."

Cleod grinned. "You admire his boots. Perhaps we just leave the man."

Kilras let out a bark of laughter. They had never left behind anyone who employed them, though men like Wern Glassman offered prime temptation to risk their reputation. "Without his boots."

"Wouldn't they be large on you?"

"But the thought is pleasant."

"The most entertaining one I've had in days." Cleod shook his head as he picked up his hat and settled it onto his head. "I'll get started."

"Cleod, I am sure Ejor and Semmio are fine. We'll get through it."

Cleod looked at his feet for a moment, his boots caked from the dry dust of the trail. He raised his eyes and met Kilras's gaze, nodded once. "We always have," he said and turned to his work.

2

Leiel – 9 years – Autumn, 1165

LEIEL SAT ON THE EDGE OF HER BED ON THE FIRST DAY WITHOUT HER MOTHER, and clutched to her chest the book Ilora used to read every night. The sun streamed through the window and across Leiel's back. Birds offered their chaotic bright chatter. The volume in her hands was the only thing in the world she wanted to be real.

Her mother's words to her on the steps of the Tower whispered through Leiel. *"This is only fear, my love, and fear cannot stand if you face it well. I love you. And nothing can take me from you forever."*

Change had twisted Leiel's world, and no day could ever be as safe and comfortable as the ones that had come before this one. Tears slid from the corners of her eyes, for the silence that had greeted her waking and all that it meant. Beyond even the memory of the horrible events of the previous day, the lack of kitchen clatter, of her mother's voice, was a sign that today was different.

Torrin, the blacksmith, had told her it would be like this. That the little things would be the hardest. No songs rose up from the kitchen. There was no laughter shared between her mother and Elda, the cook. Leiel could hear the hammer strike out in the hot shed where Torrin worked the black iron into rings and knives and shoes for the horses.

Other sounds came to her now. The thumping of hooves in the yard must be her brothers, Gial and Klem, leading the animals to morning pasture. A creak of floor boards from the room beneath her was her father shifting at his desk. Had these sounds always been here in the mornings, buried beneath the cozy, happy notes of her mother's movements in the kitchen? She knew they had. But, always, her mother's soft chatter to the household cats and unfettered soprano singing had been the vibrant chords that made each morning come to life. Gone now, silent, except in memories that she feared would fade all too quickly; the absence of her mother's voice cut Leiel in a way that even watching the flames on the ridgeline had not.

The fire that took Ilora's life had just been light against a dark sky, too far away for screams to carry. But this too quiet morning, *this* was change. This was fear. This was death.

A sob took Leiel's breath and she swallowed hard to fight it back. Along with the memory of song in the pre-dawn grey came her mother's voice. *"Now, there, Leiel. Strength is what you'll need from here forward. This fate of mine, it has come to others before. Don't be angry for me. Remember that I love you, and I would never, never leave you but for a great need and cause. Keep your heart wide open to that knowledge and one day, I promise, you will understand."*

One day. When was that? In the warm light with only the birds to sing her awake, it must be a million mornings away. Leiel lowered the book and freed one hand to swipe at her face, knocking away her tears. Her mother had told her the fire was not what it seemed. She had said it was not a terrible death, but simply a change. That was true in stories like the one she held. But only in stories. The ashes that had once been her mother blew on the morning breeze, cold as those from last night's hearth. How could that be anything but real?

But part of her whispered that her mother's words held more than empty comfort. Ilora had never lied to her. So, the world was horrible today and would be for many days to come. Leiel set her jaw and swallowed tears. Someday she would know why her mother—her strong, stubborn, wonderful mother—had allowed herself to be led up that mountain with barely a word of protest.

A final tear dropped onto the cover of the book. With the edge of her shirt, she blotted it dry, then set it aside. Her mornings would be different now. There would be no more songs. She would hurt and be sad. She would cry for days and weeks and years. But, one day, she *would* understand. She promised herself she would.

Leiel peered around the jamb into the blacksmith shop. Torrin was stoking the fire; he paused to wipe a hand over his forehead, leaving a black streak on his temple. She hesitated, uncertain, but before she could decide whether to stay or go, he turned and saw her.

"Hello, Li." He paused. "It's a terrible day."

The determination she had found in her room faded at his words. She dropped her gaze as tears gathered in her eyes again.

His footsteps came toward her and his calloused hand touched her face. "A hard day to get out of bed."

All she could do was nod. If she spoke, she would say things she could not put back inside herself. There was so much—her last glimpse of her mother as they led her into the Tower, and since then, her father's cold silence. And Klem's rage at her. Gial burying himself in the work of the farm and not talking to anyone. And the morning. This strange, bright, bitter morning that had greeted her when she opened her eyes.

When she stepped into the kitchen, Elda had tried to hug her. But Elda's arms were the wrong arms and her voice was the wrong voice and the only thing Leiel could think to do was run here. Because Torrin wouldn't try to hold her. He wouldn't yell. He wouldn't ask questions or try to explain away anything. He would just be there, and he would let her be there, too.

"Have a seat," he said. "I've got a hinge to repair."

She looked up at him, her eyes filled with tears that she did not want to let fall. "It broke?"

"Yah. Too many years of hard use and anything will break." He shifted his hand and patted her head. "But most things can be fixed, with enough time and hard work." He tipped his head toward the stool just inside the door. "Settle in. No one is going to come looking for you. Not today."

Her heart was a rock in her chest, as hot and heavy as the iron Torrin worked. Because today could not be fixed. Ever.

Outside, the weather was turning, cooling and coming in line with the season as it should have been without the influence of the Draigon. Here in the forge, heat still pulsed, like it had across all the Spur for the last several months. This was the last place that felt familiar in all the world.

She climbed up on the stool by the door.

Torrin didn't say anything else, just waited until she was seated and went back to his work. The clang and echo of his hammer on metal etched the air, and she let the beat of it settle her trembling heart.

3

Cleod – 6 years – Late Summer, 1163

THE LITTLE GIRL WASN'T PRETTY COMPARED TO THE OTHERS IN THE SCHOOL yard, but she was the only one who looked right back at anyone who looked at her. Most of the other girls were standing, careful and quiet, close to the school building, their clothes ironed and neat. The strange girl's clothes were well made and her skirts were clean, but her boots were worn from more than working in a house, and her shirt elbows were stained and patched. She was seated on the log at the edge of the grass, scuffing her feet over the ground.

Cleod sat down at the far end of the log. She met his gaze and grinned at him. "It's my first day," she said. "My brothers say it's okay for me to be scared. But I'm not scared. Are you?"

That threw him off and he sat back a little. Who was this girl? "Why would I be afraid?"

"Because it's your first day, too," she said as though that should be obvious to anyone.

He blinked. "How did you know that?"

"Because you don't have any books either," she said, and if anything, her grin got bigger.

He looked around then and realized she was right. Everyone waiting outside the school had books tucked in satchels or under their arms. Everyone but the two of them, and three other boys who he knew were also there for the first time. He looked back over at the strange girl and smiled back. "That was smart to see."

She nodded.

"I like being smart." She pushed her hair back. It fell immediately back across her eyes.

This time he laughed. "I'm Cleod. My father is a Woodcutter. Who is your father?"

"My father? Why?"

"Why?" It was the silliest question he had ever heard. "Because then I'll know who you are."

She frowned. "But I'm not my father. I'm me."

"Who are you then?"

"I'm Leiel," she said and her grin was back.

He realized she had gotten him to do just what she wanted. He couldn't let her do that. That was not how things were done.

"Who's your father?" he asked again, just as the teacher stepped out on the porch and rang the school bell.

She shrugged and hopped off the log without answering.

He had never seen anything like it. Girls were not supposed to act like this. "Hey!" he shouted and leapt up to follow her. In only a few steps he had caught up to her and found himself looking down at her by half a head. She had seemed as tall as him when they were both seated. "You can't do that!" he told her.

She did not ask what he was talking about, which meant she knew exactly what she had done. "Why not?" she asked, flashing her eyes up at him from between wild stands of hair that had sprung free of her braid.

He opened his mouth to reply and realized he did not know why not. Just that what she had done, was *not* done—girls did not introduce *themselves* before introducing their origin.

Laughter was her reply, and she skipped ahead of him up the steps into the school. He was still trying to understand what had just happened in the brief encounter as he followed her inside. His attention quickly shifted from the odd girl to the school building. He followed the other students down the hall that ran parallel to the front wall of the building, and entered the main room of the school. It was bigger than he had expected, with tables and benches lined up in three rows facing a large open space at the front. On the far wall hung a huge piece of grey slate with a name written on it:

~Joesenth Aroth~

That was the teacher's name. Cleod smiled to himself. In this moment, he was proud that his father had taken time to teach him some reading before he came to school. He had been angry at first, at the time taken away from fishing and other things more fun than books and studying and visiting the library in Adfen. He worked hard enough at his chores that he did not appreciate more hard work when he wanted to be playing. But standing here now, he was glad. He could read what was on that board. It was a list of names in pairs—and he could read his name there, matched with another:

~Leiel Sower~

So, her father had a farm. But what did that mean, his name next to the strange girl's?

"Well, enough then. Attention!" the man at the front of the room said. "Those of you who have been here before know how seating works. For the new members of our class—if you can read this board, find your name. You will notice that the pairs on the board match the number and position in the room of the tables you see. Once you have found your name, take your seat. If you *cannot* read the board, please remain standing, and we will begin your first lesson with that skill in a few moments."

Cleod counted down the list, then moved to the forth table in the left row. The strange girl, Leiel Sower, was already seated there. He looked at her for a minute, and he could tell she was trying to hold down the grin he had encountered just a few minutes before. "Looks like we're table partners," he said, trying to sound confident and knowledgeable. Somehow he wanted her to think he was smart. Why was that important? He wasn't sure. But she had already proved she was smart, and he had the feeling that she would like him better if she knew he was smart too. Which he was. He just had to show it.

A loud scrape sounded as he scooted out his end of the bench and sat down. He almost asked her if she could read the board too, but realized the answer in time to bite back the words. Of course she could, or she would not be seated where she was.

She dropped her eyes to hands clasped on the table, and he could tell she was trying to keep that lively smile in check. "How long have you been reading?" he asked, and knew it had been the right thing to say. Her eyes sparked as she glanced at him. Brown eyes. Prettier than her face. Something skipped in his mind—something strange and scary and wonderful.

"My mother started teaching me. Last year. She reads me stories and shows me how they are marked on the paper."

A year! A whole year she had been reading already. His few months of knowledge seemed so small compared to that, and to her clever wit and obvious confidence. He would have to learn more and work harder at home. It was suddenly important that he know as much as she did or more. He wanted to say things to her that would matter and that she would like. Where were all these thoughts coming from? He started to reply, but at the front of the classroom, Joesenth Aroth began speaking again, and Cleod forced himself to listen. That was why he was there, after all. And now he had a new reason to learn everything that he could.

Beside him, the presence of Leiel Sower was like a firefly in the night, snatching at his attention with bright flashes that had nothing at all to do with the place where he sat. His stomach turned and fluttered. School was going to be more interesting than he had thought.

4

Leiel – 8 years

"I TOLD YOU. I SAW HIM WHEN WE DELIVERED WOOD. BOHRIN AND BERK WERE kicking him."

Leiel frowned. The Harver brothers were brats at school, but she had never thought of them as cruel. "Is the dog mean?"

"I would be, if I was kicked all the time," Cleod said. "But I don't think it is." He leaned past her a little and peered around the corner of the barn.

She did the same and stared at the bone-thin dog that was tied to a post and lay in the damp dirt. He gazed back at her from a face encrusted with blood and mud. The dog got to his feet and looked at them, and then wagged its tail a few short swings. Her heart gave a little quiver. "I don't think so either. We have to save him."

Cleod pressed his lips together and looked at her. His eyes squinted a little and he nodded. "I can get him." He started around the corner of the barn.

Leiel caught his arm and dragged him back beside her. "Wait! We have to know where to take him first. I can't have him. Can you take him home with you?"

Cleod shook his head. "No. But Grochan at the library likes dogs. He would take him."

"You asked him?"

He gave her the look she knew so well, the one that meant he believed he had thought it all out, regardless of whether he actually had or not— like when he wanted to pull down the old mill by the pond and use the wood to make a fort in an oak tree. He was figuring out how to do it, until he realized the building belonged to her father and she might get in trouble with him.

She bumped him with her elbow. "*Did you* ask him?"

"Not yet.,"

She grinned. "But you're going to do it anyway?"

"It will *work*."

She laughed, then put both hands over her mouth to squelch the noise. "Shhhh," she said, and stopped up another giggle.

"Watch the house," he said, holding back a smile himself. "Whistle if you see anyone."

She scampered along the back wall of the barn and looked toward the house. There was no one in sight, and she could not even hear voices. Storekeep Harver was probably still at his store in the city, and the boys were fishing. She and Cleod had seen them heading to the creek. Where was Wife Harver? Leiel glanced back to see Cleod disappear around the corner of the building. She sucked a breath and whipped her gaze back toward the house.

No sounds came from behind the barn for several seconds, then she heard a high-pitched yip and the dog started barking. Her eyes went wide, and she fought the urge to run to the back of the barn and see what was happening.

The front door of the house creaked open and a woman stepped onto the porch. She stood for a second, then walked straight across the porch and down into the yard and turned toward the noise. Leiel stood frozen a moment. Remembering her role, she pursed her lips and tried to whistle, but her mouth was too dry and all that came out was a squeaky whoosh of air. The woman was getting closer. Leiel turned and raced for Cleod.

Behind the barn, he was tugging at the stake pounded into the ground while the dog pressed itself to Cleod, furiously wagging its tail and barking. Why hadn't they realized the dog was tied with a chain, not a rope?

"She's coming!"

Cleod looked up, his face covered in mud and his eyes wide. For a second he stopped tugging, then went back into action, this time working at the buckles that fastened the dog's collar. The animal wiggled and frantically licked Cleod's face. It was nearly impossible for him to get a grip on the dirty leather.

Leiel would have laughed if her stomach was not flipping into knots. She rushed forward to help. The dog leaped around at her approach and rushed against her. Mud claimed her feet and the dog her balance, and the next second she sprawled on her back with the animal licking all over her. Cleod yelped, and she saw his wide eyes peering down at her over the dog's back.

Before either of them could think what to do, a woman's voice cut the air. "What's going on here?"

Leiel gasped and pushed at the dog, then struggled into a sitting position and wrapped her arms around the trembling animal. Cleod scrambled and put himself between them and the woman standing with hands on hips at the edge of the beaten dirt circle.

"Well, children?" Wife Harver demanded. It took Leiel a moment to realize there was more amusement than anger in the woman's tone.

"We—we're—" Leiel started.

"We're rescuing this dog," Cleod said and straightened his back. The dog wiggled in Leiel's arms and shoved its head against the back of Cleod's knees. He staggered a step but caught himself and squared his shoulders again.

The woman stared at them for several seconds, then the smile she had been holding back broke through. "Well, someone certainly needs to. The boys found him in the woods a week back, and they seem to think he's a toy. I've worn my arm out whacking their backsides over it. Let him free children, and I'll find some story to tell about him getting away on his own."

Leiel stared past Cleod at Wife Harver. He shifted his feet and Leiel could almost see that he wanted to glance over his shoulder at her, but he kept looking right at the woman. "You're going to let us take him?" he asked.

The woman's smile widened. "I am going to let him escape with you."

"And you won't ever tell?" Leiel had to know.

With a shake of her head, Wife Harver's expression softened. "Not ever."

"How come you let Bohrin and Berk hurt him?" She got to her feet in the slippery mud. The dog splashed more mud on her skirts as it danced beside her.

Cleod turned and stared at her. "What are you doing?"

"I want to know. She's being nice. But she let them hurt him."

"Were you listening, child?"

Leiel and Cleod turned their attention back to the woman. She folded her arms, but her smile did not fade. "I said I've been beating them blue. But those boys of mine, they only listen to their father. He's always in town. Take the dog, children. Hurry up now. And stay off the road to the city when you leave. The boys will be coming back that way." She shook her head. "And don't tell me who you are. Go on now." She turned and walked back toward the house.

Leiel looked up at Cleod, but before she could speak, the dog leaped onto his hind legs and jumped against her. She stumbled and would have fallen again, but Cleod caught her. They tottered together but managed to stay upright as the dog barked, spattering mud over them and trying to wedge itself between them. Cleod looked down at her, a huge smile on his face. "Since we're both a mess, want me to hold him while you get his collar off?"

"Good luck with that," she said, but she nodded. He had a better chance of managing the animal than she did. He wrapped his arms around the squirming creature and tried to hold him still. The dog jumped and tugged at the chain, leaning into the collar and breathing hard.

Cleod laughed. "Calm down, dog. We're saving you."

Leiel frowned. "He's going to hurt himself."

"No, he won't. He's just excited."

"But he can't breathe."

"He can breathe better than when the Harvers were kicking him. Here, get him unhooked."

A few moments and two more sprawls in the mud later, she managed to work the collar open. Cleod loosed his grip, and the dog erupted into bounding circles, barking. Laughing, Cleod grabbed her hand and headed for the woods. The dog raced ahead, then back to them, then ahead again. She smiled and smiled more, and then skipped a little to keep up with Cleod's longer stride.

"I thought we were in so much trouble!"

Cleod nodded, his eyes wide. "Me too! She really let us go." A note of surprise lingered in his voice.

Leiel nodded. "She's nice. I wonder why Berk and Bohrin are so bratty when their mother is so nice?"

The shadows of the woods closed around them, and Cleod let go of her hand to push aside a low hanging branch and duck under it. The dog bounded ahead, weaving around trees and shrubs and occasionally looking back at them. "Maybe having a nice mother doesn't make anyone nice."

Leiel scrunched her face. "My mother is nice, too."

"And Klem can be mean, like the Harvers."

That was true. Klem was lousy sometimes, when he did not get his way. And he said stupid things when he was mad. But Gial was nice most of the time, and she was too. At least she thought she was...

"I guess it's not about having a nice mother."

Cleod didn't say anything, just hopped over a log and turned to wait for her. His face was a little pinched. She had seen that look before. Her face got hot. "I'm sorry," she said.

"No, you're right. Being nice doesn't mean you have a good mother or not."

"You really don't remember her at all?" She crossed the log and stood beside him.

"A little." He shrugged. "My father tells me about her sometimes." He paused and smiled as the dog raced back to them. Cleod knelt to scruff behind the animal's ears. "I remember she liked apples. She used to cut me apples in the fall."

Leiel nodded. Her mother did that too. And cut the peel off all in one strip. "I think that's something mothers do. Mine does. For me, and for Klem and Gial."

Cleod looked up at her. "I like your mother. I think my mother must have been like yours."

She wanted to hug him, but he would not like that right now. She nodded instead.

He smiled. "I bet she knew a lot of stories. I bet she laughed like your mother does."

Leiel giggled. "*No one* laughs like that."

Cleod got back to his feet, and the dog took off ahead of them again. "You do."

The warmth that filled her chest flushed to her cheeks. It was the nicest thing she could think of anyone saying to her.

5

Cleod – 38 years

CLEOD WAITED AS NAE WEDGED THE PLANK AGAINST THE EDGE OF THE WHEEL. A few moments of grumbling and cussing later, he managed to get a firm enough fit. Nae backed away, and Cleod braced his feet against the rocks he had piled in the mud and laid his shoulder into the back corner of the wagon. Even unloaded, the weight was significant. He nodded to Rimm, and the other man leaned into the other side of the wagon. Calf deep in the sludge that had once been the river bed, the stench of rot and dead fish assaulted Cleod's senses. He inhaled a foul breath of air and called to Kilras who sat in the wagon seat.

"Now!"

Kilras snapped the reins over the backs of the oxen, once, twice, and the tired animals put their weight into their harness with snorts of protest. Cleod drew a breath and lifted, pushing with all his strength. He heard Rimm grunt with effort. A new line of sweat burst along Cleod's already damp brow, and his legs and shoulders burned with effort. But the wagon shuddered, then began to move. He drew a breath and pushed, let the air out of his lungs with a shout of effort. The planks slanted against the wheels, creaked as the weight of the wagon landed on them, but they held. The oxen dragged forward through the muck, and the wagon, at long last, followed.

Cleod took a staggering step as it moved away from him, heard a curse and looked over his shoulder to see Rimm stumble off balance and sprawl face down in the mud. Cleod burst out laughing, the first moment of the long day in which he had felt any amusement. Rimm glared up at him as he struggled to right himself, not an easy task in the sucking mire. The young scout put an arm down and it disappeared to the elbow, leaving him no traction to even back up to firmer footing. He flopped forward, raised a mud-covered face, sucking for air and swearing. Cleod doubled over, wheezing with laughter, and it was several moments before he caught his own breath enough to wade through the slime and offer Rimm a hand up.

The look in Rimm's eyes said he would as soon pull Cleod down with him as accept assistance, especially since Cleod could not stop laughing. But Rimm reached up and let himself be hauled gracelessly to his feet.

"Only seventeen more," Cleod said.

Rimm threw back his head and groaned, then laughed himself. "There's no point in me changing clothes then."

"By the time we are through here today, we'll need to burn everything but our boots."

"All the gods forbid," Rimm said, swinging his arms to sling off what filth he could. "We'll not get more than normal pay for this."

"Be glad it's Kilras you ride for," Cleod said. "At least we'll get extra water rations to wash with. Other Dorns, you'd sit in your own filth for the next week. The next springs we can count on after seeing this are in Melbis."

"If *they* are still there," Rimm said.

Cleod looked around at the other scouts and traders struggling to move the wagons over what stable sandbars Kilras had been able to mark with pickets. Even with careful planning and chunks of the burned beams from the ferry house laid out as markers over the most solid terrain, the going was brutally slow and vile.

"At least when we get enough oxen across, we can use the remains of the ferry to haul the heaviest goods over."

Behind them, there was a heavy clatter as the wagon they had just freed reached solid ground at the edge of the riverbank. They would have to cut a ramp up that wall of packed dirt to get it out of the gulch, but at least another wagon stood on dry ground.

Kilras hopped off the wagon and turned the care of the oxen over to Nae. Cleod raised a hand as the Dorn looked over at them. Kilras broke into a wide smile at the sight of Rimm, then turned away laughing.

"It's good to be in charge," Rimm called. "You get the dry jobs."

"Best dig out those planks and get on to the next," Kilras replied. "Since you're already dressed for the job."

Cleod gave Rimm a slap on the shoulder, sending a few chunks of mud tumbling away, then slogged over to help free the boards before he lost himself to laughter again. He smiled at the oaths Rimm muttered under his breath as he followed.

They struggled through the morning, and a third of the wagons had been pushed and dragged to the far bank when it was time to break for food. The meal of cold beans and rice was consumed in exhausted silence. Then Kilras ordered half the scouts back across the river to begin pulling the old ferry level so it could be used as a skid to transport the heaviest goods. The rest, he set to digging a ramp up out of the river channel.

Tired though he was, Cleod was glad to accept work with a shovel over returning to the slop of the river bottom. He settled into the rhythm of digging, his brekko once again tight over his nose and mouth to keep at bay the worst of the dust he kicked up. Above the mire of the ancient river bed, the ground was brittle. It unwillingly accepted the bite of the shovel blade and broke loose in dry chunks that crumbled to powder as he tossed them aside. No pile of earth built up beside him as most of the soil blew off as grey silt in the breeze.

The low talk of the men rose and fell in measure with the difficulty of breaking free each section of earth. Cleod's arms and back burned. The old scars across his hips, usually only an annoyance of tighter muscle, ached deep and stiffened his movements. He sighed and allowed himself a moment to straighten and survey the work.

Scattered over both banks of the river, the merchants and scouts were busy shifting goods, digging, and organizing. The main cook wagon was still on the west bank, though the smaller, secondary cart had been pulled across. A split camp would be an aggravation, but it was unavoidable, at least for the next few days. The scouts where exhausted. To a person, they were giving their all to the rough work of the day. Even the outriders were taking turns from perimeter watch to handle a shovel or carry goods. For the ones scheduled for sentry duty, there would be no sleep until well after darkness fell.

Only Wern and a few of the frailest traders had refused to assist. Kilras had seen that the wagons of the oldest travelers were the first brought across. They were now busy setting up camp. Wern's response to the situation had been predictably petty, and Kilras had informed him that his goods would be the last to make the crossing. The man himself had been ordered to remain on the west bank. The scouts had been given permission to tie him to his wagon if he attempted to force the issue. The glee the second scout, Jordin, had expressed at the thought made Cleod smile.

"Cleod."

He looked up. Kilras stood on the bank, his face grim. The Dorn tipped his head toward the half-dug ramp in invitation for Cleod to join him.

A firm thrust sent the spade into the ground. It swayed, then steadied upright. Cleod left it and made his way up the crumbling grade.

"Trouble?" he asked as he joined Kilras.

"Maybe," Kilras said. "Sehina found something. I hope it's old, but—" He looked out across the ruined landscape, the pitiful remains of what had once been the mightiest river in the region. "I don't think it is."

"What?" Cleod pulled down his brekko and met the other man's gaze.

In reply, Kilras turned and beckoned the younger man to follow. Cleod moved after him, a tightness gathering across his lower back, as though his body knew what Kilras was about to show him.

In silence, they moved north along the river bank, pushing though the desiccated remains of river cane and dying trees. Past the rope corral—where the horses stood nose to tail, flicking flies from each other—they followed a bend in the riverbank. Just out of sight of the camp, Kilras led the way down the steep embankment.

Sehina was waiting for them where the cracked earth bled into the muck. The bronze of her braid flicked across her back as she turned to watch them approach. Her expression was as grave as Kilras's.

Cleod stopped walking. He knew, without having to see it, what Sehina had discovered.

Kilras turned and looked at him, measuring. Because he knew, just as Cleod did.

"No," Cleod said, shaking his head. The scars along his hips seemed under pressure, flaring through his skin. He could feel every deforming ripple, a heat no less painful for the fact that he knew it was only in his mind.

"Look around you, Cleod. The Seebo—the land—what's this but Draigon Weather?" Kilras said as he took the last steps to join Sehina. The brutal truth, faced at last, after weeks of hoping the signs around them meant anything else.

Sucking in a ragged breath, Cleod forced himself forward, his senses singing and every fiber of him wanting to do anything but move toward the tracks he could now see in the mud. Tracks large beyond imagining. A dozen of them. More. And long troughs in the muck that could only be made by the tail of a giant beast. He took in the scene. The ripple marks fanned across the mud caused by the pressure of the downbeat of powerful wings.

Draigon Weather. Drought and famine. Fear and panic. Draigon Weather. The thunder of wings. A memory that would never die. Old training flexed at the edges of his mind, a tingle in the air, and colors began to shift in the landscape.

He turned away, cursing—Sehina for finding the sign, Kilras for bringing him to see it, himself for being unable to live down the failure that had shaped his life.

Kilras called his name, but Cleod kept walking. Kept moving. He had to get away. Find a place far from everyone, before the shuddering horror of that day so long ago overcame him.

Cleod

CLEOD WRAPPED HIS FINGERS OVER THE TOP BOARD OF THE WAGON'S TAILGATE, closed his eyes and hung on as the Gweld trance came crashing over him. Through all the long years of his life working the trade routes with Kilras, these moments had never faded in intensity. Ten years of training in the Enclave—a white hot intensity of *purpose* had been welded into his soul—to hate the great winged beasts that ravaged the land. And not just a hatred of their actions or the periodic destruction they wrought, but of their very existence. To use the abilities expanded by Gweld to destroy them.

A Draigon here. Draigon Weather. Draigon tracks in the riverbed. The Seebo running so low there had never been anything to compare. Wing Wind.

His mind was ablaze, washed in dark fire and a memory of suffering so brutal it left him without breath. He let himself ride the wave of memory, until, yet again, it scored through all his hard-won peace and ripped him to shaking.

He lay crumpled among the rocks on the blazing ridgetop, his blackened hips twisted beneath him and the smell of scorched flesh in the air. His flesh. Her flesh. His vision blurred and grew mottled, and he could not tell if the grey flecks that blew across it were real or a product of ruined sight. The very air seemed to be on fire and his lungs labored to draw in a breath that was only smoke. There was no sound. He tried to stay sitting upright, but his spine buckled and he slid into a darkness that brought no peace.

Splinters exploded under his hands and the part of him still aware of where he actually stood, was vaguely grateful that he still wore his gloves. He hissed in a breath and dropped his forehead against the shattered wood.

Need rose up out of his belly like smoke from an erupting mountain, fierce and suffocating. Had someone waved a mug of ercew under his nose, he would have fallen into it in desperation.

The bar was dark and crowded, as so many taverns in the Spur seemed to remain at all hours, but Cleod limped through the press and wormed his way onto a dirty bench in the far corner. Tears stung his eyes at the pain of the motion, and the scratch of bandages over his barely-healed skin left his breathing tight and uneven. He was supposed to be resting. The healers had been specific that his wounds were too extensive to wander with, even partly healed and covered. The risk of infection was too great. The wrong actions could kill him still, despite all their best work and the time invested.

But death was preferable to the pain—not just in his body, but that which twisted his mind into ever unfurling nightmares. He had lain in the bed in the hostel across the street and found no relief even in sleep. There was no peace, only terror and the gut-churning recollection of ultimate failure.

Outside his lonely room, he heard the passage of daily life. The sounds of the winter streets drifted against the closed window, filtering in with the cold. Parents scolded children; merchants clucked to their mules as their carts rattled up the street; late night revelers stumbled, singing and shouting, out of the tavern across the street. The acts of everyday life shook him; even the simplest things demanded energy he could barely force himself to expend. Weeks passed so, until another memory arose and filled every moment—of Jorry, the old drunk who all but lived in the Greystone Tavern in the heart of Adfen. For as many years as Cleod could recall, the old man had sat at the bar in that dingy haven of drink. Jorry drank and drank, fell into unconsciousness for hours, then woke and drank some more. But there was always a smile on his face, and he never cared for any trouble that might erupt around him. Personal battles, politics, lost love, even war—none of it touched him. He lived in a cocoon of oblivious drunkenness and all the horror of the world simply washed over him.

Cleod had ripped off the bulkiest of his bandages and struggled into what clothing he could gather and stumbled out into the street. His steps were lurching and each had sent a searing ache through his hips and into his gut. He had staggered forward, one goal in mind, and made it to the doorway of the tavern. his vision so blurred he could not even discern the name on the sign over the door.

Now he sat in rocking agony on a dirty bench and ordered ercew. And in that bitter drink he found the last peace he ever thought he would know.

His shoulders bunched and knotted until they twisted the muscles of his back, and it was all he could do to stay standing. Was it the fatigue of the day, the exhaustion of his body that had brought him so low? It was not as though he had not encountered Draigon-sign in the years since he had joined Kilras's company. It was ever present throughout Arnan. Wing Waves on the coast. Heat Storms in the plains. Rumors of Sacrifices made throughout the land. So what was different today? He had known from the moment he saw the devastated state of the Seebo, what the cause had to be. Why this reaction? He had long since learned to control the wild responses his Draighil training engendered. And ercew—ercew he had learned to forgo with an effort he did not wish to expend ever again. So why this wracking rage? Why this brutal need attacking every part of him?

Shaa.

It was the size of those tracks. The span of the rippling impressions left in the black mud of the river bottom. Wings beyond huge. Beyond monstrous, like the beast they carried into flight. Only Shaa was that large. Only Shaa could spread wings and flatten forests, draw a breath and melt mountainsides. Only Shaa had the power to twist his soul to fragments.

The fire swirled around him and the screams seemed to speak not of horror but of mercy. She was pleading—not for her life, but for his. Tormented sounds that had nothing to do with the physical fire that surrounded them, but rather with the agony of the loss tearing at them both.

Shaa—she was calling out to Shaa. A bargain being made. A choice that somehow he knew would destroy them both. And the fire that swept toward him leaped and buckled, and he lived, ravaged and maimed, but not past healing. But her screams shifted and changed in pitch and pain and the fire claimed her and everything he had promised in the world was gone in a flare of violent heat.

He screamed. Rage and terror and remorse ripped from him a sound formed in the darkest part of his soul. He did not care who heard him, what fears the sound might awaken among his fellow travelers. What was inside him this moment was too terrible to be contained and he had no will to try.

Kilras would forgive him, would understand as he had understood so much for all the years of their friendship. If the screaming kept Cleod sane, kept him sober, kept him alive, Kilras would stand beside him and shout down heaven and earth as needed.

Friendship became the bridge, the obsessive loyalty that held all other, more destructive, needs in check. And so when strong hands grasped Cleod's shoulders, he neither flinched nor struck out, as was his trained instinct. He rolled his body back into his friend's waiting grip and let Kilras support him as he shook.

"Take ease, Cleod," Kilras's voice slipped past Cleod's shattered senses and soothed the heat that tangled around his spine. His mind gave up the struggle and his body surrendered to exhaustion.

Cleod

"DRAIGHIL DO MORE THAN HUNT DRAIGON. MORE THAN TRAIN TO KILL THEM. They study the patterns of the Draigon, and the histories of all the Sacrifices ever made. The mind of a Draighil holds more knowledge of the acts committed by the Draigon than all the libraries in Arnan." Kilras's voice filtered through the ragged edges of Cleod's consciousness. Beneath his back was the comfort of his wool bedroll. A blanket covered him.

"Draighil are forged to be deadly—body and mind. There's little room for anything in their lives but the killing they're trained for. That Cleod survived that indoctrination and still holds his sanity is nothing but astounding. He's a man who was re-forged by the Ehlewer Enclave to kill any who interfered with his goal. He's one of only a handful who survived to walk away."

The crackle of a fire reached Cleod's ears. The shaking was gone, and the rage, replaced by an echoing emptiness and a dragging thirst. He heard Rimm's questioning reply. "Survived?"

"Some don't live through the training. Those who do, usually die facing the Draigon. Walk away? He's the only one in generations."

Silence held a moment, then Rimm asked, "If he is everything you say—how is he here with us? How has he worked with you for all these years?"

"Because he had already made a choice to control himself when I met him—even if his choice was killing him. He chose drink over continuing his life among the Ehlewer. And he was wasted flat when I found him. If he'd been sober then, he would most likely not be sane. And I'd never have lived through approaching him."

"You make me sound like a maniac in need of chaining," Cleod whispered without opening his eyes. "Tell the boy that is only half true or he'll never feel safe to ride night guard with me again."

Kilras chuckled, and Cleod felt the older man's hand on his arm. "That he ever felt safe with you shows his youth."

Cleod uttered a choked laugh and cracked open his eyes. Night had fallen and the sounds of a settled camp came to him through the darkness. "You are a fan of hiring the worst fools, Kil," he said, and rolled to his side to push himself upright. The world tilted, and the light of the fire burning a few paces away dimmed.

"Easy—" Kilras's arm steadied him and, after a few seconds, Cleod nodded as his surroundings righted themselves.

"What happened to you?" Rimm asked.

Cleod frowned, looked over at the young man seated on the far side of the fire. No anger sparked despite the rough timing of the young scout's question. "Overlash," Cleod said. "An unpleasant effect of sudden awareness of things I try very hard to forget. Draighil training does not leave much room for responses to Draigon sign that do not lead to violence. I can back it down, but there is always a cost." He sighed and combed his fingers back through his hair. The grit he felt there did nothing to improve his mood. "And it always leaves me wanting a drink."

"So you're back to your usual self," Kilras said.

Cleod scowled at him. But the older man was right. Wanting a drink was nothing new, especially after a hard day of work, unpleasant surprises included or not.

"There's some Siboran whiskey in the—" Rimm started, but Cleod cut him off.

"No, Rimm. No drinks for me, ever. You wouldn't like the man I am under the hand of strong beverage. I know I don't. A plain canteen will do."

"Cleod's a drunk," Kilras said to Rimm. "He'd drink himself to death given the wrong chance."

Cleod smiled at the amazed expression on Rimm's face. He had probably never heard of a Ruhelrn that flawed. To have Kilras admit such a weakness in the Lead Sword of the company was a shock. But it had long been part of their partnership, that they would never hide who Cleod was, what he was, or what his failings were. A weakness kept secret was one that could be exploited. But one made public left no opening for abuse. Cleod had long since proved he was capable of coping with whatever pressures the work threw at him. And on the bad days, like today, the worst in many a year, Kilras was there beside Cleod to make sure his will held.

"I am worse than a drunk." Cleod said to Rimm. "I am a drunk who is master of Gweld-tranced swordwork, and is willing to skewer anyone foolish enough to cross him. It is not something I admit to lightly, but it's not a secret by any stretch. Don't find yourself unsettled on my behalf. Half of Arnan knows my failing and the other half will guess soon.

"I am a trained killer. And I have the skill to tear you apart with one hand if I decide to turn it loose. It's best you take my craving seriously now that you know about it. To do otherwise will endanger you and anyone around me. I'm careful, and it's been years since I slipped, but it's not something I want to ever take a chance with. If you ever see me with a drink—back off. I guarantee I won't be rational."

With a sigh, Cleod took the canteen Kilras offered him and drank long. The liquid settled one thirst but left the darker need in him unsatisfied. Always unsatisfied. An ever present reminder of all that he had lost and all he had achieved since. He took a quiet pride in the fact that the need was always there, but always also in check. It had been a decade since his last misstep, and he planned on adding many more years to that silent and continual victory. He lowered the canteen and wiped the remaining moisture from his mouth. "I'm anything but a good man in that state."

"I never would have considered it if I hadn't been told," Rimm said. "You've always shown more self-control than any man I've known."

"Years of practice," Kilras said. "He's not always been so self-contained."

"Save the frightening tales for another night, Kil," Cleod asked.

"Only because of the day you've had," Kilras said in agreement. "And the one I've got planned for you tomorrow."

The rest of the wagons were still on the other side of the river, Cleod recalled. And there was a new watch to be set—this time on the skies. With a disgusted grunt, he asked, "Is there at least water enough for me to sponge off? And perhaps some food?"

Kilras nodded and gestured over his shoulder. "Nae set up a wash station on the riverbank beyond the trees. There's a fire lit there, and Jordin's attending it until everyone has had a chance to rinse clean. Sehina saved you a meal. Get cleaned up. I'll dig through your trunk and send Rimm here over with some fresh clothes."

With a weary nod of gratitude, Cleod got carefully to his feet. His balance held. He passed the canteen back to Kilras. "I'm grateful."

"As you always should be," Kilras said.

Cleod shook his head and walked away. Behind him, he heard Rimm ask, "He's strong enough?"

And Kilras's amused reply, "More than."

8

Cleod – 8 years

CLEOD AWOKE TO THE SOUND OF HIS FATHER, ELLAN, CURSING. THE OATHS ripping through the sweltering air of the house were so biting and inventive that all Cleod could do for several moments was lie in bed and wonder where his father had learned such phrases. Then he realized he was soaking wet with sweat, the bed clothes damp with it. He sat up. The humidity was so thick in the air he thought he should be able to see it.

When he had gone to bed the night before, the sky had been cloudy, a cool drizzle falling. The air had smelled so much like rain that he assumed it would continue all through today, if not for days to come. Now white-hot sunlight blazed around the edges of the shutters, and the temperature had swung back toward the oppressive heat of high summer.

The slow-moving storm that rolled out of the west to collide with the ridge lines of the Spur had been massive. What could have changed the weather so greatly in a matter of hours?

The front door banged; his father's boots slammed across the porch and crunched onto the packed dirt yard. That was even more strange than the sudden rise in temperature. The amount of rain that had fallen yesterday and last night should have left the yard sodden and muddy for days. The fact that Cleod could hear his father's footsteps on hard earth sent him scrambling for his clothes.

When he unlatched the shutters on the small window and swung them open, the change that had been wrought in the familiar landscape took his breath away. So thick was the air that the light shining through it seemed to bend and waver, tinting everything a sickly hue. The bright greens of the leaves were muted to murky yellow. Earth, sky, forest—all bore a tint of citrine that seemed to guide the unnatural heat deep into his bones.

Across the yard, his father was frantically working the pump beside the barn. It had rained yesterday. Rained half the night. Why did the trough need filling? Cleod left the tiny bedroom and went out into the living area. His boots were where he had left them to dry beside the wood stove. He pulled them on and laced them, and went outside to join his father.

"What's wrong? What's happening to the air?" Cleod called across the yard. The ground was bone dry, and he could hear the brittle crackle of leaves in the trees. He looked around. The summer greens were not just muted by the strange cast in the air, but had actually lost their brilliance. They were brown and wilting in the vivid heat. It were as though the life had been drained from every green, growing thing on the holding.

"Cleod!" His father shouted. "Get the buckets from the barn and the hand wagon. Fill every bucket you can and take them to the icehouse. Empty them into the old cistern under the trap door. Hurry!"

There was an urgency in his father's voice that Cleod had never heard before. He ran to his father. "What is it? What's happening?"

"Wing Wind," his father said. "Draigon Weather! Get moving. We've got a few hours at best before we lose the well."

"But—I thought—"

"No boy, the stories aren't just legends we tell to entertain children. Get to work!"

Cleod sprinted into the barn. Draigon Weather! All his life the tales had been just that—stories. Stories of great flying beasts bent on destruction. Winged serpents from whose glowing flesh emanated a merciless heat. Their wings spanned entire mountains, each beat driving killing gusts of scorching winds over the land, desiccating everything in their path. This was a Wing Wind—heat blown over the land by the powerful fanning of a Draigon's wings. This was the vengeance of an ancient and angry god.

He scrambled through the barn, gathered every bucket he could, and tossed them into the cart he used to haul wood for the kitchen. A thought struck him, and he raced back out of the barn to the house. From hooks on the kitchen rafters came every vessel and pail he could find. Those, too, went into the cart.

By the time he returned to the pump by the barn, his father had the animals corralled close and was leading them one by one to the trough to drink their fill. Cleod pumped his buckets full, then dragged the laden cart to the shed behind the house and began filling the ancient cistern. He had asked his father many times why they did not just fill it in. The ice they collected from the river in winter often slid down into it, as did the occasional farm cat. Crawling down to retrieve either was an unwelcome adventure.

"We'll need it again someday," his father had said. *"Only a fool isn't ready for Draigon Weather."*

Now Cleod was grateful his father had not listened to his grumbling. Cleod's back burned, and his legs and arms ached from pumping and dragging, lifting and dumping. But, gradually, the old cistern began to fill. His father finished with the animals and joined him. They took turns working the pump or towing the cart to the ice house.

Beside the pump, dripping sweat and burned by the blazing sun, Cleod took the cup offered by his father and drank deep. Even cold from the depths of the earth, the water warmed too quickly to be truly refreshing. But it was liquid he desperately needed. He drank and drank, looked up at Ellan. "I never believed you. The stories."

"Most don't, until they see it," Ellan said as he raised and lowered the pump handle, his motions even and efficient, just as when he cut wood.

"How many of them are true? How many of the stories?"

Ellan looked at him over his arm as he worked. "There is no way to know about every story told in Arnan. But the Draigon. The Draigon are real, and sometimes one returns."

"Shaa? The Draigon King? Is he real? Is Shaa doing this?"

"You best hope not," Cleod's father said. "If this is Shaa—that cistern will be dry long before we see any hope of a change in this weather." He handed Cleod another full bucket. "Back to work."

Cleod

WAVES OF HEAT RIPPLED THE AIR ABOVE THE SQUARE AND THE ODOR OF sweat-soaked bodies floated thick as fog through the crowd. Not far from the edge of the Square, Cleod stood beside his father and stared up at the stone tower that loomed over the space. It was the most impressive building Cleod had ever seen. Five stories taller than the next tallest structure in Adfen, the base sprawled four times wider than any other building. The slick, grey granite sparkled with mica chips where the sun struck the surface as it soared toward the sky. At the very top, an enormous wooden crossbeam extended out to either side of the structure, like the arms of a person spread wide to enjoy a strong breeze.

He couldn't think of anything he wanted more at this moment than a strong breeze. The air seemed to have weight, pressing in on his small body and trying to crush him. His throat was sticky and thick, but water brought little relief. Even from the deepest wells, it was warm.

"Why are we here?" he asked his father. "What's happening?"

"The Council has made a decision," Ellan said. "They have chosen someone for the Sacrifice."

"Sacrifice?" Cleod did not know what that meant. Then it came to him. Another part of the legends he had once discounted. The part he still had not thought was true. "You mean they really give someone to the Draigon?" He was unable to believe that such a thing could happen. "They have picked someone for the Draigon to kill? To make the rain come again?"

His father nodded. "Yes, boy. They have done it many times. Sometimes it even keeps the Draigon from getting angry enough to bring such drought as this. But the last one, down in Sibora, must not have been enough. They had to choose another."

"Who?" Cleod looked up at the Tower. "Are they in there deciding?"

"That's why we're here. Everyone in Adfen and the Spur is required to be present for the selection. When they tell us who it is, it's our duty to make sure the one they pick doesn't try to run away."

"Our duty? Yours and mine?"

"All of ours," Ellan said. "Everyone here. The Council will choose the one they know will help us all by satisfying the Draigon. It has to be that person. Sometimes that person is too afraid to understand that they have to stop the Draigon Weather to save us all."

"Someone has to die to fix the weather?" Cleod asked again. How did that make any sense? "Why? Why did the Draigon make the drought? Did we make them angry?"

"Have you forgotten the story of Shaa, the Draigon King? When the Farlan came to free Arnan from the Draigon, Shaa was very angry. The war killed many people and many Draigon."

"But the Farlan won. Why does anyone have to be sent to the Draigon now?"

"Yes, the Farlan won. But Shaa was not killed. And the Draigon still have the power to hurt the land. But once someone is given to the Draigon, they will go away for many years."

"But how do they choose someone?" Cleod looked up suddenly at his father. "What if it's me? What if they choose me?" He envisioned himself trussed and helpless, like a sheep at slaughter, and a giant, smoldering, red beast descending like a falling spear to destroy him. He could almost hear the thunder of its wings, feel the boiling heat of its breath. He trembled, and a moisture not made by the heat filled his eyes.

"No. No, Cleod." His father dropped to one knee and took Cleod's shoulders in his calloused hands. Through a shirt already soaked and sticking to his skin, the extra weight of his father's palms, meant to be a comfort, instead seemed to add another layer to his dread. "No, boy. You're safe, as am I. The Draigon only accept girls for Sacrifice."

Had the skies opened and poured cool rain into the parched land, the relief that washed over Cleod could not have been greater. He would not be chosen today. He would not be chosen *ever*. He drew a shaking breath. "Never boys?" He wanted to be certain.

Ellan smiled and gave his shoulder a brief squeeze. "Never."

Cleod nodded, his fear allayed. But something else shifted uneasily inside him. "Why do the Draigon only want girls?"

Whatever answer he was expecting—because girls must taste sweeter, or because girls don't fight as hard—it was not the one Ellan gave. "There are some girls, son, who do not know their place in this world. They don't work hard. They just cause trouble. When Shaa ruled the land, those were the ones he ate. So now, it is said, he misses their spice. When he gets hungry, those are the ones he wants."

"So only the bad girls get chosen?" Somehow, it was important that only someone who was bad should be sent to the Draigon. That made sense—that bad girls were punished and the Draigon was appeased at the same time. It meant that he did not have to feel sad about whomever the Council was going to choose.

Ellan nodded. "Yes. And never boys or men. So you have nothing to worry about." He smiled, got back to his feet, and turned his attention back to the Tower.

Cleod tried to do the same, but his thoughts kept returning to the fearful image that had filled his mind in the seconds before his father had eased his terror. A giant monster descending. The shaking fire of the air. The scream of the wind over the creature's wings. What if it was like that? What if that was what the girl was going to see? What if that was what she was going to feel? Was anyone bad enough to deserve that?

He tried to think of a girl he knew whose behavior was so unacceptable as to have earned that kind of death. He could think of no one. Not even Brea, the healer's daughter who was so disagreeable in school and even dared to call Joesenth wrong, was that bad. So who could it be? No one he could think of. So it must be someone he did not know. Maybe one of the older girls who was no longer in the school.

Something low and deep rumbled through his body, steady, building. *Drums?* A cry rose from the people nearest the Tower, and swelled through the crowd until everyone around Cleod was shouting. Ears throbbing with the power of the noise, he rose on tip toe and strained to see what had caused the uproar. A short, wide run of steps ran the length of one side and fanned out from the Tower's door. Between the shoulders of the men in front of him, he caught a distant glimpse of a man standing at the top of the stairs. He wore black pants and a red tunic that hung to his thighs. This must be one of the councilmen.

The man raised his arms and the roar of the crowd increased. He smiled and nodded a few times, then brought his arms down in a series of pulsing movements that gradually quieted the press of people. The packed Square slowly grew hushed.

Cleod found that he was holding his breath and he let it out in a rush. He could almost smell the anticipation in the air around him. Who would it be? Who was the bad girl who would be selected?

The man on the stairs began to speak, and his voice echoed off the walls of the Square, powerful and loud. "The Council of Adfen, in accordance with the laws of Farlan Rule and Pact with the Beast, Shaa, has made selection from among the eligible women of the Spur to appease the monsters in this time of crisis."

Cleod did not know what all the words meant, but they were spoken with certainty.

"We have chosen she whose Sacrifice will be certain to return the Spur to well-being and peace for many years to come. Offer up your gratitude now. *Ilora Sower*—come forward and accept the honor you have been called to receive."

Ilora Sower!

Cleod gasped. That was Leiel's mother. *Leiel's mother!* He did not realize he was shouting the words out loud until his father caught his arm and hushed him. How his cries had been heard over the clamor of the crowd, he did not know, because everyone around him was cheering, arms raised. Then they began to chant. "To Shaa! To Shaa! To Shaa!"

But the name they had called was Ilora Sower. How could she be the one they had selected? He had been desk partners with Leiel since their first year at school. Her mother used to walk Leiel to school, before she got old enough to come so far by herself. Ilora Sower had always been kind to him. She had smiled and told funny stories and always thanked him for being such a good friend to Leiel. Ilora Sower. How was it possible that Ilora Sower was bad? How could she have done anything so terrible she was to be given to the Draigon?

He tried to see what was happening near the Tower, but he was too small, and the crowd surged and rocked around him. He grabbed his father's arm and tugged hard. Ellan looked down at him. "It's Leiel's mother! My friend Leiel. They've made a mistake! It can't be Leiel's mother."

His father shook his head—whether because he had not understood or because he did not agree—Cleod could not tell. Cleod pulled again on Ellan's arm. Someone had to stop this. Someone had to tell the Council they were wrong. Besides, Ilora Sower was not a girl. She was a mother. There had to be a mistake. "They're wrong!" he shouted. "Please stop them. They have to be wrong."

Ellan knelt and grabbed him and shook him. "Cleod, stop. They are never wrong. If they have chosen this woman, it is because she is what the Draigon wants. That means she's done things that we don't know about. That means this is what must be. Look—" He lifted Cleod so he could see over the mass of people.

At the base of the Tower, a woman was climbing the steps. Ilora walked forward without glancing back. She looked straight ahead, ignoring the mayhem around her. She did not look sad or afraid. She looked calm, as though nothing of what was happening was a surprise. Behind her, a man stood on the last step with a boy several years older than Cleod and two smaller children. Cleod recognized the younger ones, Leiel and her brother Klem. The two of them were screaming, struggling against their father as they tried to fight free and go after their mother. The older boy stood wide-eyed, just watching, mouth open in shock.

Cleod watched as Leiel seemed to churn in her father's arms. He thought he could hear her cries over all the others. A few mighty tugs and she broke free, raced up the steps to her mother's side, and threw her arms around her waist. They had only a moment before the Farlan guards pulled them apart, and Leiel was dragged, shrieking, back to her father and brothers. Her father barked something to the older boy, and he grabbed Leiel from the guard and all her struggles were then useless.

Ellan must have grown tired, because he lowered Cleod back to the ground.

"No, I need to see," Cleod said. He had to know what was happening. He had to see what they were doing to Leiel.

"I am sorry," his father said. "I'm sorry it was your friend's mother. But there is nothing more to see. They've taken her into the Tower."

"What about Leiel?" Cleod turned back toward the Tower, craning his head to see any glimpse of her. "Where is Leiel?"

"Cleod!" Ellan put a hand on his arm, but Cleod shook it loose, pushed through the throng, weaving and dodging as he made his way toward the Tower. He burst free at last, into the open area at the base. But she was gone. They were all gone, even the Councilman. He turned to find the crowd was thinning and his father was storming toward him across the old stones. The whipping Cleod had coming now was not something that could be avoided, but it didn't matter.

He had to find Leiel.

Once more Cleod swept his gaze over the area, but Leiel was nowhere to be seen. Where had they gone? Had the whole family been taken away?

"Son," Ellan's voice was gentle. That was not what Cleod had expected. He tried to blink away the tears that had formed in his eyes as he looked up at his father.

"I am sorry about your friend. But her mother must have done terrible things. You can't stop it. But maybe you can help your friend."

"How?" Cleod dragged a hand across his eyes, trying to pretend he was wiping away sweat.

"If you're her friend, be one. Lots of people won't be. Be good to her. Things are going to be hard for her."

"Why?"

"Because when a woman is sent to the Draigon, any daughters she has are also not to be trusted. Who knows what Leiel's mother might have taught her?"

"She taught her to read."

Ellan smiled, but there was not much happiness in the squint of his eyes. "Nothing wrong with that, boy."

Cleod stared up at him. "You're not angry at me?"

"No," Ellan said with a shake of his head. "Not today. Not about this." His big hand scuffed through Cleod's hair. "Come. Let's go home. You won't find her. The family has been taken to the Sanctuary."

"What will happen there?"

Ellan shrugged. "No one knows. The families never tell. Afterward is when your friend will need you most."

"What did she do? What could she do that was so terrible? Leiel's mother has always been nice to me. How can someone nice be so bad?"

With a hand on Cleod's back, his father guided them through the dispersing crowd. "It's hard to know everything about a person. No one can know everything another man or woman says and does. No one shares everything. There are things you do not tell me. I don't tell you everything either."

Cleod was silent for a few steps. It was true that he had done things his father did not know about. And certainly his father did not know everything he ever said. But did that mean that what he had done was bad, just because not everyone knew about it? "But I'm not doing anything bad in secret." Was his father? What if he was?

Ellan stopped walking and looked down at him. It was as though he had heard Cleod's thoughts. "No. And neither am I. And maybe Ilora Sower didn't know how bad she was being."

"How could she not know?" Cleod asked. His voice sounded sharp to his ears. If someone was bad, wouldn't they know it?

"Because she is a woman. And there are things that men are allowed to do, that girls are not. Things that are acceptable for me, and for you, but that are dangerous for women. Men are stronger than women. We think about things they don't. If she forgot that, or was not taught the right things, she could have done dangerous things without meaning to."

"But if she didn't mean to, how can she be bad?"

Ellan sighed. "The Draigon do not care if she meant to or not. If the Council chose her, then she is the one the Draigon want. That's why there are so many laws for girls. Because the ones who don't follow them attract the attention of the beasts. When *they* take an interest in someone, Draigon Weather comes."

In the blazing heat of the stone Square, salt from sweat and tears now crusted on his face, Cleod looked up at his father, trying to make sense out of what he was being told. If Ilora Sower was bad without knowing it, if she had never been taught what was wrong...what if she had taught Leiel the wrong things? What if Leiel was also being bad without realizing it? Did that mean that Leiel might have to go with her mother to the Draigon? "Do the councils ever take two girls to the Draigon?" he asked.

A gentle smile was his answer. "No, only one. You don't have to worry about your friend. Especially not now."

Now what did that mean? "Why?"

"She will be very sad that her mother is gone. But it will be a good thing—for not just the Spur, but for her. Her father and brothers will keep a better eye on her. They'll make sure she doesn't make the same mistakes as her mother. You can be her friend by helping her do only the things she is supposed to do. You know the laws, and you can remind her of them."

"You're not angry that I'm friends with Leiel? Even though her mother—her mother was the one today?"

Ellan shook his head. "No. I think it's a good thing you're her friend. You can help her stay safe."

Cleod nodded. *Be Leiel's friend. Keep Leiel safe.* He would do those things. He would do them forever if he had to.

10

Leiel – 9 years

THE AIR WAS A BLUR—OF LIGHT, OF NOISE, OF TEARS, AND OF FRANTIC
movement. Huddled in a corner on the cold stone floor of one of the
shrine rooms, Leiel tried to control her sobbing. She sucked breath after
ragged breath, only to have her fragile hold on composure unravel just as
she thought she was gaining control.

Her mother! They had called her mother's name! How was that possible? How could her whole world have exploded into chaos in the matter of
just a few seconds? Did the Council not know that Ilora was her mother?
Mother to Gial and Klem? Friend to so many others? Addor's wife? Was
her father not one of the most respected merchant farmers in the Spur? In
all of Arnan, even? What were they thinking? How could they have made
such a mistake as this?

How long had it been since the announcement? How long had she
been sitting helpless in this corner? A few minutes? An hour? More?

Voices rose and fell at the far end of the room, and she tried to focus on
them. They had to be discussing her mother. They had to be correcting the
mistake. She tried again to stop crying and managed to take a few breaths
that did not turn into sobs. She had to hear what was being said—had to
know what they were going to do to fix the great error that had been made
in the Square.

A few steps away, Klem was curled up on a stone bench, his face grey
and blank and untouched by tears. Gial sat beside him. He was shaking,
his face mottled and streaked.

It must be her father's voice she was hearing from the far end of the
room—her father and many strangers. And what she heard in the voices
was anger and panic and grief. The undercurrent of strident emotion that

laced the room tangled with her own emotions and set her nerves to burn.

Unable to remain still now that the initial shock was shifting into a desperate need to act, to do *something* to fix what could only be a terrible misjudgment, she scrambled to her feet and started across the room toward the knot of adults standing by the door.

Her movement must have aroused something in Klem, because he jerked upright so quickly that both she and Gial jumped in surprise. Then Klem lunged for her, his hands outstretched and face a twisted mask. She screamed and tried to turn away as he slammed into her, grabbed her tight and shook, shook, shook. He was yelling, sobs slurring his words, and she could not understand what he was saying.

"Stop!" she begged, trying to shove him off. "Stop, Klem, stop! You're hurting me!"

"You killed her!" he shouted. "You! It's you!"

Gial's hands wrapped around Klem's, and he pried them loose, sending her stumbling. Seconds later adults swarmed over, separating them. She was tugged away by an unfamiliar grasp, not as gentle a one as she might have hoped for.

"Here, girl. Sit down here and stay clear of the men. You are best served by remaining in one spot and silent." She looked up into the white-painted face of the priest, made even paler by the celadon color of his robes. His expression was stern, and though she looked for kindness in his eyes, she found none. Always before the priests had smiled at her, indulgent and amiable. The disapproval she saw now was one more horrible new thing in her world today. "What's happening?" she asked, unable to raise her voice above a whisper or keep it from trembling.

"Your brother is angry," he said. "Stay here and quiet. You will only arouse more ire if you continue to initiate disorder."

"I didn't do anything," she said, trying to understand, her voice rising. "There is a mistake. My mother isn't—"

"She *is indeed.*" He cut her off, his voice no longer just firm, but now also laced with disgust. "And you are the mistake she made. Your family knows that now. Be glad the Council only sends one at a time to the Draigon." He stood straighter, as though being near her was somehow likely to taint him.

Thoughts staggered inside her mind. What was he talking about?

Why had Klem tried to hurt her? Didn't they understand that her mother *could not* be the one to be offered up on the mountain? Whatever Leiel had done wrong, she would fix later. Somehow, they must save her mother. She looked around. Across the room, her father was standing before Klem and Gial, speaking too softly for her to hear. More priests stood around, some whispering to each other, some simply staring at her.

She pushed to her feet, shouting before she realized she was even going to speak. "You have to help! You have to stop it. Mother is good and she cannot go to the Draigon. Whatever I did, I'm sorry. I can fix it. I will fix it. You just have to help my mother first."

"Silence, shameful creature," the priest said.

"Jaidu." Another priest stepped up beside the first. This one wore the grey shoulder yoke of a Scholar. "She is too young to know. Her mother's failings on her behalf are more than she has knowledge to understand or yet combat. To blame her for knowing only what she has been taught is unreasonable. The truth has been explained to her family, and it is now for them to take her and cleanse her of the stain of her mother's actions." The new priest looked down at her. "Calm yourself, child. There has been no mistake. The choice of your mother for this offering was not made lightly. She is the Sacrifice designate and she will be delivered to her fate. Save your tears and your misplaced loyalty. She has done you great harm without you knowing it. You will find your life to be better and simpler once she is gone."

Leiel stared up at him, stunned. Only half the words made sense, but she knew none of them were good. Inside her, a thousand thoughts and feelings tumbled like grains through a gristmill. She knew what he was saying was not true, knew it in the deepest, most knotted part of her. But he sounded so certain, so sure. Why would he say such things if they were not in some way true? Was he trying to trick her? Why was everyone looking at her as though she had a sickness they could catch? Why had her father not taken her into his arms as he was now holding Klem? Where was her offer of comfort in a world gone insane?

Her mother *was good*. Had only ever *done good*. Leiel knew it the way she knew the feel of her breath sliding into her lungs. That could not be anything but true. And yet... Why was everyone so sure? So stoic and solid in their belief that Ilora had done something to deserve the fate publicly declared on the steps of Adfen Tower. What did they know that Leiel did not? Her certainty of her mother's innocence was a bitter kernel of confusion. Once again, she burst into tears.

Through blurred eyes, she saw the scholar priest nod and beckon the first priest away. No one came to take their place at her side or offer her any solace. The kernel inside her grew hard and dark in the shadow of that lack of compassion. Whatever they told her, whatever they said or did, she knew with all that she was that her mother would never have left anyone so alone and forlorn as she was in this moment. Whatever vile practices they sought to destroy to stop the Draigon, it was not her mother who was guilty of them.

For that alone, she would only ever owe the Council and the priests hatred. She choked down her tears and pulled herself straight, pushed her hair out of her eyes. Alone at the edge of the room she watched the priests surround her father and brothers and speak with a quiet sympathy to which she was somehow not entitled. Everything had changed. Everything. In just the short hours since she stepped into the Square with her family, she had become a stranger in her own life.

They took my mother, she thought, a spark awaking inside her. All of them took her from me and now we are enemies. She had never known what that word meant. Enemy. But now she tucked it deep and let it fan whatever new thing had lit itself inside her.

11

Leiel – 10 years

THE TRAIL THAT RAN THROUGH THE WOODS ALONG THE CREEK TO THE CORN mill had been well-used before the new mill was built closer to town. Addor had been angry about that, to see a new milner come to town and build a bigger works. The new one was powered by the river instead of just the pond drainage; it ran faster. Her father had finally just bought part ownership of the new business. The little family mill had since fallen into ruin, its grind stones pulled out and moved to the new location closer to town. Now the pond that had once fed the rotting flume was frequented only by ducks and loons and an occasional stray cow.

Sweat soaked the back of her dress as Leiel followed the path winding through the woods. Through the trees to her left, she caught flashes of sunlight on the water. The thought could cripple her heart—that her last walk along this trail had been with her mother. She swiped back a tear. So many thoughts like that found her now. The entire farm was a patchwork of memories she could not avoid.

She emerged from the cover of the trees into the half-overgrown clearing near the remnants of the old mill. A few sparrows startled and flitted away through the too-dry brown brush, and some katydids, ambitious in the afternoon light, fell silent for a few seconds, then resumed their peeping chatter.

She looked at the water for a long moment. Still so low. Like every creek and river. The heat had been stifling all year and was brutal this late in the harvest season. The pond, never large, had shrunk day by day as the heat and drought dragged on. *Draigon Weather.*

She wished she had never heard that phrase. Wished she did not know, all too intimately, what it meant. It was more than lack of rain and crops dying in the fields. It was the end of everything.

Leiel turned away from the pond and made her way toward the old building. Its walls were still straight and solid, though the saplings and thorny weeds had grown close against it and vines crept up its sides. The main door stood open. She paused and looked inside. Wind blown leaves covered the floor. One of the shutters over the window on the back wall hung loose and banged lightly when a small gust blew through the open doorway. The place smelled of dry rot and dust.

Two years before, she had met an old drifter setting her camp in the place. Leiel had escaped her mother's watchful eye and come to gather the wild raspberries that had sprung up in the abandoned clearing where wagons had once parked with their loads of corn and wheat. She had come through the tall weeds singing a rhyme she had learned from Elda and tapping a stick ahead of her to chase back any lazing snakes. A slight smile on her face, the woman had been standing at the edge of the water, her head tilted toward the sound of Leiel's voice.

So unexpected was her presence that Leiel stopped in her tracks and stared. The woman had eyes so golden they were almost green. They were startling eyes, not just for their color, but because they were part of a face that was otherwise unremarkable. The hair that framed it was watery dark, but short and without gloss or curl. The mud on her boots and skirts and the dust that dulled the rest of her clothing spoke of a long journey behind her. She met Leiel's wary gaze with a calm assessment.

Despite the fact that Leiel was on family land and the stranger was the one out of place, Leiel felt as though she was the trespasser. The woman, dirty and unkempt, had a calm about her that rivaled even that of the priests at the Sanctuary. She looked like she belonged exactly where she was. Leiel had the unnerving thought that the woman would look like that even if she were standing in the brightest palace in all of Arnan.

"Is this one of your places?" the stranger asked. Her voice was the husk of wind through pine trees. It seemed to gather itself from a long way off and blow over Leiel, moving through her on its way to anywhere else.

"My place?" Leiel asked. "It's my family's mill. The old mill. No one uses it any more. But it's not *my* place."

"Not the mill." The woman turned to fully face Leiel. "This place of quiet water and wild things growing. This place to climb old apple trees and pick ripe berries. Yes, this is a place where berries would be happy to grow, made sweet and bright by water and light."

Leiel started. How had the woman known she was there for the raspberries? Then she realized she was holding a berry basket and dressed in tall boots with her skirts tucked around her legs for easier maneuvering between the brambles. Anyone who had ever picked a berry would recognize what she was about. As for the apples, the trees were obvious along the far side of the pond, where the old orchard had once reached down to the water's edge. Like the mill, it had long since fallen into disuse. She did not think it had been cared for since long before her birth. Perhaps even before her parents' births.

"It's not my place," she said again.

"Yes, it is," the woman said. "It is special to you, and you are probably the only one who will worry at all that I might cause any harm in being here. The menfolk you think own this place would see only a frail drudge who might leave some waste behind a tree. You, however, can see that I might be dangerous. So it is only right that I ask your permission for the camp I wish to set here for the night."

For a few seconds, Leiel stared at the woman. Finally, she just answered the last statement. "I think it would be all right for you to camp here," she said, just as it registered that the stranger had just admitted she was dangerous. "How—?" she started, lost the words and stopped.

The woman dropped her head back and laughed. And if her voice was haunting, her laugh struck something straight through Leiel's soul. It was bells and growls and rushing water all rolled in one booming expression of pure abandon. "How am I dangerous? Oh—daughter of free spaces— there is nothing more dangerous than a woman walking in the wild."

Leiel stared at her. Never had she heard anyone speak in such a way. Especially not a woman. Even her mother was not so bold with her words. "Who are you? Why are you here? Where do you come from?"

The stranger tipped her head again, once more studying her, as though she was taking in things about Leiel that she hardly knew herself. "I am called Gahree. As for why I am here...perhaps I have always been here. Perhaps I always will be. Perhaps my home is wherever I find myself at the moment."

Gahree folded her arms and it was as though she settled into the very earth. "Are you fond of stories, wild daughter? Does the mother who pretends not to know you sneak off to seek sweet berries in these woods tell you tales so old and so odd that they cannot be anything but true?"

A footfall on the path behind her startled Leiel from the old memory, and she turned, half expecting to find the odd woman standing behind her. But years had passed since that peculiar encounter and the person behind her was very different from that odd woman. It was the only person whose presence was not an intrusion on her privacy.

Though he was younger than she, he was much taller, and it seemed he grew a bit every day. He stood in the middle of the path and met her gaze with wide eyes. They looked at each other in silence for several seconds, then he suddenly reached up and pulled off his worn cap. His tousled hair flopped into his eyes.

"I—uh—I—" He stopped and frowned. "You said you sometimes came here," he said at last. "I came to find you. I came to tell you I was—I am—I'm sorry about your mother."

It was the first time she had heard those words from anyone who mattered. Someone who was a friend to *her*, not just to her father or the family as a whole. Cleod had taken the time to come find her—the time to care about her hurt—and he had sought her out in the woods and said the words she had not realized, until this moment, that she so desperately needed to hear.

She put her hands over her face and choked on a sob. Footsteps scrunched on the path. She felt a hand on her arm, just below her shoulder, and the tears she had been holding back for weeks burst forth. She couldn't speak, could hardly breathe, and she curled into herself, trying to turn away so he couldn't see. But he moved with her. The hand on her arm slid across her shoulders. And he enfolded her in an uncertain hug. That was truly more than she had expected from anyone, and she gave in to her pain and put her face onto his chest and let herself sob.

"How did you know where to find me?" Leiel asked. She looked over at Cleod where he sat beside her, leaning against an ancient oak by the edge of the pond.

"I remembered you said you came here to be alone."

"How did you know I would want to be alone?"

He shrugged, reached out to pick a brittle blade of grass, and twirled it in his fingers. "I thought that's what I would want if—if—I—my father...I would want to go somewhere and just be alone." He looked over at her suddenly. "Do you want to be alone? I can leave—"

"No," she said quickly. "Having you here is almost like being alone."

He frowned, and she realized what she had said. "Like having another part of me here," she said. "Like you're not someone else, but some bit of me."

He looked at her a moment, then nodded. "Is that why you can cry in front of me? No one at school has seen you cry yet."

She thought about that. It was not that she hadn't cried. She had cried so much that her face and throat were raw. But she hadn't cried in front of anyone since the Sanctuary. Because to show tears was to show not only her grief, but also her fear. And, most of all, her anger. Her desire was to take hold of the entire world and shake it as though to rattle a ripe apple from a tree. To shudder and pound all the injustice from her world and have what fell out be her mother, alive and happy and back home where she belonged.

Cleod tipped his head, and his mouth pulled down a little. She guessed he had seen it in her just now—the frustration, the outrage. What would he do now that he had glimpsed that most carefully guarded part of her? Walk away? Tell his father? Tell *her* father? Somehow, that would be the worst of it. Addor allowed her to be sad, but not full of ire. That was something she tried her best to keep from him. Somehow, that was important.

"I cry," she said. "Why does anyone need to see it?" She almost succeeded in keeping her voice from shaking. She reached up a hand to push back her hair.

"They don't, I guess. But you would do better at pretending you weren't mad if maybe they saw you be sad more."

She stared at him. Whatever she had expected him to say, it had not been that.

"Why do you think I am angry?" she asked. In her attempts to hide her rage, had she only invited more scrutiny?

"Your face gets crinkly around your left eye when you get mad. Like when Joesenth won't let you answer a question even when he knows you have the answer."

She scoffed. "He only does that because he's afraid for a girl to be smarter than Councilman Swillon's bratty son." She put a hand over her left eye. "I really get crinkly?"

"Just a little. From all the time sitting beside you in school, I noticed. I don't think anyone else does."

"Oh."

"You can stop it now that you know you do it. You can learn not to show it."

"How do I do that?"

"Do you remember I used to break my quills from pressing too hard when I wrote? I used to do that when I got angry—like the time the Harver brothers took my hat at lunch and filled it with mud? I broke three quills, and Joesenth made me cut and sharpen ten to make up for it."

"You don't break quills any more," she said.

He nodded. "I learned how not to show when I get mad."

"Tell me how," she said, reaching up to wipe a bead of sweat from her forehead. Even in the shade, as close to the water as they could get, the air was stagnant.

"Pretend they're something else."

"Who?"

"Everyone. Anyone who makes you angry. Pretend they're squirrels. Squirrels in pants. Or squirrels milking cows. Or whatever it is they're doing. Squirrels scolding you. Then you can relax and your face will be more normal."

She laughed, picturing her father with a bushy tail and his cheeks stuffed full of nuts, blustering at her from his place at the far end of the table, the way a squirrel chattered from a tree limb when she too closely approached his cache of nuts. But the image faded quickly, replaced by another thought.

"Squirrels don't drag you away and kill you," she said quietly. "Squirrels don't care if you're angry or not. But people do. People don't want me to be angry, and I am. And I don't know what they will do if they notice like you did."

"I know. It's why I came to find you. I was in Harver's store today with my father. Torrin came in. Father asked him how everyone was doing and he said well enough, considering. That's what he said—'considering.' But he also said he was worried you weren't letting yourself be sad enough and your father was beginning to think you might need to be sent away to somewhere you could be more—" He paused, trying to remember the words he had heard. "More—no, better—*better* guided through your grief.

"So, I knew you were angry and that they were noticing. I came to tell you about thinking of them as squirrels." He shrugged again. "I didn't think you would cry."

She had not thought she would either, not in front of anyone. But he was different. He had been thinking of her, and known something about her that she had not even realized, something that was a danger to her and could rend another too terrible revision in her world if it was not changed.

"Why are you helping me?" she asked. "My family is—with my mother being chosen. You shouldn't want to spend too much time with any of us. The weather hasn't changed all the way yet."

"It hasn't been long enough. My father says Draigon Weather takes months to change, even af—after your mother was taken up the mountain."

"I'm not sure that I can think of squirrels for enough months." The unfairness of her loss pressed on her, a tightness in her chest. "Why is everyone so sure that it's women who have to go to the fire? Why is it only women?"

He pulled back a little, as though surprised. "Because everyone knows that's what the Draigon want. They don't want men. Men are too—too—" He stopped and frowned.

"Too what?"

"Too strong," he said at last.

"Strong?" Heat filled the base of her throat and drove back the weight in her chest. "Why would a creature that can roast the whole Spur think any human is too strong?"

"But men can be Draighil. We can kill them. We have killed them! And I—" He hesitated and Leiel realized that whatever he was about to say was the real reason he had sought her out today.

"What about you?" she asked.

"I'm going to kill that Draigon. The one that took your mother. When I am grown, I am going to kill it."

She stared at him. Did he really care that much about what had happened to her mother? Did he really care that much about what happened to *her*? She shook her head. "But only the Draighil know how to kill Draigon. Only they know how to do that."

"The Ehlewer will take me. I can talk to Soibel, the Elder who comes to get wood from my father. He knows I am strong enough. I can train to become Draighil."

"But Cleod, you're not Farlan. Only Farlan can go to the Ehlewer and learn."

He shook his head. "Not anymore. There are not as many Farlan as there used to be. And only some of them even *want* to be Draighil. I heard Soibel tell my father many times that he wished more of the candidates for the Enclave were as strong and smart as me."

Leiel stared at him. She could believe that; Cleod *was* all those things. Still, she shook her head. "Even if they took you, you would be gone forever. And it's dangerous. How can anyone kill a Draigon? It would be so long—years and years. You would have to give up your whole life to do that. What about owning your own store? You told me that was what you wanted to do."

He shook his head. "I did. But not after—it's *wrong*, Leiel. No one should be taken like that. Taken away and given to a monster. I can be Draighil. I can do it. And once I am—I am going to kill it. I am going to find the Draigon that killed your mother, and I am going to kill it for you." He got to his feet and reached down, pulled her up with him. "When I am grown, I will be a Draighil, and no one will ever have to be chosen again."

She wanted to grab hold of him and not let go for a long, long time. But she didn't. Because it wasn't possible. It was a generous idea—but she didn't want him to do it. She didn't want him to be able to join the Ehlewer. It would take him away. It could get him hurt.

"Thank you," she said. "But there aren't really Draighil anymore, are there? If there were, why didn't one come to save my mother?"

"I asked Soibel that. I asked why, when the Council took your mother, a

Draighil did not come. He said they did send for someone—the best hunter in Arnan—Orrah. But the Council panicked. They took your mother before he could get here. Because all the Draighil in the Spur are old men now—teachers but not fighters. And Orrah lives all the way west to the ocean."

"They tried to save my mother?" She could hardly breathe at the thought. She had never even considered that someone might have tried to stop the Sacrifice. Her father had been so resigned to the doom her mother faced, that he had never spoken of the possibility of stopping it. Ilora herself had not fought the Council's decision when it was announced. No one had raised any cry at all against the condemnation of her mother.

"Yes, Leiel," Cleod said. "And if there were more Draighil, if there was one closer—they could have done it. And *I* can do it. I can learn. They will have me."

"What about your father?" Maybe the woodcutter would stop his son.

"I'll convince him." He smiled. "And when I am Draighil, I can make sure a girl never gets killed again in the Spur. And I can make sure the Draigon who killed your mother is the first I kill."

"How? How can you do that? Why would you?"

He frowned at her. "Because you're my friend. You're the only real friend I have." He smiled again, and she felt a strange shiver of warmth ease the knot in her chest. "And I don't like it when you're sad. I don't like it that you're so unhappy and that you hurt so bad you can't even cry. I don't like it, and I can't fix it. But I can kill that Draigon, and someday I will." His face seemed to tighten all over with seriousness. "Soibel says there are ways to tell them apart. He will teach me." He reached out and touched her arm again, and she felt tears gather in her eyes. Her whole face was hot and she could only nod at his next words. "I can do it. I can learn, and I can make sure the monster is punished. Maybe I can kill all the Draigon."

The thought was too much, that someday Arnan might be free of the horrible beasts. "If that could happen..." She shook her head.

"So much could change." His voice trembled with excitement. "When there are no Draigon left—girls won't have to worry about not following the laws and becoming so bad the Draigon come. Maybe there won't have to be so many rules anymore."

Leiel started at his words. "What do you mean?"

"The laws. The laws are to keep girls from doing things that make the Draigon angry. Why do you think they only ever want girls? My father told me. When Draigon Weather comes, it is because—" He stopped as though he was just realizing what he was saying.

But she understood already. What he thought. What everyone must think. That Ilora had done something bad to cause the Draigon to take an interest in her. Something so terrible that it had caused a drought that had nearly wiped out all crops and wells and rivers in the Spur.

She took a step back, and he paled. "I'm sorry," he said. "I don't think your mother meant to be bad. But why else would the Draigon come? Why would the Council choose her? Maybe she did something by mistake—something she was not supposed to do."

Her thoughts froze her. What if Gial and Klem and father believed the same thing Cleod did—that her mother had been doing things that were against the laws, and had brought the Draigon down on them all? Was that why they would not talk about mother? Was that why they were treating *her* so differently now?

"My mother was not doing *anything!*" She said the words—but they were not completely true. Because her mother had *always* been doing something that was just a little outside the rules. Just a tiny bit. The way she insisted Leiel keep going to school long after all the other girls had stopped attending. The songs she sang. Her refusal to wear what Addor declared to be 'proper clothing' but which she called 'silly and inhibiting.'

Leiel had the sudden urge to laugh. Because what she had done every day with her mother, what her mother had taught her, even the bedtime stories she had told—those things meant *Leiel too* was doing things that were considered wrong. She had been doing them her whole life, and she was doing them still. Even coming to the pond today was an act that would be looked down upon, punishable by a whipping under her father's strict new discipline.

Her anger at Cleod dissolved. "You're trying to keep me safe." The relief that flooded his features made her want to cry. "You don't have to do that. And you don't have to try to be Draighil. Just promise you will stay my friend."

"Of course I'll be your friend. I can be Draighil too. I will always be your friend."

She nodded at his words. He meant them. She could see it in the set of his jaw and the smile in his eyes. But no comfort touched her heart. Always was a long time, and being Draighil was being something different for always.

12

Leiel

"**S**HE'S SO *ODD*." THE WHISPER FLOATED FROM THE HUDDLE OF GIRLS, SO MUFFLED that there was no way to tell who murmured the phrase. Leiel smiled as she continued across the dirt lot away from the school.

"I think they're talking about you again," Cleod said when she joined him on the log.

"They are. I hope they talk about me all the time."

"You do? Why?"

"Because it keeps them from talking to you."

"They talk about me, too," he said. "Because I talk to you."

"There have to be more interesting things than us to talk about. Cooking or books or something."

"I saw a book that's interesting," he said.

"How can you tell just by looking at it?"

"The priest who runs the sanctuary library—he hired my father to cut wood. We delivered it yesterday, and I had to carry some in to stock the wood box. I saw it there."

"An interesting book in a library?" She laughed.

"It was different. It was open on the desk with a lot of other books and papers. But this one had strange words in it."

"What do you mean strange?"

"I didn't know any of the words. Some of the letter symbols looked the same as what we use, but a lot were different."

"You went peeking around on a priest's desk?" She stared at him. "What if he caught you? The priests are mean."

He shrugged. "He was talking to my father. No one notices me when I am working. I am just the boy who carries wood."

She shook her head and her hair fell into her eyes. He was always saying things like that, but a lot of people noticed him. They watched him. They stopped and talked to him. And when the other girls talked about him, it was not to discuss how strange he was. "You get noticed." Her curiosity took over, a tingle in her mind. She tucked her hair back and eyed him. "Could you tell what the book was about?"

He shook his head. "Not really. But the priest couldn't either. There were all kinds of scribbles in one notebook, with lots crossed out, like he was trying to figure out what it said, but couldn't."

"He was trying to understand it?"

Cleod nodded. "But he couldn't."

"I wonder what it said? I thought the priests could read anything."

"Maybe not this," he said. He swung one leg over the log and lay out along it with a foot on either side, grinning up at her. "I bet you could though. Learn to read it."

She stared down at him, then reached and flicked her finger across his nose.

He swatted at her hand as though she was an annoying bug. "Stop it. I am trying to tell you something."

"About a secret book."

"It's not secret. I saw where he put it, when I came back inside. I was bringing in another load of wood, and I saw him throw it in the burn pile."

"He burned it?"

"He would have, but I was loading wood. I put kindling on top of it. I buried it so it would be a few fires before he got to it."

She turned on the log so she peered directly down at him, her face hovering right over his, her nose pointed at his forehead, her eyes meeting his. "Why would you do that?"

"So I would have time to find another book that had a cover like it."

Her eyes went wide. "You switched the book?"

He nodded, his face distorted by the strange angle from which she viewed him. He rolled onto his stomach and propped his arms on the log, forcing her to sit back a little out of his way. Now they were eye to eye right-side up. "Sure I did," he said. "He didn't want it. I thought you might."

"You took it for me?" She stared at him. He couldn't have. That was insane. The punishment for stealing from a priest was...was...she did not even know what it was. She had never heard of anyone doing such a thing. But it would be terrible. Her stomach knotted and flipped. If anything happened to Cleod, she wouldn't be able to stand it. "What if he changed his mind? What if he opened it again before he burned it? He'll know you took it!"

Cleod shrugged. "Why would he care even if he did?" he asked. "He couldn't read it. Why would he worry about the woodcutter being able to?"

Despite the worry churning her belly, his words made sense. She looked at him a moment more. "You took it for me?"

He was trying very hard not to look smug, but his eyes were bright, and his lips were twitching. She found herself grinning and reached out and shoved his shoulder. "Well, where is it, if you took it for me?"

He was grinning now, too. "I hid it. You'll have to guess."

She shoved him again, and this time he went with the motion and rolled off the log, gaining his feet and hopping away from her as she leaped up and followed him. "Cleod, tell me," she said, grabbing for him. He winked at her, and she would have glared at him had she not been so delighted by the idea that he had done something so brazen as to steal a book from a priest, on her behalf.

"After school," he said in promise. "Those girls have enough to talk about without me giving you things in front of them."

She laughed. "That's the best reason to do it that way."

He winked. The smirk on his face was agreement.

"You *do* have it here!"

"It's in the hollow place," he said and glanced over his shoulder at the log.

She lunged past him toward the spot he indicated, hiked up her skirts to scramble over the log. The crumbly bark scraped at her bare knees as she bent and thrust her arm into the opening in the wood. A few seconds of groping and her hand found a bundle wrapped in oilcloth. She pinched her lips tight and pulled it out. The small, wrapped rectangle was little bigger than her open hand, and her fingers shook just a bit as she peeled back the cloth to reveal an unremarkable, leather binding.

"Well, take a look," Cleod said, from above her.

She looked at him, then reached up with her free hand and yanked him down to sit beside her on the log. "You really took it!" she said, and folded open the cover. The pages inside were yellowed with age, but the ink was dark and readable. Or it would be if she understood any of the words. As he had said, some of the letters looked familiar, but none of the words made sense. Turning pages, she slowly browsed through the book. No drawings or printer's marks, just sentence after sentence of the strange language laid out in an indecipherable taunt. But it mattered not at all.

She folded it closed and hugged it to her chest. "Thank you."

He was smiling. "You like things you're not supposed to. And this is something no one else knows how to know."

A laugh burst forth, drawing more stares from the other students. Another comment floated to her ears, something half-heard about 'being crude.' Leiel wrinkled her nose at the nearest group and let out a laugh that ended in a snort.

"You only make them worse when you do that." Cleod shook his head.

"They don't need an excuse. They're bothered by me because they want to be." She hugged the book even tighter, rocking a little around it. "As long as you're my friend, I don't care."

13

Cleod – 25 years

THE ROCK DIGGER WAS CROWDED. MINERS, TRAVELERS, TRADERS, AND soldiers were all crammed together on the battered benches, packed belly to hip against the tables and the bar. Every bit of the wood—floors and walls and furniture alike—was worn dark with decades of grease, sweat, and smoke. If the stench of unwashed bodies and stale beer was enough to overpower a newcomer to the tavern, most of its patrons were long since too drunk to care. Barmaids and barmen shouted orders to the cooks in the kitchen, the crowd, and each other as they maneuvered through the jammed levels of the common rooms. The crowd had grown to well over the capacity of the seating in the Rock since the storm had broken over the mountains and set to dousing the entire region.

Tucked farthest from the great hearth that blazed in the center of the boisterous throng, Cleod drained the mug of ercew and raised his hand to the harried serving boy passing by. He caught the boy's attention and raised the empty mug. "Best not let me get too dry."

The young fellow scoffed, clearly unimpressed. "You and the rest of this sodden lot," he said and pushed through the press toward the bar.

Cleod frowned, trying to form a response, but his thoughts wouldn't coalesce into anything he could speak. The server was gone before Cleod could shape words. He was drunk then. That was good. But he was not drunk enough. The chatter from the man stuffed in next to him at the trestle was still half comprehensible. And that was, by half, too comprehensible.

The miner who was slumped over and snoring on the other side of the talker, had a mug before him that was only half empty. Cleod reached around and snatched up the drink. One to hold him over until the next round arrived.

Angry shouts and grumbling erupted from the far side of the common room, pulling Cleod's unwilling attention. A new band of men had entered the tavern, bringing with them brisk air and cold blowing rain. Shouts to 'Close the door or come to rot,' came from those unfortunate enough to be seated near the entrance. Far from the fire though he was, Cleod was glad he had arrived early at his seat. At least it would remain dry.

Finally, the last man entered, and the portal was shoved closed. Though they were blurring around the edges, Cleod recognized that the newcomers were dressed a bit too well for the Rock. Not that their clothing was any more expensive than most of those in the bar, but it was, by lengths, much cleaner. Heavy canvas pants and black vests, boiled wool jackets under oilcloth slickers. He saw the long haired man in the lead—dressed in the same uniform style as the others but for a burgundy leather hat with a black band—scan the crowd as though looking for someone. But any curiosity about the new arrivals faded as the table boy arrived with the fresh mug of ercew. The appearance of the potent, bitter ale reclaimed all of Cleod's attention. "Bring me another," he told the boy as he accepted the tankard.

His lips found the frothy edge of the crockery, and he sucked in a large swallow. It burned down his throat and settled hard in his belly. To men in fancy clothing getting wet, Cleod thought, and to getting drunk as the abyss will let me on the way to the bowels of eternity. He slouched deeper on the bench and settled in to drink in earnest.

He was most of the way through yet another mug, and the talker beside him had joined his friend in oblivious slumber, when a hand landed on his shoulder. He tilted his head up to see the long haired leader of the newcomers standing over him. Up close, the man's clothing marked him as a drover—a well off one by the look of him. Probably a Dorn—a trail lead—from the way he held himself. He was relaxed, his gaze steady and intense, as though he expected those around him to pay attention when he spoke.

Cleod shook off the stranger's grasp. "No room here," he said, making an effort to keep his words from slurring. From the look on the man's face, it did not seem he had succeeded.

The intruder frowned. "Cleod Draighil?" His expression indicated that he was half-hoping he had the wrong man.

Which he did. Draighil! Cleod gave a rumbling laugh that ended in a belch. "Hardly," he said. "No Draighil here. You need a drink, man. Move along to the bar."

"I need Cleod Ehlewer. Formerly of the Ehlewer Enclave. Lead Draighil of the Spur Region and now, apparently, a slobbering drunk."

Around them, a few of the less inebriated souls had grown quiet and were watching the exchange with sudden interest. A prickle of something that might be anger formed like a headache behind Cleod's eyes. "I *said*, no Draighil here. *Move on, stranger.*" The 't' in the word sounded only as a suggestion, but he focused as best he could on the man and offered what he hoped was his fiercest glare.

With a weathered hand, the man reached up and shoved back his shoulder length brown hair. He made a scoffing noise, then tipped his head toward Cleod.

"He's too drunk to do harm," he said. "Bring him."

Only then did Cleod realize the rest of the men who had entered with the long-haired leader stood around him. He gave a shout of protest as they grabbed him under the arms and dragged him to his feet. The bench wobbled as they pulled his feet across it, but the weight of the sleeping drunks kept it upright. "By all the gods of old I'll—" he shouted as they manhandled him mostly upright. One put a hand over his mouth to silence him, and, when he proved incapable of staying vertical on his own, another picked up his feet. He thrashed and croaked out muffled threats as they bundled him unceremoniously through the crowd toward the stair that led to the ratty, rentable bedrooms.

The crowd roared with laughter and cheered the strangers on. As they carried him up the stairs, the leader tossed a pouch of coins to a barmaid.

The bucket in the corner of the room could not contain the stench as Cleod heaved up the day's excess consumption. His body shook and sweat streamed from his temples, and he tried to ignore the humiliation of presenting his illness to an audience. The long-haired Dorn sat in the room's only chair. He was seated as far as possible from the mess being created in the corner, and his back was to the door, blocking any chance of exit.

Cleod shook his head. He barely had the strength to roll off the bed and crawl to the bucket to throw up. Ercew induced a lovely drunken state—best managed by staying in it. The process of getting sober from the beverage was the most brutal he knew. It had been months since he had faced it, having managed to maintain a steady state of near oblivion for as long as he could now recall.

But the stranger in the chair offered him no relief. Only the bucket that he periodically swapped for a fresh one, and a few cups of icy water. Food was an unbearable thought. Cleod smelled the smoke from the fire in the room's tiny stove, but discerned no warmth from it. Chilled and sweating, shaking yet strangely able to see and hear everything around him with a clarity that was unnerving, he propped his shoulder against the wall by the foul bucket. He was not quite able to sit upright, yet unwilling to face his tormentor while lying on the floor.

"Who are you?" he asked, his throat raw in the wake of the bitter bile that had scoured it. "What do you want with me?"

The dark-haired man spoke with easy authority, as though he found himself in situations like this every day, sitting watch on puking drunkards. "My name's Kilras. I'm top Dorn for Haggris of Bajor."

"Why are you doing this?" Cleod managed the phrase before a new wave of nausea forced his head back over the pail.

Kilras waited until Cleod finished. "I need a man with your skills. Since you seem to have abandoned your profession, I thought you might need work."

Cleod would have laughed if he thought he could do so without heaving up more of the week's binge. Work? The last thing he could conceive of was work. He had failed as Draighil. Failed at the one thing he had spent his life training to do well. Failed in the worst possible way. Work? For a trail drover? What did he know of that? What use could this man possibly consider him to be?

"How long do you plan to keep me here?"

"As long as it takes."

"For what?"

"To get you sober enough to discuss my offer."

This time Cleod did laugh, though it made his head pound and his stomach jerk. "Keep your offer. I'm not whatever it is you're looking for."

"We'll see," Kilras said. "When you're done spewing your guts."

Cleod started to snarl a response, but choked as more bile rose in his throat. He lurched over the bucket again, and this time, when he finished, he did not have the strength left to do anything but lay his head on the stained floor and groan.

The sun beat through the small, grungy window, slammed into Cleod's eyes as he cracked them open. He groaned and rolled away from the brutal brightness. Blankets shifted around him. Someone had moved him back to the narrow bed. Not only that, but they had taken his clothing. He was naked under the thin covers. Naked and clean. How someone had managed the feat of bathing him was beyond understanding. Just peeling off the grimy clothes must have taken an act of will. Sponging down a body that had not seen a bathtub in months would have required an iron stomach.

His mouth was dry and fuzzy, like a badly-knitted wool sock. He worked his tongue around it as he shifted, trying to sit up. His arms shook as they lifted his weight; his vision swam, but no nausea came. His stomach felt plucked and drawn. He guessed he had nothing left inside to expel.

"It rises," said the voice he had hoped had only been part of a nightmare.

He looked up. Kilras was standing by the window, hand still on the shutter latch.

"You're the brute responsible for this damnable light," Cleod said.

Kilras grinned, and there was too much amusement in the expression for Cleod's mood. "How do you feel?"

"Like I need a drink." His head was no longer pounding. In fact, his mind felt clearer than it had in weeks. Which was exactly what he had been trying to avoid. Whatever the stranger was trying to accomplish, his actions were working directly against the purposeful indifference Cleod had spent so much effort and coin cultivating.

Kilras shrugged. "That's not going to happen. At least not any time soon."

"Just who are you again? Kilras is it? Kilras? What do you want with *me*?"

The older man turned fully to face him. "I answered this question already."

"Anything said to a man while he is vomiting into a bucket should not be expected to be remembered with clarity."

"A *man* are you?" The trail lead chuckled. "Not a drunken coward on the run from his past, but a *man*? We'll see."

Anger flared through Cleod's stomach and he shoved himself into a sitting position. "If I am not a man, why are you here? What do you want with me?"

"Draighil."

Cleod couldn't stop the flinch that hearing that title caused. He cursed under his breath that the other had seen it.

Kilras met his gaze. "Not many men survive that training, Cleod Ehlewer. I don't care if you've turned your back on the Enclave. I wouldn't care if you'd never killed a Draigon. All I care about is that everyone I have talked to said that before you decided to drown your life in ercew—and cheap ercew at that from the stench you rendered up the last few days—you were the finest swordsman anyone had seen in two generations."

Kilras folded his arms across his chest. "I'm a businessman and a damn fine strategist. I won't long be Dorn to anyone but myself. I'll break from Haggris by year's end. What I *don't* have is a Ruhelrn—a lead sword—whose arm is even half as strong as my own. I need someone to ride guard with me. I need a lead defender on the escort. Want the job?"

Cleod stared at him, trying to wrap his mind around the offer. Caravan escort? Him? In a thousand years it would never have been the kind of work he would have considered. He had built his life on a grand dream—an arrow-straight path to glory and vengeance—with a shining prize at the end. Not ever had he seen himself as a soldier for hire. A paid sentinel. Those were never labels he had considered applying to himself.

Thirst rose inside him, uncoiling and demanding satiation. He gasped at the suddenness of it, the wild urgency. Tension wound through him and he shuddered. Neither had he dreamed the word *drunkard* would be an apt description.

"I need a drink," he repeated.

"I've talked to people who know you. They say you're loyal to a point of absurdity once you commit to something. I'm not asking you to be a mercenary. I want more than a hired sword. I want someone I can someday consider a partner. I want someone I can trust."

"Trust?" Cleod shook his head. That was something he had sworn he would never do again—let anyone trust him. Make any promises. "Trust me? I failed the only person who ever trusted me."

"And you've been trying to drink yourself to death ever since. Loyalty like that isn't something bought and sold. Come with me and let me earn that from you. If we don't get along, fine, you can go back to drinking yourself into insensibility. If we do—I'd like the chance to help you save your life."

The words hung in the air between them and for a moment neither of them moved, then Cleod swung his legs over the edge of the cot. "Where are my clothes?"

"That depends."

"What in the names of a hundred dead gods does that mean?" Cleod glared at the man. "You want to save me from myself, but you don't know where my pants are?"

The trace of a smile crossed Kilras's face. He moved away from the window to the small wash stand and picked up a neatly folded bundle. He tossed it toward the bed.

Reflex took over and Cleod caught it out of the air. He looked at the items in his hands. Tan canvas pants and a grey linen shirt. A black vest. "What's this?" he demanded.

"Your new uniform. If you accept my offer," Kilras said. He gestured to a burlap bag at his feet. "Or these. I had them washed. But there's only so much soap can do for ten months worth of stains and mildew." He met Cleod's gaze. "If you put on the new ones, I'll have these burned. So it depends—on which you decide are your clothes."

Something to decide. How long had it been since Cleod had made any decision except about how many more drinks to consume in a day? It felt like forever. Life was easy without decisions. Without responsibility. Without any opportunity to fail, or let anyone down. But without any *opportunity* at all. He looked up at the stranger standing in the middle of the room awaiting his choice. "I still need a drink. I can't ever imagine *not* needing a drink."

"This won't be easy, but I'm willing to work through it if you are. We've a long trip ahead of us, back to the coast and south to Bajor. I expect you'll fall down several times before you learn to stand again. But if you try, I won't give up on you.

"So make a choice and put your clothes on. I've wasted four days just waiting on you to get sober enough to have this conversation, and the rest of my people are restless."

Cleod drew a breath. He was tired. Tired beyond words. But for the first time in so very long, he felt like a living being, not a specter. "I need something first."

"Name it."

"I could use some water."

Kilras grinned and turned to pour him a cup of water from the pitcher on the wash stand.

Cleod watched him for a few seconds, then shook loose the linen shirt and slid it over his head.

14

Cleod – 26 years

LONG MONTHS IN THE SADDLE HAD ABUSED AND THEN RECONDITIONED CLEOD'S body. Now the sway of the bay mare beneath him was starting to become familiar, as was the easy rapport he shared with the Dorn who rode beside him. He still had difficulty accepting how well he and Kilras had settled into working together. Nothing was simple in their interactions—Cleod found himself in daily battle with a desire for liquor that sometimes nearly drove him to violence. Those moments, it was Kilras alone who dealt with him. Kilras who held him while he thrashed against the restraints the older man applied to keep him from riding hard for the nearest tavern. Kilras who tolerated his fits of rage, and the sobbing that overcame him in the night. Kilras who worked every day with him, for weeks, retraining scarred hips to accept long periods in the saddle.

Cleod could ride for hours now without having to lie out in a wagon and rest. He was coming back to himself a little more every day. He was getting to know the other outriders and the cooks and the healers who formed the rest of Haggris Ritt's caravan team. One thing he had learned quickly—Haggris might own the business, but Kilras owned the loyalty of those who rode with him.

"Sehina is your best tracker," Cleod said, looking across the expanse of open land toward the great harbor city of Bajor. "She's also your lead horse breaker." It had puzzled him at first, that such an important member of the caravan team was a woman. Never had he seen a woman in such a position. But Kilras had scoffed at his questioning, and Sehina was more than competent.

Kilras nodded. "The best breaker this side of the Seebo."

"And yet you have relegated her to chopping onions for the cook wagons."

"Using the same logic that applied at The Rock Digger where I found you. Place your people where you can best use them to measure trouble if it's coming. Did you think all the servers in that hole were male for the barmaid's pleasure?"

The question was one Cleod had never considered. He turned the idea in his mind. "The tavern keeper kept the women behind the bar to make sure he knew where the worst lechers would likely sit."

"The entire place was segregated to keep trouble to a minimum," Kilras said. "Women behind the bar where they had easy access to weapons. Older boys running food and drink. No table big enough to allow a large gang to gather. Small rooms with only one exit for the gaming tables."

"So why have you got Sehina cutting vegetables?"

"We're in Bajor. There's a horde of new merchants looking for a spot in the next outgoing caravan. They'll start arriving tomorrow around lunch time to be interviewed."

"And Sehina is your choice to make extra food?"

"No one trails with me who doesn't respect my people," Kilras said, looking over at him.

Cleod fell silent again, turning that statement in his mind. Among the Draighil he had been required not just to learn by rote, but to draw reasonable conclusions from very little information. "You put the person the merchants are most likely to disrespect in a position they will see as commanding the least respect. And you see what they do when she—what? Tips a tray of cut onions over their heads?" He looked over at Kilras. The older man was grinning. Cleod laughed. "Sehina doesn't mind you using her in this capacity?"

"No more than you'll mind when I tell them you're a drunken, disgraced ex-Draighil with scars so tight you can't walk a mile without buckling."

"Tell them?" The bay stumbled as Cleod yanked hard on the reins and turned the horse into the side of Kilras's mount, stopping them both on the verge of the road. A blistering heat dimmed his vision, and he started to shake as he stared at the Dorn. "You plan to tell them—" Cleod choked on the words even as they formed. He had begun to think he might be able to trust this man with his loyalty.

Kilras leveled his gaze and held it. "You've nothing to fear or be ashamed of. You or Sehina. Why ride with anyone who thinks otherwise? No need to hide who you are to put the useless at ease. It won't surprise me if a few self-important bead sellers won't be able to see your value. And they'll lose the privilege of riding with us."

The anger drained from Cleod. Who was this man who had dragged him from the Rock Digger and battled to keep him sober? "Is this what you do? Take in strays and wanderers and failures and build them back to something of worth?"

"I knock the rust off well-made tools. You. Nae. Sehina. All too good to be wasting away through the inability of others to see your worth. Or your own Draigon-blinded inability to see it."

Cleod flinched at the word Draigon, and the bay shied hard again under him. He fought down the fire that erupted in his gut as teeth clenched and moisture beaded across his brow. The effort cost him. His hands on the reins spasmed. He was grateful when Kilras reached out and caught the mare's bridle and kept her close.

"Easy now."

Cleod couldn't tell if Kilras's words were meant for him or for the horse. Either way, the calm tone in which they were uttered helped back down the trained fury that threatened to break loose inside him.

After a few seconds, he was able to draw a composing breath and nod to the man beside him. "You did that with a purpose."

"You need to learn control," Kilras said. "What little you learned at the Enclave, you drowned in ercew."

"What *little* I learned?" Cleod's temper flared again. "What do you know of Draighil training to say something as ignorant as *that*? I spent ten years—"

"There's control of your skills, and there's control of your emotional reactions. The Enclave had both—over *you*. They *wanted* your rage. As much as they wanted your sword and your talent and your loyalty. They wanted you to hate those beasts beyond any sensible measure. It worked. Maybe you had a head start on it because of what happened when you were young. And what happened to you on that mountain tempered it like steel. You're volatile. I'll keep prodding you until you get a rope around those reactions."

Cleod stared back at him, shaking in the saddle, his face burning into a flush. Because Kilras was more correct than he knew. Cleod's emotions were as unpredictable as a lightning flash. And their impact could be just as violent, if he allowed it to be translated into action. But it was more than the trained Draighil response to even the word Draigon that destabilized him, it was the shame and the guilt that his failure at that work had engendered in him. "You play a dangerous game. I am not safe in that state."

Kilras laughed. "If what I wanted was safe, I wouldn't have come looking for you. I don't mind that you're dangerous. I value it. But I want you *aware* when you are. Get used to my provocations. Down the trail, you'll be grateful."

15

Cleod

ᴀ SHIMMER ON THE HORIZON, NOT JUST A TRICK OF THE LIGHT AND AIR, BUT actual motion. Cleod raised a hand to signal halt and the lead wagon slowed beside him.

"Trouble?" the driver asked.

"Perhaps, Jahmess," Cleod said. "I am new to this part of Arnan."

"You're a fine Ruhelrn. I trust your judgment. You should, too."

Nae rode up, his bearded face scrunched with its typical expression of displeasure. "What have we?"

"Something strange." Cleod smiled at the older man's rumbling tone. Though Nae had been with Kilras longer than any other scout, his unwillingness to do more than the letter of what was asked of him had kept him in a junior position for years. A fact that didn't seem to concern Nae at all.

"Out here?" Nae snorted. "What's not strange?"

"A mirage inside a mirage," Cleod said. He turned his head to study the horizon with just the edge of his gaze. Again, the shimmer within the shimmer. If he tried to focus on it, it vanished. Was it even there? The land was strange to him, flat and smooth with browned, waving grasses that grew as high as his horse's knees. The heat seemed to catch in the seed heads and linger, contributing to the eerie undulations where the sky met the earth.

"You're not making sense, boy. The Dorn will need more than a funny phrase on your lips to draw us up for long."

Cleod frowned. Something was not right. He could ride ahead and see, but if he rode into trouble, he would have no way to warn the caravan. A glance around showed him a rise of land just to the north. He could ride higher and try to gain a better perspective...but the same problem offered itself—distance from the group. The landscape was too open for him to hide his actions from any eyes that may be watching, but what option did he have?

"Is Kilras back?"

Nae shook his head. "Repairing that wagon wheel probably took most of the morning."

"Well, if he gets back before I do, tell him I went up for a better look." Cleod pointed to his intended destination.

A grunt was Nae's reply as he turned his horse and rode back down the caravan to see if the Dorn had returned yet.

The driver of the lead wagon spoke up. "We'll wait,"

Cleod nodded. "Be ready. I wish I could tell you for what." He put heels to the bay mare and moved away from the caravan at a lope.

Something took over. He didn't let himself think, just angled away from the wagons in a perpendicular line. The hill rose north and west, and he let himself drift behind it. If hostile eyes were watching, he hoped it would seem he was seeking the easiest way up the rise. But what he really needed was a moment of privacy not so far removed from the group he was charged to protect. The mare's swinging stride rocked him as his mind tangled with the problem before him. He had to know what lay ahead, yet something warned him that to venture forth and seek it directly would be unwise.

For the first time in years, the rhythm of his heart took over, and his consciousness skipped away. The white light that lit the edges of all movement in Gweld swarmed over him. Two choices: acuity—to see the actual world around him in a detail so intense it would leave him shaking, but able to react with a speed beyond thought; or projection—to throw his awareness outside himself and leave his body to fend for itself, trusting his training to keep him on the horse and safe. The decision happened in an instant. His perception leapt, and he was moving across the plain at a speed at the edge of cognition.

Far, far, the distance to the horizon. Colors were too bright, sounds too crisp. His heart beat half the rhythm of the turning world and he expanded his attention, seeking the thing that had triggered his unease.

At first there was nothing discernible. The grass fanned over the earth in all directions, and the sun beat down like a hammer. Nothing stirred but the wind and the clouds in the sky. And yet—

A humming started on the edges of his mind. Then he felt it as though beneath his feet—a tremor, a whisper, something active that could not be seen directly. An instant later he saw it, a subtle change in the rhythm with which the grass waved. Underground and massive, something was shifting the very earth. And it was advancing in violent surges that sent ripples through the air, then faded into the heat wave of the mirage.

Drearloc. Ground locusts. Vicious insects that burrowed through the earth as they migrated—until they sensed a herd of animals above and burst forth to devour them alive. And a caravan was nothing but a herd of people...

The realization threw him back into his body with a violent jerk that sent the mare skittering sideways. He gasped as pain rebounded inside his skull. Too long. Too long since he had accessed the talent. Too long since he had tried to control the skill. He reeled in the saddle and the mare stumbled sideways to a stop.

"Gods of old be praised," he said, clinging to the saddle horn. "Sehina trained you well, little horse." His vision swam and clouded and he fought to contain the Overlash. He had to get back to the caravan. Had to warn Kilras. There was no time for weakness or hesitation, but his body would not respond to his will. Shaking, he fought for the strength to grip the reins and guide the horse. He cried out his frustration, and was again grateful for the solid nature and training of the animal with which he was partnered. She seemed to sense his need and turned on her own to return to the others. Whether it was a simple instinct to return to the familiar in a time of stress or a true understanding of what he wanted, he did not care. She made for the caravan.

As the wagons loomed closer in his blurred vision, he saw two riders break away and head toward him at speed. It seemed a lifetime before they reached him, and when they did it was Kilras who reached out and grasped his arm, steadied him. "Old Gods! Cleod did you seek within the Gweld? Is our danger so certain?"

"Drearloc," Cleod whispered, struggling to form the words. "Traveling—I have only read of them—but the sound—the earth—"

Kilras cut him off as he turned to the rider beside him. Cleod could not see clearly enough to tell which scout it was. "Back! Tell Jahmess. Turn the wagons and make with all speed for the rocks where we camped last night.

Everyone rides." The other scout whirled his mount and galloped back to the wagons, shouting orders.

He turned back to Cleod, his brow scrunched and his lips tight. "Can you stay in the saddle?"

"I will," Cleod said. He would not be the reason for any delay. It could be fatal.

"Drearloc," Kilras said, and let fly a curse to blister skin. "Out of season and by all rights impossible. Hang tight."

Cleod twisted his barely responsive hands in the mare's mane as Kilras grabbed her headstall and sent both horses thundering back to the group.

Turmoil reigned. Shouts filled the air. The bang and tangle of wagons moving too fast. Hooves pounded the earth. Somewhere a child was shrieking.

"Spread them out," Kilras called. "Single riders off the road—leave the easy way to the wagons. Ride! Cut loose the spare oxen and drive them. There's no time. Make for hard ground. Dump anything you can spare."

Cleod hung on as Kilras dragged the mare up beside the map maker's wagon. "Kimla, take him, then push for the rocks. There are Drearloc on the move. He just saved our lives."

Hands gripped him, and Cleod found himself half-dragged, half-pushed onto a rocking wooden surface.

"The mare," he gasped. She was too good to fall to such a fate as Drearloc.

"Sehina has her," the map man's voice came to him. "Hold on."

The wagon clattered into stunning motion. He had not known such a vehicle was capable of speed. His last thought before the pain pulled him under was to be grateful for things he did not know.

He awakened to the sound of wood impacting stone. The sun was high in the sky, and around him was a chaos of sound in action. Words he could not decipher echoed through the air, and it was the echo that reassured him. The rocks. They had reached the rocks. Relief dragged a ragged breath from him, and he curled into himself as the Overlash shook his body. Blessed gods it had been so long! He had been Draigre—a green candidate—the last time he had been so overwhelmed. But the years of neglected skill and the drink had taken their toll, and he was lucky to not be heaving his breakfast over the map cases that lay spilled around him.

"Cleod—" Kilras's voice was quiet. Cleod lifted his face and saw the Dorn crouched beside him on the tailgate of the wagon.

Cleod nodded. "I'll be all right. I should have warned you what I was doing. But I didn't know myself until the decision was made."

"You did right," Kilras said. "You trusted your instinct, and gave us the warning we needed. It's what I hired you to do." He gestured behind himself and someone Cleod could not see placed a canteen in Kilras's hand. He pulled the cork and slid his arm under Cleod's head to lift him enough to take a drink. "No one else could've done what you did. They would've been under us before we could react. You saved a hundred lives today."

Grateful, Cleod swallowed the water. "Losses?" He was afraid to ask, but needing to know.

"Two oxen. No people. No horses. You did well."

Cleod closed his eyes and nodded. He had done well. How long had it been since he had done anything well? Years. So many long, hopeless years. He needed a drink. But he did not want to ask for one. In this moment, the water in the canteen he held in shaking hands was not what he wanted, but it, and the presence of the man—no, the *friend*—beside him, was enough. Tears gathered in his eyes.

A hand touched his arm. "Rest. We're all safe now, thanks to you. Rest easy. There'll be time to talk later."

Cleod curled tight into himself, the canteen held close. The comforting weight of a blanket settled over him, sheltering him, and he let go, sliding toward the healing safety of sleep.

16

Leiel – 10 years

L EIEL WAS UNSURE WHAT SHE EXPECTED FROM HER BROTHERS, BUT THE ICY silence that greeted her as she stepped into the barn was not it. At first, she thought the cause of the tension she sensed was only between them, perhaps the result of some disagreement about the new distribution of chores that had been laid out in the last few weeks. The months since their mother's death had seen even the smallest disputes burst into full-blown shouting matches. As the weeks dragged forward in this new life they were living, it became clear to Leiel that their mother had been for the family the point on which civility balanced. Leiel imagined her brothers on one side of a scale and her father on the other. Between had been Ilora, and Leiel saw herself scampering back and forth between sides, sending the arms of the device tilting and shuddering. Always before, Ilora had been there to fling out an arm and catch her before she went too far. Block Klem and Gial, or Addor, before the strain of any one disagreement led to complete discord.

But now Ilora was gone, and with her, all the wise care and diplomacy. And the silence in the barn, Leiel realized, held an anger that had been brewing for a long time.

"Elda sent me for Klem," she said. "She says she needs him to bring in wood."

The younger of her brothers tossed his unruly dark hair out of his eyes and glared at her as he stabbed his pitchfork into the bale of hay he was forking out. "Elda *sent* for me? Who is Elda to send for anyone?"

"Klem—" Gial leaned over the edge of the loft. His tone was stern and held a note of warning, inherited from their father.

"Well who is she?" Klem demanded. "No one. Just a cook and a house keeper. Torrin won't even marry the whore, she's so useless."

Leiel sucked back a breath, and the blood drained from her face. It was no secret that Elda and Torrin were more than friends. Never had Leiel heard anyone speak badly of either one. Much less Klem, for whom Elda had only offered love and support through all the horror of the past months.

"Don't you dare!" she said. "Elda takes care of us. She takes care of so much now, now that—since—" She stopped, still hardly able to make herself speak the words. Every time she said them, her mother's death became more real, more horrible. And its effect greater in her life.

"Since mother was roasted alive on a pile of rocks and wood on a mountain top?" Klem shouted. "Say it, Leiel. Say it! Say she's dead. You never say it. She's dead, dead, dead, and it's *your fault!*"

She backed away from the stall where Klem stood even though he had not taken a single step toward her. Backed away as though his words were actual blows. A clatter sounded above her, and Leiel looked up to see Gial swing over the edge of the loft to descend the ladder. Instinctively she moved so that he would be between herself and Klem.

"Stop it, Klem!" Gial's boots hit the sawdust covered floor of the barn. "You can't blame Leiel."

"I can. I *do.*" Klem threw down his pitchfork and stalked out into the aisle between the stalls. "Mother let her learn to read. She made father *send her to school.* Girls are not supposed to read and go to school and—and—they're not allowed! They're not allowed, and mother made father pay off the Council so she could act like—like—like she's one of *us.*" Klem stepped right up in front of Gial, not letting the fact that Gial was a full head taller than him and three years older intimidate him in the least. He scowled—past his older brother—at Leiel, and she drew her shoulders in, trying to make herself smaller. Never had she heard such things here at the farm. Oh, certainly they were whispered throughout the town, even in school. She was one of only a handful of girls who had ever been allowed to attend classes. And all but one other had stopped coming to school years before. Only Brea, daughter of the head herbalist to the Council, still sat at lessons every day. That was proper. Healers were expected to be more educated than most people, because the lives of others—especially the wealthy—depended on their knowledge. But Leiel had never, before this moment, considered the reasons she too was still allowed to attend school.

"You know it's true," Klem shouted. "*You know it too.* You've thought it as much as I have. Mother was chosen because she was too—trying too much to be like a man. Because she wanted Leiel to be like a man. It's her fault they chose mother, and you know it. They should have taken Leiel." His breath rasped harsh with his words as he glared at her. "I hope you burn one day. I hope you pay."

Gial stood still, like a rod of iron embedded in the earth, and he said nothing. And Leiel knew, by his silence, by his refusal to agree, that Klem was right. Gial *did* blame her. Just as Klem did. Did everyone? Torrin and Elda? *Father?* Her stomach flipped into knots. Were they *right?* Was it her fault that mother had died the way she had?

This fate of mine, it has come to others before. Don't be angry for me. This is a great gift. Her mother's words. Her mother's promise. No. Leiel refused to believe she was the reason her mother had burned. Ilora had accepted her fate and blamed no one for it.

"No," Leiel said, her voice barely a whisper to her own ears.

"What?" asked Klem, dodging around Gial before the older boy could stop him.

"No," Leiel repeated, this time finding her voice. She gathered herself, though it took all her will, and took a step toward him. "It's not my fault. I didn't kill mother."

He hit her then. No warning. No shout or rearing back, just a fast slap across her left cheek that sent her stumbling against the door of the stall beside her.

Heat flared through her belly, and she vaguely realized that Gial was moving to grab Klem, but he was reaching for the wrong sibling. Without a sound, Leiel hurled herself at her brother, fists flying and with the full weight of her small body committed to the attack. She felt the skin of her knuckles split open as they connected with Klem's teeth, then the two of them were on the barn floor tumbling into a full brawl. She punched and punched, sometimes her fists finding her brother's flesh and sometimes the hard floor. Tears streamed down her cheeks, and her wrists shook and cramped with the effort behind her blows.

Klem landed another strike against the side of her ear just as Gial took hold of her and yanked her to her feet. He half-tossed, half-shoved her away, and she stumbled toward the door before catching her balance against a wall. She heard Klem screaming. Gial too. She turned to see Gial, arms wrapped under Klem's armpits, holding the younger boy up off the ground to keep him from charging after her. Feet kicked in the air and arms flailed, but Gial held tight and all Klem could do was shout and glare and threaten as he struggled to reach her.

She knew he shouted threats, not by the words which were so muddled she could barely understand them, but by the volume of his shrieking and the twisting of his face. Another roaring jumble of sound reached her, and she realized it was not just Klem's anger that muffled her senses, but the fact that her ears were ringing from the blows he had struck. A hand landed on her shoulder. She looked up to see her father looming in the doorway. She stared up at him, trying to make sense of what he was saying. Vaguely, she realized that Gial was answering and Klem's shouts had diminished. Then Addor grabbed her arm, and before she could form a thought, he dragged her out of the barn.

Addor leaned back in his leather chair and the old floor squeaked in response. Leiel sat still, hunched in on herself, bruised hands folded in her lap. She could feel her father's regard, but she did not look at him.

"You know, little one, that Klem is not angry at *you*. He is angry because your mother is gone. Gial and I are too big for him to fight. And Torrin and Elda too. He is only yelling at you because he has no one else he feels he can be angry with."

Leiel kept her eyes on her hands, sucking in short breaths. Why was it okay for Klem to be angry? Why did *he* get to yell and hit and hurt? Why couldn't she? *Their* mother was dead. *Theirs*, not just *his*. They had all lost Ilora—Gial and Klem and Father, and even Torrin and Elda.

"You have to be patient with him. He has always been the most sensitive of you three. I know he is older, but you have a stronger spirit."

She looked up at him then, her burly, bearded father. He was dressed in his usual style—dark canvas pants, a fine spun shirt, and a colorful, woven vest—appropriate for either working outside or accepting visitors to the farm office. She always imagined that, in his travels as a merchant, he had commanded deep respect. Visitors laughed at his stories, and in town, everyone greeted him by name, smiling and excited to be in his presence. In her mind, should he stand beside one of the kings of the old realm, the king would have been in awe of Addor's authority.

He was looking at her as he always had, with a resigned frown of amused tolerance. But it felt different today. Today it made her angry—knotting in the pit of her stomach angry. She waited for Cleod's squirrel trick to bubble through her imagination as it so often did. This time it failed her.

This was another thing that was different now that her mother was gone. Her father's loving looks now had an edge to them, a judgment that had been previously less obvious. Yes—because she realized suddenly, it had always been there—a hint of patronizing in his interactions with her. Had her mother tempered that as well?

Yes. The answer rose clearly from the knot in her belly. It makes no sense, she thought, for Klem to be allowed to say such hateful things to me. To mean such hateful things. To hit me. It's not about my spirit. Mother made certain I was allowed to have one—and you tolerated it—only just that—until now. Until she is no longer here and you can now let the boys behave as you have always believed they should. With unrestrained authority and whatever level of cruelty sees them through the day.

Because their anger is more important than mine. And their pain and their needs, too. And I am finally in the place I would have been my entire life, if mother had not been mother, and determined to see me free.

Something skipped inside her mind, and she spoke before she could rein in the words. "So Klem is allowed to hit me now?" Her voice shook despite her best effort to keep it steady. Her face flushed hot, and tears gathered in her eyes. She would not show him that she recognized the change in him.

"Not *allowed*, girl. But if he does, just know he does not mean to hurt you."

"But he did hurt me," she said, raising a hand to touch her left cheek. It was swollen and tender. A great bruise would cover it by evening.

"And you hurt *him*." A hard note formed in his voice. "Your mother talked me into letting you be raised to play and work the farm as you wished. And to be schooled with the boys. But perhaps you learned too well how to be like them. You loosened one of your brother's teeth today. Whatever he might have said or—"

"He told me I would burn," she said. "Like mother. He said he *hoped* I would."

Addor's cheeks flared red.

He was as outraged as she was! Now something would be done about Klem. Now there would be—

Her outrage snapped to despair as he leaned across the desk, forefinger pointed into her face. "Never interrupt me again," he said. "You might burn, if you do not learn your place in the world! I warn you, Leiel, you will not be as your mother was in this house. You are my daughter. *Daughter*, not son. And you will obey me and your brothers in all things. And you will not antagonize Klem. You owe him an apology which you will go make this moment. Then get out to the barn and help Gial with the milking."

She shrunk away from him, pressing her back into the chair. But she held his gaze, even as her eyes filled with tears and a few escaped down her face. She swallowed and held still, staring back at him. He was not, in that moment, her father, but a great beast, freed at last from the illusion of domestication. His growls were no longer humorous grumblings. They shook the room. They shook her.

She shuddered in a breath, two, then managed a whisper. "Yes, Father."

"*Go*," he said and slammed back into his chair, turning his attention to the pile of papers on his desk. It was as final and brutal a dismissal as she could imagine and—almost—she let herself hate him as she rose from the chair and left the room. What stopped her was the same memory that had carried her through every day since Ilora died.

"*One day, I promise, you will understand,*" Ilora had said, hugging her close before she was taken away for ever. "*I promise.*"

Her mother never lied. And if she had promised that her death would someday make sense, then, surely, someday it would make sense that she could have married a man like Addor, and somehow bent his will to hers.

The study door clicked quietly as she pulled it closed behind her. For a moment she just stared down the hallway. There would be answers. In the meantime, there was survival in this house—this new world left by the absence of the person she now realized had been the true power in the family.

How did you do it, Mother? How did you run this entire house? Father and Klem and Gial—this entire farm?

There were secrets about her mother that she had never imagined. What else did she not know about Ilora? What else did she not know about her father? Too much. She raised her chin and brushed her hands on her skirts and started down the hall to find Klem.

The expectant curl of Klem's lip was almost enough to make Leiel blacken his other eye. With Elda attending his injuries, he sat on the chair in the front room of the farmhouse and said nothing as Leiel approached. His swollen lip and the bruises that were already darkening the upper corner of his eyebrow would have been satisfying in a minor way had he not been wearing them like a soldier who had received an honor ribbon for a great battle.

Klem had always been a little bit likely to take advantage of any opportunity to win attention and get his way. If crying worked or yelling or most especially brooding, he had always been willing to use that trick to play others' emotions. He was doing that now, sitting too straight in the great stuffed chair that was their father's.

Squirrel on a pile of rotting acorns, Leiel thought and the image formed clearly in her head. She could envision a great fluffy tail arching over the top of the chair. Did squirrels get black eyes?

Suddenly her frustration fled, and it was all she could do not to start laughing. Had she been able to use Cleod's squirrel trick in the barn, she might not have found herself in her current situation. But then she would also not have learned what she had about her father and, most especially, about her mother.

The sad smile Elda offered Leiel as she walked into the room was almost enough to bring tears to her eyes again, despite the happy illusion she had conjured of her brother as a rodent.

Squirrel master Klem, she thought. King of the nuts. High chatter-master of the fifth tree past the tomato garden. Lord of many holes dug.

Her lips twitched, but she forced a frown. Leiel knew by the raising of Elda's eyebrows that she had caught the shift of expression. Well, Elda, at least I got him to come into the house like you wanted. Leiel wanted so badly to say the words that she nearly smiled again, but she restrained herself and moved past Elda to stand before Klem.

"Well?" Klem demanded. "What do you have to say? I heard father raise his voice. That means you were as bad in his office as you were in the barn. Does he plan to mark you with the whipping you deserve?"

Behind her, Elda gasped, but Leiel spoke before the cook could interfere. "I am to apologize to you," she said, and then found herself continuing in a manner she had in no way intended. "I am to tell you I am sorry because you are too sensitive to stand up to the punching I gave you. Father is afraid it will damage your mind if my thrashing of you is allowed to stand as a victory."

Elda's next gasp ended in a choke on a laugh she throttled back too hard. Klem went bright red, whether with embarrassment or anger Leiel could not tell.

Had she really just said that? The unmeasured words felt *right*. "So, I am sorry, Klem, that I knocked you down and bruised you. I promise, if there is a next time, I will try to avoid shaking loose any teeth." She was doing half of what her father had ordered. She was making an apology, but as for not antagonizing Klem, that notion had flown the instant she had visualized him as a fluffy-tailed tree rat.

"I have to go help Gial with the milking. I am very glad you decided to come inside and help Elda, like she asked. It's useful for her to have help when she needs it."

Klem stared at her, his mouth hanging open in astonishment. Leiel smiled at him, turned and walked out of the house. She considered slamming the door behind her, but it seemed like a petty thing to do in the wake of the victory she had just achieved. A small win, yes—just Klem with his jaw gaping wide at her words. But it felt better than she thought anything could in that moment.

Behind her, Klem yelled for their father and his footsteps pounded the floor as he ran for Addor's study.

The whipping Klem had said she deserved was certainly coming her way now. But it had been worth it to learn another thing—that she was stronger than she had thought, even when she was afraid. Maybe part of her mother's secret to taking charge in the family had been doing only one half of what was demanded of her. And doing even that half in a way that was never quite expected. Perhaps it was a first step toward the understanding Leiel had promised herself. Whatever all that had happened today meant, she would take the lessons of it, no matter how hard, and make them useful. Was she terrified of her father? Yes. Could he hurt her in a dozen ways? Yes. Klem too, if he decided he wanted to. But fear was not going to stop her from doing or saying anything. Not after today.

17

Leiel

Fɪʀsᴛs ᴀɴᴅ ʟᴀsᴛs ᴡᴇʀᴇ ᴛɪᴇᴅ ᴛᴏɢᴇᴛʜᴇʀ ᴀs ᴛʜᴏᴜɢʜ ᴡɪᴛʜ sᴘɪᴅᴇʀ sɪʟᴋ. Tʜᴇʏ were linked, always. It was something that Leiel had come to understand. The last moment of her mother's life had become the first of Leiel's without her. There had been a last day that Klem smiled at her and a first when he began to hate her. Today's sunrise had been the last she would ever be allowed to sleep past, for tomorrow morning would be her first in charge of the kitchen. This was the last time she would ever walk into the school house as a student. Tomorrow she would no longer be welcome—if she had ever been. Tomorrow her days would become only about work— about chicken houses and vegetable gardens and wood for the cook stove. Not that she minded those things. They had always been part of her world. And if they had remained that, *parts* of her world, she might be able to envision a future where she could continue to enjoy them. But they were about to become everything she did and everything she was allowed, and because of that, she could think of no way she could continue to love them.

In her future, she could see furtive nights curled close to the hearth in the darkened kitchen trying to snatch time reading the books she had already begun to hide in back cabinets of the pantry the way a squirrel hid nuts for a long, cold winter. Would she become like a squirrel, skittish and desperate to gather one more morsel to sustain a harried life? Her mother had read openly, learned every day—myths and songs and histories—but that freedom died with her. Even Gial and Klem were now forbidden to read anything not related to the running of the farm or that might assist in the accounting.

Addor removed the books from the household library. They had been piled behind the blacksmith shop, and Torrin had been ordered to use them in the forge, or burn them outright. It had not taken much pleading for Leiel to talk him into staying silent about her midnight trips to steal back her favorite volumes. She wrapped them in oilcloth and hid them—in the rafters of the chicken coop, under the floor boards of the pantry, behind the jars in the earth cellar. It was unthinkable that she should be without those stories, that they should be denied the light of day, or the ability to ferment in the minds of any readers ever again. So she stole them. And memorized them as she could. And took them to heart in the way she had once taken her access to them for granted. Because she had an idea that they mattered more than she had ever imagined. That the reason her mother had taken the time to collect and save those stories was for more than her own pleasure. And the reason she had made certain Leiel had been allowed to attend school for so long was the same. The stories mattered. More than most people could ever imagine.

And if her own life was at all a story that might have been sung by the old poets, today was a closing of a phrase. She stood outside the school building, its weathered boards bright in the morning light, and tried to actually believe that she would never again after today walk inside and take her seat at her desk and *learn*. What was it about knowledge of the world that was too dangerous for her to have? Why, just because she had been born a girl, was she not allowed to understand the world and its workings in the same way as her father and brothers? As even Torrin the blacksmith or Ellan the wood cutter?

So she faced her final day as a student with a tight throat and a churning stomach, her emotions jerking inside her, from resigned sadness, to rage. She could not keep the feelings from her face as she walked up the three steps to the door and opened it.

The two younger boys in the entryway that ran the width of the building, stopped talking and just stared at her when she came in. Before today, she might have considered them friends. But now she was just a curiosity, a creature out of place and about to be removed from their lives forever. She turned her back and ignored them, hung her coat on the peg that had always been hers. With her books tucked under one arm, she rounded the wall that separated the entryway from the classroom.

Immediately, the usual morning chatter fell to a hush. Most of the boys just turned their gaze to the front of the room, but a few, Klem included, snickered and scowled at her. Only two students held her gaze with anything resembling kindness. Brea, the herbalist's daughter, nodded to her; her face was full of sadness and sympathy. Though Brea was closer to Gial's age and they had never been close, they had been, in a way, partners in a battle against the standing expectations of the community. Leiel was not the only one to lose something on this day. Brea would be alone here now, and Leiel's heart ached for the loss they would both suffer tomorrow.

And Cleod. *When I am grown I will be a Draighil, and no one will ever have to be chosen again.* His words from the day of his visit to the pond all those months ago came back to her.

She held his gaze for a few seconds, and his expression shifted into the same hard, determined mask it had on that day by the pond. The hardness was not for her, she knew. Of all the people in the room, even Brea, Cleod was the only one who she knew with complete certainty did not begrudge her presence in the least. He had never tried to make her feel that she should know less than she did, understand less, care less. The hardness in his face was for the cruel facts of their circumstances which demanded that she now be relegated to the shadows. It was possible he resented it more than she did.

She managed a smile as she sat down beside him. He reached across the table and placed a small piece of smoky quartz in front of her. The unexpected gesture brought a tightness to her throat, and she blinked back a sudden urge to cry. But she couldn't. Not today. She could not show that her unjust expulsion from this place was as painful as anything she had ever felt.

"Thank you," she said quietly, knowing that if she tried for any more words they would stick in her throat like honey to a spoon, sweet but messy and not meant for sharing.

"It's the Wild Stone of the Ehlewer," he said. "When I am one of them, I will have one mounted on the hilt of my sword, and the pommel of my horse's saddle, and wear gauntlets studded with them. And when I kill Shaa and all his kind, you can look at that and know I kept my promise."

Leiel sucked in a breath, and this time could not stop the heat that rose in her face or the water that filled her eyes. "You don't have to," she said, her voice shuddering a little. "You don't have to do any of that Cleod. I know you are my friend. You don't have to promise your whole life away."

"It's not promising my life away," he said, a new note in his voice she had not heard before. Something firm and uncompromising. "It's promising my life *to* something. It's the first time I feel like my life can mean something. And I want it to mean something to you."

She stared at him, and the chatter of the schoolhouse faded from her senses. All the muttering of the other students, their half-heard comments and sideways looks no longer occupied any of her attention.

He was willing to give his entire future to a profession that would take years of training and was both brutal and dangerous. He was willing to do that to ensure that the horror that had happened to the mother of his friend would never happen to another woman. He was willing to give himself over to life in the Ehlewer Enclave to get revenge *for her*.

Before she could form a reply of any kind, Joesenth called for attention at the front of the classroom. Gradually, conversations stuttered into silence and attention turned to the teacher.

Cleod broke her gaze and turned his attention to Joesenth. For several seconds, Leiel looked at him, seeing him for what seemed the very first time. This is more than friendship. The thought was almost unfathomable. The thrill that jolted through her was like nothing she had felt before. It filled her with heat and her heart seemed suddenly determined to pound out of her chest.

"Leiel!" Joesenth's gravelly voice snapped her back to where she was, and she looked up at him. "I would think, on your last day among us, that you would be more concerned with learning what you can today, than with dream gathering. Or would you rather just return home this moment?"

A snicker came from her right. Klem. The elation in her chest twisted itself into a tight, slithering mass. That was what she had to look forward to from now on. That condescending laugh and satisfied smirk. For a moment she could not breathe. Cleod nudged her under the table, and her dismay was replaced by a white heat that burned behind her eyes and almost set her to shaking with rage.

Then—*squirrels*. In her mind, the whole room was suddenly filled with furry-tailed rodents. Their chatter was pointless, a worrying over nuts and twigs. Joesenth's glare was a frenzied ogling, his threat no more meaningful than if she were a bear and he a squirrel squawking from a tree branch. Yes, he could send her home. But he would do that anyway in a few hours. His threat was actually an empty one. And that thought, in parallel with the image Cleod's suggestion at the pond had brought bursting into her mind, drove the anger from her.

"No, sere," she said, her voice calmer than she could have ever demanded it be. "I am sorry, sere."

Joesenth looked at her a moment longer. She could not tell if he was hoping she would argue or was just puzzled that she hadn't. At last, he turned away and began the day's lesson.

Leiel sat still for a moment. A smile spread over her face.

Without hesitation, she reached across and took Cleod's hand. She curled her fingers around his and squeezed. Warmth spread up her entire arm and seemed to kindle a space at the base of her skull as he returned her light grip in kind.

Today she would learn all she could. And she would keep learning. And she would not look to the future alone. Because this was her last day as a student. But it was her first day as part of a future that was something more than just her own. Firsts and lasts. They were tied together. Like she and Cleod.

18

Cleod – 10 years

"I NEVER EXPECTED THAT YOU WOULD EVEN THINK SUCH A CHOICE WAS POSSIBLE for you," Ellan said, as he placed his freshly sharpened ax in its place on the shed wall. He shook his head and began to gather up his tools.

"You don't look surprised," Cleod said. He had expected a very different reaction from his father—anger, disbelief. Not this unflustered acceptance.

"I am not surprised by the choice—not after the way you reacted when your friend's mother was Sacrificed. But I didn't think you would realize it was even possible for you to choose a life outside this."

Puzzled, Cleod leaned back against the wall. "But I heard you and Elder Soibel talking about me."

Ellan smiled. He tucked his grinding stones into the toolbox on the workbench and closed the lid. "I mentioned that you were upset by what happened in Adfen Square."

"You told him I might want to be Draighil?"

"I told him you had instincts that were more than those of just a woodcutter." He looked over at Cleod and there was something in his expression that Cleod had never seen before. It was not quite regret, not exactly resignation—perhaps a hint of longing. And Cleod had never thought Ellan wanted for anything. "I know what it is to want to be more than what you are. How do you think a mere woodcutter aspired to marry someone like your mother?"

"My mother?" Cleod straightened. His mother was only the shadow of a memory. Often he was not sure if what he recalled about her was real or just what he had been told.

"She was an herbalist's daughter, remember?" Ellan said with a laugh. "You're old enough now to understand what that means."

Cleod considered. Yes, he had known his mother was an herbalist's daughter. But it had never meant more than anything else he had been told about her. Now he thought about it. It meant she was educated—well beyond most other women. Well beyond what was allowed for most tradesmen. It meant that her future would have been assured. Filled with more money and privilege than almost anyone not born Farlan. "I—" He stopped.

"She decided to marry me, son. *Me*. The woodcutter's son with plans of being no more than a woodcutter himself. Because I like this work. And I am content with it. Because we loved each other and she decided that love was more important to her future than money and an easier life. There's a reason you have never known anyone from your mother's family. When she married me—well, she was as happily rid of them as they were of her."

The idea rocked Cleod, that his mother had been someone who was thought to be better than his father. Why had he never considered that he had family he had never known—and probably never would? It had simply never come up. He had his father and his grandmother—before she died. No one else. His mother had gotten sick long before he was old enough to know her, and he remembered more about her funeral than about his life with her in it.

"Would Leiel be considered too much better than me?" he asked before he even realized the thought was fully formed. Where had that come from? But he knew. There was something about the merchant-farmer's daughter that he could not imagine doing without.

Ellan laughed. "Not so far that it would matter." He paused and shook his head. "Two very different things—marriage and work and family, or becoming a Draighil."

"But after I kill Shaa—I'd be doing it for her—for what happened to her mother. And after—"

"Cleod, there is no *after* in the Enclaves. Such work and training—it changes a man. Changes his needs and priorities. Draighil don't marry, son. They don't have families."

But he wasn't supposed to be allowed into the Enclaves either, and that was happening. "I could be the first. Woodcutters aren't supposed to be Draighil anyway."

"No, they are not," Ellan agreed. "But it wouldn't be a wise idea to plan on being the one to change every tradition." He smiled a little. "Though, if they're willing to risk taking you on, I suppose you can try."

Cleod nodded, thoughtful. He knew little of the rules of the Enclaves. All he really knew was that they trained people to kill Draigon, and that was want he wanted—*needed*—to do. Whatever the laws of the Ehlewer, he did not see any reason why he could not find a way to do what he needed to do and still be friends, or more, with Leiel.

"If I join the Enclave..." Cleod paused. "Will everything be all right here? You don't have any help besides me."

"If you can talk yourself into the Ehlewer—if that's really what you want to do—then I'll be proud of you. Don't worry about me or this little farm or the wood lots. I've got many years of cutting timber left in front of me. Decide what you want to do, then do it. Don't let concern for me and a few cows and logs keep you from doing what you decide you need to do."

"You really aren't angry?"

"Never," Ellan said. "You want more than you were born to. I raised you to think for yourself and make your own decisions. If I thought those decisions would be only about which trees to cut and how to decide a fair price for your work—that was me being short-sighted."

It was true that his father had always let Cleod make his own choices. Ellan had even let him stay in school for years longer than most tradesmen's sons. There was trust in that. A history of trust in Cleod and his ability to make good choices. So Cleod had to make sure that the choice he made now was a good one. That meant he had to take the rest of what his father had said and think it through. He needed to learn more about the Enclaves.

"Can I go to town—after I feed the cows?" Cleod asked. "I need to go to the Library."

Ellan smiled, and Cleod was unsurprised when his father nodded.

"You are not Farlan blood," Soibel said. "But you are strong. You may be smart enough to survive the training." The elder eased back in his chair and eyed Cleod.

More lamps burned in the spacious stone chamber than Cleod had even known existed in the entire town. The walls were hung with brilliant tapestries woven through with scenes of old battles. The table behind which Soibel sat was intricately inlaid with symbols that Cleod had no knowledge to interpret. He swallowed and met the old man's gaze.

"You said that before, at my father's. I want to join the Ehlewer. I want to learn how to be a Draighil."

"Does your father know you have come here tonight?"

Cleod nodded. "Yes,. He heard what you told me—that I am strong enough to be Draighil. He said you were too smart to take me."

Soibel laughed and lifted a scarred finger to tap his temple. "A man of uncommon wisdom is your father—especially for someone who works with his hands more than his mind." He tilted his head onto his fist and his gaze became measuring. Cleod forced himself to hold still and stare straight ahead despite the fact that the old man's gaze made his skin tingle. Cleod's clothing was too dirty for this neatly swept bright space. His accent was too coarse, his manners bumbling at best in comparison to that of the old Draighil. But he could do it. He could learn whatever they could teach him. He could learn anything he needed to keep his promise to Leiel.

"You are...bolder...than the Enclaves usually want even their brightest candidates to be. And you are not Farlan. I am not certain we could ever know where your allegiance lies."

"Where would you need it to be, to take me on?"

Soibel's reply was crisp. "With me."

"And how would I prove that? You don't know me, and I don't know you."

Soibel smiled, but his eyes were hard. "True. And you have no blood-line to swear against, as all other aspirants are required to do. So how can I take you into the Enclave, Cleod Woodcutter? When you have no line of loyalty to the Farlan?"

"You can decide to let me in. You are the oldest of the elders. You can just decide I will be trained. And then I will be."

Soibel laughed. "Bold," he repeated.

"Why would you not want that? Is there only one way for a Draighil to fight a Draigon? Are they so stupid that one way beats them every time? If that were true, no Draighil would ever be killed."

"Oh, we want *some* of that kind of thinking, but not so much that it interferes with what we must teach any candidate in order that he might survive and be trusted as one of us." Soibel leaned forward and laced his fingers together. "You have no knowledge of what being Draighil truly means. You have *no idea* what you are asking to become. And your choice to do this is not based on a desire to live such a life for your own sake. You would throw away everything you were meant to be to take vengeance for the care of a...*girl*."

Cleod started. How did the man know about Leiel?

"You seem surprised. You should not be. The Ehlewer have many sources of knowledge throughout the Spur.

"You do know, woodcutter, that if you were to be lucky enough to be chosen to train among us, you would never be able to claim any girl as your own? Draighil cannot marry. We live only to learn to kill the Draigon and to pass on what we know of doing it. We live only to keep Arnan safe. Arnan in its entirety and not *just one woman*. You have given the girl, Leiel, your promise that you will kill the monster that took her mother. Your promise is an oath to her—but in joining us, all your oaths would become ours. You cannot keep your promise to this girl, Cleod, and not betray her trust. You must give up your promise of friendship in order to keep the one to avenge her loss."

Of all the things that Cleod had considered in thinking about what it would take to become a Draighil, this one that had never been part of his planning. Becoming a Draighil would be hard. It would require that he leave home, his father. That he leave school. That he work harder than he had ever done in his life. All these things he knew and was prepared for—prepared to even consider in greater depth. But not this. Not the idea that, in trying to bring justice to Leiel, he would have to leave her—in fact and in spirit.

Could he do that? He was nearly the only person she trusted. He had promised her so much...did she really expect that he would be able to give her all of it? He didn't think so. But he had hoped that he *could*. He had meant every promise he had ever made to her, and he had hoped to keep them. Was that the first thing becoming a Draighil meant, giving up those hopes? No. If he could become Draighil, he could find a way to be with Leiel.

He remembered the hollow, shocked look on Leiel's face that day in the Square when her mother's name was called. The horror she endured as Ilora was led away to her death. Her quiet despair through all the weeks that followed. He could not imagine anything more terrible. Not even her heartache if he should walk away to do this thing that he now realized he *must* do. The only way to erase the pain she carried daily was to destroy the cause of it. Destroy the Draigon. To do that, there was only this path, only the Ehlewer and the Enclave training to become Draighil. However much he might hurt her in pursuit of that goal, the relief he brought to her heart would be worth it.

"It would be worth it," Cleod said the words aloud and met the Elder's gaze.

"Too bold even for you," Soibel said. He waved a hand toward the door. "Go home, boy. Your request will be brought to consideration at the next Enclave meeting."

Cleod did not move. He needed more than just a casual assurance that his entreaty would be taken seriously. "You'll stand for me?"

Soibel studied him. Cleod could feel the measurement in the cold gaze. "I will."

"Your word—on the Wild Stone?"

Soibel stared. Cleod held firm and stared back. He had studied hard to come by that piece of knowledge, to be used in just this moment. He did not know exactly what the Wild Stone was, only that in the lore he had discovered, oaths on it were taken seriously.

"An oath sworn on that Stone is unbreakable, as you will discover, Cleod Woodcutter, *if* you are allowed to strive among us toward our greatness."

"Your word," Cleod said again.

Soibel grinned. "On the Wild Stone," he said. "Bold."

19

Leiel – 10 years

"NOT SO ROUGH," ELDA SAID, TOUCHING HER FLOUR-COATED FINGERS TO THE backs of Leiel's wrists. "Kneading dough doesn't mean punching it into the butcher block."

Leiel pushed out a breath that was half grunt. "I hate baking. Why can't I just cook the meat?"

Elda chuckled and bumped her slender hip against Leiel's. "Well most people eat more than just meat. If you're to run this kitchen, you'll have to know how to do everything."

Leiel punched the dough again. "I won't be working in this kitchen forever."

"That might be true, but you can't assume it," Elda said. "Here, let me show you." Leiel sighed as Elda's hands settled on top of hers. "Firm, but not hard, see? Like this. You have to pay attention to the texture and the moisture so it rises properly."

"Elda...I don't care about the bread."

"I know you don't." Elda laughed. "But what else are you going to do down here all day? I don't think you will care for your father's reaction if the bread is a hard lump. So you might as well pay attention and learn something."

The fact that the older woman was right did nothing to improve Leiel's mood. She used to love coming to the kitchen, tucked into a room under the house, when it had been full of laughter and her mother's songs. But it had not been her mother's *place*—not the spot to which she had been relegated—it had been her refuge. Once, Leiel asked her mother why she sang only in the kitchen. *"Because then I can put the song in the very food we eat,"* she had said. *"Can't you hear the pies singing?"* Now every moment Leiel spent in the kitchen was a reminder of the harsh reality of her mother's absence. There was no longer joy in the warm scents and familiar labor.

"Maybe someday, when I have my own house," she said, "I will like kitchens again."

Elda laughed and stepped away to let Leiel take over the working of the bread again. "And when will that be? This is your house."

"But it won't always be." Leiel picked up the flour bag and shook a bit more onto the butcher block. "If I get married, I can leave here."

"Leiel—" Elda's voice went quiet, and she spoke gently. "Leiel—you aren't going to marry. Not ever."

Leiel froze, the flour bag in her hand. She looked over her shoulder at Elda. "What do you mean?" Cleod's face flashed through her mind.

Elda shook her head, dusting her hands on her apron. She set the bundle aside, turned Leiel gently to face her. Her warm fingers touched Leiel's face. "Leiel—you're Draigfen—the daughter of a chosen Sacrifice. Such women don't find husbands."

Leiel drew away from the older woman. What was Elda talking about? *Such women*? What did that mean? She stepped back. "What are you talking about? What kind of woman do you think I am?"

"*We* are," Elda said gently. "Did you never wonder why I have no family, Leiel? My cousin—thirty summers ago—my cousin, Gemda, was taken as your mother was. Up the mountain. She met the Draigon. And none of us—my sisters, my cousin's daughter—none of the girls within a generation of Gemda ever married or had families. No one will have us. We are tainted by men's fear that we will somehow share that fate."

Leiel stared, and then shook her head. It couldn't be. She had lost too much. Lost Ilora, her closeness with her brothers, her freedom on the farm. She could not lose hope too—hope that someday she would have a home of her own far from the farm and the prison it had become. That someday she might have someone to care about and who would care about her. "That can't be true. I know a boy who—"

"It won't matter," Elda said. She folded her arms and shook her head. Her dark hair flashed its fine tints of grey in the lamplight. "Even if he would have you, his parents wouldn't let him marry you. The Council would not allow it. You are *Draigfen*, girl. You're ruined—since the moment they called your mother's name." She stepped toward Leiel and raised a hand as though to touch her. "I'm so sor—"

Leiel didn't wait for that sentence to be finished. The heart tearing itself apart in her chest could not bear the further burden of pity. Whirling on her toes, Leiel fled to the far corner of the room. She thought of running farther, but her father was home, and she could not face him, not at this moment. Because she would rage at him and scream at the unfairness of it all, and he would not care. She would earn more of his anger. The weight of knowledge pressed upon her, that she could not even safely leave this room, much less this farm—and so she was truly trapped. If Elda was right, what hope did she have, with a future as dismal as the dough she had just kneaded?

"Why do they hate us so much? Why do the Draigon hate us?"

"It's not the Draigon who hate us," Elda said, and there was such certainty in her words that Leiel turned back to face her.

"How can you say that? They kill. They killed my mother! And your cousin. They have killed women forever, and they will keep doing it."

"The Draigon are just what they are." Elda sighed. "It's the Council who decides which woman goes. And they always choose women who are smart and strong. Never someone meek and polite and proper."

Leiel stared. With the surety of instinct, she understood that something had shifted in her relationship with Elda. The other woman had been just a laughing side-note in her life, someone always there, bustling and seeing things done. Elda had never been a vital part of her life, not like her mother. But now Elda was more—perhaps she had always been more—if not to Leiel, then to her mother. Hours spent in the kitchen together, working throughout the house and the garden. Days and weeks and years. Stories shared, jokes and laughter. Problems talked out and solved. How could Elda *not* matter to her mother? Thinking back, Leiel could not imagine how she had been so unaware that she had not seen it.

Leiel leaned back against the wall. "You and my mother were friends."

"Your mother saved me," Elda said. "I never had anyone to tell me what I just told you—that no one would ever want me—be *allowed* to want me—because of my cousin. I had to learn that on my own." Leiel shifted as Elda crossed the room to lean against the wall beside her. "Your mother and I were friends when we were young—younger than you. Years later, when she married your father and came to live here, she asked me to come with her and work in this house. A long time had passed since Gemda was taken and some of the stigma had eased—enough that I was not considered ill-luck just to have around. So for me, there was some escape. Thanks to your mother."

"They took her." Tears filled Leiel's eyes but she blinked them back, let the anger in her belly burn them back. "They took her away. Why Elda? Klem says it's my fault. So did the priests."

"It's not your fault—it was *their* choice," Elda said. Her voice was firm and calm, her mouth a hard line. "Anything else is just a story they tell to keep everyone under control."

"How do you know?" Leiel looked up at Elda, really looked for a change. How had she never noticed the sharpness of Elda's gaze? How smart she was?

"Your mother and I used to talk about it. We tried to understand why the Council chose who they chose. We could not make sense of it. So your mother started asking, when she went to the Market, about other women who were given to the Draigon. She started to hear old stories and songs. She started to learn things, and she brought them home and taught them to me. And then to you."

"They took her because of the stories?" Leiel whispered. Her stomach twisted.

"No." Elda shook her head. "They took her because they could. It doesn't matter what stories she knew. It only matters that someone on the Council did not like your father."

Her father? What did he have to do with any of this? "I don't understand."

"What else could it be? No one cares what a woman knows. The Council took your mother to hurt your father."

"But who would want to hurt my father?" Leiel asked. Even as the question passed her lips, she knew it was the wrong one. Because however much some on the Council might dislike her father, there had to be easier ways to hurt him than sending her mother to the Draigon. That meant they had chosen her mother for their own reasons. But what could those be? Ilora had never hurt anyone. She would never have spoken against anyone on the Council. The only thing she could have done wrong was learn things she was not supposed to know. Or ask questions about *why* things happened the way they did. Or about *who* they happened to—and the who in the stories Ilora had told were not always the same as in the stories Leiel read in school. So the stories must matter. They must matter very much.

"I think you're wrong," she said. "I think the stories are very important."

"They are," Elda said. "Because your mother loved them, and they will always remind us of her."

Leiel nodded and did not argue. But Elda was wrong. There was more to it. Leiel knew it. And she would find out what.

20

Leiel – 11 years

THE SUN WAS LOW IN THE SKY, DRAPING LONG SHADOWS ACROSS THE STILL surface of the pond. But this evening the familiar setting had lost its comfort. Cleod stood beside her, and she was trying to wrap her mind around what he had just said.

"You're really going to become Draighil." Leiel formed the words with quiet awe. Never had she thought it would actually happen. He was not Farlan. He was not born to a tradition of warriors and fighters. He was a woodcutter's son. The promise he had made her when he gave her the quartz stone slipped through her mind.

The kind part of her was glad for him, that he had found a way to step outside the boundaries of the life he had been born to. The jealous part wished she, too, could find a similar path. But mostly what she felt was weight over her entire spirit, like grey clouds hanging low over a mountain. His dream would take him to the Enclave. And while it was only on the northern edge of the Spur country, it might as well be another land. Because it would be months before she saw him again, before she could talk to him again. And who would he be then? Who would she become without him? He was her only ally. He was the source of her laughter and her calm. And he was leaving. As he had promised he would. She did not want him to go.

She hadn't thought, when he had made that promise, that it would ever be possible for him to keep it. But she should have known better. He had never committed to anything he did not intend to achieve.

Like the dog.

"I promised that I would," he said. "You don't seem happy for me."

She shook her head quickly. "No—it's not that. I *am*—I just—I never—" She closed her eyes for a moment then looked back at him. "I am going to miss you."

He smiled then. "I won't be going far—only a day's ride. People can visit me."

"People can. Not *me*. I'm a girl. No one will let me travel that far."

"Then I'll come home and see you. And we can write. I'll have so many things to tell you. Just imagine the things I am going to learn. A sword! I am going to learn it all. I will be the greatest Draighil the Spur has ever seen."

She smiled at that, because he was probably correct. In school, he had always been one of the quickest to learn new things, even better than students years older. He was the swiftest runner in all the races at school, and strong from working with his father chopping wood. If anyone could wreak havoc on all assumptions, it was Cleod.

"You will," she said, and as she said it, she knew it was true. There was something big and wonderful in him. She had known that for years. Was there a word for it? Intensity? Or passion? Perhaps even greatness? She did not know what to call it. But she had admired it and counted on it since the first day they had met.

"That smile is more what I hoped for," he said.

She looked up at him, irritated as always that he was so much taller than her. "Come sit down. I am tired of looking up at you."

Their oak tree was fresh with new leaves. Beneath it, the curve of the gnarled roots formed a familiar seat. Folding her legs, she dropped to the earth and waited for him to join her. His lanky frame was not graceless in its descent, but it lacked the simple ease with which hers settled to the ground. As ever, he grumbled as he joined her. "You're closer to the earth."

"You breathe in clouds when you walk."

He laughed, and for a moment it was as if nothing had changed, as if next week he would meet her here as always and tell her what he had learned in school, bring her books, and tell her silly stories. And she would help him solve the number problems Joesenth made up for no more reason than to annoy those who hated them.

No more. All of that would be no more after this afternoon, and she met his gaze with a welling of sadness in her throat. "Cleod—I don't know how to miss you."

"It won't be that long," he said with a shake of his head that dropped his hair into his eyes. He always let it grow a little wild before he bothered to cut it. Would that be allowed in the Enclave? The Elders she had seen in Adfen all wore their hair cropped close and neat. Was that how his would be too?

"Are you listening to me or dream-gathering again?" he asked. "I said I'll be back in a few months."

"I was thinking about your hair," she said, then laughed at her own foolishness.

"My hair?" He tipped his eyes up as though he could see the top of his head, then blew the unruly strands from his face.

"It needs cutting."

"It always seems to."

She smiled at him and shook her head. What was she doing? Worrying about stupid things when he was here to tell her about the most important decision of his life. Reaching out, she caught his hand in hers and met his gaze in the dying light. The peeping of spring frogs began at the edge of the water, and something splashed on the other side of the pond. She squeezed his fingers. "Tell me what he said—the Elder—when you asked to join. Tell me everything."

21

Leiel – 12 years

Fourth Market Day in Adfen was always bustling. The weekly markets were busy enough, but Fourth Markets drew the largest crowds. Mountain musicians came down out of the Spur, informal gatherings that often turned into dancing in the dusty streets. The farmers with smaller holdings, or those who harvested wild plants for weeks to gather enough to sell, all made a point of coming to the last market of the month. The cheese maker saved his most cultured offerings, and the bakers made sweet cakes in great variety.

As long as she could remember, this day of each month had been her favorite. The air rang with happy chatter and the clatter of animals in the traces, while the warm perfume of fresh bread and rare spices filled the air. The sound of singing rose over the common spaces of the town, large and small. And there was ever a sense of newness, of things to be discovered, wondered at, and sampled and savored.

Leiel looked over at Gial where he sat beside her on the wagon seat. His face did not wear the scowl that had become his normal expression. On Fourth Market day, he was relaxed—more the brother she remembered from better times. It was thanks to him that she was even allowed to come to town at all. Since before she could speak, she had been blessed with the best eyes in the family for livestock. When she was little, she would wander among the chickens, and the ones she ended up playing with were inevitably the best layers. Even though Addor had restricted her freedom, in this one thing he could not deny her usefulness. And so, on this one day, she left behind the boring duties of the kitchen and the house, and accompanied Gial to town.

The wagon swayed with the rhythm of the mule's pulling as they negotiated the streets jammed with sellers and ware-seekers alike. Familiar greetings were offered and received, and at last they crossed under the old, stone archway that marked the entrance to Old Adfen. There, the streets were cobbled, not dirt, and the grey buildings were all of stone instead of weathered wood. The heart of Old Adfen was also the heart of Market activity. Only open as part of the Market on the Fourth week, Adfen Square was a marvel of complicated stonework.

In the center of the Square rose the ancient Tower, with its huge beam that formed a crosspiece at the top. It soared over the rest of the city, its grey stone glinting with mica chips. What the structure had been used for in ancient times, no one had ever been able to tell her. Halfway up, a balcony wrapped around it. Sometimes she would look up and see the members of the Council in their deep-red tunics looking down on the market. The hard thoughts that came to her when she saw the Councilmen would get her whipped if they were ever known. Whatever the Tower had been, it now housed the Council's meeting rooms, and, on festival days, provided a vantage point for the Farlan guards as they watched over the haggling and revels below.

Leiel tried to ignore that it was also the focal point of the ceremony that had taken her mother from her. Her stomach crashed in knots every time she entered the Square. But the place was so different during Fourth Market—from that terrible, sweltering day when Ilora's name had been called—that Leiel could sometimes forget where she was. At least for long enough to get through the day.

She shifted her gaze from the Tower to sweep it over the Square. Ringing the space were the best Market stalls in the region. Roomy, built of stone, with shelves along the back walls, the stalls were roofed with wood, not thatch. They were dry in any weather, and were the most sought after venues in all the Spur. Once a trader was granted a space in one, as long as he or she did not miss a Fourth Market, the place was reserved by contract until the death of the signer. When spaces came free, new owners were determined by lottery. Addor had drawn a space the year Leiel was born, and the family had enjoyed the advantages granted by such a location ever since. Warm in winter, cool on the hottest days, and located beside the finest chandler in the region, the site had been a boon to their prosperity for the last twelve years.

They rattled across the Square. Gial nodded to friends and fellow traders. With a lurch, they halted at their stall. Leiel did not wait to be asked before she jumped down and began to unload the wagon. No matter that he cared enough to help her escape the farm on these occasions, Gial was no longer the loving brother of her childhood. His temper was quick to light, his patience all but nonexistent. She thought of him now as a badger, calm enough if he got his way, but easily roused to viciousness if threatened or crossed. Keeping out of his reach was wise, as was quick action when there was work to be done. This month's offerings were the finest selection of squashes in the region, and a young sow nearly of breeding age. The squealing that erupted from her crate as Leiel removed the wooden boxes stacked in front of the sow, brought a grin to the girl's face. "Stop complaining, Sobbie," she said. "You were born a girl, so no one is going to eat you over the winter."

That brought a sound that might have been a laugh from Gial as he unhitched the mule, and a definite chuckle from Ils, the old chandler in the next stall.

"Bothered to name this one, did you?" he called.

Leiel nodded to him as she toted a box of acorn squash into the stall. "I knew she was going to have a long life. And Elda says 'A sow with a name is a sow with a future.' Sobbie's been cared for well and is going to have a lot of piglets to keep someone fed."

"Your Elda always was a wise woman. You're smart to learn from her, Leiel." Ils put a tray of candles on the table at the front of his booth. "You need any help with Sobbie's crate?"

"I'll get it, thank you," Gial said to Ils. "Leiel, make certain the pumpkins aren't stacked too high when you set them up. I don't want any falling and breaking." It was a warning that she was not moving fast enough. Time to stop chatting.

"Yes," she said, and focused her attention on the work at hand. Not that any work that needed doing would stop *him* from chatting once Ils's granddaughter, Corra, arrived to help. Up into the back of the wagon Leiel went. She shoved the pig crate toward the tailgate then began sorting boxes.

She was handing down the last box to Gial, when she caught sight of the woman on the edge of the Square. Dirty hair, watery dark and longer than was manageable, loose along her back, she stood looking up at Adfen Tower. A large pack was propped against her leg, and it was by that pack that Leiel recognized her.

Gold threads, so out of place in the dusty fabric, caught the sunlight that filtered into the old mill. The pack was tilted against the wall; the intricacy of the embroidery on it was unlike anything Leiel had ever seen. Even the detailing of her mother's finest dress did not compare to the fine work that made up the golden tree stitched into the canvas top flap. From the bark on the trunk to the branches and the hundreds of tiny gold leaves that bedecked them, every part of the design seemed to shimmer and shift as though alive.

"Beautiful, is it not?" Gahree said. She sat beside Leiel in front of the old fireplace, where a small blaze nipped merrily among the partially crumbled bricks. "It's a reminder of the finest work of genius ever conceived. A work that will never be finished and which grows more beautiful with each moment that passes."

"What work?" Leiel asked. She leaned over and reached out to touch the glittering tree, but stopped herself.

"Go ahead," Gahree said. "Your touch will do it no harm. Best that it comes to know you anyway."

Leiel glanced at her, but didn't hesitate longer. She was growing used to the woman's cryptic way of speaking, and it no longer left her curious, only amused. And the lure of the shining threads was too much. She laid her fingers over the image and a tingle swept up her arm. Beneath her touch, the leaves seemed to rustle and dance. She could feel them, as though they were in fact part of a living tree.

She yanked her hand back and looked over her shoulder at Gahree. The woman was smiling her knowing smile again.

"What is that?" Leiel whispered. She glanced back at the pack. The tree was still. Had she imagined what she felt? Had the stunningly perfect detail of the needlework allowed her fanciful nature to run away with her senses? Certainly now, the tree was just thread stitched onto fabric.

"An art long forgotten," Gahree said. "A history. And a promise that the future is something we are always growing toward."

Leiel looked at her. "You promised me stories."

"No," Gahree said. "I asked if you loved them."

"Leiel! Mind your work." Gial's angry voice snapped her back to her place in the wagon, and she quickly adjusted her grip on the box before it went tumbling.

"I'm sorry," she said quickly, handing it to him. He glared at her as he took it, and she was glad his arms were too full for him to raise a hand against her. She might have risked a glare at his back as he moved away, but more important than vengeful thoughts, was the presence of the woman in the Square. Leiel whipped her attention back toward the Tower, half expecting to find Gahree vanished.

But she was there. And she was looking back at Leiel with the same, all-too-insightful gaze so well remembered from that strange day by the pond. The years that had passed since that meeting once again dropped away.

"Which stories has your mother told you, wild daughter?" Gahree placed another handful of sticks on the little fire, folded her legs under her, and sat back down beside Leiel. "Stories of sunrise and creation? Or why the bees love the flowers? Perhaps, the tale of how the stars are born?"

"Yes," Leiel said. "All of those."

"But what of the directions and how the world is balanced? Do you know those stories?"

Leiel shook her head, fascinated now. Her mother knew many stories, and she shared them with an endless enthusiasm that rivaled the devotion of the Farlan fighters. How wonderful it would be to have a new one to share with her!

Gahree laughed a little, and again the too-intimate sound struck through to Leiel's spine. The woman reached out and took Leiel's hand and began to speak. "In this land of Arnan, the fish traders know all the land runs downhill to the sea. They know this to be truth because the sea brings the rains and fishes for food and glorious goods from distant lands. By the sea, the legends are of water creatures and wing-waves and tides that run black when sailors are about to die. So the sea folk know they sit at the edge of the world.

"But the mountain folk know different things. They know all the land runs upwards to where clouds form to cool the summer heat. There, the snows feed all the rivers of the land. The mountain people tell of bears who speak in human voices, and mighty peaks that belch fire. Of ancient rivers of ice their ancestors once

walked while hunting. These are the shared stories that mark the journeys taken in
every story they tell. The mountain people know they hold up the edge of the sky.

"And then there are the people who live on the plains and see the sky rise to
the peaks, and the roads roll away to the ocean, and they have decided that the
whole of the world slopes one way or another, and are certain they are the center
on which the world hinges. They are glad they live in such perfect balance. Their
stories are of great swarms of burrowing creatures that devour the land, hot sun
that cracks the earth, and winters so cold people's lids freeze to their eyes.

"But all of these people share one tale, Child of Stories. Is it a story you might
know?"

Leiel stared into those green-gold eyes, and she knew without doubt which
story the strange woman meant.

"Shaa," she said. And she kept her voice quiet. "Shaa, the Great Draigon that
seeks to destroy all the world."

Leiel held the woman's gaze for a heartbeat. Gahree smiled, and shook her
head. Her hair, much longer than when they had first met, flew around
her face in wild tangles. Then she lifted the embroidered pack and walked
across the Square toward the smallest booths. She did not look back.

What was she doing here? Here in the heart of the Fourth Market of all
places? Leiel had not seen her since that one meeting at the mill, the fall
before her mother died. Certainly, Gahree had never been a seller at any of
the markets Leiel had ever attended. Had the woman been in the Spur all
this time? Perhaps attending only the smaller markets?

If so, what could she possibly sell? She had no wagon, no goods. Only
the strange rucksack, which could hold little more than the necessities of
travel. What in all of Arnan was she doing here?

Leiel hopped off the wagon and raised the tailgate, locking it closed
with the iron latch pins. She looked across the Square again, watching
Gahree disappear in the crowd. Whatever the woman's purpose, Leiel did
not have time, this moment, to discover it. Gial called her name, and she
went to him where he was stacking the last of the boxes in the stall.

"What were you looking at?"

She hesitated, then decided the truth was the best answer—part of it
anyway. "A strange woman. She smiled at me."

"A strange woman smiled at you?" Gial scoffed. "Of course. What else would keep you from what you are supposed to be doing? Am I to be grateful you didn't decide to run off and drink tea with her?"

She frowned at him. What did he think she should have been doing instead, in that minute she had spent in the back of the wagon? Making shoes for the mule? Knitting a new pair of socks? What had he been doing before he noticed her distraction? Chatting with Ils, or, more likely, the chandler's rather lovely granddaughter. Tension shifted between them and she realized he had caught her look.

"I'll move the wagon," she said. Before he could decide whether to just yell at her or actually hit her, she ducked around the back of the buckboard. She walked to the mule's head and took up his lead. Clucking quietly, she led him toward the stable that served the common area. Another thing that made the Old Adfen Square unique, was the space to park trade wagons and keep pack animals. Two liverymen watched over the animals and wagons, leaving their owners free to sell their wares. The use of the stables was yet another reason the Adfen Square stalls were considered the finest in the region.

The sellers in the other booths were all familiar to her. Some, like Ils, were old friends. Some were competitors, other merchant farmers who sold goods similar to those of her family. But even they smiled and waved as she passed.

The mule knew the way to the stables as well as she did, so she did not have to pay much attention to where they were going. They wove across the Square, and she scanned the crowd for any glimpse of Gahree. She had to be here. No one came all the way to Fourth Market only to leave before sales officially began at midmorning. But the dark-haired woman was nowhere in sight.

With a sigh, Leiel threaded her way down the narrow alley that led to the courtyard where the wagons were left for the day.

"Hello, Arri," she greeted the stableman. "How many do you have today?"

"Not many yet," the grey haired man replied. Though his hair was the color of storm clouds, she did not think he was even as old as her father. "And only one waiting here for you." He pointed to the far corner of the courtyard.

Leiel opened her mouth to ask what he was talking about, but the words never came because she already knew. She looked where he pointed. Gahree was seated on the tailgate of a dray, her pack beside her, legs kicking in her long skirts. She grinned at Leiel and waved her over.

"Here, Arri," Leiel said. "I'll bring you an extra pumpkin if you take care of Old Doghead for me."

"Make it two," he said as he set aside the water pipe that he was never without. He took the mule's lead from her.

Nodding in quick agreement, Leiel made her way through the parked wagons. Her mouth was suddenly dry. It had been years since she had spoken to the woman awaiting her. Years full of sorrow and sadness and change. New ideas. Scary thoughts. Strange ambitions. Years since a meeting that had lasted only a few hours...and yet...

What was turning in her chest, setting her heart racing? Why was her breath shortened and coming fast? Happiness? Hope? It had been so long since she felt either that she had forgotten these things accompanied it.

But why? Why had just the sight of Gahree, without a word yet spoken between them, awakened those things inside her? Because she knows things. Things no woman is supposed to know. Things perhaps no one at *all* is supposed to know. She sees things, and she hears things, and she has no fear of sharing them—with you.

Leiel all but ran the last few paces to the strange woman.

Gahree laughed as Leiel drew close, and the sound was as she remembered, ringing and shaking and bold. "Daughter of wings—I am glad to see you remember how to smile."

Leiel realized she was indeed smiling, truly smiling for the first time in as long as she could remember. These days, only rare letters from Cleod gave her reason to do that. And yet here she was, standing before a woman she had met only once, holding herself back from throwing her arms around Gahree and sobbing. "Where have you been?" she asked. "Where did you go? I looked for you—"

"I am not to be found, wild daughter, but I will always find you." Gahree patted the space beside her on the bed of the cart. "Sit and tell me what you need to tell me."

"I don't have anything to tell."

"You have everything." Gahree held out her hand. Tears filled Leiel's eyes, and she reached out and took it, let the woman draw her up to sit beside her. "So begin to speak. Your sorrows will not be belittled, and your joys will not go uncelebrated. Sit with me, and for as long as you are here, you will be safe, and your stories will be safe."

Leiel folded her legs under her and bent her head for a moment. Where to start? What to tell? How long before Gial missed her and sent someone to find her, or worse, came himself?

"I don't have time," Leiel said. "I have to get back to work."

"It is an ill thing to have no time for stories." Gahree shook her head. "Tell me just one, then. And when you come next to Adfen, I will be here. And I will be here every time, until you tell me all the stories you feel the need to share."

Leiel lifted her head and stared at Gahree in amazement. After years with no contact, now she was here with an offer to meet every month, and share Leiel's pains and fears and joys? What was this? Why? Why now?

"Mountain peppers," Gahree said as though Leiel had actually asked the question. "The finest in the Spur. Rare and not sweet. I will bring them to this market each time you come. I will bring them all through the winter until people will wonder how they are possibly so fresh. Then you can come to me every month and trade your goods for mine—and so, too, your stories. I make you a promise the way a tree promises to make leaves again in the spring." She leaned close to Leiel. "Stories, as many as leaves on a tree. Old leaves, and new. Old stories, and new."

"Leaves like on your pack?" Leiel asked. She looked around at the worn bag tucked into the corner of the cart. "Is this your wagon?"

"For as long as I am seated on it."

"But—"

"You owe me a story, wild daughter. Tell me what you need to tell me in the time that we have."

Leiel looked back at her. What did she have to tell this strange woman? Why was Gahree so certain Leiel had something to share? "I don't know where to begin."

"There are no beginnings. There are only starting places in the middle of longer tales. Tell me something. It will matter."

The questions that filled Leiel's mind seemed endless, and she could not find a way to sort through them to voice just one. So she gave up trying and said the first thing that came to her. "There is a secret—about my mother. She saved stories. She saved them so I could save them, too."

Gahree nodded. "And how did she save them? In a box? On the wind?"

"In my heart." It was the first time Leiel had said the words out loud, but it was not the first time she had thought them. "My brothers don't know the same stories I do. I used to sit in the kitchen late at night with my mother and listen. She sometimes spoke and sometimes sang and sometimes she had me sing with her. Her stories were bright and made me laugh and smile. With her, I could always laugh and smile." She ducked her head and thought a moment, about this thing she had learned by accident that now suddenly seemed to be important.

"I always thought the stories she told me were the same ones she told everyone—my brothers and my father. Even Elda in the kitchen with her." Leiel stopped, thinking. A few months ago, she had been walking to the chicken house, singing one of Ilora's favorite songs. Gial had stopped her in the yard and demanded to know where she had learned it.

"But they were not the same," Gahree said. Her voice held no surprise.

Leiel shook her head. "No. Not the same. I sang Gial a song of the woman who saved the Sanctuary in the time of the Great Rain. When she said her poetry, it called up power to seal together the roof when none of the priests could figure out how to fix it.

"Gial got so angry. He grabbed me and shook me and demanded that I tell him where I had learned such a song. It was a mockery, he said. An offensive tale that shamed me when I sang it.

"I told him I learned the song from our mother." Leiel shivered a bit at the memory. "He hit me and started shouting. He said I never could have. That mother could not have known such a song and I was terrible for trying to blame her for teaching it to me. 'Where did you hear it?' he kept asking. And he hit me again, and again, when I told him from mother."

"What made him stop, if he did not believe you?" Gahree asked, and there was a spark in her gaze that Leiel could not decipher.

"I learned a secret about my mother. I learned it when he hit me. I learned that she held me apart from my brothers and told me things she never told them. I learned that she had secrets, and that somehow I was one of them. And that meant I knew things about her that they never would. So I told Gial the truth—that I learned it from a woman he never knew. A stranger."

"And he believed you. Because it is easier to believe in someone you do not know, than to believe that someone you thought you knew was more or less than you imagined."

Leiel nodded, thoughtful as she looked down at their clasped hands. "You speak so strangely." She raised her eyes to meet the woman's green-gold gaze. "Are you doing what my mother did? Are you setting me apart?"

"You hardly need me for that." Gahree laughed again. "An easy enough task for a woman dancing in a man's world. To be apart is a simple thing when you are born to be so. You never had a choice."

A light laugh escaped Leiel's lips, and she nodded. "So my mother was only making me more of what I already am?"

"And herself as well. What you must know of your mother's secret is more than just the stories she meant, but what she meant by sharing them. That is an idea for you to carry with you. While you work and while you sleep. Until you see me again."

Leiel's entire body lost tension, even the muscles in her feet relaxed. The air seemed cleaner, the sky brighter. She could really breathe for the first time in months. She was open—light—as she looked back at Gahree. Leiel was speaking with someone who cared about what she had to say. She was listening to strange words that perhaps held wisdom, and she had a promise from the odd woman that both would happen again.

She released Gahree's hand and slid off the wagon. "We'll meet here again? Next Fourth Market?"

"No. Next month you will find me selling peppers in a stall across the Square from yours. And you will have to spend a long time bartering with me to get the best ones—a barter of stories."

"And when will I hear *your* stories?"

Gahree grinned at her. "When you bring me something worth my bartering for."

What that could be, Leiel could not imagine, but the statement held challenge. And the prize for discovering what someone like Gahree might want to trade for was, she somehow knew, worth far more than money.

"I will find something." Leiel took a step forward and gave Gahree a quick hug before she turned and ran back through the maze of wagons. Gial was surely missing her. But whatever punishment he decided to mete out, what these conspiratorial moments had given her would be more than worth it.

22

Leiel

S HE HAD NOT REALIZED WHAT A RARE THING HOPE HAD BECOME UNTIL SHE FELT it again, riding through the Old Adfen Gate and into the Square. The shadow of the Tower angled long across the paver stones and up the wall of the building bordering the southwest side of the Square. That was where she would be—Gahree, with her wild hair and green-gold eyes, and perhaps several bushels of fresh peppers. Leiel smiled and an anticipatory laugh escaped her before she could stop it.

Gial looked over at her, and she realized what she had done.

"What's funny?" he asked.

She shook her head. What to say? She fell back on something that had struck her years before. "The shadow of the Tower," she said and pointed. "The way it bends over the buildings—it looks like it is trying to hug them."

Gial shifted his gaze to follow her gesture. After a moment, he smiled as well. "It does, a little." He glanced back at her. "It's good to have something to laugh at in this place."

Leiel started and met his eyes. The Square. Of course. When their mother's name was called here, in this place, she had hardly realized where she was. And what horror she remembered of that day was about the hours afterward, in the Sanctuary, where she had been accused and isolated and cursed. For Gial—that had been a place of comfort, and the worst of that day had happened *here*. Why had she never thought of that before? Maybe the anger and the short temper he always displayed on Fourth Market day were not all about her, but about having to be in the Square. She tried to think of something to say, but nothing came.

He must have seen it in her face, because he scoffed and turned away, clicking to the mule. "Figured it out at last, did you?"

"Maybe it's not me you hate."

"Hate?" he asked, and she heard the surprise in his voice. "I don't—I have never hated you."

"You do," she said, before she had a chance to think. "Just not as much as Klem does—or as much as you hate this place. But you do." She should have kept silent, but her words held truth. She couldn't take them back, and she ducked a little, anticipating the blow she was sure would follow.

It didn't come. "I didn't want to. When we were small—"

"Yes," she said. When they were small, there had been room for laughter and joy and gentle teasing. "But I know what they told you—you and Klem and father—the priests. And I know what they told *me*. I'm used to being hated. And I am used to being sad, too—just like you."

He said nothing to that, turning his attention back to driving the wagon. Whatever sentiment had just passed between them was all there would be. With a firm tug, he turned the mule into the stone stall.

Tears misted her eyes. She did not even wait for the wagon to stop rolling before she swung her leg over the back of the seat and hopped into the bed, folding her emotions tight into her chest. Somewhere inside her was still the lightness she had felt coming into the city, when she saw the Tower's shadow. Despite the shift that had just occurred between her and Gial, there was something more important here today. A strange woman, with peppers, and stories, and something Leiel could not yet fathom, but knew mattered very much.

"I'll unload," she said. They had brought no animals to sell today, only more gourds and late season tomatoes. "I can get it all, if you want to check the merchant boards."

"Well enough. Leave the wagon here today. It looks like rain, and I want it dry when we reload. Just take the mule," he said. The wagon shifted and creaked as he climbed down, but she did not look at him. If she did, she might ask more. Say more. Press more. Whatever might come from that was not what she wanted out of the rest of the day. "I'll be back by opening hour," he said. Leather slapped over wood as he tied off the mule's reins, then his footsteps moved away.

She waited until she could no longer hear them over the chatter and clatter of the arriving sellers, then she got to the ground and began to unload the wagon. For once, they had arrived at Market before Ils, and she was grateful to be alone with her work. Her thoughts were too full for easy chatter this morning. Should she even try to meet Gahree today? Leiel smiled a little. Of course she would. What else did she have to brighten this day now? Even Ils's good humor would not ease the sadness of what had passed between her and Gial.

Organizing the crates for display did not take long. By the time Ils rolled his hand cart into the stall beside hers, she had the wagon in its place and was unhitching the mule.

"Well, young one," the chandler said with his usual laughter. "What have you to trade today?"

"Morning, Ils!" she said in greeting. "I brought a pumpkin pie. And don't worry, Elda made the crust this time."

He laughed and propped his arms on the edge of his cart. "Still no skill for the baking?"

"I can't have skill in everything. You told me that yourself."

Again he laughed. "I did? I must be wise, then, yes?"

"Yes." Her smile flashed. "Eight pillars. And six tapers."

"Four pillars and two tapers," he countered.

"Four and four," she said, tipping her head and meeting his eyes with the steady trader's gaze she had mastered in bartering with livestock sellers.

Ils chuckled and nodded approval. "Fair. The pie is boxed?"

"Boxed," she promised.

"Five pillars," he said, and she laughed.

Gahree had settled herself in the heart of the shadow. Green-gold eyes flicked up at Leiel from where the woman sat on the ground, her peppers spread on a blanket. The blanket was grey, like her clothing and the old stone walls of the Square. The peppers were clean-scrubbed shades of red and yellow and green, gleaming like gems in the hot shade of the stall awning. But those eyes made the peppers seem dull. How was Gahree going to hide the strangeness of those eyes?

Leiel frowned and glanced around the booth. It was small, but still... "How did you get Hemmel's space?" How had Gahree, so odd and unknown, acquired a booth in the Square when so many traders waited years for such an opportunity?

"This fine location?" Gahree said. The strange echo in her voice was amplified by the enclosure. "It's been in the family for what seems forever."

"Hemmel is your family?" It had never occurred to Leiel that Gahree was anything but a lone traveler. No—that was not quite right. Gahree was certainly more than that. It was the idea that she might have family or friends that Leiel had never considered.

The woman laughed a little. "Oh I see. You thought I was a singular oddity. Well I am that, in my own way, child, but not a lonely one." She gestured to the spot beside her on the blanket. "Join me. What have you brought this day to trade?"

"I have late corn," Leiel said quickly. "And acorn squash—and a fresh pillar candle." She stepped into the booth and sat down.

Gahree glanced over at her and her eyes were no longer strange. They were bright, yes, cheerful and full of life, but the metallic glint that made them so very *different* was missing. Leiel saw no more or less than a dusty, mountain woman.

"What did you do to your eyes?" Leiel couldn't imagine how such a thing was possible. The change was more than illusion, it was fundamental. That was clear the moment Gahree spoke and her voice, while warm, had lost its echoing musicality.

"Only what is necessary. Rarely more than that—very rarely."

"But how—?"

"Wild daughter, this is the least important of the things we have to learn about each other. Tell me, what stories have you brought me today? We must trade for more than peppers, sweet or hot though they might be."

Leiel thought a moment. "It *is* about the stories after all. Elda said the stories didn't matter."

Gahree chuckled as she sorted a few more peppers from her pack and arranged them on the blanket. "By color, or size, or flavor—so many ways to organize—peppers are easy. Just lay them out. They are only what they are and nothing more. Not like me or you. Peppers don't care for stories. Do you remember the first one I told you?"

"In the old mill. About the balance of Arnan."

"And what story did you tell me?"

"The story of Shaa," Leiel said, an ache suddenly forming in her chest. She closed her eyes, and for a moment, was back in the old mill on that summer day.

"In the days long ago, Arnan was overrun by monsters. The people were enslaved by the Draigon and all the days were filled with sadness." Leiel chose her words carefully, trying to remember the story exactly as she had been taught it. She glanced at Gahree as she spoke, trying to judge if she was getting it right.

"The Farlan were explorers who came in search of trading partners, and when they found Arnan, they were horrified by the Draigon and their control over all the people. So they brought fighters to the land to kill the monsters and free the people."

"Many were killed, on both sides—Farlan and Draigon. And the Farlan thought they had won. But the king of the Draigon survived—Shaa. And it is Shaa who still leads the Draigon to this day. So it's Shaa who all people from the mountains to the plains to the sea, must watch the sky for." She shrugged a little and looked at Gahree as a wisp of smoke from the fire drifted up between them. "That is the story of Shaa."

Gahree threw back her head and laughed until the rafters echoed.

"And is this the same story you would tell me now?" Gahree asked, and the wind was back in her words, the shimmer in her eyes.

"No." Leiel pulled her head up and narrowed her gaze. Her voice scratched in her throat. "No, I would tell a story of how Shaa took my mother, and the best of my life. You would not laugh at that one."

"I might." The strange woman did laugh. "If you chose a very silly voice for the Draigon."

Leiel frowned at her, but the woman's expression had turned so forcibly serious that Leiel found her lips curling into a smile. Gahree's gaze flickered to hers and the spark there was unmistakable. Leiel held back a few seconds, then started laughing and Gahree joined her.

"Another story, then," Gahree said. "What do you wish to tell me?"

"I think it's your turn to tell me one." Leiel folded her arms and looked at the older woman.

"Oh, not yet. Not *yet*, daughter of wings. Remember—a barter. Keep all your candles and tell me a new tale."

"I don't—"

"Never say you have no stories to share. Stories are like air. They are everywhere and in everyone, and they are as necessary as every breath you take. Tell a simple one—such is a better trade for peppers than any candle."

In the heavy shade of the Tower, the moment she had shared with Gial came back to her, and she thought of a summer day long ago, when her mother was still alive, and her family had still loved each other, and the day was so perfect that even the motion of the clouds took her breath away.

It was a rare afternoon. The sky was a blue that she had only seen in paintings, with high clouds that tumbled from horizon to horizon and cast slow moving shadows over the ground. All day, the entire family had been relaxed and full of laughter. Her father even left his office to come out and do his work on a table moved to the porch. She had caught the usually serious Torrin humming something while he worked. In a shift from her father's normal insistence of formality for a late meal, her mother and Elda had dragged the big table into the yard and were setting out a feast to make eyes pop.

Leiel skipped across to the barn to fetch her brothers, in awe that a day such as this could exist at all. From the moment she swung her legs out of bed, everything had been special. The temperature was perfect, the air smelled sweet, and even the birds seemed to be singing a promise of good things to come. Even with the day drawing to a close, the joy of just being left her without words to describe the happiness filling her.

She danced up to the barn door and hopped inside. "Gial! Mother says we'll eat soon."

He waved to her from the end of the barn, where he was putting away the grain buckets. His hair, the same brown as hers and just as in need of trimming, draped into his eyes. He shoved it back. "What did Elda cook up? I hope it's special on a day like this."

"Mother says it's a surprise, but I smelled spice pies for sure. Where's Klem?"

"Checking the coop for evening eggs. Go tell him. I bet on a day like this the hens laid double."

She laughed. It was still so beautiful out that she would take any chance she could get to prolong the sense of wonder of the day.

"Don't take too long," Gial shouted after her as she ran back outside. "Or I'll eat all the spice pies before you can get any."

She rounded the corner of the barn and headed toward the chicken coop behind the house. Leiel sprinted across the yard, and her mother looked up and laughed at her darting past. "I have to get Keehee!" Leiel called. Her mother nodded.

Klem was just emerging from the tightly built shed.

"Keehee!" she said, her fast breathing making her words bounce. She could almost imagine them bounding through the air toward him. "Time to eat! Oh, it smells so good. Come on!"

"Let me wash first." He held up a basket with a few eggs in it. "I'm all chickeny."

She laughed as she unlatched the wire gate that keep the hens in their pen. "Keehee chickeny! Funny!"

"I'm too old for you to call me that." He pulled himself up straight and tried to look serious. He was always trying to look serious. But the perfection of the day had gotten to him, too, and his mouth curled up at the edges despite him crinkling his face the best he could.

"You said I could call you that until you were ten."

"Well, I changed my mind. Nine is too old to have a silly name."

"You said ten," she said, sing-songing the last word as she closed the gate and followed him toward the pump by the back door to the kitchen.

He handed her the basket. "Well, not at school when you start going. Only here. Take these inside."

She smiled and waited as he washed, not making any move to carry the eggs to the house. As soon as he finished cleaning up, she thrust the basket back into his hands and raced away around the front of the house. "Keehee's putting the eggs away then he's coming," she shouted, laughing as he protested behind her.

Leiel smiled as she told it—the happiness of that day flooding back through her. When the last words were spoken, she blinked back tears. That day was so far gone.

"Keehee—he liked me once. Gial, too. When we were little. And mother was alive."

"You called your brother Keehee? Like the grey hawk on the wing?"

"Yes." Leiel wiped at her eyes. A slow smile found its way to her face. "He used to squawk a lot, when he was angry. His voice would get all squeaky and sharp."

The rising noise of the market all but covered up the low laughter that shook Gahree's body. "And now?"

"More growly than squeaky." Leiel gave a laugh—a short, sharp biting sound that startled her and made her clamp her fingers over her mouth.

"Oh—wild sounds from a woman should never be held back." Gahree reached out to pull Leiel's hands down. "Like the leaves of a tree, such sounds must move in the wind."

"Klem doesn't like it when I am loud."

"Because you're a girl?" Gahree laughed again, bold and ringing, and it seemed to Leiel that the entire market quieted to listen to the sound. "Nothing is more precious than knowledge, wild daughter, unless it is the unfettered laughter of a free girl." Gahree reached out and broke open a green pepper and bit into it. "Sweet as rain falling. And a better sound than any made by a griping brother."

"Do you have any brothers?" Leiel asked. "Do they let you laugh?"

"Like you, I had a brother, long ago. And there was once a time, child of laughter, when no one asked leave to show joy."

That seemed a tale even more legendary than the old story of the Witch in the Wood. But then, the story she had just told of her own childhood seemed no less fantastic to her. "Where is he? Where is your brother now?"

"Long gone. To ride the winds and stars and occasionally whisper terrible jokes in the falling rain." She leaned close and winked. "And I had a silly name for him as well."

"What did you call him?"

"Deheru." Gahree's penetrating voice was low and conspiratorial.

"What does that mean?"

"His name was Glau—in an old, old language, that means rain—so I called him *deheru*—which means 'drip'."

Leiel choked on another laugh. "You called your brother *drip*?"

"He was very small." Gahree sat up very straight and eyed Leiel with pointed seriousness.

This time the laughter doubled Leiel over, and she was giggling into her hands with her face pressed to the blanket. It smelled sweet, from the peppers, like tumbling rain. Like pepper drips. The giggling became rolling chuckles, then snorts. Tears were rolling down her cheeks. This was a state she was most certainly not supposed to be in—this ridiculous, elated, huddle of happiness. She fell gratefully into it, somehow secure in Gahree's company, knowing that whatever she said or did was sheltered in the woman's presence.

23

Cleod – 12 years

THE PAIN OF EXTENDED EFFORT WAS FAMILIAR. HE HAD SPENT YEARS ON THE woodlot with his father, and had taken care of the animals and the garden at home. He had worked until his arms ached, and his back cramped, and his fingers blistered and bled. He had suffered the cold wind of winter days and the desperate heat of Draigon Weather. Long days and short sleeps were familiar companions. But his first weeks among the Ehlewer had left him stunned by the effort it took just to get out of bed every day.

Light from the narrow slot window tipped its way into the tiny stone chamber, its weak illumination the only sign that morning was upon him again. This far back in the Spur Range, at such an altitude, there were few animals to signal the fading of the night with their song or their chatter. He missed that—knowing the rhythms of the hours and the seasons. Even those were missing here, where the chill in the air was so constant it was easy to forget that it was spring.

With a groan, and the pop of a tight hip, Cleod swung his legs over the bed and sat up slowly. In the bunk above him, the boy who shared the space turned over and muttered a curse. He was the third cellmate Cleod had been assigned since arriving, and this was the fourth room he had occupied.

"You're going to run out of ways to say that," Cleod said. On the peg beside the bed hung the grey pants and shirt that were the standard uniform of the new candidates—called Draigre by the Elders.

"I'll ask someone from Bajor for a few more versions," Trayor replied. The bunk creaked as he rolled over, and he hung his head over the edge of the bed and blinked blearily down at Cleod.

"Do they have a phrase similar to 'The sun is a rotting pus ball?'" Cleod scruffed his hands through his short-cropped hair.

"I'll find one." Trayor pulled the thin pillow over his head.

"No point in that, Tray," Cleod pushed himself to his aching feet. A dozen needle points of pain danced up his legs and into his back. Everything he had imagined it would take to earn the rank of Draighil had waned under the shadow of the actual experience. His mind was as tired as his body. Mornings and evenings were spent on physical training. Afternoons were for school. The studies here were of subjects he had not even known existed. Strategy and recounting of old battles. Puzzles to be solved and maps to be studied. Weather reading and languages from all over Arnan. The Ehlewer were testing not just his strength, but his will. And then there were the history lessons. At every meal, stories were told, of the First War—something every child of Arnan was required to learn. But these tellings were new. Detailed in a way the ones he had learned were not. The tales Soibel and the other elders shared were learned from old books, journaled accounts of the fighters who had lived the wars. But more important even than those, were the stories of the Ehlewer Draighil and the founding of the Enclaves.

Though Cleod had studied everything he could find on the Ehlewer before coming to the Enclave, the information available in Adfen's library had been lacking. The Ehlewer Draighil were learned men. The first of six Enclaves founded to train Draighil, the Ehlewer's long history was well charted, and the Enclave protective of its own and its secrets.

Never before had he been a part of something so dedicated to its history. Despite the pain that every day brought—the new bruises and the exhaustion that muddled his thoughts—he was proud to be here. This place had purpose—and it offered him the way to make sure he satisfied the purpose he had chosen for himself.

He stepped into his pants, pulled on his shirt and grabbed Trayor's clothes from the other hook and tossed them onto the top bunk. "Get up. I won't do without breakfast just because you're lazy."

Enclave rules dictated that room partners were responsible for each others' actions. If they did not arrive in the meal hall on time and together, neither would eat.

Cleod sat back down on the bed to pull on his socks. His fingers cramped as he laced up his boots. He spread and flexed them.

"Tray!"

"Right, I'm moving," the older boy said. "You're damn bossy for a cefreid."

"Oh and how many cefreid have you known to compare that to, Farlan brat?" Cleod said. He no longer bothered to take offense at the slang term for one not of Farlan blood. His answer was the flimsy pillow swung down toward his face. He dodged the makeshift weapon, caught Trayor's wrist and yanked him half off the bunk.

"By the—" Tray sputtered struggling to shove himself upright.

With a wink and a grin, Cleod pulled his friend the rest of the way to the floor. Tray managed to grab enough blankets to slow his fall and land only with a grumbling thud. He was scrambling to his feet amid his bedclothes and Cleod's laughter, when the cell door cracked open and the floor warden, Hebben Ehlewer, stepped into the room.

Cleod jerked to his feet, pillar straight, and stared at the wall. Tray was still muttering and untangling himself, but he staggered into place as he registered Cleod's change in position.

"More energy than the morning usually arouses in you two," Hebben said. "But significantly less coordination. Get dressed and get to breakfast. Then both of you report to Rhol Ehlewer for balance drills before your sword training."

"Yes, Elder!" Cleod said in unison with Trayor. It could have been worse. At least one of them was dressed. Had they both been in their small clothes, it was unlikely that an extra hour of training would have been all that was required of them.

"Get moving," Hebben pulled the door closed behind him.

Tray kicked away the blankets the moment the door clicked shut. "Rot and fire. My legs will shatter if I have to stand on just one for more than a moment."

"Next time get out of bed."

Another round of oaths was tossed into the air as Trayor found his clothes and pulled them on in quick jerks. Cleod took pity and remade both their beds, while Trayor searched for his footwear.

"Come on," Cleod said, grabbing their coats from the shared trunk by the door. "We'll just make it if we run."

As on so many other mornings, they were not the only ones rushing to make the morning meal. By now Cleod had realized all the shuffling of cellmates and chambers was designed to keep them struggling each day. Every time he and a roommate became accustomed to each other and what they had to do to work together, they were reassigned. The same was true with their rooms. They could never become passive about shortcuts or planning to the last moment how long they could oversleep and still not be late. Nothing was static. Anything could change at any moment. The only thing he could safely expect was that nothing would stay the same for long.

They ran down the hall and staircase, their breath steaming white in the cold morning air. While the individual cells were heated by hot water piped under the floors, the hallways were not, nor the privy chambers, which made using those somewhat traumatic.

The sprawling granite buildings of the ancient complex hugged the side of the mountain just below the crest of the ridge. Terraces carved into the stone served as gardens and training grounds as the seasons allowed. The dormitories were divided by student year and formed a ring around the classroom and dining buildings. The Sanctuary was located by the spring-fed pond just inside the walls. By the Up-Mountain Gate was the oldest building of all, a black stone Keep that housed the elders and the Enclave Library.

Crossing the frozen ground toward the meal hall, Cleod looked up, hoping for a glimpse of sun. But the promise made by a brightening sky remained unfulfilled, and the clouds above hung low and grey.

"Did you grab your gloves?" he asked Trayor as they reached the big wooden building. The other boy shook his head as they entered. Noise swelled around them with the warm press of many bodies and the scent of spiced bread. "I didn't think."

Cleod sighed. "Go back. I'll wait."

"No," Trayor said. "Better cold hands than a cold belly. We're in for it with Rhol already. I'll be all right."

Cleod nodded.

"We can share mine if the temperature drops too far. Trade off." He peeled off his coat and folded it over his arm as they found seats at one of the sprawling tables.

"They won't let us." Tray plunked down beside him. "Frez and Willem tried it last week on the spear grounds. They both ended up without and on half rations. We don't fight the Draigon in teams, remember? They're trying to teach us to be responsible for ourselves."

"Then why tie our meals to coming here together?" Cleod reached for a hot loaf and an apple.

"Weeding us out," Trayor said. "Those that can't manage their partners can't manage a Draigon."

"How are we managing so far?"

"Better tomorrow," Trayor said. "Eat."

One foot lifted and held out before him, Cleod bent his knee and lowered his entire weight toward the earth. He held his back rod-straight as he descended, kept his movements slow and his muscles tense. The chill wind beat against him, tried to push him off center. He focused, held steady, sank from his hips, careful to listen to everything happening around him.

Drawing steady breath, he raised his heel off the ground, until his body was stable over just his toes, then unbent his knee and pushed his body straight. With careful precision, he reversed the pattern of movement, and repeated it. His leg trembled and his thigh muscles burned, his foot quivering in a constant series of tiny adjustments. After the tenth sequence, he reached back and slid the wooden practice sword from the sheath on his back. He had not yet earned his own harness set, and from day to day, the borrowed equipment never had the same balance or weight. He suspected that was another strategy to keep him uneasy and adaptable.

Starting into the movement series again, this time adding the beginning level sword pattern he had learned the week before, he faltered. Off balance immediately, he stumbled forward and had to fling both arms out to keep from falling. He clamped his teeth shut to keep from uttering a curse of frustration.

Rhol provided one for him as he stormed across the practice ground, hand-whip poised for use. "By all the gods of old and their now destitute spawn! Do you practice not at all, boy? You'll bring nothing but shame to the Ehlewer with maneuvers like that one. Do you want to be Draighil or a kitchen whelp?" He struck a solid blow over Cleod's shoulders and stepped so close Cleod was afraid to draw breath as he scrambled back upright. "I don't care if you were born *cefreid, Farlan, or half-god.* You are *nothing* on this training ground until you have earned it. Whatever you were before and whoever you think you deserve to be—you are *not* that. Not now. Now, you are less valuable to this Enclave than a two-legged dog, and you cost us more to feed.

"Do you think these sessions are the only practice you need? Do you think you can just work here on this ground and hope your body has the strength to do this when called upon?"

Cleod shook his head, trying desperately to reorganize his body and mind to resume the drill, but his nerves were jangling like bells down his tense spine. "No, Elder Rhol."

"Then *focus,* boy!" This time the whip landed on Cleod's wrist. The sting spiked up his arm. His fingers went numb, and he nearly dropped the practice sword. "Indeed, this is not a game. Do you think a Draigon will wait for you to get this right? Or care a wink in the dark for your hurt feelings and sensitive skin? Pull straight! Concentrate! If you cannot manage this pattern twice on each side by the end of the hour, you will return here, instead of eating last meal, and work on it until you *can.*"

Shaking, Cleod drew taut the muscles around his center and focused inward. Rhol Ehlewer's shouting continued, but Cleod drove the words to the back of his mind. How much of the problem was that his body was tired, weak? How much that he was thinking too much? Where did the two problems mesh and where must they be separated? Within the pattern of the movement and his own determination lay the answer he needed. And even if he failed this moment, and the next, all possible deficiencies were simply there to be triumphed over. There existed no other option. Success was all. For the promise he had made to Leiel. For himself. For the future of the Ehlewer.

Falling again, he did not wait for the blow or chastisement, or even to curse his own flaws, he just moved back into position and began again.

Again he slipped and returned to the pose. On Cleod's third attempt, Rhol moved away, turning his ire on Trayor. Shifted off center by the moving weight of the sword, Cleod knew he was destined to have to return in the evening. But it would be worth it. All would be worthwhile when the moment came for him to keep all the promises he had made.

24

Cleod – 13 years

"IT STARTS TODAY!" TRAYOR LEANED ACROSS THE TABLE, HIS WHISPER BARELY classifiable as such.

"Might as well shout your secret," Cleod said without looking up from the text he was studying. "What starts today?"

"The real training." A hand snaked across the tabletop and flipped the cover of the book closed under Cleod's nose. "*Gweld training!*"

The irritation that scrunched Cleod's eyes into a glare vanished as he looked at the other boy. "You're sure? Today?"

A fierce series of nods was his reply, Trayor's white-blond hair bouncing in the sunlight streaming through the library windows. "I saw Soibel readying herb bundles. Not sage or silkweed—something darker. It has to be the *cuila!*"

Cuila. The vision plant. Rumored to be used in the aftermath of the Gweld trance to calm the terrible Overlash. For as long as Cleod could remember, he had heard stories about Gweld, though none of the older Draigre offered true details. Those who had mastered it were unwilling to share their secrets before the younger boys began the training. Those who were still learning returned from training sessions violently ill and cursing. "You're certain that's what it was? Not some new plant species we need to learn to identify in the field? Some new remedy?"

"No—I am certain of it. They were wrapped with dry straw and green willow bark. To light quickly and burn smoky."

Cleod tipped his head and studied Trayor. "And where were you spying from that you saw all this in such detail?"

Trayor chuckled. "I wasn't spying. I was on my way here, and he stopped me and asked me to help carry baskets of herbs."

Cleod joined in the laughter. "Well, that's more than a guess then. You really think it will begin today?"

"Or tomorrow. It's our third summer. It's the next thing we must learn."

"Do you know anyone before fifth summers to have mastered it?"

"You know I don't." Trayor leaned back in his chair and shook his head. "You're the only one looking for short routes to knowledge. Is there a book in this place that you haven't read trying to learn how to skip ahead in all our subjects?"

Cleod frowned. It was true that he studied beyond the required work, looking for more information about the training yet to come, and about the Enclave. He had uncovered a long, stern history of wise men who had given their lifetimes, and sometimes their lives, to understand how to destroy the monsters that plagued Arnan. But shortcuts—none of those. The only way he could see through to mastery of all he wished to learn was long practice. Patience given over to time. If he had enough of one to use the other wisely, he might someday find a way to speed up the process. Already, the things he studied hardest—strategy and swordplay—he found came quicker and easier the more he practiced them.

"There's no skipping anything. There's just more and more work." He held up the book he had been reading—a history of the first Draigon killers. "Think about it, Tray. All the Elders—the Draighil who have come before us—how hard did they have to work to learn so much? And then they had to figure out how to teach it to us. They are great men—You should read the things I have."

"We learn all about the Draighil in school." Trayor shrugged. "Of course they are great men. They are the best of the Farlan. Why do you think I wanted to come here? There have not been, for a long time, enough Draighre to fill the Enclaves. Now that the Draigon are coming back more often—it is good to see so many here now."

"Maybe you learned all this in school," Cleod said in correction. "I am just a low born cur, remember? Cefreid learn the common history. Not the stories of warriors."

"Well you're here now." Trayor reached across the table, and punched Cleod's arm. "Come on! We've just time to get to noon meal if we leave now."

Cleod grinned and got to his feet, packed the book into his satchel among the rolled maps he was studying. Heat rushed through his chest. Gweld at last—the true secret to destroying the Draigon! "What do you think it will be like? Mind-work like the histories? Or body-work like the sword and spear?"

"The Gweld?" Tray shoved back his chair and shook his head. "From the look of the fourth summers returning, it's more like violent puking."

Cleod grimaced. "For a highborn Farlan, you speak as low as any field rat."

"I learned from the best of the low, Woodcutter." Trayor dodged away toward the door of the library before Cleod could react.

"At least I can rise above my station. You can only fall from yours."

"Move it, cefreid!" Trayor shouted back, and ducked outside as the librarian rounded the stacks and moved across the room with a glare that would melt stone.

Cleod yanked his satchel strap over his head. It was barely settled on his shoulder before he sprinted for the door. The Elder shouted, but Cleod dodged across the threshold without looking back. He would pay for that later. He was too much of a fixture in the library to avoid chastisement for long. But, for mealtime, and probably his first round of Gweld training, he was free. If the violent sickness he had witnessed in so many others was an accurate prediction of what was to come with the new skill, he might wish instead for whatever menial punishment the scholar Elder might have chosen.

The thought of the sickness and the pain should have terrified him. But somehow it thrilled him instead. He strode across the green grass of the Enclave's common area, and the sun beat warm on his face. Gweld was the reason he was here. It was the most important thing he must learn if he was to become the Draighil he dreamed of being. Gweld trance was what drove a Draighil's awareness into the state of readiness that allowed him to out-think and out-maneuver a Draigon. It allowed him to span, with the mind, a space greater than he could see or hear. To combat and to kill.

Swordwork he knew and could improve every day. Knowledge of landscape and weather and strategy, he could study on his own. But the Gweld was the secret knowledge that set the Draighil above all other warriors. It was the thing he most needed, and he would face any hardship to master it.

25

Leiel – 15 years

"IT'S NOT HER PLACE!" KLEM SAID. HIS VOICE ROSE IN VOLUME AND IN PITCH, THE strident sound out of place in the warmly lit room.

"Do you want to be the one to do it?" Addor demanded, leaning forward in his chair and pointing an arthritis-curled finger at his youngest son. "Leave the bookwork to her instead? Take over managing the milking and harvest and birthing the pigs?"

"She's a *girl.*"

Leiel had become resigned to the way Klem said that word, as though he were speaking of something rotting under the woodshed. But the venom in it now surprised even her. For years, she had been relegated to the house and kitchen, in charge of the cooking, and the mending, and assisting Elda with keeping the old house clean and in order. If she had learned to take a quiet pride in the efficient ease with which everything about the household was managed, she had never gotten over the loss of her freedom to roam the farm. To ask questions and seek answers. To go to school. That her father was now proposing an expansion of her responsibilities set her almost twitching with anticipation. But she said nothing, just sat at her place across the table from Klem and tried not to look amused at the chastisement he was receiving.

"A *girl,*" Klem repeated. He shoved to his feet, almost knocking over his chair, and paced the length of the room. "You would let her take on too much—just as you did mother. You'll lead her into violation of every law we've been trying to obey since the Sacrifice and even the old gods would not be able to save this family if she starts down that path."

"What mother did or did not do on this farm has nothing to do with what the Council decided." The words escaped Leiel before she could stop them.

"Silence yourself!" Klem rounded on her, his face flushed red. "This concerns you not at all."

"Oh? Who, exactly, are you discussing then?"

"Both of you. Enough!" Addor's voice was still strong. Where his body had failed him, his will had not.

"This isn't acceptable," Klem said, coming back to the head of the table and staring down at their father.

"What do you propose then?" Addor demanded. "Your brother must see our goods to the coastal markets. My Draigon-damned hips won't let me do what needs to be done any longer. You want nothing of the daily work this place requires. And I am glad for that—your talents are too formidable in other areas to be wasted on just building callouses. But someone must take charge. I can't do it from a sickbed any longer."

"We'll hire someone. A man with the knowledge we need to—"

"By your own calculations, any man with the knowledge we need is beyond our means to engage," Addor said. "Not if we want to see enough profit to keep you attending the Academy. What would you prefer? A hired foreman who'll keep your sister where she rightly belongs, or Leiel monitoring the fields and the cattle, so you can stay in school? Since you're so set against this proposal, make your choice. Wounded propriety, or your future."

"You'll never make Councilman with only a merchant farmer's education," Leiel said.

She was unsurprised by the backhanded blow her father landed across her mouth as he turned on her, tone vicious. "And you! If this is a change you want, you would do well to hold your silence as your brother suggested."

She raised a hand to her bloodied lip and nodded, shifted her eyes to Klem again. The satisfaction she saw in his expression would have roused her anger if she had not been feeling smug herself. It was worth the slap to see Klem's need for control buried under Addor's authority.

"Klem—you'll continue as you are, in charge of the accounts and attending to your studies. Leiel will take over a good portion of my work *and* remain responsible for the continued functioning of the house. Gial, when he returns will be notified of the changes, though while he is home, he will be in charge of all exterior duties."

With a snort of outrage, Klem turned and stormed from the room. When the door slammed shut behind him, Addor turned to Leiel. "I expect you to live up to this opportunity. My infirmity has given rise to a need to go against my better judgment. Do *not* disappoint me. You will regret it."

She met his gaze. His threats were still worth fearing, but she had learned that if she was willing to tolerate the consequences, she could push back. Doing so kept her frustrations from boiling to the point of explosion. The blow he had landed tonight was reason enough for her not to hold her tongue. "How can I ever disappoint you more than I already have by being born a girl?"

He raised a shaking hand, but she pushed back from the table out of reach. "You only get to hit me once tonight, father." She got to her feet. "I'll start work on the planting schedule in the morning."

"Leiel!" His shout followed her from the room, but she did not turn back. He had changed her duties, and he could not go back on that decision without incurring the ridicule of her younger brother. That was something Addor could not stand. Klem was more condescending to Addor every year and, once her brother was a Councilman and no longer needed Addor's approval—or money—he would not have any respect left for the older man at all. The animosity she now faced from her brothers was going to be more than unpleasant to rebuff, and she could expect little help from her father beyond what she had just received.

She had hardly closed the door behind her when a strong grip wrapped around her wrist, and she was jerked sideways against the wall. Klem's face was inches from hers, his breath hot in her face, over the cut on her lip. "Proud of yourself?"

A tug of her arm failed to achieve her freedom, and she glared at him. "I leave pride to you. Let go of me. Even if you break my arm, it won't change anything."

"Your disrespect for the way things have to be will ruin us," he said, his voice low and insistent. "It will ruin *you*."

"You've wanted that for years. You promised I would burn someday. This should put me well down that path."

"It was you." Klem shook her. "You that—" He drew a ragged breath, and a hint of pain flashed in his expression before it was gone. Years had passed since she had seen any real glimpse of emotion in him. It startled her. Something turned a little in her heart.

"Do you remember," she asked, "when that dining room was the best room in the house? When we were all together and the table was full and all the candles were lit?"

He released her and stepped back, and she glimpsed again the layer of anguish under his rage. "I remember," he said, but no shared warmth touched his voice, only bitterness. "I would be living it still, if it were not for you. Run the farm, Leiel. One day I will see you get what you deserve." He turned and stormed away.

She rubbed her bruised wrist and tried to control her shaking. She had never understood why Klem had decided to hate her. His anger had grown, year to year, and become ever more blended with his determination that he would find a way to see her pay for whatever it was she had done to earn his enmity. One day he *would* be on the Council. Then she would have reason to actually fear him. Until then, she took what pleasure she could in sidestepping his domination.

Pulling herself back under control, she moved down the hall and stepped out the front door. She paused on the porch and breathed deep of the moist spring air. It tasted like victory. It tasted like hope. If Cleod were here to share it with, the day would be more than satisfying; it would be superb. But he was not, so she took what the clean air and the expansion of the boundaries of her world offered and was, for the moment, content.

26

Leiel

"YOU'RE A SIGHT."

Mud flew as Leiel started upright. Buried to her ankles in the pig pen, with her skirts tucked up, hands equally covered from rescuing the piglet who had tried to burrow under the shelter, she stared through the glare of sunlight at the man on horseback. No—not yet a man, but far more than a boy.

"Cleod?"

He reined the horse around a little so the sun was no longer directly behind him and smiled down at her. "Hi, Leiel." His voice had changed, deepened and broadened, but it was familiar to her bones.

She gave a whoop that sent the pigs scrambling. "I was doubting I would ever see you again!" How long had it been? Years that seemed much longer. And he was here in the farmyard—of course on a day she was dealing with the livestock. Two slogging steps brought her to the gate, and she was through it before he had stopped laughing. He backed the horse up as she approached.

"Oh, no," he said, shaking his head. "Get away from me. You're a mess."

"Ha! I haven't seen you in ten forevers and you're afraid of a little mud?"

"You look like you slept in it." He turned the horse again, evading her.

She held up her filthy hands and shrugged. "All right! Get down and help me wash off." With a grunt, she turned and went to the water trough. A bucket hung on the hook by the pump. She dipped it full and set it aside.

"I'm not coming anywhere near you until you're half-clean," he said. He slid off the horse and walked toward her, but slowly.

She looked over her shoulder at him as she dunked her hands and began to scrub. He was as neatly dressed as she had ever seen him, all in grey, with black boots, and a knife tucked into his belt. "Look at you. No wonder you don't want to roll in the mud. When did you get home? You're not done training already?"

He chuckled. "We all got leave to visit our families. I got back three days ago. Father sent me to town for some supplies, so I thought I would stop and see you."

She pushed up her sleeves and sluiced her arms, then dumped the bucket, muddy water washing across her boots and knocking away the worst of the muck. "Town is the other direction," she said. A couple flicks of her hands speckled her skirts with water. He had made a special trip to see her. Her heart skipped lighter as she turned to face him fully. "Now do I get a hug?"

He studied her for a second, then she simply ran forward and grabbed him before he could refuse or protest.

"Ooof!" He laughed as she squeezed the breath out of him. Then his arms went around her and he returned her hug in kind. "You're still getting me dirty."

"If you actually care, you'll just have to bear the mess."

He laughed again, and the sound rumbled through his chest and into her ear. Like his voice, his laugh held more depth. She pulled away and looked up at him. "How long are you staying?"

"I go home tomorrow."

"Home? You mean you're back to stay?" She held her breath, afraid to hope, but he shook his head.

"No. Home to the Enclave."

She tipped her head, her brow creased by a frown. "The Enclave is home?"

He shrugged, reached up to pat his horse's neck. "It's where I live, now. And for a lot more years."

Did simply living in a place make it home? That was something she would have to think about. But she nodded. He was here! Here to see her!

"I went to the pond, like we used to," he said. "At dusk. But you didn't come."

"I never go to the pond any more. I didn't know you were home, or I would have tried to sneak over."

"Sneak?"

"Father doesn't let me leave the farm much any more," she said. "Come sit!" She took his hand and tugged him toward the bench outside Torrin's shop. She glanced around, but Klem was nowhere in sight. He was probably up to his eyes in his ledgers. As long as lunch arrived on time, it was unlikely he would notice Cleod's presence. Torrin's hammer sounded from inside the shop. That would help cover the sound of conversation.

The horse clopped behind them, and Cleod took a moment to wrap the reins around the tie-pole near the shop door before he joined her. "That makes sense. I thought I would find you in the kitchen," he said as he sat. "You said that's mostly what you do now."

She nodded. "It is—or was until a few months ago. But my father has been sick. His feet and legs are swollen up. And his hands. He doesn't travel any more. And he can't do farm work. So that leaves me."

"What about Gial and Klem?"

"Gial does the trading now. He's gone all the time." She leaned forward a little to look past Cleod toward the house. "Klem—"

"Klem never liked to work."

She grinned at him. "Still doesn't. But now he has the excuse that he's in school and keeping all the books. No time for mud and pigs and farming. He was pretty angry when I got put in charge of all the dirty work."

"Why? If he's not going to do it, what does he care?"

"I enjoy it. He doesn't like me to enjoy anything."

Cleod frowned. "Well, it is strange that you would."

She sat back and looked at him. "Strange?"

"Well, you're—"

"If you say 'You're a girl,' I will throw a piglet at you."

"But you *are*."

She folded her arms and glared at him. "Then *who* exactly is supposed to do all this? The hands already work the fields all day. Torrin is needed here." She waved a hand at the blacksmith's shed. "There's no one else. When did me being a girl matter to you, ever?"

He smiled. "I always knew you were a girl."

"But when did you decide it *mattered* for anything?" Here he was, neat and proper, hardly started into their conversation and already she was half-mad at him. Something skipped inside her. What was she doing? Who knew when she would see him again?

"It's always mattered." There was something serious edging his tone.

Now what did that mean? She shook her head. "Well, I never knew it. Not with you." She sighed and tipped her head. "I chase pigs and cows. What do you do all day at the Enclave? I haven't had a letter from you in months."

"They don't let us write many letters any more. We have a lot more to concentrate on. Distractions are bad." Some of the tension left his expression, replaced by a brightness in his eyes, and a lift at the edges of his mouth. "We are learning Gweld now."

"Gweld? That's the trance skill you wrote me about?"

He shook his head and leaned a little toward her. "It's more than that. It's the most important part of Draighil training. Because of the Gweld, Draighil are faster and stronger than the beasts."

She tried to imagine that—a skill that would make a person more dangerous than a creature that could destroy entire regions of Arnan with the heat of its body, and the beating of its wings. What must it be like, to learn that kind of power? "How do you learn it?"

He drew back a little. "I can't talk about that. But it's hard. It makes you sick, until you learn to control it."

"It makes you sick?" Her chest tightened. That was not an image she wanted in her mind—Cleod tired and ill.

He nodded, but there was no concern in his alert expression. His energy pushed at her, eager and certain. "Of course. Nothing worth learning comes without price. But the Elders have a plant that helps. It's called Cuila. They burn it after the training and it—"

"Leiel! What is this?"

She jumped and Cleod lurched to his feet, turning to face the voice that had interrupted him. Addor stood on the porch, and his face was mottled and his mouth a hard line.

"Sere—" Cleod began.

"Save your breath." Addor came down the steps and hobbled toward them. His face as firmly set as each plant of his canes on the ground. "What are you doing here, Cleod Woodcutter? It is not proper that you make yourself welcome on my property without announcing yourself to me first. It is even more improper that you turn unsupervised attention on my daughter."

"We were school friends, Sere," Cleod said, pulling himself straight and walking forward to meet Addor. "I meant no disrespect to you."

"She is Draigfen!" Addor said. "You disrespect yourself, as well, coming here like this." Shaking his head, he halted a few steps from Cleod.

Leiel stood, breath caught in her throat. "Father, I only—"

"Be silent!" Addor glared at her. "This is what comes of allowing you out of the house. Klem was right to be concerned." He turned his attention to Cleod. "Such rash behavior as this can mar your future. I would have expected the Ehlewer to teach you proper action. Get back on your horse, boy, and don't come back."

"I am sorry, Sere. I should have considered—" Cleod flicked a glance at her.

"Don't look at her," Addor said, his voice rolling across the farmyard with a strength that was no longer matched by his body. But his tone brooked no dissent. "I said back on your horse."

Cleod nodded, the motion as stiff as his stance, and he walked quickly to his horse, swung into the saddle.

Tears gathered in Leiel's eyes. Addor stared at her. Behind him, the front door of the house swung open and Klem stepped out. His gaze met hers across the yard, and he smiled without humor.

She wanted to run to Cleod, beg him to take her with him. She could out-pace her father, but not Klem, so she stood caught between the need to move and the knowledge that anything she might do was useless.

Cleod turned his horse, was moving out of the yard.

"Cleod—" His name slipped out, barely a whisper on Leiel's lips. For a moment she was afraid he had not heard, or would not acknowledge her, if he had. But he looked at her, just a brief flash. His expression had gone tight and hot, his face flushed and tension pulled at his eyes. He gave the slightest tip of his head, then kicked the horse into a canter and rode away from the farm.

Leiel watched him go, heart pounding like a drum in her chest, a rhythm that seemed to skip and change with her breath, with the heat rising in her gut. She gritted back tears and fought the trembling that threatened to render her impotent. "He's my friend," she said. Somewhere in the back of her mind she recognized that Torrin's hammer had fallen silent; the hoof beats of Cleod's horse faded in the distance. What was the point of her words in the silence now buzzing the farmyard? "We were hurting no one."

"You hurt him by existing," Addor said. "That boy is becoming something worthwhile—or will be if he keeps his mind on what matters. Get inside where you belong. I have much to consider about your place on this farm."

She inhaled a biting breath and swallowed—hard tears, hard anger, hard words. Picking up her skirts, she stalked toward the house.

Klem stood in her way. She half-shoved by him, pretended she did not hear his snicker as she slammed the door behind her.

27

Cleod – 15 years

HIS FINGERS RESTED LIGHT AS BREATH ON THE HILT OF THE SWORD SLUNG ACROSS his back. The green leather wrapping under his touch was stained with sweat from long hours of practice. Familiar beyond any requirement of conscious intention, the weapon would merge with his grasp into an extension of his arm.

Cleod stared straight ahead, his gaze fixed on the entrance to the dark cavern in the rock. But his attention was not focused just there. His senses were buzzing, and everything was a soft blur; nothing about his environment could be presumed fixed or predictable.

The breeze shifted and everything seemed to streak sideways and expand. There was nothing he did not hear, even as the patterns of sound changed with the wind. A hint of cuila smoke touched his nose, then the distant odor of snow. Trance without peace, an awareness of situation so precise that the sunlight bit into his exposed skin. The woods around him pulsed with life. From the worms in the soil, to the water seeping into the roots of the trees, everything moved through him and over him and around everything else until he was the still center of the swirling chaos of each moment as it arrived.

One leaf shifted, out of place against the push of air, and he was in motion before a thought formed. Drop. Spin. An upward slash of the silvered blade. Falling back into balance. The time-slowed blur of foiled metal slipped by his head, and his blade bit backward, sideways and down, cutting, slamming into the man sent against him, so sharp it did not even drag against bone as it severed it.

"Idodben!"

The command to exit trance pierced his consciousness.

Cleod snapped back to himself. Everything around him collapsed inward in a heartbeat, an implosion of dispersed energy that knocked him to his knees, sword still in hand. Nausea rose, and he swayed and gasped for breath. His grip on the sword tightened as he used it to steady himself. Full awareness returned slowly, like water seeping through rocky ground, as the images conjured by the Elder trainer dissipated.

Beneath him, speared by his sword, was only bare earth. No sign of the attacker. Around him, no stand of trees, no leaf littered earth, only the hard, red dirt of the training arena.

With an effort, he raised his head, and looked up at the man standing on the platform at the edge of the ring. Around him, the other Draigre also stirred, shook off the trance vision, struggled to stand upright. Cleod did not try to force the transition. He knew too well what was coming to expend any unnecessary energy in a vain attempt to impress the Elders with his resiliency. Enough years had passed for them to know his strengths. His weaknesses—when it came to his physical prowess—were few. The awareness and control he had gained over the years were those of an adept—undisputed.

On the other side of the arena, the youngest aspirant, trying to rise to his feet, bent and heaved the remains of his breakfast into the dirt. Cleod smiled a little, recalling his first experience with the Gweld. The trance state took years of training to reach successfully, years of fear and frustration and illness. The Overlash had first knocked him senseless for days. Over time, days spent in the anguish of recovery became hours, then only moments. Then he learned to take the time to let the violent energies dissipate, and the pain had become manageable at last. Once he no longer feared the aftermath, he slid into the vision state of the Gweld with fearless poise. And he came out of it shaken but not lost.

As the new boy collapsed in a shuddering knot, Cleod rose and slid his sword back into the scabbard slung across his back. He and the other senior trainees turned their attention to the Elder as a pair of attendants came to take charge of the fallen candidate.

"*Draigre!*" The man raised his voice to carry over the screams now rising from the crumpled boy. "Take your places. *Again!*"

"It gets better," Cleod said as he took a seat beside the boy's bed. The pale young Draigre was propped on pillows, lines of exhaustion etched in his face. "Not soon, Hoyd, but it will happen." He turned in the chair and poured a cup of water from the pitcher on the side table. "Drink this." He handed it to the young man. Cuila smoke rolled through the air. "Drink as much as you can over the rest of the day. Even if you feel sick, keep drinking. And breathe deep. Water and cuila will shorten the time you need to stay in that bed."

"How do you do it?" Hoyd asked, drinking deep. "You're not even Farlan."

Cleod shook his head. "I work twice as hard. I get twice as sick. And I earn twice the respect."

Hoyd scoffed. "Respect? You're good, but you will never make full rank. You'll fail initiation and end up a teacher. You won't even be an Elder. Just a drill master. Everyone says so. Even the other senior Draigre. You're cefreid—born a laborer. If they give you a title, then anyone will think they can bid for Draighil. Only Farlan have the right to such positions."

Cleod laughed. Even sick to the point where he could not stand, Hoyd was Farlan to the core, absolutely certain of his superiority in all things. "You'll make a good Draighil, but you'll never be as good as me, because you'll earn it, but you'll never *need* it." He leaned close to the bed. "Why do you think Soibel allowed me into the Enclave in the first place? Because the Draighil need someone who *needs* the rank just to have a reason to live. That's me. Filling the empty space where they would prefer a Farlan to stand, but where one no longer can. Because for you, it's just a title now. And for me it means everything. Because no one needs to be Draighil more than me.

"So drink a lot of water, Hoyd, and remember that I tried to help you once. Because I know now that you won't be helping me." He turned, lifted the pitcher and reached out to refill the cup in the sick boy's hands. "I have been assigned to mentor you on how to endure the Overlash, but it seems you don't want the help of a cefreid. You'll find clean clothes in your chest. I'll see you in the practice ring when you can stand." He got to his feet and returned the pitcher to its place on the stand. If the boy was foolish enough to let him walk out the door, then he would deserve the ongoing pain of untamed Overlash. No one learned to control the tangled recoil of Gweld without assistance.

"Cleod!" Hoyd's voice held a note of frantic realization. Cleod stopped but did not turn to face him, both to hide his amusement and to make the younger boy wait for his response. "I—I insulted you. I am sorry. I—Trayor says you recover faster than anyone else. You'll teach me? Will you teach me?"

Cleod nodded, turned back to look at Hoyd. He was only a few years older than the boy, but he felt he had lived a hundred more. Time seemed to stretch and drag in the Enclave. The training was endless, merciless, and savage. It tested every part of him. It had dug into and etched every part of him. The finesse with which he had learned to manipulate the misery that accompanied the aspect of training most designed to shape his reflexes was not something he could explain to another. It was born from his ability to commit completely to something, to the point where nothing else was important, not even keeping his own life. That was not something he could teach. Not to anyone. Especially not to a boy like Hoyd who only half-trusted his own reason for being here. But he could help ease the Overlash symptoms as they manifested. That would eventually give Hoyd the space to understand his own abilities and find his own way to conquer the Gweld.

"All I'll teach you today is that you need to drink more water—right now. And all night. And especially before you practice the Gweld next." Cleod grinned and shook his head. "I'll decide later whether or not you really care that you insulted me. If I think you did, I might teach you something else." He tapped the edge of the door frame with his knuckles. "And make sure there is a bucket beside the bed. Breathe the cuila. You'll wake back up in a couple hours ready to puke your guts all over the bed." He watched the other boy go pale at the thought, and took pity on him. "Don't worry. Every time gets easier. Pretty soon you'll only vomit right after you're called out of Gweld."

Hoyd smiled faintly. "Something to look forward to." He took another drink.

"Maybe you'll learn someday," Cleod said. "Even from a cefreid."

28

Cleod – 17 years

THE CLAWS WERE REAL THIS TIME. AND THE TEETH. IT WOULD BE DIFFICULT enough to navigate the Gweld against live animals for the very first time, but nothing was simply difficult in the Enclave. The Elders meant this session to have consequences. They had not denied the possibility that death lurked on this mountainside.

The ground over which he moved was not a landscape he knew well. As Draigre, most of his time had been spent in the area immediately surrounding the Enclave compound. He had ventured off on his own a few times, but he had gone north, deeper into the mountains, not back toward the bottom of the Spur. Unable to spare the concentration to regret that lapse, he instead took to heart the lesson in it. Once titled, he was unlikely to be able to choose the ground on which he fought.

This day, more than one awareness invaded his. Shimmering, pulsing waves of *otherness* slivered his senses, and he had to fight to separate his perception from the interjections of the Elders. Always before in the Gweld, he had been surrounded by Draigre in the same state, sharing a similar, controlled experience. He had never experienced the *merging* of multiple consciousnesses. Layers of sharpened senses, his, Soibel's, Rhol's, others', sparked bright lights and echoes through his mind. Trying to focus was like balancing a hot coal on a stick in a swaying boat. He had to select, divide, sort, and yet he could not afford to narrow his attention too far, because he was not surrounded by other Draigre, but by beasts loosed with him in the mountainous bowl.

The air shifted like a mirage on the horizon. Every step changed not only where he stood, but the vantage of his every sense.

He was being stalked.

The feeling of *something watching* permeated every part of him. Discerning the location of the creature tracking him was vital, but with his senses pulsing with the input of others, he had difficulty distinguishing what *he* knew about his surroundings from the interjections of the Elders. Could sight echo? It seemed so—along with sound, and scent, and the feel of the breeze on his skin.

Daylight died. The change was instantaneous. Sunlight vanished, replaced by night shadows and the chill light of moon and stars. He froze. It *was* day. He had eaten breakfast not three hours before. This change was not real, but the projection of one of the elders, meant to add to his confusion. Cleod moved forward, eased around trees and slid through shadows he knew were not actually there. He thought of the sun and the line it took through the sky, and placed himself in the landscape. He willed the real forest to appear, and the truth of the light revealed itself to him. Those spaces between the pines were *actually* dark; those were not. Gradually, the false night bled away and he moved in leaf-scattered light again.

He could not say what warned him, perhaps the *weight* issued by the change in the air, but he found himself in motion, sliding sideways and stepping back up the slope. The sword blurred into his grasp and the swing connected. The creature screamed, and for the first time, hot blood streamed over his hands in response to a trained action. The weight of impact staggered him. For an instant, his hold on the moment shuddered, Gweld and cross-laced Gweld influence threatened to splinter his reality, but he jerked in a breath and caught hard at his awareness. The mountain canine lay convulsing at his feet, the yellow foam around its jaws speaking to the disease it carried. He drew a breath and shoved down the fear *that* realization brought. There were more ways to die today than just having his throat ripped out. The creature at his feet was twice as deadly as he had imagined.

Rain began before he could form a thought of either pride or sorrow at the animal's death. Was the change in weather real? The sun shone through the trees, yet he felt the chill impact of each raindrop. Water ran into his eyes and soaked his shoulders and sleeves, but the air still smelled dry. He flexed his fingers on the hilt of the sword. The gore on his wrists and hands remained, unrinsed, and so the rain was just another distraction. A bright flash that he might have registered as lightning if he had not already dismissed the reality of the rain burst across his vision. Not *his* sight. He was unsure how he knew—but the light was not seen initially through his eyes. A pattern of shadows. Another spatter of brightness—something moved swiftly—

Cleod whirled, dropping low as the second animal leaped, the rain snapped out of existence as he moved. A second canine's hind legs brushed his shoulder, and he heard the scrambling rush as it landed beside its dead fellow. Time expanded. Cleod gained his feet again, and every contraction of his muscles seemed to take a day. The creature before him turned as it landed, already gathering itself to spring. Every hair on the beast was outlined and clear, from the way it flexed with the animal's movement, to the way it caught the light. Cleod felt the rumble of a growl building in its throat before it became fully audible. It swung its head back toward him. Its body pivoted to follow.

A rushing of air warned him, and he could feel the push of his breath on the fibers of his lungs. He stepped toward the dog he faced and arched the sword over his back, catching a third animal across the belly as it launched itself at him. The weight of the yelping creature pulled and turned him, and he rotated with it. When the second animal sprang, its dying companion was falling through the air into its path, and Cleod was clear, light on his feet. He balanced himself and struck. The remaining animal died, cleaner and quicker than the other two.

No time was given to catch his breath before the temperature plummeted and he could see his exhalation misting the air before him. He gasped at the change.

Around him, the stench of blood was sharp in the cold air—coppery and sweet. He shivered. Reality, or vision cast? It hardly mattered. His body was flushed warm from the fight, and he could almost *hear* the different aspects of what he was seeing. There was a rhythm to the world he moved in, and a rhythm to each change sent to assault him. The cold was not real, and he need not fight it. Whatever was set before him, he would face.

Gathering himself, he flicked the blood from his blade and stepped away from the bodies, again working his way down toward the bottom of the bowl. The air bent and trembled, and it seemed with each step he took the temperature changed. It was as though the minds fighting to control what he felt and saw, were also fighting each other. Only his heartbeat and the air in his lungs were to be trusted. Only his instincts, and his familiarity with his own Gweld state, were anchors in waves of manipulation and interference.

He moved carefully, testing the ground beneath his feet and shifting his weight slowly to avoid cracking sticks, choosing his path carefully so as to not swipe branches. Around him, the trees thinned until he stood at the top of a clearing that offered a view of the lower portion of the bowl.

Clouds rolled above him, but he could still feel sunlight on his skin. The wind blew and leaves trembled, but only to his left and not his right. He was beginning to be able to discern what was before him from what was pushed upon him. His control of the Gweld was strong—and with every step he took, he was learning to use it to push back.

He smiled to himself and flexed his fingers against the sword hilt. Within the Gweld trance, his mind made leaps of connection that he could never hope to hold onto once his senses collapsed to encompass only daily reality. The space he moved in was powerful. He might have even called it addictive had it not been that Overlash required masterful strength to battle on every descent back to normality. No one, the elders said, had ever willingly committed themselves to Gweld for simple pleasure. The price was too high, too painful, and unavoidable. Only a madman would attempt to use the Gweld for anything but battle—and a madman could not long hope to survive the consequences. Moving among the thinning trees, Cleod was glad he had proved himself both sane and worthy of the training he had been granted.

Something flickered in a corner of his mind. Something clearly *not human*. He froze. Never had he touched an awareness that was not that of another person. Was it just that he had never had the opportunity, or that he had never been forced to focus so thoroughly on the different minds surrounding him? The *otherness* was a whisper against his perception. Not *human*. Hungry. Focused. Hunting.

Cleod took a step sideways, and the *other's* senses sparked. Being watched then, not just scented. Cleod went motionless again, his breath ringing his body like a bell. Did the creature hear that? Feel his lungs moving the air and smell the blood coursing in his veins? Every whispered in-halation was also motion, and Cleod could see the air tremble with the touch of his presence. What stalked him this time? Its mind was hot but not frantic, unclouded by distraction. When it attacked, *it would not miss.* Never miss. Never miss the meal.

He snatched his mind back from the strange awareness with a gasp. What he had felt was not just *other*, it existed outside reason, in a primal place he hoped he would only ever encounter in passing.

In the beat of a heart, the land beneath his feet turned to liquid, rush-ing water slammed against his knees and threatened to send his sprawling. He gasped, jumped back against the nearest tree. *Jumping,* he had pressed against solid earth to make the move, and so the water suddenly rushing all around his legs was also illusion, but unlike the others he had encoun-tered, this one held no sense of uncertainty. It was as though the elders had reached consensus as to what tactics were to be used against him. But this time—had it been minutes? hours?—had been well spent in learning how his own mind felt when it encountered theirs, and he was not so easily fooled.

Tearing! He screamed as the claws ripped into his shoulder and the weight of the Hlewlion dragged him to his knees. Saved from having his back completely shredded only by the thick leather of his sword harness, he registered his mistake even as he focused through the pain and let him-self fall, using the momentum of the cat's attack and his body weight to throw himself into a roll across the clearing. The cat, still attached and snarling, tumbled with him. Grass tangled over them and brambles tore and snagged skin and fur. The sword was torn from his grasp, and with it, any chance of killing the beast.

A blow to his back left him breathless, and he was grateful that in that instant the cat was downslope, colliding first with the half-buried rock. With a feline shriek the animal released him and leapt away. Cleod twist-ed his body and planted his feet downhill, skidding to a halt in the brush as his Gweld enhanced senses tracked the cat. Blood streamed from the wound on his shoulder. Cleod lunged to his feet with a shout of rage that echoed over the mountainside. At the sound, he watched the cat jump, its eyes wide and ears pinned. Cleod's focused vision spiraled inward until everything about him was pure energy, focused on the predator before him. Bare-handed, he shrieked again and lunged with all his strength in the direction of the animal.

The cat broke and ran, bounding back upslope with fierce strides, startled into a pure flight reaction. Cleod followed, but not in pursuit. In a dozen strides he had spotted and reclaimed his dropped sword. He bent his knees, ready for another attack as he extended his attention across the clearing, but the cat was gone. He was alone. No sense of being watched remained, and his mind was free of the Gweld touch of the elders as well. Seconds passed as he absorbed his failure. The pain of his wounds, half clotted with mud and weeds, began to creep over him.

"*Idodben*, Cleod!" A voice rang over the clearing and wrenched him from the trance.

The drop out of Gweld was more violent than he had experienced in years. It rocked him not just to his knees, but sent him sprawling to the ground. The sword slipped away again, and he cursed his weakness. His entire body shuddered and burned; pain erupted from the claw gouges over his shoulder and back. He twisted in on himself, choking back a scream.

"Take him to the infirmary," a voice said, and Cleod could not focus enough to even determine who was speaking. Hands grabbed him and lifted. He cried out again as the impact of fingers on flesh reverberated through his bones and into his brain. Too much. "Seek ease, Draigre," Someone was speaking again. "You are well trained. Find your control. Your body will heal soonest if you take control again of your mind."

With a lurch of pure will, Cleod grabbed hold of the pain and wrestled it into a deep corner of his consciousness. It was not the organized process he had mastered. It was a violent act of desperation. But he achieved what he needed—the mayhem wracking his body and awareness was sundered and contained. He drew a great shuddering breath and felt tears on his face.

"Better," the voice said. *Soibel*. Old gods grant mercy! He had failed this test in front of the High Elder himself. Cleod closed his eyes in shame and tried to speak his regret, but sudden exhaustion sapped his ability to form words. "You will heal," Siobel said. "We will speak tomorrow when you have been cleaned and bandaged."

Carried...he was being carried away from the Elder and any chance he had to beg forgiveness for dishonoring the Ehlewer Enclave's best training.

"What is to be my punishment?" Cleod asked, trying to sit up straight in the bed. The pain down his back and the pull of the bandages meant he only partially succeeded. Just like the day before—the beginning of success leading only to failure. They could take anything from him, his rank among the Draigre—his place in the Enclave—his life.

"Punishment?" Soibel asked as he stopped at the foot of the bed and met Cleod's gaze. "For a Draigre as arrogant as you are—you seem to have taken little pride in your accomplishments yesterday."

"I fell," Cleod said. "I dishonored the Ehlewer. What is there for me to take pride in?"

Soibel laughed. "You slew *three* Blayth Hounds, survived the attack of a Hlewlion, Cleod Draigre. All while in shared-vision Gweld. And you survived with not just your life, but a victory."

Cleod stared at him. How could anyone call what had happened yesterday a victory? He had collapsed in battle—allowed the Hlewlion to escape. "The cat lived," he said. "How is that victory?"

"You used skill and imagination. You fought with what you had—even only your will and your voice, when you had nothing else. That is something we cannot teach. That is something of which only the best Draighil are capable."

All night, Cleod had lain awake going over the events of the day again and again. Of all the conclusions he had reached about what his mistakes had been and why they had happened—he had never considered the things he had done correctly. And *those* things were just as important. Those moments when he had seen things clearly or gained insight. Those moments when he had *learned* something or used a skill to perfection—they mattered.

"You are not angry," Cleod said. Not a question at all, but a statement born in new understanding.

"With a Draigre of your prowess? And you a cefreid. The old gods must enjoy these moments." Soibel came around the bed to stand beside Cleod.

The elder raised a closed fist and touched it to his forehead—the Ehlewer salute of respect—something Cleod had never before received. "Well done, Draigre. I see a great future for you. You will carry the pride of the Ehlewer Draighil with you to many victories."

Cleod drew himself up a little more, though his wounds stretched and burned, and returned the salute in kind with his uninjured arm. He said nothing. There were no words for such an honor as he had just received, and he was smart enough not to try to find any.

Soibel gave a single sharp nod, then turned and left the infirmary.

Cleod drew a breath and nodded to himself. He had earned Soibel's respect; nothing he had determined to achieve was beyond him. Closing his eyes, he envisioned, not the battle with the Hlewlion in the clearing, but himself standing over the smoldering body of the great Draigon, Shaa. That day was coming. After this day's victory—all others were certain.

Leiel – 16 years

THE FAMILIAR CLANG OF METAL ON METAL RANG THROUGH THE AFTERNOON air. Torrin swung the hammer, and the curved metal on the anvil bounced and shuddered under the blow. White hot, it changed under the impact of his experienced concentration. "What rules are we breaking today, Li?" he asked without looking up from his work.

She smiled to herself and took a seat on the chair just inside the shop. The heat of the forge washed over her, and she took the opportunity to unwrap her scarf and shake her hair free. The snow falling outside was the first of the year, and while she enjoyed the quiet it brought, her body had not yet accepted the change of season. "I have no mischief planned today," she said. "I came to bring you lunch." She showed him the basket she carried, then nestled it into her lap.

He made a low noise that was part disbelief and part amusement, one he often made in her presence, and set aside the hammer to lift the horseshoe back into the coals of the forge. He shifted the grip of the tongs to heat a new area of the metal and glanced over his shoulder at her.

"That's an honor not without price."

She laughed. He knew her too well. "I need help solving a riddle."

"A riddle is it?" He turned the shoe, examined it, and removed it from the heat again. She fell silent as the sound of the hammer pounded through the air. Since she was a little girl, she had loved to watch him at work. The smooth motion of his actions and the precision with which he placed each hammer strike had always intrigued her. What must it be like to turn lumps of metal into things that mattered? Horse shoes and wagon wheels and plow blades and knives. The implements of farm life that made so much of what they did possible. Her mother had always said that they could be no luckier than to have a man of Torrin's talents be willing to work for them. They were not wealthy, and his skills were admired throughout the region. She had never thought to wonder why he had chosen to work for her family, not until recently. So she had asked him. His reply had been simple. "I like it here." So much about Torrin was simple. He seemed to need so little and expect almost nothing. And she could count on him to give her a direct answer to any question.

Even if she did not like the answer.

She watched as he worked, until the shoe was finished enough to be set in the sand tray to cool. When he had arranged his tools, he grabbed a rag and wiped his hands as he came to join her. "What is your riddle? And where is my lunch?"

With a smile, she lifted the basket and passed it to him. "Warm bread and fried chicken. And an apple."

"And the other?"

Leiel tucked her feet up onto the rung of the chair. Arms crossed over her knees, she tipped her head. "What do you offer in trade to someone who has something you need, but who needs nothing that you have?"

"That's simple," Torrin said. He took a bite of a drumstick, chewed and swallowed.

"There's cider in the jug. How simple?"

He nodded in thanks, pulled the cork from the clay bottle, and took a long drink. "Very simple. If you have nothing that he needs, you just find something he wants."

Of course. It *was* simple. So simple it had never occurred to her. Gahree *must* want something. Something only Leiel could offer. Why else would she be in Adfen, paying so much attention to a barely-educated farm girl? "And how do you figure out what someone wants?"

"You could ask him." Torrin laughed.

She shook her head. "This is a riddle. I don't think I can ask for the answer."

"Then you get to know him well enough to guess it."

Leiel sighed. How was she supposed to get to know Gahree that well? The woman was so odd. Her words were cryptic and layered in meaning Leiel only half recognized. And she was only with Gahree for a few min-

utes each month. She wished, as she did so often, that Cleod was here to offer her some crazy idea that would lead her to the answer. When the two of
them were together, bizarre solutions to problems often seemed to create
themselves. But he wasn't here. And after their last meeting, would he ever
be here again? She frowned. She could not hope for it any more. Whatever
she needed to figure out, she must do so on her own, but how could she
possibly come to understand what Gahree might want?

"Torrin, I don't know. There's not enough time for me to figure that
out."

"Well, your riddle maker must know that. He wouldn't ask you to solve
a puzzle you couldn't figure out how to solve."

Leiel sucked in a breath, then she laughed. Of course. Gahree, strange
as she was, really did want Leiel to find the answer. Gahree had stories she
wanted to share, but she would not do it until she thought Leiel was ready.
How would the woman know when that time had come?

She'll know when I bring her what she wants, Leiel thought, because
I'll know enough for her to trust me.

"I seem to have rocked something loose," Torrin said. He sampled the
cornbread and nodded in approval. "Your cooking is nearly as good as your
mother's was."

"Ha! That's Elda's hand in the baking you're tasting. And you did...help
with my riddle. I still don't know how to solve it. But you have to be right,
that I must be able to."

"No cause to give you one you couldn't. Who's got you running in circles, Li? Not that boy in the Enclave. I didn't think you had seen him of late."

"No, not Cleod. Someone at the Fourth Market. I'm trying to barter for
something, but I have yet to find the right thing to offer."

"What are you bartering for that requires this much thinking?"

She hesitated. But then, he knew about the books and had never said a
word to the boys or to her father. "Stories. Secret ones."

"Stories?" He finished his meal and brushed crumbs from his shirt
back into the cloth that covered the basket. "Yah, I suppose stories could
require some thinking."

She wanted to hug him for that, for simply accepting that she occupied herself with something probably silly and likely destined to draw the

wrath of her brothers. For not asking more questions or ridiculing her for caring about what Klem would say were 'stupid lies meant for children'. That's what Klem called all the old tales now. And he would have no patience with what he would consider her foolishness, should he find out. Torrin's disinterested acceptance of her antics meant more to her than she knew how to express.

"They do require thinking," she said and smiled at him. She got to her feet and reached up to brush a bread crumb from his chin. "Who's the shoe for?"

"Klem's mare. She loosened one on the way back from town last night."

"He was probably pushing her to beat the weather. She's not bruised, is she?"

"Nah." Torrin tucked the cider jug back into the basket and handed it to her. "She's well. I noticed it this morning, and it will be set right within the hour. In this weather, even Klem won't be riding anywhere."

Leiel nodded as she tucked up her hair and wrapped her scarf around her head. She gathered up the basket. "We are stuck with him today," she said. "He's already got Elda in a fuss, racing to keep the sitting room fire hot enough to satisfy him. He's bundled up in a pile of blankets like an old grandfather. You'd think he had never seen a cold day."

"And you?"

"I escaped to bring you lunch."

Torrin laughed. "The luck you make for yourself. Back to the house with you, Li. He'll be yelling for you soon enough. I'll carry up another load of wood when the shoeing is done."

She waved in farewell and made her way back out into the snow.

30

Leiel – 17 years

WHEN HAD HE BECOME GRACEFUL? THE BOY SHE HAD GROWN UP WITH HAD always been strong, but he had never carried himself like this, with such intention and balance. Even standing still, there was an alert poise to him that was new. It had been almost seven years since he left to join the Enclave, two since she had seen him last—that disastrous visit to the farm. Of course, there had been letters, shared bits of their lives committed to paper and passed on, but inscribed words could not express transformation such as this.

His hair was cut close now, in the style of the Farlan, and he wore clothes made from a finer cloth than she had seen on anyone not of the Sanctuary. The black pants were heavy and finely woven, the grey tunic shimmered even in the dim light. He looked confident and controlled and not at all like the person in whose presence she had once felt such ease. If he had not spoken her name with familiar cockiness, she would never have recognized him.

For a moment more she just stood and stared, taking in the stranger wearing her old friend's smile. Then she stepped forward and put her arms around him and be damned with the murmurs her action drew from the other shop patrons.

He laughed and hugged her back, but it was not the strong embrace she expected. So the change was not just in his appearance. She drew back and stepped away, looking up at him. So tall! He always had been, but now he towered over her. His frame was still lean, but there was a new hardness to him, in the lines of his face and the directness of his gaze.

"What are you doing here?" she asked.

"I got leave to visit my father. He sent word that he has not been well."

"Oh, Cleod, I'm so sorry. I hadn't heard. Have you seen him yet? Is he all right?"

He shook his head. "I am on my way home now. I was just stopping for some supplies, since I doubt the house is stocked to feed two any more." He looked her up and down, and she wondered if he found her appearance as different as she found his. Perhaps she was just as he had remembered her to be. Which would he prefer? His expression gave her no answer.

"You look well," he said. "I hadn't expected to see you in town."

She kept her tone light. "Well, I have, for years, been in charge of the kitchen on the farm. And since no one else wants to be bothered with it, part of my duties include venturing out to buy spices and rock candy for Klem."

He laughed at that, and her old friend was at last in the room with her. Warmth tingled through her chest. Old gods, she had missed him!

"He still has a taste for those sweets?"

"I don't think he can get through a day without one."

"And his temper is more than anyone should risk for the sake of a cube of cane sugar."

"Much more," she agreed, and grinned back at him. She looked around at the people in the store making up their small audience and shrugged. "It's not as though his tantrums are a secret."

His shocked expression was almost enough to make her laugh, but the shift that followed it stopped the urge short. Something else crossed his face—worry maybe. Or maybe disappointment. A chill dropped over her shoulders. "Well," she said again. "I'm finished here. I need to get home."

"Can you wait a bit? I can ride with you part of the way. An escort, if you will."

She hesitated. It's still Cleod. It's still him.

"All right," she said. "I'll be on my wagon. Since you insist on accompanying me, you can tie your horse off the back and drive the damn thing."

"Escort implies that I am riding free enough to respond to any danger that might arise."

She scoffed. "Cleod Woodcutter—this is *Adfen*. If there is a bandit to be found between this town and my home, he is likely to be five summers old and holding up my wagon for a share of Klem's candy." She tipped her head and looked up at him. "Ride with me. It will be easier to talk."

"I'm a Woodcutter no longer," was his reply, and by the fact that he had corrected only that part of her statement, she knew he would join her on the wagon.

"Very well, Cleod of the Ehlewer." She laughed. "I should have everything loaded by the time you are ready to leave. Purchase whatever you need—there is more room in the wagon than on your horse's back. You would do well to take advantage of that."

He smiled, again with the boyish glee she knew so well. "I will do so, Leiel Sower."

The chestnut gelding Cleod tied to the rear gate of the wagon was sturdily built, straight-limbed, and broad chested. Leiel had seen such horses only rarely, usually ridden by Farlan Commanders, or the wealthiest of merchants at Fourth Market.

"Has he a name?" she asked, still gazing at the horse as Cleod climbed onto the bench beside her. The seat tilted and creaked under his greater weight. "If not, you should call him Bearer—in honor of having to carry all of you about."

"His name is Mihweer."

She glanced over to see him looking sideways at her. "Oh, I see. You've forgotten what it's like to have a little person poke at you? You have always been taller and wider than me. And you have never been either stupid or cruel—so what else can I tease you about?"

"Well, never stupid," he said, wryly enough that she felt it appropriate to laugh a little.

She faced him fully and handed him the reins, noting the callouses on his hands. Their presence was nothing new—he had always worked with his hands—but the placement of the scars had changed.

"They don't let you wear gloves?" she asked, touching the thickened flesh in the web of his hand.

He looked down at his hands and shrugged. "Sometimes. It is best to toughen the skin and strengthen the grip before worrying about the protection of fireleather."

"Fireleather?" Something gave a small twist in her gut as she spoke the word.

"It's made from the belly hide of fallen Draigon."

She started and pulled back her touch. "I did not know there were such things."

He laughed and clucked to the mules in the traces, and the wagon began to roll. "Of course there have been fallen Draigon. What do you think the Draighil are for if not to create such things?"

"No," she said too quickly, unable to pinpoint what had caused the sudden unease that tingled her skin. "The leather—it never occurred to me that a Draigon could be put to such use—clothing or the like. Simple things."

"Not so simple," he said. "The items are rare—it has been too long since the Ehlewer produced a Draighil able to claim victory over one of the beasts. Not since the great Soibel Draighil defeated Gola. It's been two generations since then. We are only allowed to borrow the clothes, until such time as we earn the honor of bearing full title of Ehlewer Draighil."

She took in his words, silent beside him. The warmth of his body radiated through the crisp air, and yet a chill filled her. When had he begun to use such words as *honor*? When had anyone earned from him the label *great*? Yes, the tone of his letters had shifted over the years, become more formal as they had become fewer, but somehow she had always been able to put the voice she had always known to those letters and hear sarcasm in his chosen words. So different it was, to have him here with her and hear sincerity in his tone. "Why so long since the killing of a Draigon?" she asked at last. "I thought there was a Draighil—Meidoth?"

He shook his head. "The training is difficult, Leiel. Even those who are good do not always make it all the way through. And even men who earn the title do not always survive their encounters with the beasts. That was true of Meidoth."

She drew in a sharp breath. Cleod *would* be Draighil—that she had never doubted. But somehow she had not let herself think beyond that, to what that would really mean. Always, she had pictured him victorious and unscathed in the black uniform of the Draigon hunters, the steaming body of a vanquished monster sprawled before him. But what if that was not the case?

"Stop worrying," he said. "By the time I face a true monster, I promise you, I will be something for him to fear—not the other way around."

"How did you know I was worrying?" It irritated her that he had read her so easily.

"Crinkly in the left eye."

She laughed and the years between them fled. "I rarely see anyone as a squirrel any more. And you—you I never could."

"Too handsome, am I?"

This time the laughter burst from her in pure startlement. Now *there* was something she had never thought to hear him say. Since when had he been concerned with his appearance? But she took in again the fineness of the clothing he was wearing and the poise with which he wore it. "Oh, no," she said, unwilling to follow the conversation in that direction. She was Draigfen. "You are simply too well-spoken and, by far, not nervous enough."

They had reached the outskirts of the town. The sky seemed to grow bluer over their heads as they rolled onto the well-packed road. "That must be it."

She heard a hint of something in his voice that she could not quite identify.

"Your father," she said, "what's ailing him?"

"Age more than anything."

"Age? But how, when you are younger than I am?"

"He looks younger than he is." Cleod frowned slightly. "But he is older than your father by a good twelve summers. And the life of a woodcutter is not an easy one. He has always worked harder than any man I know. Last summer he was injured—remember I wrote you—when that tree fell on his leg? The injury was worse than he told me at the time, and he has never healed fully."

"Oh, Cleod—I'm so sorry. Had I known, I would have found a way to visit him."

"What way? Are you now allowed to visit single men alone?"

She sat straighter, uncertain what to make of his words. Was he concerned for her safety or for her reputation? "I could have found a way to make such a visit had I known of your father's need."

"It's of no matter. I didn't know myself until his latest letter. Stubborn old man. He could have asked for my help sooner. The integrity of the Ehlewer respects family."

Her heart jumped into her throat. Could she have such luck...? "Are you home to stay then?"

He chuckled and shook his head, shot her a glance he might have given a child. "Of course not. Don't be foolish. I am home to see Ellan comfortable and settled in town if he chooses, or to hire him assistance if he does not wish to move."

"When did you decide I was to be condescended to?" The muscles around her left eye twitched. She wished, after all, that she *could* picture him as a squirrel. Fuzzy tails and meaningless chatter were always a better option than letting her temper slip its bindings.

He drew back on the reins, and the wagon shuddered to a halt. For a moment he stared straight ahead, out over the flickering ears of the mule to the packed dirt of the road bending to follow the edge of the forest. Waiting, she looked at him as he stared away. At last, he pulled in a heavy sigh, and then turned his head to meet her gaze. His cheeks were flushed bright, and she realized that he was embarrassed.

"I don't know which is worse," he said. "Speaking to you so cheaply or thinking I would get away with it."

"Hmmf." She let the noise escape through her nose. "You've become proud in your new life."

His eyes narrowed a bit. "I have. The Ehlewer are worth taking pride in."

"And the rest of us? Your father?"

"I have not forgotten my promises to anyone."

She looked back at him for a long time, then nodded at last. No, of course he hadn't forgotten. But she was beginning to see that the promise he had made the Ehlewer Enclave was the promise by which he was coming to define himself. It cut her—she could not yet judge how deep—to know that his priority had shifted. What had she expected? He had been gone for years, among the Farlan, living and breathing and bleeding Enclave teachings.

Gahree had warned her. *"The Enclaves bend even the best hearts, wild daughter. Do not let surprise overwhelm you, if you someday discover that such has happened to your friend."*

"But you're only here for a short while. How long? I've missed you."

He nodded and smiled. "I've missed you, too." He shrugged. "I can't stay long. A week—two at the most. It all depends on what needs doing and how stubborn Ellan will be about doing it."

She snorted, and raised a hand to cover her nose. "You would know nothing about that."

He eyed her sideways, and she choked back another grin at the indignant look he turned on her.

"Oh please," she said. "You are the most stubborn person I know. You learned it from someone."

"I'm not the most stubborn. That would be you."

She laughed. "I'm not certain that's a compliment."

"I'm not certain either."

Again she heard it—something in his tone that made his words more serious than she expected them to be.

Change. Of course she knew it must come to them both. But how much? And how much would it matter? How much would it alter each of them beyond what could be bridged in letters and occasional visits? "I don't want to ever miss you more than I already do," she said.

"What do you mean?"

She shook her head. "So much is different now. All the training and schooling for you. My place at the farm. Your father. My father. Both in failing health. And my brothers. Errff—Klem is seeking power, and Gial is seeking escape to the trade routes. Everything is shifting so fast. How do we hang on to our friendship in all this?"

The words hung in the air.

The wagon rolled on, wheels crunching on the stony road. Birdsong hung in the air, and the wind shifting the leaves in the trees seemed to move at half speed. He didn't speak. Her breath pushed in and out, and her pulse flashed in her throat. Twisting her hands, she looked at him. "No words?" she asked at last.

Another few seconds, he held the silence. "Too many. No answers. I never thought our friendship might be at risk until this moment."

She sucked in breath. No, why would he have ever thought that? The uniform. The pride in him, so fresh and polished. "No," she said in agreement. He had set himself on this path on her behalf. "You never would."

"Do you think we can't stay friends?" He meet her gaze.

Never did I think we could not, until I saw you today, she thought. Until I heard the tone of your words.

"I think we're different. So, maybe hanging on is the wrong thing to try. Maybe we just grow up and into whatever happens next."

He laughed. "Are you becoming wise with time? I always thought sassy was enough for you."

She wrinkled her nose and grinned at him. "It was ever enough for you."

"It no longer serves either of us, to enjoy skirting the rules."

"Ha!" She swayed a little in the seat as she laughed. "Did it ever? I am not sure what we ever gained from it but our own enjoyment." She stopped, considered. "No..." She rushed on before he had a chance to respond. "That's not true. I gained, even if you did not."

"You got a book."

Leiel smiled. "I did." And I got a chance to be me, fully, in those moments when I thought only you mattered and you did not care that I was different. She wanted to speak the words as they ran through her mind, but she didn't. There was some hint of judgment in him now that she did not know how to measure.

"What?" he asked.

Tension fled her shoulders. He still knew her well enough to know when she held something back. "I was thinking I was also allowed to be myself."

"I didn't know that was ever a problem for you."

"Then, maybe."

"And now?"

"Now..." She sighed. "I still spend much of my time in the kitchen, except these trips to the shops on the west side, and when Gial takes me to Fourth Market at the end of the month."

"How does that keep you from being yourself?" He laughed.

"It doesn't. But it takes some of the joy out of it."

He laughed, clicked to the mules, and turned them up the narrow track that led to his father's house. She caught the low rail on the side of the seat and braced herself as the wagon rocked deeper in the rougher path.

His laughter put a heaviness in her chest. Their letters through the years had been full of humor and little details about daily life, but she suspected now that he had left as much out of his as she had left out of hers. The change in him was more than a new level of education, or physical training. It was in the way his eyes swept the landscape, and her, and how he measured what he saw—a subtle assessment in his gaze, new and distancing.

They rounded a stand of trees and the small woodcutter's holding appeared—small house, large lean-to stacked a third full with split wood, the little barn and corral for a few cows and sheep. They crossed the distance quickly and suddenly they had no more time to talk.

"Cleod—" she said, but stopped. What could she tell him about her life that would shift anything? She belonged to her father and brothers. Nothing she or Cleod could do would change that. "It's been good to see you," she said before her hesitation became obvious.

He drew the wagon to a stop in front of the house and set the brake. He tipped his head and looked at her. "I'll come to the farm, before I leave."

She shook her head. "You wouldn't be welcome. I am glad I saw you."

"Your father's still so strict that he would again turn away a member of the Ehlewer Enclave?"

"Not this time."

"The problem is not your father, then."

She smiled. "Klem has become very aware of his lack of status and what he must do to gain it."

Cleod tipped his head and looked over at her. "He always had a greater sense of propriety than a sense of humor."

Leiel's cheeks twitched and a smile broke through. "Gods of old, that's truer still now."

He laughed and handed her the reins, then climbed down off the wagon and reached into the back for his pack. It went over his shoulders with practiced ease and he gathered the box of supplies he had purchased. "Let me put these on the porch, then I will come back for the horse."

"I'll get him," she replied. Wrapping the reins around the foot rail, she climbed down and walked around the wagon to untie his horse. Cleod was beside her seconds later, and she raised her head to met his gaze.

"I will forever be staring up at you."

With a grin, he took the horse's lead. "It does seem your lot."

She nodded and started to speak, but past him, she saw his father appear in the doorway of the house. She remembered Ellan Woodcutter as a lean, muscular figure with a quiet voice and gentle laugh, always strong, efficient in his movements, and definitive in his actions—traits he had passed to his son. But the man framed by the door was not at all as she recalled. Hair greyed by age, a frame rendered thin by illness, he peered into the dimming light at the visitors in his yard.

Leiel lifted her chin in his direction. "Cleod—" she said.

He looked over his shoulder and stiffened at what he saw. He glanced at her, and she nodded. "Go. It was good to see you."

He hesitated. "And you." He stood a moment more, then turned and led his horse toward the house.

Leiel watched a moment, then climbed back up onto the wagon, gathered the reins, and clucked to the mules, turning the buckboard out of the packed-dirt yard. The image of Ellan's frailty hung in her mind, kicking up dark thoughts. When would she see Cleod again? His father's funeral? Never?

She shook herself. "Stop it." Feeling sorry for yourself, Leiel? What for? You have just had the incredible luck of seeing your dearest friend after far too many years. So what if it was not the meeting or the parting you would prefer? It's still good. Whatever comes, will come.

31

Leiel

"IT WAS SO STRANGE TO SEE HIM. HE WAS MY FRIEND WHEN I WENT TO SCHOOL. And after my mother died, he was the only person who still spoke to me like a friend." Leiel passed another handful of peppers to Gahree, and the other woman arranged them on the new display frame at the front of the stall. "We've been writing all these years...and I knew he had changed some. He had to have. The Enclave—it seems so different from here. All the things he has learned—so, he is different, but I can't explain how."

"Your friend is becoming," Gahree said, her voice light. She took the next bundle of peppers and hung them from the hooks above her head. The long strands swayed back and forth, colorful ornaments, bright in the shadow of the booth.

"Becoming?"

"It is what all people do. Make choices and become what they decide to become. Your Cleod Woodcutter is becoming Cleod Ehlewer. Soon, he will be Cleod Draighil, and then you will recognize him not at all."

"How can that be true?" She had always known Cleod. Always trusted him. So his words were different now. So he dressed and moved in ways she was still trying connect with the boy she remembered. He was *Cleod*. "He made me a promise. He won't break it."

"And what was that promise?"

"That he would always be my friend. And that he would become Draighil and kill Shaa for me."

"Two promises." Gahree shook her head. "Two, and discordant. They are different stories to be sung into ballad, and the paths down which they lead cannot cross at all. He cannot become a killer of Draigon and remain the friend you know."

Leiel leaned against the side of the stall, blinking back tears. Gahree put into words what had been turning in Leiel's mind since the afternoon spent with Cleod. The man who would slay Draigon and the man with whom she might have had a future, could not be the same person. Not just because of her status as Draigfen. But because he had become an honorable man. And honor had no place in their relationship. Their friendship was mischief and laughter and feckless moments of joy. Their friendship was comfort and peace. Honor was none of those things. In honor, lurked a stiffness and a distance that was not part of anything she loved.

"I can't—" she whispered. "I have always thought that when we were older, we would find a way to be happy together." Her next breath hid a sob.

"Be calm, daughter of wings, you are meant for more than your worst fears. The world is wide, and wonder is its purpose. Change is something you should embrace, since you cannot stop it. New leaves shiver on old trees every spring. Your future is never what you think it will be when you are young."

"Even for someone like you? Nothing seems to surprise you."

"Me, most of all. The world has found its way into everything I once knew to be truth, and it filters through my life like sunlight through a forest canopy. Everything flickers and everything dances."

"I don't see any dancing."

"Not even the birds in the sky and the wind in the grasses? I think you are not looking with wide eyes."

"Dancing birds won't change that Cleod is lost to me." Leiel wiped her eyes and gathered another handful of peppers. She stepped up beside Gahree and added to the colorful selection on the angled table. "I never dared to plan for anything except him."

"Tell me a story of him and of you. The old ones are always the most precious."

"Me and Cleod?" Those stories had always belonged to the most private part of herself. Never had she shared them. She could not start now. She shook her head. "No. Have I not yet earned any stories from you?"

"A few perhaps. Short ones."

"Then I would like to hear a short one. Anything I have to say will only make me sad."

"Let me speak of happiness then." Gahree hung the last string and faced Leiel. "Sit. Your brother has no excuse to miss you yet."

Once there were women who wondered about all things. They studied the stars and the sea and the rhythms of the earth. They sang and danced and were teachers and dreamers. Men worked in kind beside them, and children were raised in love and knowledge.

There was one woman, who was the wisest of all the teachers. She measured the rising of the sun and the path of the moon. Longing for a place where she could share all she knew consumed her. On a shining spring morning, she set out on a journey. She traveled all of Arnan until she found a place where the ground did not tremble, and the seasons had strong changes, and the soil was rich. She found a mountain where grey stone, flecked with white and silver, endured wind and snow and rain. There she asked the earth for a gift, and a boulder broke free. It tumbled down before her, to the base of the mountain where in each direction the landscape changed. North lay the mountains, west the forested plains. To the east rolled a river, and the south was graced by open fields. In that spot, she touched the great stone and spoke over it words of strength and hope, and it settled deep into the earth, with just a corner showing. Around and above it she laid other stones, until the landscape was tall with the works of her hands.

Others came to join her and added their skills to hers. A town arose, built of stone and wisdom. Teachers came. Students came. They gathered in the center of the town, around the first stone the woman had placed, above which rose a tower. Every year, as the town grew, so grew the creation at its center. It rose and cast shadows that swung over the town with the movement of the sun and the turning of the seasons. It told the hour, and the month, and marked the festivals of winter fading and harvest.

So happened the building of the first great city of knowledge in the land of Arnan. Built on the whim and wisdom of the one woman who dared a dream, then built it.

"Where was this city?" Leiel asked.

"You are seated in it." Gahree flicked her gaze toward the Tower.

"*Adfen.*" Leiel's voice was soft with wonder. "Is it true?"

"Her name was Desga. And you know truth when you hear it, Leiel of

Adfen. You always have. How do you think all trouble has started in your life?"

"What do you mean?"

Gahree laughed. "Oh daughter of free spaces, you will never live well in this world of false rules and pride. It is your nature to seek justice, and where little is offered, you will find only frustration."

"A woman built Adfen?" Leiel frowned. She had never heard a story of the founding of the city. She had never thought about it. Adfen simply *was*. It had always been. But of course that could not be the case. Someone had to start building here. Someone had to lay the first stone.

"Desga Hiage—renowned scholar of her age, and curious traveler. If you walk to the base of the Tower, you'll see her name in the ancient script. And her words of blessing. At the north corner. The first stone." Gahree pointed.

Leiel stepped up beside her and looked at the Tower. She scanned the base, then raised her eyes and followed the Tower's height into the sky. Light flared around the edges of the stone where it blocked the sun. Leiel shook her head. "I can't read anything but Farlan. If something is written there, I won't be able to understand it."

Gahree cocked her head and raised her eyebrows. "Ah well then, that is our next task—to teach you old words and script. For there is something written there. You will see it low on the darkest stone as you pass by. It is faint now with the passing of time and the rub of rain and wind, but you can still see it. Take note as you return to your brother. Remember the lines of the runes. In the time we have left, come sit with me. I will start you on learning the old as though it were new."

She moved back, and settled on the blanket spread at the back of the stall, and opened her pack, digging through it. Leiel watched her a moment, then looked back at the Tower, then to the crowded Square and the shoppers passing by. Never in all her visits to Gahree had a single shopper interrupted them at their talks and tales. But the moment Leiel walked away, she could look back over her shoulder and see the stall being swarmed with people excited by the unusual color and freshness of Gahree's delectable wares.

"Why does no one ever stop to buy while I am here?" She moved back to take a seat beside the woman.

"Because my shop is not open while you are here," Gahree said without looking up from searching her pack.

"But how do they know that?"

"Because I do. Ahhh—here it is." She pulled out a small book covered in a fine dark leather. Not much larger than her hand, the paper gave a crackling flutter when she opened it. "Here is a great tool of learning. A thing of great beauty, well made to offer knowledge. When you understand this work, you will have knowledge to better understand much more." With a smile that invoked sunlight in the dusky space, Gahree handed Leiel the little volume.

The leather was soft under her touch, and had a subtle texture that made her want to run her hands over it. She opened it and looked down at the pages. On the right, were words she knew, the Farlan sentences neatly printed in dark ink. On the left hand page were different words in a strange hand. The writing was also neat, but the words and the shape of the letters were strange. Strange and yet familiar. The book Cleod had stolen for her! The symbols were the same. Her throat went dry, her heart began a dance in her chest.

"What does it say?" She looked at Gahree. If she could learn this language... "What language is this?"

"It says what it says. The story is the same, Farlan and the old tongue. Line by line, in simple statements, each page is a mirror of its partner. Find time and some patience in your heart, and you will see where the two meet and understand the old words as easily as you do the new. It is called *Fennar*, the words you will be learning."

Leiel's eyes went wide. "You mean you will let me use this book to learn?"

"Oh, yes," Gahree said, amusement dancing in her eyes. "This you must learn, and what better way than in your own time and by your own mind?"

"This is mine?" Leiel hardly dared to believe that such a fine thing—such a wonderful book as this—might be her own.

"Of course. I have carried it with me to find it a home. You are its home. I know you will value it and the knowledge it was made to impart. And you will find within its pages the very story which I told. But this time spoken in more poetic words than mine. And also within are more tales as well, other wisdoms and some great humor you must take care about. Laughter might knock you senseless."

Leiel's grin split her face. "This is mine. *Mine*," she said, trying to believe it. She stared down at the words, wanting more than anything to curl up in a sunny corner and study the text. "Gahree—this is the best gift anyone has offered me since I was a little girl."

"The first of many bests to come. But this one, you must embrace first."

"I will. I do." She hugged the book to her chest and smiled, and smiled some more. She could not stop. No matter that she had been gone too long from her duties at her family's booth. No matter that her face would bear bruises by nightfall. This volume in her hands was worth today's consequences because she could already see the wealth of new knowledge to which it would lead. "I must go."

Gahree nodded, reached out and put a hand over Leiel's on top of the book. "Do not rush this—the learning and the joy it brings."

Leiel nodded, her heart and breath trembling in her body. This was important. This was *powerful*. This was something that could change her world. Old knowledge. Forbidden. Things that would make Klem's hair go white and her dreams at night be of laughter and light, instead of fear.

She squeezed Gahree's hand and got to her feet, tucking the book safely into the back of her skirt. "In a few months, I will be able to read the stone," she promised, and laughed in delight at the thought.

"I expect it. Now, go."

32

Cleod – 18 years

Blue-grey skies swirled with storm clouds rising out of the valley and lingering on the ridge lines. Cleod stood on the terraced west ridge above the practice field and watched the weather come. Far off, the sun was setting and, with the fading light, a change was building over the land. Citrine lit the edges of twilight. Flashes of lightening slashed horizontal furrows through the clouds.

His hands clenched into fists at his sides, and he stared at the distant front rolling out of the west from the sunset. Sickly green light and the scent of heat—already much of the Spur country would be feeling the change. Tomorrow, the day after at the latest, and the effects would be felt even here at the Enclave. Tension lined his jaw, pulled at the edges of his eyes. To at last be able to get a chance to cut down one of the monsters...

"What is it?" Hoyd asked, stepping up beside him.

Cleod looked over at him, realized that Hoyd was too young to have a clear memory of the last time the sky had turned.

Running buckets to the cistern. Air so thick that walking was like moving through honey. Clothing that clung like another skin and turned rancid from sweat within moments. Crops shriveling in the fields. Anger and frustration and fear.

Then, there had been no one of age able to fight the monsters causing it. But that was not true now. There were again Draighil in the Spur. This time, the outcome would be very different. "It's why we are here," Cleod said and turned his gaze again to the west.

"What?" Hoyd stared in the same direction.

"Draigon Weather," Cleod said.

The indrawn breath beside him spoke of Hoyd's shock. "How do you know?" Hoyd's voice shook with excitement or fear. Perhaps both.

"I have seen it before. It came when I was a child."

"Cleod! Hoyd! What delays you?" Trayor called across the field.

Hoyd whirled and shouted a reply that spoke his uncertain emotion in the face of the very thing that signaled their years of training were not wasted. "Draigon Weather! Cleod says the sky to the west signals Draigon Weather!"

"What? Cleod, is it true?" Trayor shouted.

Cleod looked over his shoulder. "Yes."

Trayor and the others on the practice field broke into a run, pounding over the packed earth and up the low slope to the top of the ridge. Cleod nodded as Trayor stopped next to him, his breathing rushed and loud.

"Old gods grant us pardon," he said as he saw the line of the front hovering over the setting sun. "It is. I never dreamed to see it again so soon in this lifetime. Something has happened—in Adfen, or Sibora. Maybe in Gwindor. Someone has brought this upon us. It's not been many years since the last."

Cleod nodded. "Some of them are too young to remember." His heart blazed in his chest. The knowledge he held now, the skill, was the saving wisdom of the people of the Spur, and he would wield it with all the acumen of the past decade of training.

"Did you see it, Cleod? Tray?" Hoyd asked. "Did you see the Draigon the last time one came?"

The questions burst from the youngest candidates as Hoyd's inquiry loosed a flood of frightened curiosity. "How big was it?" "Did you feel a wing wind?" "Did you see it take the girl?" The words spilled over the small group. Trayor tried to answer them, but their young curiosity outpaced his attempts to reply. Cleod said nothing, his eyes still on the warning in the clouds.

"What in the name of the founders is happening here?" Elder Rhol's voice rang over the ridge, and all but Cleod whirled to look at him.

"Draigon Weather!" Trayor called. "Cleod spied it oncoming with the sunset."

The Elder joined them and studied the distant landscape. "You're right, Cleod. Your eyes have been well trained."

"It could be Shaa," Cleod said, his tone low. His memory of that color in the sky was clear. The tones were the same. Were he close enough to smell the air, the fiery notes of sulfur would be the same as well. A series of gasps issued from those close enough to hear his statement.

"What brings you to that conclusion?" Rhol's voice held doubt.

"The light—before the lightning—pale green—like wheat grass just before it begins to brown and die. I recognize it from when I was a child."

"You cannot know that with certainty. Until the elders examine the signs in the morning, it is best to assume nothing." Rhol's tone held dismissal.

Cleod shifted his attention from the dying light to the old man. "If it's Shaa," he said, putting all the conviction of his certainty into his words. "That Draigon is *mine*."

Rhol's eyes narrowed as he held Cleod's gaze. "That is not your decision to make."Once the Draigon sign is verified, the elders will select the best candidate to meet with the Council in Adfen."

"And who would that be if not me?" Cleod demanded. "You, Rhol? None of you here had the strength twelve years ago to even face him. Who here is better prepared than I to stand for the Enclave and return the title of Ehlewer Draighil to its place of honor?"

"You are *not* the one to decide such things," Rhol repeated, his face flushed. But Cleod knew his words were truth. Few other candidates were as prepared or skilled as he.

Once the Draigon's presence was confirmed, someone would have to be officially Invested as Draighil. The Spur's warrior Enclave could not again afford the humiliation of standing aside as the Draigon claimed a life—no matter how corrupt that life might be.

Of the Draigre, only he and Trayor were ready for the next step. But if the Draigon was Shaa—then that beast was Cleod's to kill. He would do whatever it took to make certain he was the one to stand for the beast's death.

"As you say, Elder Rhol," Cleod said, but he couldn't speak the words with his usual respect, not with the light of his destiny painted against the clouds behind him. The chance to do honor to the great traditions of the Draighil lay at his feet, and he found he could no longer think of the Elder standing before him as his superior. Cleod was ready. Ready to his bones, and he would make sure the rest of the Ehlewer knew it as well.

"Indeed, as I say!" Rhol raised his hand whip and placed it against Cleod's cheek. "As you value your place here, you'll speak no more in such a tone. What we lack in youth, we own in knowledge. If you wish to take up the sword with full honor and title, you *will* respect that, or you will find yourself using a blade on nothing more dangerous than vegetables."

Silence fell as the boys held their breath. Cleod held himself still. Though he knew he was right, he had overstepped. And he valued the honor of the Enclave too much to do anything to threaten the respect of the Elders more than he had already. He gave a short nod and dropped his gaze. "Apologies, Rhol Ehlewer. I spoke outside my knowledge."

Rhol stepped back and jerked his head toward the compound. "Indeed you did, Draigre. Now *move*! All of you! You have just time to wash before evening meal."

The group turned and scrambled back across the practice field. Cleod moved a bit slower, following at the back. He would have preferred to linger and watch the last of the light fade, but delaying would further anger Rhol, and that was not wise. Not with the Draigon on the way. The Ehlewer must stand this time, and Cleod had to be the one to signify their return to greatness. For too long, the Draigon had raised fear across the land. That must end. There could be no order, no peace in the Spur, in Arnan, until the people knew there were once again Draighil worthy of the name, walking among them.

"What are you doing?" Trayor's fierce whisper came at Cleod's shoulder as they made their way down the slope toward the walls.

"I'm right," Cleod replied as quietly.

"Will it matter if you make Rhol so angry that he speaks against you among the Elders? There are three of us ready to test for investiture. They could decide to not even let you test."

"Two of us," Cleod said, correcting him. "Bonniri doesn't have enough control over the Gweld yet. Not to face Shaa."

"You're so certain it's the king beast?"

"The light is the same."

"Then it's you and me." The initial excitement had faded from his voice to be replaced by a sober note of realization. Cleod smiled to himself. The idea of a Draigon was no longer abstract, if ever it truly had been.

"This has almost seemed a game, until now." Trayor shook his head, a gesture blurred by the dying light.

Cleod could see his breath in the air now, and he took a moment to appreciate the mist. Against the lamps shining through the windows of the building ahead, it held an ethereal beauty. Soon that would fade in the fierce light of what was to come. He remembered heat so vicious that the night seemed brightened by it. Heat so intense he could barely breathe. The cool air around them was suddenly precious, and he blew a stronger exhalation toward the sky just to see the vapor form. "It's never been a game. The Draighil must rise strong again. We have to be the ones to change things. The chance is ours, to gain distinction for our kind again."

"Cleod, when you talk like that, I think someday you will hold Soibel's position and scare the life out of Draigre at every turn."

Laughter rumbled in Cleod's chest, and he smiled. "But I'm not wrong."

"You're not." Trayor stopped walking and looked back the way they had come. Cleod did the same. Light spilled over the frozen ground as the other boys pulled open the door to the hall. Their chatter echoed against the rocks. Across the yard, Rhol entered the House of the Elders. The early night was quiet but for the wind.

"You claimed the right to the Draigon," Trayor said.

Cleod looked at him. They had shared years of hardship and success, lived and eaten and struggled together. But were they friends? At the end of all the years of training, were they compatriots or competitors? "I did."

"I'm as well-trained as you. As skilled in the Gweld. And I'm faster than you."

Hoyd's words from years before drifted through Cleod's mind. *You'll fail initiation and end up a teacher.* No. He would die before he let that become his future. He shook his head. "I won't disagree. And you'll probably be the greatest Draighil to ever protect the Spur. But Shaa is mine. And I'll earn the right to face him, no matter what it takes."

Trayor was silent a moment. "Is this where we become rivals, then?"

Cleod found himself smiling. "We've always been rivals, you damn fool. You're Farlan and I am just a cefreid. You should have figured out from the start that we were supposed to be at odds."

"Har! I used to hate you on principle, you arrogant filth." Trayor laughed. "But it's difficult to stand just on bloodline against someone who can match you skill for skill." He shook his head and lifted his eyes to the clouds swirling above them. "But I suppose it's time. We can't both be the best."

"No." Cleod studied the other man. Trayor was only slightly shorter. His white-blond hair and his pale, Farlan skin almost glowed in the low light. Through the last half dozen years, they had trained, and laughed, and fought together. But tonight everything between them was changed. Cleod drew a breath and tipped his head toward the meal hall. "We might as well start now. I can eat more than you any night."

Trayor scoffed. "Lead on—we'll see about that."

Cleod started down the hill, but his mind was not on food. *Once again, Draigon, you disrupt my closest friendships. For this, too, you shall pay.*

33

Cleod

THE SPARKS THAT FLEW FROM THE BLADES AS THEY CLASHED EXISTED ONLY IN the fugue state that engulfed them. Blue flakes of dust and energy dazzled as they sprayed the air. They rained over Cleod's head as he twisted and slipped the following blow of Trayor's left hand. Whose mind generated the brittle embers? Did they exist outside Gweld?

His sword flashed again, meeting Trayor's as their gazes locked over trembling metal. "Pretty lights," he gasped out.

"Perhaps I can make them burn," Trayor shot back, and stepped forward, rolling his body and twisting the sword to strike.

Cleod drew breath, responded without thought, and again steel rang on steel in the echoing space of their combat. The shock went through arm and mind. Trayor's perception *pushed* at him, tangled his senses, as much a weapon as the blade the other held. What Cleod's body fought, his mind must also.

His gut twisted, jaw drew taut, and he forced himself to release tension as he moved to put space between himself and his all-too-skilled opponent.

Cleod let go of rational preparation and descended into pure instinct, letting his trained muscles commit to action as his mind, freed from thought, followed a pattern of response and attack that happened outside of focused time. He gasped as Trayor's blows landed, grunted with impact as his blows also found contact.

Sweat ran over his body, slicking the grip on the sword hilt. It slipped in his grasp and Trayor's blade flashed through his defenses, and blood joined sweat in soaking Cleod's side. Hissing pain, he reacted, danced away, struck back. The wound burned. It would slow him.

Too matched in skill. Both too well trained, too in control of the Gweld.

We know each other too well. Either this will end in a draw or with one of us dead. The thoughts peppered Cleod as he bent and slammed his shoulder into the other Draigre. The impact backed Trayor a step and Cleod followed. We'll not win this through knowledge or skill. Only treachery will be victor here.

Trained instinct screamed as he tripped the mental triggers to drop him out of Gweld. His world imploded and he fell back into his mind, wrenched through time and light into a world both smaller and easier to navigate. The air around him was just his again.

Trayor stumbled as though a great weight against which he pushed had suddenly given way. Given way but not given up. Cleod dropped low. Kicking out he caught Trayor behind the knees and sent him sprawling into the dirt.

Cleod's chest heaved in air as he moved to pin the other man where he lay. Cleod's sword crossed Trayor's throat, and the Gweld faded from Trayor's eyes.

An ache began in the back of Cleod's skull. He did not want to consider how brutal the coming Overlash would be after such a violent release from the fighting trance. But he had won, and the right to face the Draigon whose sign he had seen on the horizon was his.

"Cheat," Trayor gasped up at him.

"You think Draigon have any more honor?"

"I think, I wish, I had thought of it first."

Cleod winced, stepping back to let the other rise. Despite the humor of Trayor's words, a bitter bite lingered behind them. Pressing his arm against his bleeding side, Cleod backed away. He offered no assistance as Trayor staggered to his feet. If ever they had been friends, they were something else now.

"You are better than I am," Cleod said, drawing in heavy breaths to regain his equilibrium. "But Shaa is mine."

Trayor swayed on his feet, clearly also beginning to feel the Overlash. "And if it's not Shaa out there?"

"Then this will be my training run."

Something flickered in Trayor's eyes. He shook his head, and his damp hair waved like white fire. Cleod sighed in relief. If Tray had decided to push the fight further, there would be no choice of response beyond one meant to carve true harm into his body. There had been violence enough between them today.

"Draigre." Rhol's voice came from above them. Cleod did not take his eyes from Trayor until the other man looked up at the viewing platform on the edge of the circle.

"Cleod." The Elder's voice held a command.

Cleod turned slowly and raised his gaze to meet Rhol's.

"Gather your wits and find your way to the infirmary. You as well, Trayor. And take proper care of those blades. You are both to return here at first light in full dress uniform. Dismissed."

The Investiture was not the pomp and flourish Cleod had been expecting. In the center of the ring, he stood with Trayor, sharp at attention. All the Draigre were gathered, everyone in their dress finest, stood straight-backed around the training circle. Most of the Elders were there. The sun was rising over the lowlands and streaking gold into the sky. But it was quiet. He heard the wind overhead and the rustling of clothing, felt the pull and loosing of his breath. In the trees beyond the edge of the ring, a squirrel chattered.

Cleod smiled. Of course. This was something no friends or loved ones could witness. This was the moment when he joined a new family, one dedicated to saving the families of others. So on this most important of days, who else would be witness to his achievement? The squirrel rattled out another phrase, and Cleod glanced in its direction. "Hello, Leiel," he whispered. "This is the day I become what you need me to be."

He shifted his attention back to the Elders as they crossed the space toward him. Beside him, Trayor drew in a breath. He could almost taste the other man's emotion in this moment. It mirrored his own. They stood tall together, no longer friends, but certainly not enemies. Both to be named Draighil. Both fully titled as members of the Ehlewer, with the privilege of wearing the Enclave's dark leathers. Nothing would be hidden from them now. All the restricted rooms in the library, the best weapons and fireleather—accessible. As well as the highest level of training to come.

Suddenly, the lack of ostentatious celebration mattered not at all. His ears were filled only with the words Soibel was speaking, and it was everything he could do to keep the grin tugging at his lips from breaking through.

Anticipation was a vertical heat wrung up his core. The Draigon leather jerkin and pants were well-fitted but not tight. He paced the chamber from fireplace to window, feeling the uniform move with him, almost meld with him. So many years of struggle—brutal nights in the rain, hot days in the sun, and education in history and the tactics of battle, all to earn the right to wear these clothes. He wore them well. More than that—he belonged in them. He had the skills and the knowledge, the determination, required to do them honor. He would bring distinction to the Enclave and return to the Elders with the greatest victory they had ever received.

Behind him, the door opened. At last. Cleod tried to swallow, but his throat was so dry he had to clench his teeth and suck forth moisture instead. His lips parted and he blew out a low breath. He planted a foot and pivoted to face Soibel.

Still wearing his ceremonial garb, the Elder crossed the room with short controlled strides. Even weathered by time and the harsh living at the Enlcave, Soibel was unbent. The last Draighil to take down one of the beasts, the Elder had long been the public face of the Ehlewer. That he had trained only failures over the decades, had not at all deteriorated his confident bearing. Since the day Cleod had first encountered the man in Adfen, Soibel's poise and self-assured presentation had never diminished. A flick of his gaze was enough to tighten Cleod's gut.

Now the Elder met Cleod's eyes with a steadiness that demanded full attention. Cleod pulled himself straighter. Rohl, even some of the other Elders, Cleod might now face with equal confidence, but this was Soibel, who could still change Cleod's fate with the smallest word. And that could not happen. Not now. Not when he was so close to accomplishing his goal.

Soibel stopped a few paces from Cleod, clasped his hands behind his back, and spoke without ceremony. "Eirar." Uttered with a crisp flatness that left no room for doubt or argument, the name sliced through Cleod's mind like a hot blade. He pulled his head back stiff-necked as the full impact of the announcement went through him.

He had been so sure. He stood still, tension lacing his shoulders together. Not Shaa. Not Shaa after all. Almost, he asked if the Elder were certain, but Cleod bit back the words before they fully formed. Soibel would not make such a mistake.

Cleod shook his head, words rolling though his mind until he finally found ones he could speak without bitterness. "What sign determined this?" The sky had been the same, the same as when he was a boy. How could it not be Shaa?

Soibel's lips pursed, then turned in a sharp-edged smile. "We have word from Gwindor, where the Draigon has been seen in flight."

"Seen? Before the Sacrifice is announced?"

"A sign in itself. In all our records, only Eirar shows himself before battle."

Cleod frowned. Frustration would have turned him storming from the room had he faced any Elder but Soibel. All the years of work and it was not Shaa.

Soibel chuckled. "You have earned the right to engage this beast. Is it now your wish to give Trayor Draighil that honor instead?"

Too obvious then what Cleod was feeling, if Soibel would ask that question. Cleod pulled himself to full attention, gave a single shake of his head. Not Shaa. But perhaps even more important, this battle. Because he had to win—win and survive. Even to die with the beast was not an option if he was to reach his final goal. "No, Elder Soibel," he said. "I am ready to stand for the Elhewer."

Soibel raised a scarred hand and gestured to the chairs before the hearth. "Then sit. We have much to discuss about the naming ceremony. And the tribute you will afterward be due, should you succeed."

34

Leiel – 18 years

THE LAMP FLARED BRIGHTER AS SHE TURNED UP THE WICK AND FILLED THE corner of the kitchen with flickering light. She scrubbed the big kettle, then filled and hung it over the fire. She had time while she waited for the water to boil so she could scour out the last stubborn stains. From her herb bag, she pulled out the small book Gahree had given her and began to pick her way slowly through the words.

Over the last weeks, she had come to understand enough of the strange writing to dare to try reading the next story in the book without looking at the Farlan translation first. The process was slow, but she took her time, searching for understanding of the more complex words and phrases in context. Most, she was able to tease meaning from. Occasionally, she hit a word she could not decipher and only then did she resort to the right hand page. This story was a simple one, familiar, and that helped. A girl found a coin in the hollow trunk of a certain tree every time she walked the road to town. She saved the coins in a box in her clothes chest, until one day her mother found them. Asked where she had gotten the money, the girl explained about the tree. But after that day, she never found another coin on her walk.

It was an old cautionary tale about keeping secrets, and the consequences of both sharing them and keeping them. Those things Leiel knew about. No correct choice existed. It just depended on what the one with the secret wanted.

She smiled and glanced over at the kettle. It was steaming, but the water was not yet starting to roll and bubble. Tipping her head, she looked toward the door, but all was silent. Klem had gone to bed an hour ago, and the sound of Elda's low singing came from her chamber down the hall.

Leiel picked up her bag again and lifted out another volume even smaller than the first. She smiled. Cleod's reckless gift. Never had she been able to unlock the secrets of the strange words, until now.

She opened the little book and rested it in her lap beneath the first one. The single word that formed the title she could not understand, but when she turned the page, the first word was instantly familiar. *Morning.* She laughed, the sound high and light in the cozy space. She could *read it!* Shifting her shoulders to contain the sudden energy dancing through her body, she focused her attention and continued.

The story unfolded. A little girl hid from the evil witch who was chasing her. But the witch actually only wanted to help the lonely child who had gotten lost in the forest...

Leiel gasped. She *knew* this story! Upstairs in her room, on her clothes chest, was the last book her mother had given her. Here, for all these years, was the same story she had loved for so long. The little girl, Fen, went into the forest to hunt herbs for her mother, the village healer. But a storm came up, with rain so hard that it flattened the branches of the trees. The forest grew dark, and trees blew down across the trail back to town. It was too dark and dangerous to try to walk through the woods. Cold and wind drove her to seek shelter. The only house nearby was one she had always feared to visit, owned by a strange young woman who tended odd plants in her forest garden and was known to be a witch. But as the storm grew more violent, Fen knew she had no other place to shelter, and she struggled back along the path.

At the house, the woman welcomed her, but her words were so bizarre, and the food she offered so peculiar, that Fen grew uneasy. When she realized the drawings hung on the wall were of monsters and dark places, she waited until the wind eased and ran back out into the storm.

But the woman was no witch, only a collector of old art and books and recipes. She followed the girl into the weather and sought her through the night. Long and far Fen ran, until exhaustion brought her down in the lee of a great oak tree. She sheltered under its branches until the cold and chill left her shivering and only half alive.

She awoke to warmth and dry clothing, and when the fog in her mind cleared, there was the witchwoman, tending a great fire under the spreading arms of her oak. Above her, strung through the branches, other boughs had been woven with oilcloth to create a dry space. Wrapped around Fen were blankets of wool and canvas. She was so cozy that she realized the strange woman could not be the fearful creature created by panicked imaginings. And they spent the night in relative comfort, talking and laughing while the wind howled around them.

From that day, they were friends. Fen learned great things from the woman she had once feared, and together they shared old knowledge with the village until everyone in the town was wise and kind and giving.

Leiel's heart was pounding and a cold sweat chilled her lower back. Beside her the kettle was boiling, but she paid it no notice. The story—the wonderful story she knew from a hundred readings. The story in the book her mother had given her in the last days of her freedom. The story was the same, but one most important fact was different. In this book, the witch woman had a name—Gahree.

Leaves crackled under Leiel's feet as she made her way along the path to the pond. Dried grasses tickled her skirts the way the revelation at the end of the story kept swiping through her mind. *Gahree* was the witch in the story.

Leiel stepped off the path and made her way to the cracked remains of the little fishing dock at the water's edge. Though the air was chill with the first hint of the coming winter, the sun was warm on her shoulders. She sat and began to pull off her shoes and socks. What was real and what wasn't? She dropped her bare feet into the cold water.

The breeze off the pond lifted the loose strands of her hair and she raised a hand to brush them away from her eyes. The water was chill as it lapped around her feet, and the bunched fabric of her tucked up skirts made a comfortable pile underneath her. She kicked, splashing water away from the dock and watching as the drops sent waves of tiny ripples expanding across the surface. How much had her life become like that? Dozens of unpredictable impacts rolling out from odd points, meshing and colliding with each other? But then, every life must be like that, and perhaps to her it was just more obvious than to most.

Klem, as near as she could understand, had experienced only the giant impact and disruption that was their mother's death and never since had he recognized any other. When Leiel was gone—however he got rid of her—what would become his driving passion? His hatred of her was so vibrant; what would he do without it? Turn it on other girls who might be as willful and wayward as she? He was a Councilman now, one of the men in charge of deciding who was offered to the Draigon. It was more than possible.

She sighed and looked up. Fluffy clouds lazed across the sky. She could be the first in a line of women to die for her brother's twisted sense of vengeance.

Kicking out again, she let water rain down upon her. A way must exist to change that, to reorder the destiny Klem had laid out for her. She needed some magic for that to happen.

Was Gahree the forest witch, come from her wooded home to sell peppers at Fourth Market? Leiel turned the idea in her mind, thought again of Gahree's wild statements and outrageous ideas. She was a woman alone and yet she was *fearless*. She spoke of things and laughed at things and did things that Leiel had seen no other woman do. The *freedom* implied in Gahree's words and actions—that had never been something Leiel had more than dreamed to have for herself. But what if she could? What if the laughter and peace she experienced in that woman's presence could be part of every moment of her life? Why had she never asked herself that before? Gahree knew things. Secrets. The living embroidery of the tree on her pack. The way her peppers were always ripe no matter the season. How she came and went at will and the Farlan guards in the Square never questioned her, or even seemed to see her. Those were secrets not just worth being curious about, but worth understanding completely.

Reaching up, Leiel once again pushed stray hairs from her eyes.

"You are meant for more than your worst fears."

What if they were more than just words of comfort? What if, all along, Gahree had knowledge that could give Leiel's life the direction she longed for?

The water lapped her feet, tugging her senses, offering answers. Gods of old! Leiel shook her head. Of course Gahree had! Had she really ever been so young and naive as to think any of her meetings with the strange woman—from the first one right here at the pond, to the initial one at the market—had been accidental? There was *purpose* in Gahree. In her choice to listen to Leiel's stories. In her choice to share her own with Leiel. So caught up had Leiel been in the miseries of her life, so grateful for the moments of reprieve Gahree's company offered, that Leiel had never considered why they were offered.

"And when will I hear your stories?"

"When you bring me something worth my bartering for."

What was that? She had offered her own stories, and knives hammered by Torrin's fine hand, and even the best wine she could smuggle from her father's cellar. Nothing had sufficed. Gahree needed nothing. Wanted nothing. Except...

It's me. I am what she wants. It felt right. Gahree wants me to be willing to hear her stories. Not just listen to them. She wants me to understand them. The way I am still trying to understand mother's stories. That's the trade. My willingness to open my mind to more than what I have known.

When was the next market? Months away—spring. An endless stretch of time given the new thoughts ricocheting through her mind. How was she going to hold out that long? She would study the book more, learn everything she could. A tingling swept up her spine. The possibility of— *possibility!* When had she ever had that?

35

Cleod – 38 years

"You're Draighil," Rimm said.

Cleod flicked his gaze to the young man riding beside him. This conversation had been lurking since they left what remained of the Seebo. Every time Rimm looked at him, Cleod saw the questions swirling in the scout's eyes. "I was."

"Kilras says you're never not Draighil, because of what you know."

Kicce snorted and shuffle-stepped beneath Cleod, attuned to his rider's moods. "I suppose Kilras isn't wrong." Rimm's skills as a scout were unrivaled among Kilras's men, so it was easy to forget his youth in the face of that competence. But the excitement speckling Rimm's words was a reminder of how young he was.

"What's it like? How many Draigon did you kill? Why did you leave?"

The horizon flickered and, for a moment, the color of the sky shifted toward silver-green. Cleod closed his eyes and drew a slow breath, willing back the Gweld awareness that pushed at his mind. The same questions, every time, from anyone who found out what he had been. The young ones were always the most shameless in their inquiries. He had responded to these curiosities through the years; but doing so was harder this time, with the memory of the Draigon sign at the Seebo still fresh.

"It's like work. I killed one."

"You actually killed one? You killed a Draigon? Did you use your sword? The one you carry now?"

"Yes." Cleod looked over at the scout. At least Rimm seemed to have forgotten that he had asked why Cleod left. "This sword." He shook his head. "Don't bother asking me for the tale. It's not one I'll tell. You might hear an old ballad in a tavern some time, if you get lucky."

Rimm frowned. He opened his mouth, then snapped it shut again. He dropped his gaze and pinched his lips tight.

Cleod smiled a little. The smarter ones did eventually figure out they were being rude. "You're not the first, Rimm," he said. "There'll be a hundred others that follow with these questions."

"Gods of old, I'm sorry. I don't know why I—"

"You're curious. I would be too, in your position. Not many former Draighil are riding around Arnan."

"No," Rimm agreed. "I never thought I'd meet one. I wanted to be one, but my mother told me it wasn't possible, because I am not Farlan." He cocked his head and looked at Cleod. "You're not Farlan."

At that, Cleod smiled. "No. Cefreid through and through, according to the Farlan. But exceptions are made, if the Enclaves want you."

"So I could have been—"

"Be glad you aren't. It's a lonely and dangerous path. Even those who survive training, often don't survive their duties."

"But you did. Why did you quit?"

There it was again.

Cleod turned his gaze back to the cracked trail before him. "Another story you'll have to hear from the bards."

"Will they get it right?"

A very Rimm question, wise beyond his years. "It's doubtful." The truth was impossible to explain. It was something more felt in his bones than known by clear thought, even for him. Leiel had died, and he had failed, and everything that had mattered had slid away like a rockslide down the Spur. The Enclaves, for all their knowledge, were built on half-truths. Yet the changes they had worked in him were deep and abiding. There was no room for the losses and lies to coexist inside him in a way that would have allowed him to continue to retain the Draighil title. He could never explain that. He would never bother to try.

Rimm was speaking again, but the words flitted unheard through the air as the skin along Cleod's shoulders prickled. Again, his color sense shifted, and this time it was not simply in response to Rimm's unwanted questions. He drew Kicce to a stop, then turned the horse to face the rear of the caravan. He scanned the horizon.

"What is it?" The all-business tone of Rimm's words snapped through Cleod's attention.

"Not sure." There was nothing behind them, not even trees for anyone to hide behind. He raised his eyes to the sky, seeking any shimmer of motion, and flicker of something that did not fit. But there was not even a cloud. And yet... Even without delving into Gweld, he knew it. "Someone is out there."

"Following us?"

Cleod nodded.

"You're not just trying to get me to stop asking questions?"

Cleod scoffed without turning his attention from the searching for the *otherness* that had touched his mind. "There are easier ways for me to do that. We're being watched."

Rimm peered into the distance. "Where from? There's nowhere for anyone to hide."

"Hmph," Cleod said, as he turned the gelding. "You're young. Keep your eyes open." He rode up the line to talk to Kilras.

36

Cleod – 18 years

THE GIRL CURLED AGAINST THE ROCKS WAS BEGGING. CLEOD COULD TELL BY THE tone of her cries, though he could not hear what she was saying. Her hair, copper bright, caught the light of the setting sun as the beating wings of the white Draigon showered sparks over the clearing. The black leather of the Draighil uniform retarded the impact of the particulate fire raining from the molten body above. Between the ivory scales, the glow of smoldering flesh burned the very air.

"Hello, Eirar," Cleod said, into the wind. His jaw was tight, and his whole body seemed to blaze from the center outward through his skin. The roaring that filled his ears had nothing to do with the actual sounds around him.

The great beast's wings pounded, gossamer in the sweltering air, and it hovered—impossibly—over the canopy. It opened its jaws and roared and the sound was an echoing beacon that spiraled Cleod into the Gweld.

Focus beyond purity. Anger so fierce it bordered on love. The creature above him was encompassed in the hollow sweep of his perception and the breath, the heartbeat, of the monster became his own. Cleod smiled and the action rang like a bell, sending waves through the air, rippling over the Draigon's seething flesh. Three steps running and Cleod launched for the trunk of the great beech tree, his limbs flexing on impact as he pushed off and hurled himself into the descending path of the silver beast.

So clearly did he discern every fraction of the moment, that the sword seemed to *unfurl* as he drew it. The fine metal rippled out of the sheath, shuddering intoned harmony through the air. Cleod spun as he fell, not trying to strike, but instead ricocheting off where the mighty wings met the Draigon's body.

The Draigon shrieked, startled, already in motion, its action designed to counter an attack Cleod *had not launched.* Eirar twisted toward Cleod and the shining blade now being raised to strike. Cleod landed, his knees bending to take the impact of the fall and spring him upward into the strike that followed. The polished edge caught flesh, a bright rend torn over the squared face of the monster. Heat boiled through and from the blood; Eirar threw back his head, slinging Cleod and the stained weapon back into the forest.

Sweltering incandescence chased him, and all around him greenery withered and crisped, curling into crackling dust that crumbled through the air like smoke. He flung an arm over his face and rolled away from the blazing wave. The Wing Wind picked him up and slammed him through the trees. The air blew from his lungs as he crashed to the ground. For a few seconds he could not move. Around him, Gweld measured each second of his helplessness, propelling his lungs back into action. He forced himself to roll just as a massive leg crashed into the ground where he had sprawled.

Everything shimmered, from heat—from Gweld. The dying forest steamed around him. On his feet in seconds, he fled the onslaught. Behind him, around him, over him, Eirar roared again. Cleod turned into the noise and let his Gweld enhanced senses lead him through the wall of thermal energy. Glad for the Draigon leather uniform that clothed him, he closed his eyes and trusted it and his training.

He reentered the clearing on the monster's flank, only a few paces from where the girl chained to the boulder cried out to him. He flashed a glance at her. Her eyes were wide, pleading, but her shouts were drowned by the thunder of the Draigon's wings above them. Cleod's attention refocused, layered now with the cries of the girl and the billowing of the Draigon's wings. Into motion. His body took over, training outstripped thought as he dodged swiping claws and the slash of teeth as long as his arm. For all the Draigon's size and strength, it was not nimble, and Cleod moved fast over the earth just beyond reach of its strikes.

Under the near wing, in the tender bonding of joint and back, the sword again pierced through to bone. This time, the Draigon's screech spoke more than startlement. This time the damage was deep and brutal. The great glimmering wing collapsed over Cleod and that alone kept him from again being flung away as the monster rolled in agony, knocking him off balance.

For a moment, something kissed his mind, snapping his focus into a tumble of emotion. Somewhere, his name was whispered, in sadness and in awe. The shift lasted only seconds, but it was enough to freeze him, sword sliding from the now bloodied white body, tearing flesh as it came free. Then Eirar was once again in motion, forcing the damaged wing to flight and when the great, silver tail swung round and low, Cleod did not react in time to avoid the swipe that lifted him and sent him crashing over the tree tops. The earth reached up to claim him, and he plummeted, torn by tree limbs and a collision with the ground that cracked skull against stone. Despite will, darkness fell.

Seconds or minutes later, his ears rediscovered sound and his mind recovered thought. Where was the sword? How far was he from the fight? He turned, seeking, and found the blade by his bloodied hand. The Draigon leather gloves were bright with gore. He smiled. He could hear the noise of the beast and the girl, not so far off as he had feared. He opened his mind and, as he regained his feet, Gweld responded, rushed in like water to fill him. He held silent as he turned back to the fray and charged through the dying trees.

The monster must have thought him dead—how long had he lain fallen?—because the girl still lived. As Cleod burst from the forest, Eirar's response spoke of distracted focus and pain. Cleod leapt. Fire streamed through the white flesh of the monster's back as he landed on it. He raced along the giant's spine as it roiled beneath him, turning its head on its long neck to measure him. A fatal glance. Cleod plunged the sword into Eirar's golden eye and twisted it through to the brain.

Eruption. Heat and screaming and rolling agony. Cleod did not hesitate, just yanked back the blade and tumbled away from the writhing giant. Its death was blazing panic. Its thrashing tore the earth. Trees exploded, and the air turned to smoke. Leaping away, he sprinted around the creature toward the girl.

Covered in blood and sweat, she huddled against the rock, beyond screams now as she stared in horror at the Draigon's death throes. Her face was a slack mask, and for a moment, he thought the blood was hers. But when he touched her, she thrashed away, striking out at him in silent frenzy. So far had her fear taken her that she did not yet realize she was safe.

He sheathed the sword over his shoulder and grabbed her wrist, dodging her kicks and worked the complex series of twists to free her from her iron bindings. When he lifted her into his arms, her screams began again—still pleading tones, and for the first time he understood her words as they flashed in Gweld-bright colors through his mind. "Not this! Not this! It can't end like this! Let me go! Please let me go! I must go!"

He forced words, though speaking from the trance was like pushing ice through fire without melting it. "You're safe now. You are saved."

"Never safe!" she cried. "Never again safe!" She fought him, crying, struggling in his arms.

To have faced such terror as this day, untrained and with no hope—that would twist anyone's mind. For a girl such as this...would she ever recover from the horror of this attempted sacrifice? He held her tight until she went slack in his arms, giving up the struggle in a fit of weeping. Behind, in the ruined glade, the Draigon gave one last shudder, matched by a final sob from the girl in Cleod's arms. He looked over his shoulder in time to see the beast's last breath leave its body. The fire between the white scales went dark. The only sound left in the clearing was the creaking of trees and the crackling of small fires set by falling embers.

The beginning of an ache shot through his skull—the warning of Gweld collapse. He realized the blood on his face was not just the Draigon's. His entire body was bruised, his coat torn at the shoulder. He could see exposed muscle, a wound—part gash, part burn—though as yet, he felt no pain. With potential agony held at bay by trance, whatever damage his body had sustained made no impact yet on his actions.

"I have you," he managed to say, and tensed his muscles to gain his feet, her weight deathlike in his arms.

"You killed Eirar," the girl said, still sobbing. "I didn't think the Draighil were real like that. You killed Eirar."

He said nothing. Slow steps carried them away from the remains in the charred woods. He *had* killed Eirar. He—Cleod Ehlewer—Cleod Draighil—had done what he had trained so long to do. The monster lay dead behind him and a living soul shuddered in his arms. He was the first Draighil in generations to kill one of the winged giants. Not since Soibel had destroyed Glau had a Draighil succeeded in such a vanquishing. Was it any wonder the girl had not expected him to win such a fight?

He could hear his heartbeat now, pushing his blood through his veins. Physical awareness was returning—and with it emotion. A tremor went through him. He had *done it*. His chest swelled and his breath came hard through it. The smile that tugged at his face despite the first tingles of pain from his wounds was irrepressible. His name would be known throughout Arnan, and tales of this day told and retold in the Enclave for centuries to come—how he had slain a monster few any longer believed slayable. The girl would sing his praises. Generations would speak of his prowess. He lifted her a little higher and pulled his back straight as he moved through the trees. Toasts would be raised in his name. Ballads created and recited. And this was just the beginning—the start of his victories and the honor he would bring the Ehlewer.

Ahead, the trees thinned. He heard the voices of those who had gathered to witness the battle. The air dimmed around him as Gweld began to collapse. But his body did not, this time, follow his mind into weakness. Carried forward on the thrill of his victory, the burdens of injury and the girl in his arms were as nothing, and he stepped from the final cover of the forest into the cheers of waiting hundreds.

37

Leiel – 18 years

THE RAIN HAD NOT SLOWED IN THREE DAYS. IT SLUICED OVER THE SHINGLES and tumbled down the edges of the stall, filling the worn places in the flagstones until puddles overran and swept in short torrents over the Square. Outside the cozy booth, people hopped the small rivers and rushed from dry stand to dry stand, trying in vain to gather their needed goods without getting soaked.

The small fire Gahree tended in the back of the space spread more warmth than Leiel would have thought possible. The damp faded the moment she moved into the stall and she had hardly stepped toward the fire before her clothes began to dry.

She stopped and touched her hair. Only seconds before, it had been slicked across her head and dripping down her back. Now it was barely damp, as if it had been drying in the sun for several minutes after a swim. "Anywhere else, I would have said that it was not possible," Leiel said. "But I would not be surprised if you told me you could control the weather."

"So, it is not this place that makes you believe in the impossible." Gahree lifted her worn kettle from the grill set over the fire and poured the steaming water into the tea cups on the plank beside her. The air filled with the scent of sharp spices—cinnamon and fresh mint and something with a sweet, peppery overnote.

"No." Leiel came forward and folded her legs to take a seat beside the fire. Warmth spread through her fingers as she wrapped them around the offered mug; bright scents twisted through her nostrils, and she closed her eyes to immerse herself in them. Fresh harvested pumpkins and crushed catnip. Cedar and smoke. Damp earth, like a path walked from a field to the mountains.

"A new blend," Gahree said. "You are traveling with the story."

"The Spur. Like moving north on a windy day."

"You have been?"

"Once, when I was very young. My mother took me. She wanted to pick mushrooms, and we walked forever. She stopped at a large flat area and just looked at the sky for a long time. The air smelled like this tastes." Leiel sipped the warm liquid and savored the slide of it down her throat. She opened her eyes and met Gahree's, the green-gold depths moving like leaves dancing in the summer sun. "You know things, Gahree."

The other woman smiled.

"You told me you would tell me your best stories," Leiel said, "when I had something to trade that was worth them. But there is nothing you need; I have learned that." She smiled. "But you've wanted something from me, and it took a long time to realize that what you wanted was not a thing at all. It was me. You were waiting for me to understand that what you wanted was only me to be ready to hear your stories. You wanted me ready to accept all the strange things you do here and all the strange things that happen around you. And to understand that even your teas are stories. And to tell you I am ready for you to tell me why you sought me out that day at the pond."

Gahree brought her hands together and laughed a little. "So, what you have brought me to trade is a mind willing to hear things both strange and difficult. Truths lost to time."

"Are your stories true?"

"As true as yours."

"Why did you come to me that day? Why have you been here in the market all these years?"

"Arnan is not what it was." Gahree raised her mug and gestured with it, a slow sweep of the booth that encompassed the space and the rain falling outside and the world beyond. "And every change, even those wrought with the best intentions, has consequences beyond imagining."

"Why? At the pond. What consequences? What change?"

"Because your heart is wide and your mind always seeks and you speak from your soul no matter the cost. And girls like you grow into women who make men nervous. Such women, in this Arnan, are too often made to pay a horrible price for who they are. For a girl whose path leads that way, it is often better that she be distracted by the best truths of the world, and led toward the biggest of them."

"You found me to protect me."

"I found you to prepare you to hear a story," Gahree said. "Because you are part of it, now. And eventually everyone in a tale must discover their part in it."

Leiel hesitated. Was she truly ready? Did she really want to know? She hugged herself. "Tell me the story."

Gahree smiled, knowing and gentle. "It begins in a way you already know." She lifted the kettle. "Fresh tea is best, for a telling as long as this."

Leiel was silent as she handed over her mug and watched Gahree refill it. When it was back in her hand, Leiel said, "Is this a story about how I become a leaf on your ever growing tree?"

"Child of wishes, you have ever been so." Gahree laughed. "What you will begin to learn now is what wind blows over you and makes you shimmer in the breeze."

"And how does this story begin?"

"As legend. A beautiful one. But you will not enjoy hearing it, even if you think you are willing."

Leiel nodded. "I think I am afraid of your stories. But I think I am more afraid not to hear them." She looked into the fire, then back at Gahree. "Are you the witch in the forest, Gahree?"

Green-gold eyes sparkled as the face around them crinkled into a smile. "I am the witch in *every* tale."

"Even in the story you are about to tell me?"

"No, in this story, I am something much more. Hear my words, daughter of dreams. Let them wash over you and do not speak out until they have passed. They will hurt. They will heal. Hold yourself strong. These moments ahead will not be easy ones."

"I'm afraid."

"Then you are ready." Gahree set her mug aside and smiled. "You will want to flee. Or to beg me to stop. But wait. Wait, Leiel Sower, and truly listen, because a story like this is meant to change the world."

Leiel gathered herself, sat up straight, and drew in a long breath. Was she really ready? Yes. She had to be. She nodded.

With a tip of her head, Gahree began speaking, the song of her voice filling the space like a chorus of wind. "In the time before history was something that people forgot, the Draigon were the guardians of all knowledge. They learned the ways of all things, from the travels of the animals and the cycles of the plants, to the patterns of the winds and rains, and the flaws and perfections of people. They grew large with knowledge, wrinkled and scaled with the weight of accumulated wisdom. They sprouted wings to be able to carry all they knew across the breadth of Arnan. They burned with desire to understand and share, to spread knowledge, and teach any who would learn.

"Schools were founded—on mountain tops, in valleys, on islands, by rivers, on the open plains. And the teachers, the Draigon, came and lived among the people, and all those of Arnan grew more aware of the greatness of the world. The people sought art, and kindness and, even in their acts of war—for war has always existed—were more just in the choosing of their battles. Women and men worked together, learned and loved together. And, if peace did not always reign, happiness won out over sorrow more often than in most places in the world.

"But change has ever been the way of all things, and even the best of nations cannot last forever. And so, from the Far Lands, beyond even Dyil-Across-Water, came two ships. And on these ships were men who did not know the purpose of the Draigon. And when they saw them, they called them only monsters and would not hear that they might be wise.

"Of all the places the Far Landers had sailed, Arnan was the strangest, the most beautiful and the most terrifying. The Far Landers came seeking, not knowledge, not understanding, but riches. They witnessed the peace and abundance of Arnan and looked on it not with wonder, but with envy. And that envy turned to anger when they learned the bounty they saw all around them was not based in wealth, but on the teachings of monsters. They had no understanding of what it meant to ask for something and have it given in return. They could not believe that what they saw offered was all there was to see—all there was to offer—and that it was offered freely.

"So they sailed away in anger, and though two ships left Arnan's shores, many times a hundred returned. Their sailors were also soldiers, and their purpose this time was not discovery, but conquest.

"The Draigon, for all their might, had never been creatures of battle. Their fights had ever been against ignorance, and not for blood or domination. But fight they did, for the people of Arnan. Like the people, most Draigon did not learn the ways of battle easily, and so, like the people, they died. For years the war raged, a losing war from the very start. Until the places the Draigon had built and so loved were almost all in ruins. Until only the strongest and fiercest few Draigon remained.

"Too few, to stop the Far Landers. Only just a few, to take charge of what remained of the accumulated knowledge of Arnan and retreat to the highest peaks and darkest caves. Teachers they had been, and guardians they remained, dying slowly in the farthest wildernesses, exiled from their charge to counsel and spread understanding.

"Then one rose among them who had best learned the ways of the Far Land invaders, and how to fight them. A leader who refused to surrender to despair. Teachers the Draigon had been, and a teacher this one became again. But this time what was taught was survival. A way to mark a path through all the ages to come. A way to preserve the old knowledge and find new acolytes to join them. A way to do their best to carry wisdom forward. They must turn to what they had always valued most—knowledge, and seek an answer to their continuance. They studied and considered, experimented and failed. They learned to think in new patterns and use their bodies in new ways. They grew, and they changed, and they discovered power they had never before dreamed they could possess.

"Therein lay the great danger—the possibility that they would do as the Far Landers had done and simply take what they wanted because they could. After all, the course the leader laid before them was not grounded in any precedent of kindness or hopeful choice. Survival would be all that mattered for as long as the knowledge they held safe was endangered. Yet they could not simply retake Arnan. For while the Draigon were learning what they must do, the Far Landers had settled through all of Arnan.

"The Far Landers rebuilt the cities and ports they had burned. They brought back trade and travel and schools. And, as the victors of the war, began to retell the history of the conflict. No longer were the Draigon the teachers of old, keepers of knowledge and friends to any person who wished to know them. The keeps the Draigon had built as centers of learning, in the new tellings, became the prisons of old from which the Far Landers had liberated the people. Ancient rituals became known as spell craft and the singing of old songs was forbidden. Statues and sculpture and paintings were destroyed. Books were burned and writing in the old language was punished with beatings and even blinding. But Arnan was a whole society again, no longer the wasteland left by the First War. And the Draigon had never been made for vengeance. Their desire was to keep safe what they most treasured—old knowledge and the memory of freedom. Both would be needed when the world turned again for the light.

"And so, when the Draigon returned, they found their Arnan was dead, and their only allies were old and hidden away.

"But to the old ones the Draigon went, and from them, the Draigon learned to move among the Far Landers. They learned that it had all but been forgotten how the strangers came to the shore, how they were not of Arnan, but from far away. Once strangers, the Far Landers were now the heroes of the land—soldiers of Farlan, warriors, and councilmen, and kings. Only kings, never queens, for women had been relegated to the edges of society. Among women, memories lingered longest, and many had long refused to believe the Farlan lies. In those memories, lay danger to the new rulers, and hope for the Draigon at last.

"So the Draigon watched and learned, growing stronger in the hidden places. They sought out the women whose memories were the strongest and whose wills were most tenacious. They came to those women and spoke to them of times of old. The truth of the legends long since buried. The hope they had, and a dream to sustain it. The Draigon knew they could not drive the Farlan from Arnan. Too great was their old enemy. Too much time had passed. And they had no wish for another war. But their need to protect and pass on their knowledge was strong. Together with the women, they formed a plan. Fear became their weapon. The Farlan had named the Draigon monsters, so monsters they became.

"Where direct battle had failed to bring the Draigon victory, they chose disruption instead. Their great blazing bodies beat forth heat to surpass the fires contained beneath mountains. Massive wings pushed the fevered winds over the lands, boiled away rivers, seared crops, roused waves in the ocean that battered ports and smashed ships into splinters. The Draigon wrought destruction and famine and suffering, and in return they faced a new threat.

"As the Draigon learned the ways of the Farlan, the Farlan learned theirs. The Enclaves were founded to see the Draigon destroyed. The Draighil arose, well trained and fearless. And so the Draigon, the great teachers, died again. But this time it was part of a plan, a Sacrifice made to set in motion the saving of the old ways. For Draigon do not live forever, but knowledge must.

"So the Draigon came in force to the great city of Sibora and they demanded a meeting with the Farlan King. Rather than agree, he sent his best Draighil forth. But the Draigon he faced was the great teacher, the mighty Shaa, and the Draighil fell.

"Two more Draighil the King sent to fight Shaa, and two more died. At last the King agreed to come forth. Shaa presented him with a choice— agree to a Sacrifice of the Draigon's choice, at a time and place of their choosing, or face a drought that would boil the life from the land. Though enraged, the King agreed, because he could see he had no choice. But he made Shaa agree to one condition—it would forever be the right of the Farlan to send a Draighil to defend the chosen Sacrifice. And if the warrior killed the Draigon, they would make no more evil weather in that region for an entire generation.

"And so it was agreed, and the Draigon retreated from the land. They stayed hidden in their secret places and the heat faded and the rain fell again. Life returned to Arnan. But with a difference. Over the land hung the knowledge that the Draigon would come again. And when they did, someone would face Sacrifice. But for some, a chosen few, there was also hope where none had been for generations. The Draigon would come again, and someone would be born to freedom at last."

Leiel was shaking, tight, frantic trembling that rattled her teeth and shuddered every part of her. Stop. Stop stop stop. The word kept rolling through her mind. She could no more control it than she could her desperate shaking. She tried to speak, tried to rise. Nothing happened. All she could do was squeeze shut her eyes and roll onto her side and tremble.

"Ever the same, when this tale is told, the panic called up by the hearing of it," Gahree said. "No one is ever ready to hear a truth that rends the fabric of the world."

"You witch," Leiel choked out. This was what she had waited all these years to hear? This was the story so closely held and bartered for? Lies. Self-serving lies and poison. "How could you?" She rolled onto her back, her arms clutched hard across her body as she tried to contain the convulsive shaking. Try though she might, she could not stop it. It wracked her, relentless. Bile rose in her throat. Her body was out of her control. Even her voice shook. "You lied to me. Lie—lied for so l—long. Ahh no!" Sobs exploded from her, giant gasping waves. She gagged.

Gahree came to her, eased her onto her side and pulled her into a tight embrace.

"Don't touch—don't—" Leiel could not form the words through the congestion of her tears and the heaving of her body.

"It's touch you need," Gahree said, her sparkling voice gentle in Leiel's ear. She could feel the woman's warm breath over her skin and her arms were strong and unbreakable. "Let go, Leiel Sower. Let go and believe when I say you are not the first to feel this pain. Sometimes the truth burns like fire."

"The Draigon—Draigon killed my mother. How can—?"

"*No,*" Gahree stroked Leiel's hair. Her words were lit by laughter. "No, Leiel—your mother is not dead."

38

Leiel

RUNNING. LEGS CHURNING. AIR LIKE FIRE IN HER LUNGS. RUNNING AND RUNNING and running. Shouting people. The hot press of bodies and angry voices. A narrow alley, close and dark. She slammed to her knees, smashed into the wall beside her. Bruised everything. Scraped everything. Her heart was on the edge of explosion, wild in her chest, out pacing even her sobs. She rose and ran.

Alive! Not possible. Not possible that Ilora still lived. Among the monsters to which she had been Sacrificed. Among them. One of them. Like Gahree—alive!

Leiel ran. Everything about and inside her was in motion. The world was a blur and she a leaf in a storm blowing through it. Memory pursued her and she ran.

It was not the kind of sunset Leiel was used to seeing. She was familiar with warm golds fading into the purple-blue of twilight. Or vivid reds that burned bright against cottony clouds before whispering to nothingness. The sky this night was green and hazy. The sun drifted through the murk and slid into oblivion, and lightning sparked. But the smoky dust lingered, and with it came a heat unlike anything she had ever felt.

Summer nights on the edge of the Spur country were often heavy with humidity. Clothing would cling to flesh like another layer of skin, and sweat would form at the base of her spine until she wanted only to peel off her layers of skirts and splash into the stream that ran behind the farmhouse. But this heat was something new. It was a brutal, creaking hotness that got behind her eyes, and was so thick in the air it was hard to draw a filling breath. Even her bones seemed to be sweating.

She stood on the porch and the wave of it rolled over her. From behind her, her mother raised a hand, wiped a sudden beading of moisture from Leiel's brow. Leiel looked up at her.

"What is it?" Leiel asked.

Ilora met her gaze for a few seconds then looked back out toward the western fields. "Draigon Weather. It's the beginning of Draigon Weather," she said quietly, then flashed a brief smile. Her hands clasped and then dug hard into Leiel's shoulders.

"What is Dragon Weather?" Leiel looked up into her mother's face. Ilora's eyes were wide and bright, her jaw trembling with tension. What was this? Fear? Excitement and joy? What did it mean?

Ilora smiled. "The best and worst of all things, Leiel." She drew a breath and released her grasp. "Go find your father. He needs to see what's coming."

"But what is—?"

"Go on, daughter," Ilora said, in the tone that meant she was not to be argued with.

Leiel turned and went back into the house to find her father. When she glanced back over her shoulder, her mother had moved to the porch rail. She leaned into the strange wave of heat, a smile back on her face, as though she was waiting to greet a friend she had long hoped, but never actually dreamed, she would ever meet again.

Though Leiel's legs were no longer carrying her breakneck through the streets, her heart still pounded, and her breath was rushed and loud. Where was she? Some corner of Adfen she had never before found herself. The street she walked was narrow, but clean. Small shops—selling strange goods, dried herbs, and bizarre fruits with which she was unfamiliar—bordered it. In the market, she had seen so many items, so she thought she knew everything that might be for sale in the whole world. But not here. Not in this odd little alley with bright curtains in the shop windows and complex scents filling the air.

The place was as strange and new and frightening as everything else that had happened today, or as the memory that had crept up on her and flooded her with *truth*.

Ilora had known what was coming. Just that. Known and anticipated. Known and *welcomed*. Gahree's story was as real as the worn cobbles beneath her feet. Of course. Of course. Why else had Gahree visited her for so many years? Gahree came even before Ilora was chosen. Leiel remembered telling her mother about that day at the pond. Remembered how Ilora smiled as she listened. Remembered how she laughed at the end and said, *"An auspicious meeting, my daughter! Keep the memory close."*

And now—not only close, but vital, necessary, *thrilling*, not only the memory, but the relationship with Gahree.

A tremor tingled Leiel's stomach. Should she be angry? If so, then something was wrong with her. Because beneath the fading shock, was not fury, or betrayal, but a heady lightness that brought everything around her into sharp focus. She wanted to run again, but, this time, not away from anything. She wanted to jump and wave her arms and shout her wonder to the city. All the twisted emotions she always found in her thoughts about what had happened to her mother were now settled. The confusion and frustration that had been Leiel's everyday companions for so long, were at last countered by something she had not had in so long—a hope that would never again fade. Because Gahree's story was more than explanation—it was an offer. *A choice.* And having that more than balanced any need for anger.

Leiel looked up, seeking the position of the sun above the narrow buildings. Was it only just past noon? Gial would be missing her, but not so much that she would earn a terrible beating. She glanced into the nearest shop. The woman seated by the door smiled and raised a hand in greeting. Leiel returned the gesture. She would ask directions here. Perhaps choose a few odd spices to explain her absence, and mark this place in her mind for a return visit. While the world was changing, she might as well change with it.

My mother is alive. She is changed—a free woman—a dangerous thing. And I, too, can be such a thing. And I can see her again and have all my questions answered at last.

Leiel

"SOMETHING'S WRONG," TORRIN SAID AS HE PULLED ON HIS BOOT.
"How do you know something's wrong?" Leiel sat down in the chair beside his on the porch.

"You never come find me before lunch unless something's wrong."

Leiel shook her head. "I am that predictable?"

"Yes. Plan to tell me?"

She sighed. "I don't know how."

"Beginning is how."

A brief smile crossed her lips. "I am not sure where that is either."

"Then where you start doesn't matter." He whipped the laces around the hooks at the top of the shaft and reached for the other boot. "Best to say something."

She nodded. He was right as usual. But how did she share any of what Gahree had told her? All night she had tried to sort it all into something she could accept. But to tell it? How could she?

He had finished lacing his boots. The stillness of his usually active frame spoke expectation. She looked at him and held his gaze. "Do you remember, a long time ago, I asked you for help, finding something to trade?"

He nodded. "I thought you gave up on that."

"No." The shake of her head gave her an excuse to look away. "It just took a long time, to find what was wanted."

"You found it and now you wish you hadn't?"

"I found it. But I am not sure what I wish. I learned something, and I am not sure I want to know it."

"Learning new things never bothers you, Leiel."

"This is an old thing."

"Ahh. Old things are the hardest."

That brought her gaze back to him. "What do you mean?"

"Old things keep coming back up because they are usually the things that someone already figured out a long time ago. Someone got it right. Everyone since tried to do better. Sometimes there's a new way that works. Sometimes the old ways are the best."

"But everyone wants to find an easier way?" Leiel asked. "Because learning the old things is so hard?"

"Sometimes."

He did not ask her what she had learned, so she smiled at him. The knot in her belly eased for the first time since she had heard Gahree's story. "I know things I never wanted to know. And knowing is going to change everything."

"Everything?" He tilted his head.

"Me. It's changed me."

"Not the best parts."

The short laugh that escaped her lips surprised her. "I hope. I'm afraid. What I learned—I can't look at anything the same. I thought I knew what happened to my mother. I thought I knew what was going to happen to me."

"What happened to your mother was not what you thought."

"No," she said, and then realized he had not asked a question. She sucked in a breath and stared at him. "Did you know?"

"My grandmother was Draigfen. In Bajor. She was taken when my mother was four years old. Later, my mother had a friend who wanted to barter. The way your friend wanted to barter. And when she understood what her friend wanted, she learned things, too. But a Farlan soldier attacked her. She was hurt, and she was pregnant. She ran away from Bajor to Adfen. She was the child of a Draigfen, so no one cared enough to follow her. Everyone here thought she was a widow. She found work as a wash woman, and she had me, and she told me the things she knew."

Leiel stared at him, her body stiff and her thoughts tumbling. Her mouth was hanging open and she snapped it shut. The click of her teeth made her jump, and her cheeks flushed hot. He looked back at her, waiting, calm as ever, as though he had just told her nothing more stunning than what he'd had for breakfast.

Her hands were clenched. She shook them loose, trying to distract her body enough to organize her mind. With an effort, she found her voice. "I—this is why you came to the farm. Like Elda," she said. "This is why you stayed."

He smiled and nodded. "Yes."

"You've always known."

"So have you."

"Not this. Not all this."

"No," he said. "But enough. Now—"

"LEIEL! TORRIN! Come quick!" Elda's frantic shout came from the main house. "It's Addor."

Torrin pushed to his feet. Leiel was right behind him as he jumped off the low porch and ran toward the house.

40

Leiel

AS ADVERSARIAL AS THEIR RELATIONSHIP HAD ALWAYS BEEN, A TIGHTNESS FILLED Leiel's chest as she watched Addor's coffin being lowered into the earth. The sky was brilliant blue, the air chill and clear with the fading of winter. In the trees above the grave, song sparrows struck up the first notes of the oncoming season. Around her, the knot of people huddled for warmth in the wind. Torrin and Elda stood with her. Across the grave, Gial and Klem stood beside the priest who was speaking the final words of the burial ceremony.

Her mother had not received such honor as this. How was it right that a man as brutal and unforgiving as Addor deserved the presence of all these people? Of councilmen and merchants? Of traders and musicians, even? How had he earned the right to such ritual when Ilora had been dragged away to perish alone on a mountain top? Gahree said her mother was not dead. But, in this moment, that possibility did nothing to lessen the ache of injustice spreading through her.

The pressure in Leiel's chest grew, and she bent her head to contain it. Elda slid an arm across her shoulders and hugged her. Leiel did not look up. Comfort was not what she needed, because the feeling filling her was not sorrow, it was anger. All these years... What had he done, this man? Had he cared for anyone? Even Klem and Gial? Had he done any good or created any hope? She had seen the account books—he had not even managed the petty act of generating wealth.

"He tried," Torrin said, his voice low.

That brought her head up. She looked at him. "*Tried?*"

"To keep you safe." Torrin tipped his head to where her brothers stood beside the priest. "From all of them. If he hadn't gotten sick, it might have worked."

She stared at Torrin. "What do you mean?"

"He was a spiteful fool," the smith said with a shrug. "But he tried to keep you close to home. Now, he's gone. And you have to be careful. Klem means to hurt you, however he can."

As though she did not know that. But the first thing...was it possible? Had Addor, after all, in some twisted way, cared for her? With a shudder, she turned her gaze from Torrin to her brothers. Gial dropped the first shovelful of dirt into the hole. It thudded on the wood with no echo. Klem was staring at her. In that hollow instant, and for the first time, she knew it was true. Addor's protection had been real, warped though it might have been.

"Torrin—how can I be careful?" she whispered. "You know what he's planning. Careful won't matter in my life any more than it did for my mother. Or yours."

Elda spoke into her ear. "You're not alone. And they need you. Nothing changes. The farm must be run. You are the only one left to do it."

"Until they sell it." She knew that Gial wanted the freedom of a traveling merchant and Klem wanted the power and convenience of the city. "And what will I be then? Part of the asking price?"

"A servant in Klem's home," Torrin said.

A chill drained her strength as it swept over her, setting her to tremble. *"Be calm, child of fire, you are meant for more than your worst fears."* Gahree's words came back to her. So far away the humor and comfort of the woman's presence seemed, and yet her words lingered. They soothed. They eased the pounding of Leiel's heart. They mattered. The way Cleod's once had. So far away he seemed in this moment, as she must have seemed to him when his father passed. But her first thought of comfort had not been of him, but of the strange woman in the market. The weight of that realization made her draw a breath, then another. Her heart slowed its pounding.

She would be no servant. Klem hated her too much. He was not patient enough to keep her around even to abuse. "No," she said. "He's a Councilman now. He wants me sent up the mountain."

"He'll try," Torrin said. "You have choices. You know that."

"I know," she said. Gahree's story. Cleod was Draighil. "And none of them will be painless."

Leiel settled herself at the table and forced herself to sit upright against her body's desire to curl her shoulders and huddle. Gial paced on the other side of the room, short, stiff strides that scuffed the rug. His back was log straight, and he refused to look at her.

She tried again, pitching her words low. "Gial—please. I need to know what you're going to do."

Still no response, just a new tension visible in his shoulders that meant he had heard her. She sighed, looked down at her hands resting on the table. Gial might be the oldest, but it was Klem who would decide what happened today. The wood under her fingers was polished and unscarred, kept in fine condition through years of her care and her mother's before her. The house was spotless. The old wood floors were buffed, and the windows gleamed. The hands of women, forced to care for the minutia of crevices and dust. The dirt of the barn floor and the ash of the forge had always been more to her liking. But the house was home and if she lost it... Her stomach twisted. That loss was coming. She could hear Klem's footsteps in the hall and when the door opened, she forced herself to look up at him.

He smiled, and it reached his eyes. It had been years since she had seen true happiness in him. Would that she could find joy in that.

She drew a breath; the knot in her stomach rotated. Though her fingers twitched on the wood, she willed her hands not to clench, instead pressed her palms into the tabletop. The last time she had faced Klem from this chair, it had been with her father beside her as he announced that he was placing her in charge of the farm.

"You'll stand when I enter the room," Klem said. "And you'll not meet my eyes unless invited to do so."

She stared at him. Not even half a day since Addor's burial and it was already beginning.

"Let her be," Gial said from the far corner of the room. "You'll have your way with her soon enough. This day we only decide how to divide up the farm. Neither of us wants this place. The sooner we settle business, the sooner you can gloat."

"What do you care how I speak to her?" Klem said. "You can't stand the sight of her any more than I. The difference is that I am stuck with her. You'll ride away from Adfen soon enough, and I'm the one left to handle her mischief."

"Leave me the farm," she said. "You can keep ownership, and I'll run it, just as I have been. Gial can go his way. Klem, you can move to town and never have to see me again."

"Like a squeaky floorboard, you never *stop* your noise," Klem said. "Don't speak again. If you had ever known your place—"

"I'm not a *thing*." She pushed to her feet and looked between her brothers. "I am not something to be divided up or sorted out like cows or chickens or furniture. I'm your *sister*. I don't care how you feel about me—you don't get to treat me like an animal."

"If I wanted to treat you like an animal, I would have you slaughtered with the cattle," Klem said. "You will not speak again."

"I will speak as I must. You hate me. So be it. Bide your time. Take your revenge. But let us be rid of each other this day. I'll stay here, and you can both be free of me."

"It's the money," Gial said. "We must sell this place in order for both of us to have enough to move on."

"She is owed no explanation." Klem rounded on Gial. He crossed the room and stepped up face to face with the older man. "If you were capable of running the trade routes with half the results of father in his youth, I would have the wealth I deserve, and we would not be losing valuable property just to have enough to survive in comfort."

"And if you were anywhere near the bookkeeper that you are the talker we would never have been dependent on the fickleness of the markets," Gial said. His voice dropped low. "Step back, brother. You are no more in charge here than I am."

"Both of you are fools," Leiel said. "Fools with no hearts. I would pity you if I had the will left to do so."

Klem turned, and his stare pushed at her. Her heart ticked faster in her chest until she could almost hear it. There had to be something she could say or do, something that would stop the backsliding loss of what little freedom and self-respect she had managed to garner these last years. But no more words came. Nothing said would matter. No one could help. Cleod was of the Enclave now. Torrin and Elda were as powerless as she. Gahree—Gahree was perhaps about to be lost to her as well. If Klem took her to town, would he let her attend the market? Maybe. It was the one thing that might hold for the future. She wrapped her mind around the hope in that thought and found the strength to meet his gaze. "Fools," she said again, knowing she was as much one herself for speaking so in this moment.

Three strides brought Klem around the table. She raised her arm to block a blow, but it never fell. Instead he caught her wrist and yanked her to him, chest to chest so she had to look up at him. "You'll clean my house," he said. "You'll scrub my floors and wash my clothing. You will sleep in the cellar with the coal, and you will be *grateful that I allow you that much.*"

"Until you try to kill me."

"Until I deliver you to your promised fate." He shoved her away and she stumbled before she caught herself.

She refused to rub her wrist, though it ached. She held still, glaring at him, then she turned and stormed from the room.

"I did not give you permission to leave." His voice was like a whiplash through the air.

She turned in the doorway, her heart pounding and her face hot. "You've never granted me permission to do anything. Why would you start now? And why should I care if you did? I hope you rot—both of you." Pivoting, she yanked the door closed behind her, taking satisfaction as it slammed, drowning out the worst of Klem's snarled reply. No matter. She would hear it all later. She would hear it for years if he had his way. And he would. Gial was already gone, his heart and mind on the road, and he would not come to her aid.

The words etched on the base of the Tower rolled through her mind as she descended the steps to the kitchen. *The days are long, the nights unnerving, but in the center of the darkness, I found a great dream. The rock here is solid, and it whispers my name in the wind as the stars shine down. It says 'Desga—this is home—this is where your wings will spread and lift you to new heights. Build here and reach high. Land here and teach all. These hardships shall pass and new dreams are wide. It is only when you are at your lowest that you see the fineness of the horizon above you.'*

Elda stood in the middle of the kitchen, hands wrapped into her apron when Leiel came down the stairs. Her stomach was still tumbling and she took a few breaths to try and calm her nerves as she crossed the warm space. Elda reached out and hugged her hard, held on for a long time. The warmth of the woman's arms surrounded Leiel, and for a moment she stood enveloped in caring. Her shoulders relaxed a little.

"Thank you. You always know what I need."

"Are they selling?" Elda asked.

"Yes. It's what we thought."

Elda pulled back and met her gaze. "And you?"

"I'm to go with Klem into town. I am sure he will want you as well. I am fine at scrubbing floors, but Klem knows I can't cook."

The older woman laughed a little, then frowned. "What about Torrin?"

Leiel shook her head. "Torrin belongs here. Anyone who buys this place would be a fool not to keep him on. What would he do in town?"

Elda sighed. "He's the best smith in the region. He could make a good life in the city."

"He won't leave the farm as long as he is welcome here." Leiel stepped back and reached up to push her hair out of her eyes. "I don't know how much time we have. Will you be all right? Him staying here."

Elda smiled and nodded. "Torrin has no name for the priests to trace, Leiel. Nor do I. We have been all we can be to each other. Maybe someday we will get to be that again. Don't worry about me. We have to use the time we have to hide all your books among my things. You should start right now, digging them out of their hiding places."

Leiel laughed. She turned and seated herself on the bench by the wall. "I hadn't even thought about that yet. I was hoping, somehow, that I could convince him to let me stay here." She waved her hand to encompass the room. "To just leave me here with the rest of the things he finds useless. I don't know why I had any hope of that working."

"You're no good at not hoping." Elda went to the stove, opened the fire door and bent to add more logs. She adjusted the damper and glanced back at Leiel. "Even when it's pointless."

"Well I had a good teacher." Leiel watched the woman work. "You cook a lot when you're worried."

"I cook a lot when *you're* worried," Elda corrected.

"Ha!" It was true she liked to eat while she plotted how best to get around Klem's rules. Leiel smiled, got to her feet, and crossed the room to the hearth. She lifted the candelabra from the mantel with both hands. The wrought iron was warm, and she tensed the muscles in her back to take some of the weight off her arms. Carefully, she turned and placed it on the table, then worked her fingers along the back edge of the base until they hooked into a small groove in the metal. Applying pressure, she lifted slightly, and the well-oiled compartment slid open. She pulled out Gahree's leather bound book and the volume Cleod had liberated so long ago. And a small bundle of cloth that held the crystal Cleod had given her. That went straight into her deepest skirt pocket. She picked up the books.

"These two first, Elda." She tucked back a stray strand of hair. "Can you take them now?"

The older woman nodded and accepted them with gentle hands. "I know just where to put them. Keep an eye on the fire." She moved past the stove and down the narrow hallway that led to her room.

Leiel watched her go, then closed the panel on the back of the candle stand and lifted it back onto the mantel. There were other books she would have to retrieve from their hiding places, but the most important ones were now safe. She fingered the small knot of cloth wrapped around the stone in her pocket. If only that were true of everything she cared about.

41

Cleod – 38 years

CLEOD DREW THE SWORD. IT GLEAMED IN THE FIRELIGHT, REFLECTED FLAMES dancing the length of the blade. The crystal mounted atop the leather-wrapped hilt glinted dully. He stared into the smoky stone. It was not known for sheen, even when cut and faceted as this one was. The Wild Stone grounded, forced focus. It increased the mind's clarity within Gweld trance and burned away doubts. It was a tool as much as was the sword itself.

He leaned back against the wagon wheel and laid the sword across his knees and ran a finger over the crystal. Common in the Spur, the Stone was rare elsewhere in Arnan. Many times, he had been offered payment for it—payment that outstripped what he could even get for the sword itself. At times, when the ercew had nearly drowned him, he had considered such a deal. But he had never completed the transaction, never been able to part with either the blade or the Stone. Why? Why, when he had thrown away or given up everything else he had valued, had he held on to these things?

Because you knew some day you would see what you saw at the Seebo. He sighed, wrapped his hand over the sweat-stained green leather that bound the hilt. The full weight of it settled into his fingers. He rolled his wrist slowly. The length of the weapon turned in his hand, and he could feel the tendons and muscles in his arm working. Strength and control. Those things he still had. And knowledge. And this sword. Did it really matter that a title no longer graced his name?

Shaa had returned.

Red light over metal. All things on fire and the scent of pain and fear and death. A sound pierced his mind, high-pitched and fine-drawn—a scream. A cry of fire within fire. Green-gold eyes, fierce and fearless, stared into his.

"Cleod?" Rimm's voice.

Cleod raised his gaze from the blade and looked up at the scout standing across from him. Tension pulled the edges of Rimm's mouth, and Cleod belatedly registered the tentative tone with which his name had been spoken. His ears filled again with the comfortable sounds of the camp at rest. Low voices and laughter. The occasional stomp and snort of an animal. Rustling of canvas and the crackle of fires. With a grunt, he lowered the sword and slid it back into its sheath in a single motion. "More questions?" he asked as the blade clicked home.

Rimm's face relaxed, and he shook his head. "Not now. Kilras wants you. He's in the maps again."

Cleod tucked the sword into his bedroll and slid both beneath the wagon behind him. He got to his feet. "What now?"

"Something about alternative camp sites near Melbis."

Cleod nodded. He stepped over the wagon tongue and turned toward the cookwagon. Kilras preferred to do his most intense thinking in the presence of fresh coffee. "As many people as will be arriving in the next few weeks, water and forage will become an issue."

"How many do you actually think will be coming to Melbis? It was hard enough for us to get across that mess at the Seebo."

Cleod glanced at Rimm, pleased with the young man's alert consideration. "Not everyone comes from the west. And many who do prefer the southern route. Too many bandits along this way."

"So why did we come this way?"

Cleod shook his head. "It's usually faster, despite the danger. Especially since few choose to pick a fight with Kilras any more."

"We'll be early arriving," Rimm said, side-stepping to avoid tripping over one of the wagon cats who sprinted from the grain cart in pursuit of something only it could see. "Old gods rest in peace. One of these days some cat is going to tip me onto my face. Why would Kilras care if this route was faster?"

Cleod chuckled. "Would you want to spend another week with Wern?"

"Ooof," Rimm agreed. "I'd rather ten cats trip me."

This time Cleod's laugh was full, turning the heads and shifting gazes from warm fires. "I could second that."

"Why'd Kilras take him on anyway?"

"He put on a fine show of being reasonable back in Kittown. The other traders there vouched for him."

"Why would they do that? Won't Kilras consider that when next any of them want escort?"

"He will," Cleod said. "But he'll also take into account that this is Wern's first trade run this far from home. He's always sent others to this festival, but this year decided to go himself. The trip is a bit more arduous than I think he expected."

"Arduous? For an old man, you like big words."

"For a young one, you're barely annoying."

"Ha. So, what happens after Melbis? Wern's left to find his own way home?"

Cleod shook his head. "Never. But after the festival, he'll either mend his ways and travel with us, or keep his pride and lose all his profits trying to join another caravan. After Kilras lets the other Dorn know what Wern's like to work with, none will take him except to make him broke."

Rimm laughed. "So—Kilras teaches him a lesson that will either cost him his attitude or his coin?" He shook his head. "Our Dorn is a singular man."

"That's a big word for you."

"I'm learning from the best."

They rounded the last wagon. Kilras looked up from the maps splayed over the tailgate. Three lamps were burning in a semi-circle at the tops of the papers, casting bright, if flickering, light. "The best at what?"

"Talking big," Rimm said.

Kilras shook his head. "You've made a poor choice in opponents. Cleod's got more experience than any twenty men when it comes to that."

"What are we looking at?" Cleod asked, gesturing to the maps.

Kilras grinned and tapped the papers. "I don't want to stop west of town."

Cleod frowned and stepped closer. Rimm moved around Kilras's other side to see better.

"Why?" Rimm asked. "Looking at this, camped west, we'd have access to the largest springs. Why not take that advantage?"

"There are more important things." Cleod pointed to a location just to the south of the best water sources, where a stand of forest was marked on the map. "Here?"

Kilras nodded. "Most other caravans won't have seen what we did, Rimm. Once they start talking to our merchants—"

"Once they start talking to Wern," Cleod said.

"At the worst. But any one of them will want to talk about what's left of the Seebo. I'd rather have a bit less water and a lot more shade, as well as a place we can duck into for cover if things turn toward panic."

"Couldn't anyone just use the woods as cover to sneak up on us?" Rimm asked.

"They could, but given the terrain, it would probably be more effort than it's worth. These three springs are small, but they've been reliable."

"Stop at the western springs on the way in," Cleod said. "We should fill all the barrels, and scout the southern springs, make sure they're still flowing. After the Seebo, I wouldn't be willing to bet everything that they are. We're ahead of everyone. We can move camp before anyone else arrives if the water is there to the south."

"Well enough," Kilras said. "Now what about your other issue? Any thoughts?"

"What issue?" Rimm asked.

"Our watcher." Cleod shook his head. "No. I haven't seen anything that might tell who or why."

Kilras eyed him sideways, silent for a long moment, then he nodded. "And beyond seeing anything?"

"Someone's there."

"Not something?"

Cleod breathed hard in, considering. *Something.* It could be a thing, a monster, the eyes of a Draigon. But it felt more intimate than that. "Maybe. Whatever it is, it seems not to be interested in doing more than watching for now."

Another nod from Kilras. "We'll wait then. Not worth sending anyone looking. Get some sleep, both of you. This trip isn't going to get any easier."

"After what we went through at the Seebo," Rimm said, "I'll settle for the rest of this trip not smelling like rotten fish."

"No promises on that front." Kilras turned back to the maps, sipping at his coffee.

"Goodnight." Rimm headed away into the night. Cleod watched him go, then turned to go back to his own small fire.

"And Cleod—" Kilras's firm tone stopped Cleod. He looked over his shoulder at the Dorn.

"I mean it. Rest."

"Don't worry about me, Kil."

"Normally, I don't. But when it comes to you and Draigon, I choose to."

"I don't intend to use Gweld. Not for what's probably a scout from one of the horse tribes trying to get a look at our stock so they know what the competition is for the festival."

"Probably." Kilras nodded, held the look a moment longer, then turned back to his work. "Goodnight."

Cleod stood a moment longer, then walked back through the fire-flecked night. Fewer voices floated on the hot air, and it seemed darker than before. A good night for sleeping, if he could tame the unease still scratching at his mind.

42

Cleod – 19 years

CLEOD PUSHED BACK THE CHAIR AND ROSE TO GREET TRAYOR AS THE OTHER MAN came through the tavern door. Trayor looked around, nodded when he met Cleod's eyes. A new confidence added determination to Trayor's stride as he crossed the crowded room, weaving between the tables of half-drunk revelers.

"*Draighil!*" Cleod greeted, unable to contain his smile. "Congratulations, Tray. You've earned your scars." He raised his closed fist to his forehead in salute. Laughing, Trayor returned the gesture.

"I never knew what you meant when you said that," Trayor said as he reached out to grasp Cleod's wrist. "Now it makes sense." He released his grip and raised a gloved hand to touch the left side of his face where the still healing burns had left their permanent mark.

"You couldn't leave me more than a few months to bask in the glory of being the only Draighil to successfully take down one of the monsters?" Cleod asked as he resumed his seat. The memory of that fight, the hot blood and the beast's dying, still sent a thrilling tingle up his spine. He smiled wider.

"You're barely back on your feet." Trayor pulled out a chair and joined him. "They needed someone else."

"You walked away with less damage than I."

"Well, I'm better than you. I killed Aweir in less than half the time it took you to take down the white beast."

Cleod laughed and raised his hand to signal a passing server. The man was perhaps a few years older than him, but he moved quickly, eyes down, shoulders tense, to take Cleod's request. Gods of old, the power of the uniform he now wore. "Two glasses of your finest Vorden. Gora Vineyard, if you have it," he said. "Tyrdth, if you don't."

"Sere. Right away," the man said. "Do the Seres need anything else?"

Trayor waved a hand in dismissal before Cleod could reply. "We will inform you when we do."

Cleod laughed a little as the server moved away, heading directly toward the bar despite requests being called out from other patrons. "Did you know it would be like this?"

"You are cefreid. For the Farlan, every day is like this."

"Steaming piles of Draigon shit," Cleod replied. "You've never been treated so well."

Trayor grinned back at him. "But I am quickly getting used to it."

"We've earned any accolades offered us." Cleod leaned back and took in the moment. In the cool of the dark tavern, even the smoky air was sweet. They were two victorious slayers of the deadliest monsters to ever stalk the land. Entire regions owed the two of them their survival. Their names were even now being immortalized in song—the bard in the corner had spent the past few hours trying to rhyme Trayor's name with—well, anything besides 'betrayer.' If the singer got the lyrics straightened out by evening, Trayor would be in for a pleasant surprise.

"How healed is your shoulder?"

Giving his arm a roll from the upper joint, Cleod nodded. "Almost back to full strength. The leg is still coming along." He passed a coin to the server as the man returned with a tray holding the requested wine, then lifted a glass and tipped it to his nose. Rich and bright, the scent of berry and smoke opened his senses. "Hmmm...Gora, just as I hoped."

Trayor picked up his drink as well and raised it in a toast.

The click of their glasses held a tingle of music and sent the scent of the fine vintage wafting across the table. "And as well-earned as our scars."

Cleod tipped his glass and took a sip, letting the rich liquid coat his mouth, savoring the tannins that dried the top and back of his palette. "One thing I truly appreciate about our Elders has been their willingness to impart their knowledge about things beyond Draigon slaying."

"Cefreid," Trayor scoffed. "We Farlan were weaned on such as this."

"Which is probably why you don't know how to appreciate it."

Trayor laughed. "You have never failed to entertain me." He set his wine glass on the table. "We will enjoy comparing battles now. I am sure we can learn from each other—all but my speed, which you'll never match."

"Or you, *my* endurance."

"Ha! What woman ever said that?"

Cleod laughed, but the sound was awkward to his ears. Trayor caught the odd note and shook his head.

"Still unwilling to tell tales of the back rooms of the Red Dove? We're men now. That's what men do. There's a story to be told I am sure, of you and Cirilla? Or Ahheli? Perhaps both."

"Oh, there are," Cleod agreed. "But nothing that needs to travel as far as what sharing them with your ears would mean."

Trayor sipped his wine. "I think you are just as jealous of my skill with women as you are of my skill with a sword."

"I was named Draighil before you," Cleod reminded, tipping his glass at the other man. "And mine the honor of the first kill."

"How else was I to judge how much effort I must use to best you in future contests?" Trayor asked. Though he grinned when he said it, Cleod saw truth in the fine tension around the other man's eyes. Compatriots and brothers of the Enclave they might be, but also now, forever rivals.

"And what for you tonight?" Cleod asked. "Wine and song? A woman?"

"Perhaps all three. Perhaps three women."

The bard in the corner struck a first nervous note and hummed a little, glancing their way. Cleod offered him a nod and the man quickly turned his attention back to his instrument. "The musician is set on crafting you fine praise. I am not sure he expected to have to sing two songs of great heroes tonight."

"Two?" Trayor shook his head. "This is Oryok. We are three months ride from Gwindor. Who here do you think even knows your name?"

That was true enough. Eirar had died nearly a year ago, and a long march from here. While the ballads sung of the Draighil who had killed the beast might have traveled this far, who here would suspect that first victorious Draighil would be the man sent to assess the praise given to Trayor?

"Have they treated you well here as you have healed?" Cleod asked, turning the conversation to the reason for his presence in Oryok.

"The Elders sent *you* as envoy?" Trayor asked, unable to hide his surprise.

"Of course," Cleod said. He chuckled. Trayor's inability to keep his emotions from his expression had always been his greatest weakness. "Who better than one who has recently received proper accolade to test the worthiness of what is offered you? Oryok is a wealthy city. The Ehlewer expect honor worthy of that wealth." If Trayor's portion of the tribute was half of what Cleod had received, they could both afford to find comfort in wine, or anything else offered across Arnan, for the rest of their lives.

"The Bynkrol Enclave is displeased that Ehlewer has succeeded where they have failed for five generations. We should make our celebration short after tomorrow's ceremony. It is a long trip home, after all. And the wagon weight we can expect the mules to pull will slow us. Plan to leave at first light in two days?"

"First light," Cleod agreed. The real reason he had been chosen as envoy was simple—he and Tray were the best the Ehlewer had. The wealth of gold and fine tobacco and herbs they would bring back to the Enclave, after tomorrow's Ceremony of Praise, was too precious to be risked with a single Draighil—even one of Trayor's skill—to guard it. But two—the finest two alive—few would dare harass them.

"So tonight it must be, to drink and find the women you spoke of." Trayor leaned across the table and again touched his glass to Cleod's. "Unless you are now keeping yourself for that farm girl you pine for."

A fine tension crossed Cleod's shoulders. What had brought this topic to the table? He had made sure, over the years, to keep his mentions of Leiel casual, his letters from her private.

"Don't ruffle, Cleod. You've said nothing. Too little, in fact, considering how many letters that have flowed between you over the years. And the time you spend writing them. What do you fill them with? Poetry? Fantastic stories of what the girls of the Red Dove have taught you?"

Cleod frowned. "Back off. She is worthy of more than such comments, especially from someone who has never met her."

"Aah ha—so what do you plan to do? You can't marry her."

"Not now. I have work to do still. There are many Draigon." *Most especially, there was Shaa.*

"We can't kill them all, just the two of us. Eventually we'll be called to teach others. The Enclave needs us."

"I'll not always be Draighil," Cleod said, but the words sounded odd as he said them.

"Oh, you think not?" Trayor leaned back, shifted his attention to the musician by the fire. His next question lingered in the air, caught the first notes of a real tune as the bard finally struck up a song. "What else, exactly, do you think you know how to be?"

43

Leiel – 19 years

GAHREE WAS FASTENING HER PACK STRAPS WHEN LEIEL LEANED AGAINST THE EDGE of the stall entrance. The day was fading, the market nearly empty of shoppers as the merchants packed their remaining wares.

"It is always good to have hope," Gahree said. "So I have hoped you would decide to visit me today."

"I very nearly didn't."

Green-gold eyes flicked up at her. "Nothing is easy, in facing a truth. Even a good truth."

"I have questions," Leiel said. "You told me a story. You did not tell me the things I need to know."

"It is late this day, daughter of dreams. Have you the time to hear the answers you seek?"

"Gial thinks I have gone to get the mule. As busy as the market was today, he won't be surprised if it takes me some time. And Corra has his attention. He'll be in no hurry."

Gahree straightened and smiled. "Spread your questions like seeds, Leiel Sower. We'll grow answers into knowledge as best we can."

Leiel stepped into the booth, but didn't sit down. She crossed her arms over her chest, trembling despite the determined lecture she had given herself as she crossed the Square. The sun canted into the space at a low angle, and she put her back to it, needing the warmth. So much for thinking she was in control, for believing she was ready for any of this. She met Gahree's gaze. "I am trying to understand—if your stories are true—why my mother did this? Why would she leave us?"

"The Council fears women. They feared Ilora. And they feared what she was teaching you. That meant they feared you as well."

"Then why did she teach me anything? She could have stopped—"

"She could have stopped breathing? Stopped caring and hoping? Why should she have to? Why should knowledge be denied you—or her? It does not belong only to those in power. Do you wish to unlearn what you know, child of wisdom? Do you wish you were content in the way things are? Would you be content to have your child be so?"

"I'll never have a child," Leiel said. "I'll never have a family or a place of my own. Because she was chosen. Because she *went*."

"You're alive *because* of her choices. The Council does not need for the air to be dancing with heat to destroy a woman—or a girl. They need only a bit of bad luck, and someone to blame."

"You are saying they wanted *me*?"

"Adfen's Council would have taken you. Retrained you at best. Sold you at worst."

The world warped before her, and Leiel put a hand against the wall to steady herself. "Sold?" The word barely made it past her lips. Sold did not mean *just sold*. It meant more than slavery. It meant a brothel—or worse.

She had heard of such things—whispers of dealings in the darkest corners of the market. It happened—girls and boys. But the Council selling children...? Of course they would. There was nothing they wouldn't do if it meant keeping their power. Look at Klem. It had always been his dream to be one of them—if for no other reason than to punish her. She was too old now, for the child markets. She was just the right age to find an excuse to kill.

Her heart heaved. "My mother...Draigon Weather did not come by chance that season, did it?"

Gahree shook her head, sending loose stands of her hair into her eyes. "Your mother called the Draigon, Leiel."

Leiel pushed out air. "Because the Council had marked me."

"Because she *could*. Because she had a choice. And she used it. It is the best of dreams—full of hope. What is more vital and alive than that? A woman with choices is a woman who does not have to live in fear."

"Who are you?" Leiel whispered. "A woman? A witch? *Draigfen*?"

"Yes. And all of those things you can choose as well. As your mother did. As have so many women before you."

Leiel sat.

She did not decide to, her body just folded beneath her and dropped her to the stall floor. The wall beside her provided support and she leaned into it. Was this happening? Was she finally learning what she needed to keep the promise she had made all those years ago? The promise that she would make sense of what had happened to her mother? That she would understand the *why* of all of it?

"You're my choice, aren't you? I can see my mother again. You're not just here to teach me—you're here to offer me what my mother was offered." She didn't wait for Gahree to reply. "I need to know more. I need to know why."

"Why your mother said yes?"

"Why the Draigon—why *you*—do this. Why *this* of all things? The Draigon could destroy all of Arnan. All the Farlan. Why haven't they? Why all these years of Sacrifices? So many people hate the Draigon. They're afraid of them. They would see all the Draigon dead. *I* would love to see that. Or I would have. Now—I don't understand."

Gahree smiled. "Generations have been raised to fear the Draigon—even the descendants of those who knew what the Draigon really are, now are uncertain of the old truths. In the old days, people watched the changes of the Draigon, knew they were not something to be feared. Not so, now. Not so, for far too long." Gahree placed her pack between them, embroidered side up, and settled across from Leiel. She ran her hand over the dancing threads of the tree. "The war killed most of the Draigon, for they were not fighters. Generations passed before the few that were left learned the skills they now have to control the weather—the wind and rain. Draigon do not do this without weighing the cost. Draigon pay a price for the change they render in the weather. There are too few, now, to change all of Arnan, to control and maintain the drought for long enough to drive the Farlan away. Too many would die. Too much would be lost, here and among the Draigon. No. Draigon take what is needed, with the least damage necessary."

Leiel was shaking her head. "No. Why don't they just ask the women to come with them? There have to be so many who would leave the lives they have—"

"There may be." Gahree traced a finger over the glimmering leaves of the embroidered tree. "But the women who join the Draigon, they are here—flickering and alive with knowledge and passion and will. And they are unknown. Most importantly, that. If the Farlan knew they still lived, do you think they would leave them in peace? Do you think they would not send every Draighil and every beating heart of the Farlan army in search of them? It would mean another war. The Draigon do not want war, only to save the knowledge they hold dear and what few lives they can."

Silence drifted into the space between them. Leiel breathed slowly in and out, her mind churning, questions rising and falling with the beat of her heart.

"It is not, then, all women who are part of your tree."

"Ah, no. No, Leiel. All are part of its roots, but not all are woven as leaves on the thinnest branches."

"So who choses?"

"Draigon watch. Draigon listen, and seek out and question. When a girl is smart and daring and quick and does not allow herself to be crushed by her world..."

"They send you," Leiel whispered.

"I come here."

Leiel eyed her, knowing there was more in that simple phrase than just the words that formed it. Moments flickered in her memory—time spent here in this stall in laughter and comfort. That first sunny day at the mill by the pond. The times she had called forth Gahree's words to sustain her in difficult moments. Ilora. Ilora leaning into the rising heat as if welcoming an old friend. All of them warmed her heart, had given her hope, made her want to know more than she had. And yet—

"I don't know what to say to you, Gahree. I don't know what you are. I don't know what I ever thought you were. And I have hated the Draigon since I can remember learning what hate is."

"Is your hatred for me, wild daughter?"

"No. But there is hatred in me. What do you want of me?"

"I want you to know you have a choice. And to think of that choice in the days and months to come. And when you have more questions—I will be here to answer them."

"Klem is selling the farm."

Gahree did not speak. She sat waiting, tracing the leaves on the pack. Tracing and tracing, soft and slow and elegant.

"He won't be rid of me soon," Leiel said. "It will take time to sell it. But once he does, I don't know how much time I will have."

"Time?"

"Time before he finds an excuse to have me killed. He would like best to wait for Draigon Weather, but he might not have the patience for that. He'll find something though. If not a Draigon, some other horror that might be used as an excuse."

"Ahhh—that wait is up to you, Leiel. You have much to consider. Let your heart and mind write this story. I will be here when the tale is ready to be completed." Gahree rose and picked up the pack. "Time to make our way," she said as she slung it on. She reached out a hand to help Leiel up.

Leiel nodded and gripped Gahree's fingers. They were slender and strong, dry and firm. Leiel smiled a little as she gained her feet. A dozen decisions lay ahead. More questions. More hopes. More fears. And not enough time to ponder any of them.

44

Leiel

SUNLIGHT STREAMED INTO THE BEDROOM AS SHE LAY IN THE QUIET LIGHT, TAKING in the familiar play of brightness and shadow over the ceiling. So many mornings in her childhood she had done this, just lay still and listened and taken in the start of the day. It had been a rare pleasure these last few years, stolen moments of sleeping in until dawn on the days when Klem was in town. Now this was the last day. Klem could yell and threaten all he wanted about breakfast being late, but after today there would be no more mornings in this room. There would be new quarters for her in Klem's house in town, quarters with only one narrow window and no room at all for the furniture in this room. All but the bed was being sold with the house.

She sat up and tucked her knees to her chest, gazing out the window at the familiar landscape. All the sounds were right, from the chickens clucking behind the house to the lowing of the milk cows. The air was as sweet as she had ever smelled it. She smiled and shook her head slowly. "I'll miss the sounds. I'll miss the light." She sighed and tilted her head onto her knees.

For a moment the sound of her mother's voice seemed to fill the air, light and effortless as the sunlight now brushing her hair. That was the thing that was forever missing. And yet...those last days when it had filled the house, in the heart of Draigon Weather, those had been the most joyous she had ever heard that voice. All during that sweltering summer, her mother had laughed and showered love upon her and Klem and Gial. Love like rain falling. The stories she had told were all long and filled with humor. The kitchen had always been filled with extra treats, cookies and pies and cakes, sweet breads and fresh fruits, despite their rareness in the drought.

Ilora had been *happy*. In the worst summer in decades, with the terrible threat of the Draigon and the drought and the potential for long-term suffering looming over all of the Spur, Ilora's joy had been palpable.

Because she *knew*. Leiel blinked and raised her head. Ilora *knew*. Gahree... It was all true. She pulled in a breath, long and slow, allowing the new knowledge to wash over her. No. Not new. All the years of retelling the stories she had learned from her mother. The secret hoarding and copying of odd texts she had found in the dustiest parts of the library. All the long hours spent with Gahree. Her long letters to Cleod in the Enclave, asking every question she could think of about life there and his training. Her continued desire to learn and question, despite the consequences of doing so—no, the knowledge was not new at all. It was just, at last, complete enough to be made sense of.

My mother was Draigfen, Leiel thought, one of the Draigon touched. A woman too dangerous in the eyes of the Council to be allowed to continue to exist. She knew what was coming, just as I do. She prepared me as well as she could, and when she could no longer be here, Gahree took over. I promised you, mother, that someday I would understand, and now I do.

Her heart pounded and she blinked again, this time to clear the moisture building in her eyes. Her fingers were wrapped tight in her blankets, and she forced them to unfold. One breath. Another. The muscles in her arms and back loosened. She drew a third breath, and the turning in her stomach eased. Was it possible? It felt right, but—believing Gahree would mean that everything else she had ever believed was wrong. The very history of her people was wrong. The most horrible moment in her life—wrong.

She looked around the room, taking in the space as though it were brand new. Her gaze found the book on her clothes chest, the last thing her mother had given her. The old story that made perfect sense in a way she had never imagined. "I am Draigfen, too," she whispered. "How long has that been true? Since I was born? Did I ever have a choice?"

Of course she had. At any time, she could have changed everything. Stopped flaunting her wit, and arguing with her brothers. Stopped Cleod from joining the Enclave. Kept her place in the kitchen. Given in. Yes, she could have made different choices. But she could not imagine having done so.

Comfort lingered in the small shape and weight of her mother's book tucked into the pocket of her skirt. It brushed her leg with each step she took and seemed to whisper its tale through the fabric and into her skin.

A witch in the woods. A witch in the world. Not a bad thing at all. Maybe the best of things.

The forge was silent. Torrin stood by the shed, his arms loose at his sides, gazing north toward where the ridge of the Spur was a sharp stamp against the sky. He turned at the sound of her approach, and she smiled at him.

"Come to say goodbye?" he asked.

She nodded, a small gesture that lacked conviction. "Yes, I suppose. But it's not really goodbye, is it?"

His smile flashed and he nodded. "Unlikely to be."

She stepped up beside him and turned her gaze toward the mountains as well. They stood shoulder to shoulder.

"Where is your mother, Torrin?"

"Dead."

She glanced over at him. "I'm sorry. I had hoped..."

He shook his head, tipped it toward the Spur. "That she was up there. No. I think she wanted to be. But she was sick a long time. She sent me to apprentice with a smith in Sibora, and she died not long after I went."

"I'm sorry." She looked over at him. So much she did not know about him... All these years of seeing him every day, and she *now* thought of a hundred questions she should have asked. No time now, for that. "Will you stay here? For the new owners? I told Elda I thought you would. But is it the farm that has kept you here, or is it Elda and me?"

"I like this place. But it won't be home without you and Elda."

"Maybe she can come back and work here someday again. I can't think of a reason for her to stay long with Klem in town."

He shook his head. "It will be hard for her to leave there. Just as it would be hard for me to leave here. More difficulty comes with not having a family to trace back than not being able to marry."

"People want to know why you can't."

"And they want references. Which Klem won't provide. For either of us. If I stay on here, I just come along as part of the property. Too bad Klem won't let Elda do the same."

"He won't risk my cooking," Leiel said, and smiled when Torrin actually laughed.

"Not for lack of quality. Just for fear of what you'd add in."

She laughed too. Klem was right to be worried about that. If he knew half of what had gone into the meals he had consumed over the years... She shook her head, fighting back a grin. Then the rest of what Torrin said sank in and the smile faded. "You're not property, Torrin. You or Elda."

"No, but at least if we were we would actually have a place in the world. Low and brutal as it might be."

The words stabbed her. Because they were not bitter at all, just simple and resigned. "Maybe I can do something," she said. "One day. Maybe I can—"

"You can't worry about that, Li. It's not for you to fix, for me or for Elda. We're responsible for ourselves."

She frowned and turned to face him. It was not right that someone so good and solid as Torrin should have so few options of change in his life— all because of the Councils' whims and the vindictive control exerted by the priests of the Sanctuaries. "How is it that Klem can wheedle his way onto the Council, and Cleod can become Draighil, even though they are not Farlan? But you and Elda hardly have a choice about your lives just because you can't publicly trace your lineage?"

"We have choices. They're just not pretty ones. Or ones most people would want."

Leiel slid her hand into her pocket and wrapped her fingers around the book. She had come to give it to him, but standing before him now, it did not seem the right thing to do. Torrin's stories were not her own.

How often had he and Elda sheltered her, like the oak tree in the story? How often had they brought comfort with words and laughter and small kindnesses? Gahree might be the witch in the story, and it might be through her that Leiel would find her own choices, but it was through Torrin's and Elda's examples that Leiel had learned the determination, and the willingness to work hard, that had cleared the path for her future. "I want you to have more."

He chuckled and turned his gaze back to the mountains. "It is good that you do, but anything more is for me to find. Elda too. And we'll do well enough. We always have." He opened an arm to her and she stepped close and let him hug her to his side. "Don't worry about us, Li. We're good at getting along in this world."

"I'm not."

"No. That's why you're going to make yourself a better one."

45

Leiel – 22 years

"I AM GLAD TO SEE YOU TODAY. OUR VISITS HAVE BEEN FEW, THESE LAST YEARS," Gahree said, as she slid her pack from her shoulder and leaned it against her leg. They stood at the base of the Tower, with the sunlight just gliding over the stone laid by Desga Hiage so many centuries ago. Leiel knew the words etched there now. They were part of her the way the old language, Fennar, had become part of her. The way so many things, wished for and regretted, were now part of her. All had led her to this moment. Torrin's simple wisdom. Moonlight on the mill pond. Elda's endless good humor. Klem's passionate rage. The smell of unwashed bodies and spices in the Market. How many stories had she told herself, daydreams and wishes and nightmare tales that had made up all the parts of her and now met in this place?

"I had not planned to come," Leiel said. As for so many months, she had stayed away from Gahree's stall. But the slow acceptance of her truth had grown over the years—not simply, not easily, but certainly enough that it colored Leiel's every thought. Now, with the last rays of the sun bending into the space, she gave up resisting the knowledge.

When had the unbearable become not only tolerable, but welcome? When had she decided to trade her small life for something else? When Gahree told the true story of the Draigon? In the small alley of strange scents? While Torrin had laced his boots? As her father was lowered into the earth? Through the long days and nights between then and now, when her breath jerked within her at each of Klem's calls and beckonings? One decision, or many small ones? *Yes.*

"I could ask you a thousand things—When will it happen? When will I see my mother? Why me? Does it hurt?" She paused. "But in truth, I have only one question—will Cleod survive?" Leiel met Gahree's bright gaze. "He *will* come for me, if I go through with this. Will you promise me that he lives, Gahree, if I come to you on the mountain, and join you in the north?" Leiel drew a breath. "My loss will be for the best as far as Klem and Gial matter. I will be better for losing them as well. But Cleod—he is Draighil, and he is determined. He would say, *honor bound*. Whatever happens, I don't want to live with his death on my spirit."

Green-gold eyes sparked through loose strands of Gahree's dark hair. The sounds of the shuttering market echoed against the Tower stones. A breeze flicked through. "It is well that you should ask me this, Leiel. There are some promises that the asking for is as telling as the keeping of. You see what he was and is and might become, and you care for all those men. I will do my best, within the boundaries of your survival and my own, to keep this one Draighil from finding his end on the height of the Spur."

Leiel drew a breath and nodded. She cocked her head and met Gahree's gaze. "Could he kill you, then?"

"He could kill any of us. Eirar found her end by your friend's sword. The Draighil are as real as the Draigon, Leiel. Their knowledge is great. It is only through care and luck that they have not guessed the truth. Should they ever, they would hunt us until even our memory was wiped from Arnan. Danger exists, Leiel Sower, in allowing all who climb the mountain to survive."

"You have already promised me."

"Your request was anticipated." Gahree laughed, as she picked up her pack. "Cleod is as known to us as you are. Without him, we would not have you. He braced you up in your youth. His choice to join the Enclave left a space in your heart for us to fill."

Leiel stared. "You mean—if he had stayed..."

"You might have learned to bear your suffering in silence—lived your life as many bright-hearted girls do—half alive, surviving, but crushed by the weight of being in a world that values them not at all."

"He would have valued me."

"He *does* value you," Gahree said. "But would that have been enough, wild daughter, if he had stayed? He has made choices. His life has offered you, and us, both loss and gain. And we will do our best to see him through the coming trial. We will risk what he is, that you might become all that you are."

For a moment, Leiel went still, inside and out, then she nodded. Tension eased from her shoulders. "When? Will I see you before?"

Gahree shook her head. "The transformation is not undergone lightly. Time is needed. And strength and power. It may be long months before we meet again, Leiel Sower. Attend the weather. Keep learning. Share your stories." Gahree smiled. "You'll next meet me on the wind."

"Wait." Leiel reached her hands behind her back to where two small books were tucked into the waist of her skirt. She handed them to Gahree. "Will you care for these until then?"

Gahree smiled, and accepted the volumes. "You trust me with all that is precious to you, wild daughter. I shall guard these well, until they can be placed in your hands again."

Leiel nodded. The sight of the books in Gahree's hands was both comforting and terrifying. Her heart beat slower in her chest, and she drew her fingers into gentle fists to keep them from shaking. Stories passed on and long remembered, passed back into good keeping until such time as they were able to be shared again. Leiel turned and walked away before she could reconsider anything.

46

Leiel – 23 years

THE CHANGE SWEPT IN FROM THE WEST, GREEN LIGHT SPLASHING OVER THE clouds as the sun slid below the horizon. She could smell the brittleness of dust on the wind. Her mouth went dry as she leaned against the open frame of the window and looked across the rooftops toward where the line of torridity marched across the distant plains.

So many years since she had first seen such weather roll in... She closed her eyes and breathed in the rising heat. No more cool nights. No more easy days. She laughed. Sound shook through her chest and trembled her entire body. She clutched the window casing, the dust rag in her hand wadded in her grip. A Draigon on the horizon.

Ahead lay months of sweltering oppression. Here in Adfen, the stone buildings would make the impact much worse than anything she had ever experienced on the farm. Weeks of misery, trapped here in the smothering landscape of buildings. But at least the town had its deep, ancient cisterns.

Out in the countryside there would be drought. Failed crops. Illness. Fall would bring hunger. Unless a Sacrifice was made early, before the worst damage could be done.

Downstairs, someone pounded on the front door. She heard it shuddering in its frame. She leaned out the window, trying to glimpse who had arrived, but she could not see far enough around the corner of the house to identify the visitor. She drew back.

Tucking her rag into the pocket of her apron, she slipped out of the bedroom and moved to the top of the stairs, her footsteps masked by the sound of the door creaking open downstairs and an excited voice asking Elda for an immediate audience with Klem. Elda had no time to respond before the man stepped into the entryway, forcing her to step back out of his way. His red vest marked him as a Council messenger. His looked quickly around, his movements jerky and harried. "I must see Klem Councilman. I am here with urgent news. Quickly! The Council requests his immediate presence."

"Yes, sere. If you will wait here I will—"

Elda's attempt to restore decorum was interrupted by Klem's voice demanding to know what was causing the commotion. Leiel stepped back from the edge of the stairs as the study door swung open. She peered around the corner of the wall. Klem came striding out, his lips pressed together and a frown crowding his brows. "I assume there is a purpose to this disruption."

The messenger took a step back and nodded. "Yes, sere. You are wanted in the Tower, Councilman."

"To what duty am I summoned?"

"In regard to the change in the weather, Councilman." The messenger clasped his hands, then unclasped them, waiting.

"The weather?" Klem's shoulders tensed, and the air in the house seemed to gain density. Leiel saw Elda start as the courier's meaning struck her as well.

"The *heat*," the other man said, as though worried he had been too subtle in the delivery of his message.

"Go," Klem said, a new brittleness in his tone. "Tell them I will be there as fast as my horse can be saddled."

Leiel put a hand over her mouth to hold in the scoffing laugh that threatened to escape. The house was in Old Adfen—only a few moments' walk from Adfen Square and the Tower. The only reason a horse was needed was to assure Klem's arrival was made with sufficient showmanship.

"Leiel! Get down here. Saddle my horse and have him ready in five minutes."

She suppressed a snicker and took a breath to settle her face into a more serious expression. She moved quickly to the top of the stairs and down them, in time to see the messenger vanish out the door.

Klem glared up at her long enough to measure her understanding of his demand, then turned and went back into his study.

Hands outstretched to grasp Leiel's fingers, Elda met her at the bottom of the staircase. "The *weather*," she said. "Leiel—that can only mean a *Draigon*."

Nodding, Leiel squeezed the older woman's hand. "I saw it. To the west. Green light and rolling heat."

"Klem will—"

"I know. We'll talk later. I have to get his horse." Leiel hugged Elda and slipped past her.

The short walk to the stable beside the house gave Leiel a few minutes to feel the change in the air. Already it had the weight to it that she remembered from her childhood. Familiar in a haunting way, the very smell of the air held memories. *Ilora leaning into the heat as though greeting an old friend.* Leiel smiled.

It took her only minutes to ready Klem's horse and lead him to the front of the house. Her brother was waiting in the courtyard and the look on his face stopped her before she reached him. The gelding at her side bobbed his head in response to the tension that rolled up her body and into her arm. She loosened her grip and stepped forward, meeting Klem's eyes. His lips were curled into a smile that showed no teeth and his eyes were hard.

"*Draigon Weather,*" he said, and the twisted smile intensified on his face.

She nodded, and handed him the reins. "Do what you must, brother. And don't waste time with gloating. You are, after all, needed at a most important meeting."

He yanked the reins from her grip, and she stepped back as the horse shied a step. Klem moved past her and swung up onto the gelding, reined the animal around and looked down at her. "The most important of *your* life," he said, and kicked the gelding into a run over the cobblestones and out of the courtyard into the street.

"No, brother." She watched him turn onto the street. "That one happened long ago."

The floppy brim of the hat cast Elda's face into shadow. Leiel picked her way through the tiny vegetable garden to where the older woman was salvaging the remains of the pole beans. As carefully as they had watered and tried to protect the delicate plants, most had not survived the onset of brutal heat. But the ones that had would soon be better off.

"He did it," Elda said without looking up. She plucked a shriveled pod and placed it in her basket. Her words were as gentle as her touch on the browned vine.

"He did," Leiel said. She ran her hands back through her hair and lifted it off her neck. "When the Council calls all of Adfen to meet in the Square, I will be the one they name."

Elda sighed and raised her head. Tear tracks streaked her cheeks.

"Elda—no—" Leiel dropped her hair and reached out to put her hand over Elda's on the basket handle. "Remember you told me it was not the stories that caused them to choose my mother?"

"What?"

"You told me that, once."

Elda nodded. "Yes. I remember that."

"You were right." Leiel tightened her fingers, the sweat on Elda's hand mixing slickness with the gentle pressure. "It was not the stories. It was fear of the stories, because they are true."

"You brother is going to have you killed, and you are talking to me about wishtales?"

"I am telling you that I am not going to *be* killed, Elda. Come sit with me under the oak. I have so much to tell you."

47

Cleod – 22 years

"TRAYOR HAS ALREADY LEFT FOR THE CITY. I SENT HIM WHEN THE FIRST SIGNS appeared. But you are of Adfen, and their Council has asked for you by name. Were the decision purely mine, you would not be the one to face Shaa." The very quiet of Soibel's voice spoke to the truth of his words. He clasped his hands behind his back and shook his head, his lined face made somber with concern.

"Why?" Cleod paced toward where the Elder stood on the dais. The click of his boots on the stone floor rang in his ears. What more could he have imagined as the culmination of all his years among the Ehlewer? "Why would you think Trayor better suited to this fight? *This* is the reason I came to you as a boy." To at last be able to pit his skills and his resolve and all the long years of training against the king of the monsters that had for so long plagued Arnan... It felt as he had imagined it would. He was ready. He had proved that with Eirar. A rush of heat filled him. And the woman he was destined to save was Leiel. Of all women—Leiel.

Soibel eyed him with the piercing stare Cleod had grown so used to reading. "No," the elder said at last, thoughtful. "No, I think that I am not, after all, troubled by this series of events. You *have* no conflict in your loyalty, do you, Cleod?"

Laughter was Cleod's response. As wise as Soibel believed he was, the old man had never quite understood. Leiel was the foil around which all choices folded. Cleod *could* keep both his oath to the Ehlewer *and* his promise to Leiel. He *could* become the man he had been striving to be *and* save her at the same time. Then he would have everything. All his dreams would come true at once. And the *need* to do that, made him the only one right to face Shaa.

Soibel's expression shifted; his smile settled easily and his eyes brightened. "Very well, then. I will send you with word. You, not Trayor is to stand for the Ehlewer.

"You have learned all I could ever have wished to teach you, Cleod Draighil. You are truly worthy of that title. Your brothers of the Ehlewer are proud to have you stand for them. When you complete the achievement you have made your great ambition, you will be the greatest Draighil ever to walk Arnan." He stepped down off the platform and clasped his hands on Cleod's shoulders. His grip was still strong despite his age, and it was as though Cleod could feel the old man's pride and vitality flowing to join with his own.

"I will bring the Ehlewer great honor," Cleod said. "This I make as an oath on the Wild Stone."

He watched Soibel's eyes grow wide. But the words had been uttered and could not be called back. Such an oath was binding; to fail meant banishment, or worse. Cleod grinned at Soibel's discomfort at the promise. But Cleod had no intention of breaking it. He had never failed to keep his word, and the fact that it was Leiel he would save on the mountain was proof of that. He could not fail and therefore he would not.

Silence reigned in the chamber for a few heartbeats more, then Soibel nodded and his smile returned. "Go. Stand before the Farlan Council in Adfen. You carry the blessing of the Ehlewer."

Cleod laughed, alight with the pure intoxication of the certain victory that loomed before him. Even the thought of riding through the night to Adfen could not squelch the satisfaction of the moment.

Leiel, I am coming, and soon all our hopes will be realized, and you will be safe forever.

Trayor lifted the cups from the tray the servant boy held and handed one to Cleod. The pottery was cold to the touch. How was that possible in the midst of the Draigon-cursed heat?

"Where did you get this?" Cleod asked as they stepped to the edge of the Tower balcony. Below, the crowd moved like wheat waving in a breeze.

"There is so much about being Ehlewer that you have yet learned to take advantage of."

Cleod chuckled and raised the cup to his lips. Water. So sweet. So cool. It poured through him and he sighed. It had been months since he had tasted anything so fine. "Some Farlan secrets might actually be worth learning."

"Haa! Says the Draighil-trained cefreid." An edge marked the words and hinted that Tray would not soon forget being replaced for this fight.

Cleod ignored the tone and scoffed. "The Ehlewer are no more Farlan than the people who built this tower. We're our own entity, Tray. That's something *you* have yet to take advantage of."

Trayor shook his head and pointed down into the Square. Along the far wall, in front of the selling stalls, were clustered priests and clerics from the most prominent religions of Arnan. The priests of the Sanctuary were front and center in their citrine robes. "More, in the way they are more than just Farlan?"

"Like them, but more still than them. No one expects *us* to forgo women or fine wine."

Trayor laughed and raised his cup to Cleod. "A toast to that, with the coldest water left in the Spur."

Another swallow of the chill liquid and Cleod closed his eyes, taking it in. It had been too long. When had he last had a cool drink? The mountain stream before the welcoming ceremony for the newest Draigre? Yes. It had been that long.

Sound pulsed through Cleod's body and he opened his eyes. From inside the Tower, the drums pulsed again, deep, pushing at the stone and into the air. The crowd stirred as the sound washed over it, only feeling the pulse at first, until they recognized the vibration for what it was. They settled into stillness. From above, the slowing of the crowd's motion was a wave rolling into calm water. Ripples of movement slowed and died to eerie silence. The stillness was preternatural. But then, if not for the unnatural presence of the Draigon, there would be no need for such a gathering. Someday, when he and Tray and the rest of the Ehlewer had conquered the monsters, these gatherings would be only a terrible legend of darker times.

To the day when the Draigon are no more. He drained the cup, the icy water the best toast he could offer.

The roll of drums deepened. He passed the cup to the serving boy and gave his full attention to the ritual unfolding below. Though he had seen this once as a child, nothing was quite as he remembered. Part of it was, of course, his vantage and his position. But more than that, it was knowing that *this time* he was going to be able to save the woman whose name was called tonight. A tingle touched the back of his mind, the hint of contact, faint but skilled. He frowned and looked down into the crowd, saw nothing to catch his attention.

"Cleod, isn't it?"

He turned at the sound of the voice and tilted his eyes down to meet the gaze of the man in the red tunic of the Adfen Council. He was familiar, but it was a few seconds before recognition dawned. "Klem Sower." Of course. Leiel's brother had risen above his born station much as Cleod had.

"Klem Councilman."

Cleod smiled at the correction, made with too much sharpness to be casual. "Yes. Congratulations."

"And to you, Draighil. I would never have dreamed to see you here, given that you once consorted with my sister."

The venom that wrapped around the last word almost carried its own rotten scent. Cleod raised his eyebrows and did not speak.

"Well," Klem said. "We deserving ones find our way to rise above our provincial beginnings. She'll find her reward tomorrow."

Cleod held his gaze. So, it was true. In Adfen, the corruption had reached such a level that the selection of Sacrifices was an instrument of personal vengeance as much as it was a protective judgment on the most dangerous of women. Well, Leiel had always been made to fill both those roles. He turned away as Klem reached up a hand to clamp him on his shoulder, and stepped back up beside Trayor before the hand could land.

Cleod scanned the crowd, seeking Leiel's face. There she was, gazing upward. But before he could catch her eyes, she dropped them, her attention shifting away to the front of the Tower. What was she thinking in this moment? Did she know it was her name to be called today? Was she hoping he could be her salvation? She had to know he had anticipated this moment.

Planned for it. Trained for it.

I will save you tomorrow, Leiel, he thought. I will fulfill every promise I made you.

"Here and now," Cleod said.

Moments passed. The Tower door opened below. Leiel's brother, Klem, walked onto the entry landing at the top of the steps. The ritual words poured from him, slick and crisp as Cleod remembered them from his childhood. He had heard similar in Gwindor, though here, the echo of the past was stronger. The boy he had been, sweating and baffled in the Square all those years ago, could never have imagined the man he had become, all he had achieved. He watched the ritual, not as a spectator, but as a hero, destined to take a vital role in the forthcoming drama.

A tremor shifted through his stomach. How terrible must Leiel's crimes be that Klem would choose to voice the condemnation of his own sister? It was well that she had Cleod here to save her from her reckless actions. Klem neared the end of the ritual phrases, then spoke through the sweltering air, calling out the name of his sister.

Surprise rocked Cleod back a step as Leiel's laughter rang across the Square.

48

Leiel – 23 years

MEMORY WAS LIKE THE PEALING OF A BELL, CRISP AND BRIGHT, AND FOR A moment she was a child again, standing with her family awaiting an announcement that would change all their lives. She remembered the tension that strummed her body like a wire in the wind, and the restless shifting of her brothers beside her. Her father's jaw clenched, his temper brittle as his tone when he spoke. Of them all, only her mother had been relaxed, holding Leiel's hand with a gentle grip that shared no anxiety.

Was this what Ilora had felt, this serene certainty, this relief that something for so long expected was finally coming to pass? Some of it perhaps, but she had not been preparing just to leave a life of repression and fear. There had been a family who loved her and who she must have loved in return. Such a difference as that, Leiel could not fathom. The path laid before her was powerful and offered more than she had ever dared to dream for her life, but for her mother...had that choice truly been Ilora's, or had it been made simply to protect Leiel? Had both their fates been marked by the moment Ilora's name was called?

As though no years had passed, the crowd in Adfen Square swayed and rumbled with nervous anticipation. Unlike that hot day so long ago, there was no uncertainty of outcome in the proceedings. For Leiel, there would be, in today's announcement, as little shock as there had been horror all those years ago.

The first thunder of drums pulsed out of the Tower. All around her came the sound of indrawn breath. The motion of the crowd stilled. Tension was a hollow pounding she could almost see in the air. It flexed and shifted with the rhythm of the rising drums. She breathed it in, rode it. Whether or not they knew it, their energy, their fear and hope, was all for her.

Like the little girl she had been, she stood beside Gial, waiting. The crowd was mostly behind and around them, and she heard the whispers and speculation in the hot air. Who would it be this time? The healer's wayward daughter? The urchin girl who stole food from all the market vendors? Or could one family be so ill-starred as to have two women chosen in as many offerings? Was it possible the Council would select the reckless child of the last Sacrifice?

So much more than possible. Leiel smiled. She knew the change in expression alone would make most doubt her mental soundness. But she knew what was to come. Long years had crawled past to bring her to this moment, and in all the world, the one regret she had was not being able to share with Cleod the truth of what it meant. But she had lost him long ago, to a promise made on her behalf—one that had consumed the boy she had loved and left in his place a man so refined and defined by his position that there was room left in his life for nothing else.

She looked up. On the balcony that wrapped around the waist of the Tower, he stood with another Draighil, Klem, and the rest of the Councilmen. As she watched, Klem stepped up beside him and spoke. Cleod turned and smiled at her brother, and her stomach dropped. For a moment the world tilted, and she forgot that it was her choice to be here, just as it was his to be on the Tower, wearing that uniform. For a moment, what she felt was only the cramping nausea of betrayal. She forced herself not to turn away. No. Whatever had changed inside her, inside him, he was incapable of knowingly turning on her. Klem reached to place a hand on Cleod's shoulder, and he stepped away from the touch, offering his back to her brother.

The air left her lungs, and the last fear she held fled. She was ready now. Ready for the loss and the pain and the possibility of a freedom she had never dared imagine. Their paths had split long ago, but she and Cleod would always be something more than friends. No turning of the world could change that, not even what tomorrow would bring.

A Councilman appeared on the steps of the Tower—Klem. She just looked at him, waiting. If he wanted her to cry or beg, she would no more do that now before him than she ever had. Long since had she given up missing the brother she had once known. And the man he had become—she was free of him, now, in this moment.

"Are you well, Leiel?" Gial asked as Klem began to speak.

She smiled, but not at Gial. It was only now, standing here awaiting the inevitable, that he chose to ask after her wellbeing. The first time in fifteen years. The irony pushed at her smile until a laugh burst forth, rolling and free, just as Klem called out her name.

Leiel

THE STONE BENEATH HER FEET WAS WORN SMOOTH, THE CENTER OF EACH STEP slightly scooped, and polished. How many feet had walked this staircase? For how many hundreds of years? Her mother had climbed it, fourteen years ago. What had she been thinking? Had she felt any fear? Any regret?

Leiel could feel the passage of time with each press of her shoes into the granite as she rose into the heart of the Tower. The guards surrounding her were stiff and silent. What did they think she would do? Try to claw through the walls and leap to her death in the Square? Had her mother been this amused? Maybe. Maybe she too had this knot in her stomach and this rushing in her heart. Was it worth it? Would this be worth it now?

Leiel breathed in the cool air trapped by the Tower's thick walls, such a relief after the months of brutal heat, and she did not allow herself to slip any farther into doubt. Whatever lay ahead was better than what would have been had her name not been called this day.

The first guard halted on a narrow landing. Hot, bright light from a narrow window pierced the dimness, catching dust motes in the air and landing on a heavy door on the inner wall. Without a word, the guard pushed it open and stood aside. A single sharp sweep of his hand indicated that she should enter.

She stepped though the opening, and was greeted by a warm ring of lamplight, and a circle of unsmiling faces. The Councilmen of Adfen, every one of them, seated in a half circle facing the door. Had she ever seen all nine of them in one place before? She didn't even know half their names—only the two or three Klem had brought home to sample Elda's creative cooking. If they had ever guessed just *how* creative some of those recipes had become with Leiel's assistance, they might have arranged a reason for her name to be called sooner.

The stoic faces of the men in front of her should have quashed any amusement she was feeling, but they didn't. Her lips turned in a smile. Not even Klem's near snarl of an expression was enough to diminish her good humor.

Then a man stepped up beside Klem's chair. His face was painted white, and he wore the celadon robes of the Sanctuary. Jaidu. The name came to her in a flash, though if she had been asked only a moment before to call a single priest by name, she could not have dragged one from memory. She was a child again, meeting his eyes, hearing the casual, arrogant horror of his words. The smile slipped from her face, and she stared at him. Had he thought of her at all, between that day and this? Or had she been as unworthy of his recall as she had been of any kindness? Why had she not considered that they must be here in the Tower as well? The priests had always used their position to reinforce whatever the council chose to dictate. From the King's court in Sibora to rooms like this one, and down into the temples of every city and village, the stories passed to the citizens of Arnan were ever the same. And ever half-truths.

"Jaidu," she said, the words slipping through the silence. That was needed—a female voice to take the density from the air and give it life again. "Have you been awaiting this moment for as long as my dear brother, Klem?"

The man's eyes widened. "You are all we have been warned about."

Leiel smiled. She was, in fact, the least of what they feared. But she had come to understand that she represented all of it. "Whatever satisfaction that thought gives you will have to suffice," she said. "You'll not see me sob as I did as a child in your supposed sanctuary."

"Arrogant and twisted, even here." The words came from a nameless councilman, and she glanced at him before turning her gaze to Klem.

"What now, *brother*? Am I to be beaten one last time before you send me to my fate? Or just assaulted with more pointless words?"

"The pointless words appear to be all yours." Klem's lips twisted even more—part smile, part sneer—and the satisfaction in his eyes said more than any speech he might utter. And yet he kept speaking; the words slurred in her ears, as cruel and meaningless as she had expected them to be.

What was any of this for, this meeting in secret rooms and whispering in shadows? These men in this room, and the priests with their righteous public faces—so in control of so many other lives, and so careless with them. What was the purpose of any of this, of all the families broken and all the lives sent astray over the years? To keep these few men and their kind in power? To allow them to feel superior and in control?

A different man was speaking now—was he listing the charges against her? Yes. The reasons for choosing her to send to the Draigon. If only he knew all the things of which she was in fact guilty, not just the paranoid imaginings of her angry brother.

Then a door on the other side of the room opened, spilling in a line of daylight, and another man stepped into the space behind the council's circle. The height. The grace. She had seen him on the Tower balcony, why had she not thought that he would be here also? When had she thought she would see him again? Tomorrow on the mountain? Of course it would be him that the Enclaves sent. He would insist on that. She had hoped it might be another—the man she had seen with him, perhaps. But it never could have been.

"Despite your known guilt, the Ehlewer Enclave has decided to honor you, Leiel Sower. Cleod Draighil will stand with you and act as guardian for your life. Should he succeed in destroying the beast, you will be allowed to return to Adfen, where you will be granted reprieve to live the rest of your life in service to the Sanctuary."

So, should Cleod manage to kill Shaa, she would be a slave in actuality, not just by proxy. She met Cleod's gaze. He stood purposefully straight—poised and controlled. He did not blink, looking back at her. Was this where the training had led him, to a place where he, in fact, felt nothing to see her standing here? She wanted to say his name. But did she, any more, know this man at the edge of the lamplight? Between them stood more than cruel men and haughty religion. Cleod Draighil was not Cleod Woodcutter, the boy she had known.

Could Gahree keep her promise to let him live? Would there be any choice? Cleod had killed a Draigon. He would try with all he was to kill another tomorrow.

"Greet your would-be savior, Leiel," Klem said.

She looked at him, then back to Cleod. "Hello, Draighil."

His gaze held hers, and for a moment she could smell the musty scent of the pond, and hear his calm voice offering her comfort and advice. Then he spoke, and the memories dropped like stones into water. "I greet you, Sacrifice. I will stand for your life despite your crimes."

"My crimes are the things you liked best about me," she said. "Or have you forgotten that you once encouraged them?"

He continued as though he had not heard her. "I will triumph, or I will fall. Your life will only end if mine does. May you find the humility to appreciate my sacrifice in the face of your corruption."

His words flowed over her, and she held still, still to her core, and let them. Beside him, Jaidu smiled. She did not need to look to know the others wore similar expressions. It must be like this for them every time, the gloating in the face of what they supposed was their triumph.

How little they knew.

There was nothing more they could do to her now. Even if they chose to beat her, they could not hurt her. They were done, in this very moment—defeated by their own actions. She could say anything, now. Act as she pleased. Strip naked and dance over the stone floor cursing them if she wished. It all ended tomorrow.

She looked once again at Cleod. Only for his sake did she not explode with laughter. "Chatter, squirrels," she said. "I am the tree you think to hide in, but my leaves know your every move and your scampering gives you away." Then she spread her arms wide and turned, spinning in place in the ancient space until the guards grabbed her arms and dragged her from the room.

50

Leiel

TENDRILS OF HER HAIR CAUGHT IN THE LIGHT BREEZE AND TWISTED AROUND HER face. The window seat was cold. In the Square below, the people were shouting. Their cries swelled and ebbed. So many. It seemed she should be able to feel the pounding of their fists on the stone. She was meant now for the shackles on the ridgetop. What more could they want? They were certainly not there to stop what was coming.

A scrape of leather on stone warned her. She tipped her head to acknowledge his presence and looked over her shoulder at him. She had known he would come—there was nothing else he would do, though she wished with all she was that he had not. She did not want to see him hurt. He looked so proud and strong in the black uniform of his station. Even in the dim light of the Tower room, his eyes were vivid and intense.

"I used to wonder, when I was a child, what this place was for," she said before he could speak. "I never understood until that day the Council called my mother's name. All these years, coming here for Fourth Market... Always, this place was waiting for me." She turned, looked out the window so he could not see her expression. "You should not have come."

"I am the only one who should have come," he said, and the determination she remembered so well was steel in his voice.

She closed her eyes. How she wished he was not so strong-willed, that his resolve was less than perfect. But then he would not be Cleod. Not the boy she had once so depended on. Not the man she might once have loved. She drew a breath, rose, and turned to face him. "No," she said, keeping her voice quiet so he had to want to hear her, had to focus his attention. "It's too late. I don't want you to die trying to stop this."

"You are so sure I will be the one to die." He stepped closer and she could feel the physical strength of him.

She drew a breath. There was so much that she knew now that he did not. So much that she wished she could share. But they were not children anymore. They had both chosen their paths and, though parallel, they could not be any farther apart.

"I don't need you now," she said. "I needed you through all the years you spent working toward this moment—when you could be the hero and strike back at the harm that was done to me so long ago. But you cannot heal the harm done since by the fact that I have been alone, without the one person I thought I could trust, through all these long years."

He stared down at her. Tension rippled through his stance, and his jaw tightened. Anger, she thought, and disbelief.

"I am *Draighil*," he said, and the determination in his tone deepened, and she knew there would be no reaching him. "I promised you I would be. I promised you I would kill Draigon for you—and now when I do so, it will *save your life*. I can *save* you, despite what you must have done to earn this."

"Despite what I have done?" She half-gasped in a breath and choked on a laugh. But no anger came. "No. I don't need saving." She wanted so much to tell him the truth, but even if she could, it would not bridge the distance between them. The best she could hope for was to point him away from this path of certain destruction, or, failing that, see him to the end of it alive. "Not now. I needed saving years ago. I needed saving all the long years of growing up without my mother. In a family full of men who resented everything about me. Who hated my very existence. Who blamed me for what happened to my mother. I needed you then, but the road you chose led you away from me. I understand why. I know what you have always wanted to do for me. But I am asking you not to. I am not a dog in need of rescue. Don't stand for me on the Spur tomorrow, Cleod. We lost each other long ago."

She spoke softly, her words calm, but she feared he would not hear the truth of her forgiveness. One look into his eyes and she realized he had only heard indictment in what she had said. She turned away, back toward the window, so she would not have to see the hurt grow in his expression. He had only done what he thought would help her.

"What are you talking about?" he demanded. His fingers dug into her shoulder, and she gasped as he pulled her back around so she had to look at him. "I have *always* been your friend. Why else do you think I have done this? How can you tell me you don't need saving? They are going to give you to *Shaa*, Leiel! They are going to see you burned alive, *just like your mother!*"

"Yes." She reached up and wrapped her hands around his and squeezed gently. "Yes, like Ilora. And now I know *why*. It's *all right*. I must go. I am ready to go—more than willing. They need me to go. It's too dangerous for me not to."

They were the Draigon, who awaited her, who needed her, and those like her, to continue their survival. *They* were not the Council. *They* were not her brothers, or the people in the Square below who begged for her death. But that is what he would hear in her words, and she could not correct his assumption. Old gods, how she wanted to tell him the truth! But how could she? He was Draighil to his bones. Trained and determined. He already half-believed that she had deserved the fate the Council had chosen for her. What could she say that would make him understand that she had chosen it, too?

"People are dying," she said. "I have to go to Shaa. Don't do this. Too much will be lost if you do."

His fingers bit into her shoulders but she held his gaze and refused to acknowledge the pain. He had never meant to hurt her, and he did not mean to do so now.

After a long moment, he released her, but he did not take his eyes from her. His expression was hard and hurt. She could taste his resolve in the chill air. "I am Draighil. Not just what I do, but what I am. The Draigon must be faced, and I was meant to do it. I *am* meant to do it. I will kill it, Leiel. I must. I don't understand why you would ask me for anything else. I can keep you alive. Why wouldn't you want that?"

"Alive for what?" she whispered, as if anything she could say would change his mind. "You *are* Draighil. This is what you will always do. You made a promise to slay Draigon, and you are going to keep it. But there is no room, in doing that, for the little girl you made that promise to."

Where had it gone—the forthright caring that had been so easy between them? Her throat was dry and so were her eyes. She had long since cried herself out. The last thing she wanted was to see him in pain. "Please let me do this. Let me go. I have to do this. Any other choice is unthinkable."

He took a step back, and she could taste his rage in the air before it erupted. *"Living* is unthinkable?"

"What I have been doing all these years is not *living,* Cleod. It is survival. Yes, I have food and drink and clothing, but I am not *free* to learn or do or say the things I wish to learn or do or say. The things that make life worth living. I would rather go to the mountain a thousand times than return to Klem's house." Again, she considered telling him everything, easing both his heart and her conscience. But he was so *changed.* And the Draigon were more vulnerable than she could ever let him know.

Her mother must have felt like this, the last time she had seen her, the last time she had hugged her. But speaking the truth was impossible, just as it had been then. To do so was to endanger all of Arnan—any hope for the future. Any chance the women of Arnan had of ever regaining their power and their freedom. Any possibility that old knowledge would remain safe enough that it might someday be released again into a world renewed and once again awake to hope.

"Don't fight for me. *Please.* Save your training for someone who is not ready to leave this place." He had always been the one thing that she would have continued to live this life for. But he was not hers and never could be. The Enclave had claimed the boy she had loved. "This is not how our story ends," she said, looking up at him, trying to see through the years and the lies that now separated them, see through to the boy who had once offered her comfort in the most awful moment of her life. "This is not a children's tale. Endings aren't happy just because we wish them to be. Ending are not endings at all. You cannot stop what is going to happen—because you are not the writer of my story."

"What does that mean?" he demanded. "When did you learn to speak in riddles? This is not a fable. This is your life—*my* life."

"That is *your* story, not mine." The legend he had carved into the bedrock of his self included her, but only some dream of her, not the person she was or the one she wanted to be. Even were the world to turn and spin a web of change over tomorrow, there could be no story written now that included a life together for the two of them. Choice had changed forever that possibility.

Regret. She had never known the meaning of the word until this moment.

"I loved you," she said, and watched the past tense of the words strike across his face like a blow. She held his gaze a moment then slowly backed away, putting as much distance between them as the small room would allow.

For a moment he stood motionless and returned her stare. Then his expression hardened, but not in the way she had hoped for. Not with disgust or rage or hatred, but with renewed resolve. The last of her hope fled. He would go through with it. Try to fight, to rescue her. Try to prove that he was still worthy of her love and she of his. Though her heart was melting in her chest, she did not speak, and at last he turned and struck the door with his fist to call the guards.

She closed her eyes as it slammed behind him.

51

Cleod – 22 years

HE STUDIED HIS REFLECTION IN THE BLACK WINDOW. CLEOD TOOK A MOMENT to appreciate the image he presented in the glass. Flawless, lean, and well trained. In all his imaginings of this day, no vision had ever been as perfect as this moment, with sunrise but moments away, and he, the champion awaiting battle.

His reflection dimmed slightly as the outline of the Spur became visible against the first grey tones of the morning sky. The eastern horizon would be starting to streak red, and he wished the window of his tower room faced that direction. On such a day as this, one should step forth and greet the sun in all its glory. Today he would accomplish everything that he had dreamed of achieving. He had turned his life over to the Enclave for this day, and he would not fail. No matter what Leiel said she wanted.

How had the fearless, hopeful girl he had known grown so cynical? What had happened in the years they had been apart to make her so hopeless that she would beg him *not* to save her?

On the stone floor, his boots clicked with smooth authority as he crossed the space to lift his sword harness from the bed. He pulled the straps over his shoulders and settled the familiar weight across his back. Ancient, the blade had been bloodied by Draighil generations past, and today it would find its way into the heart of yet another beast. The edges of his vision shimmered, and he drew himself straighter to settle the onset of Gweld before it could blanket his mind. Time enough for that in the eye of the storm to come.

When he had descended into Gweld in training, always the one he stood before to guard was Leiel. In his mind, she was the only woman who had ever waited in the Draigon's path. Not even her mother, who he had actually witnessed being led in chains up the mountain, had risen in his imagination. That today Leiel really would stand in danger of annihilation seemed only to be the proper turning of fate. This day was meant to be, had been since they were children laughing together in the schoolyard.

If the woman he had spoken to yesterday had baffled him, had looked at him with something akin to pity, he knew with all that he was that this day had been predestined by something greater than them both. As the Farlan had so many generations ago come to free Arnan from the terrible reign of the Draigon of old, so would he, as trained warrior of their chosen protectors, bring down a monster bent on the destruction of order.

"Cleod Ehlewer, Draighil," he said aloud. "From cerfeid to Draighil despite all odds. You may not think you want my help, Leiel, but it has been mine to give you for longer years than you can know." She was trying to protect him. It was the only thing that made sense. Always, they had looked out for each other, and now she could not face the thought that he might die in an attempt to save her.

He smiled. He had no intention of dying. Or letting her. He carried a Draighil blade on his back, and had mastered the Gweld at a level of nuance Soibel said had not been seen in generations. A far cry from the naive woodcutter's son he had once been—from someone who needed to fear the monsters that had haunted Arnan for too long. Not only would he kill this beast, but he would kill them all. Wipe their very existence from the memory of future generations. They would name him the greatest Draighil to have ever lived, and he would stand proud—and Leiel would be beside him.

The light from the window now wore a tint of gold. He slipped on his gloves as he walked back to stare out the dirty glass at the ridge line of the Spur. It was time. A light breakfast, then the climb up the mountain. Leiel would walk behind him, and he would keep her safe. When it was over, they would speak of all the years between them, and he would find a way to help her overcome all the flaws that had led her to this day. Together they would be a true symbol for others that the Draigon were not to be feared, that correct action and strength of will would lead them all to a world where the Draigon were no more.

He opened the door of the room and stepped out onto the landing. As the Tower stairs spiraled down beneath his feet, he pulled his mind inward, pushing back his elation. Time enough for that when he stood victorious over the city with Leiel at his side.

52

Leiel – 23 years

THEY HAD INSISTED ON CHAINING HER, THOUGH SHE OFFERED NO RESISTANCE. Klem stood beside the Tower guardsman and smiled as the key turned on her wrists. Had she not long ago accepted Klem's hatred of her, and mourned him, she would have cried in the face of his obvious satisfaction in that moment.

The shackles weighted her arms and rattled in the hot air as she walked. At least her feet remained free for the climb up the Spur. Her spine tingled, unease tightening her shoulders. Knowing what was to come and actually walking toward it were different things.

Ahead of her, Cleod's back was straight, the sword in its harness perfectly balanced across it. The crystal on the hilt gleamed dully. Had her hands been free, she would have reached for the stone sewn into the lining of her pocket—the one he had given her so long ago. The children they had been....

She saw no fear in him, only an anticipatory tension reined by the grace his training had taught him.

Such certainty. Such loyal passion. An ache started under her ribs, rolling through her and filling her eyes with tears. He was magnificent before her, strong and skilled, his confidence evident in the power of his stride. If she raised a hand, she could touch him, but he was not here *with* her, only *for* her—for the girl he remembered, the child who had longed for his advice and warm laughter. The girl she had grown into had respected his pride and the strength of his will. The young woman she was now wished she could speak to him in a way he would understand, wished the person she *was* held as much value to him as the one she *had been*.

"I never could shift your will," she said.

He glanced at her, but the smile she hoped for did not appear. "A lesson you are just now remembering."

She met his gaze. Was he still in there, in this regal stranger, the boy who had offered her warmth and humor in her darkest days? "A lesson I learned too late," she said. Had she understood sooner how the threads of loyalty wove through every bit of him, could she have changed this outcome? Could she have said something? Done something? Shaped his choices in such a way that this day would never have come? Too late now to wonder at what might have been. So young they had been, and she so torn by grief. What did either of them know then? How little, it seemed, did they know each other now.

She smiled at him, to honor the memory of the friends they had been, but he turned away, and she was left only the fine-carved presence of the man he had become and the unreconciled heaviness in her heart.

53

Cleod – 22 years – Autumn, 1179

UNLIKE THE FOREST WHERE HE HAD KILLED EIRAR, THE JUTTING ROCKS OF THE Spur ridgeline had nothing to block the view of the Draigon's arrival. It came out of the north, dawn light flashing over the side of its body, the thunderous beat of its wings trading brightness for shadow along its length. Straight on without swooping or banking it came, as though the shifts in wind and the rising air currents caused by the mountains were nothing. Its wings were leathery solid, not translucent as Eirar's had been, and its body was watery-dark, scales glistening as it drew close and filled the sky.

Beside him, the rattle of chains was just audible over the great wings pounding the air, and Leiel's voice came to him, hoarse now with panic. "For the love of all things, Cleod, *run*! I don't want to witness your death."

"You won't," he said, reached back, and slid his sword from its sheath. The grey crystal that crowned the hilt caught the morning light as he stepped forward to meet the monster.

The Draigon slammed down onto the ridge with a force that shattered rock and shook loose boulders to tumble down into the valley. The last sweep of wings scattered debris into the air. Cleod swayed with the impact but did not flinch back.

The beast was huge—so much larger than Eirar that the white Draigon could have stood at full height under this one's wing. Was this Shaa? The Draigon he had seen as a child had burned red against the sweltering sky. This creature was ink dark, its green-gold eyes bright as it tilted its head on its curved neck—and glared.

Then the Draigon drew breath like a tornado sucking at the ground and began to glow. The scalloped lines between the glistening black scales pulsed gold and darkened. Copper to yellow to forge-hot orange, internal fire lit the creature in a roll of color that began around the eyes and moved wavelike down its entire body. Even the wings coursed with seams of red heat. It was horrific. It was beautiful. The beast was no longer dark—it had been reborn as fire.

Cleod gasped. Draigon heat. All comfort was sucked from the air as the beast pulsed with fire. Around it, the few low trees and shrubs began to smolder, and the scrub grasses blackened and crisped. Heat swept like the shadow of a passing cloud over the ridge and rocked him back. He shifted his balance and met the creature's eyes. Shaa, indeed.

"Welcome, monster." He heard Leiel scream his name, and then he let fly his senses as Gweld claimed him.

The horrible magnificence he had seen with his eyes was a glimmer on glass compared to the diamond precise energy that greeted him as his mind expanded into trance. Energy streamed from the creature across the entire range of his senses. The air rippled with ghostly flames. The earth trembled. His ears rang as though iron bells had been struck. From the place his body occupied, to the expanded realm of high connection, everything drew to focus and responded as Shaa opened his mouth and roared.

Sound and breath pounded Cleod. He smiled, bent his knees, and charged.

The Draigon did not move but to bow its neck until he was almost upon it, then it shifted, one step, a single beat of the mighty wings moving air and the earth under Cleod's feet. He leapt and landed rolling as the shale ground where he had stood skittered away down slope. His perception burst outward and the battle fully engaged.

The beast was too large to be as agile as Cleod, and the advantage he took from that difference he used ruthlessly. Heat scored over him, beating at him even through the Draigon leather. He struck out and missed. The ground rumbled with the steps of the Draigon. Engage and retreat. Step close and dodge. Cleod breathed smoke. Sweat streamed over his body and through it all he could hear Leiel's pleading cries. They penetrated the Gweld in a way no other voice ever had. He forced back her words, rode smell and sight and heartbeat as he stepped forward and struck again.

His sword found its target, the Ehlewer blade sliced hard through the meat of the beast's hind leg. Roaring, the creature turned on him, and the rock beneath his feet began to smoke. Gweld guided him, the monster's intentions flaring like signal fire through the wavering air in the harrowed instant before they were enacted. He moved, ahead of thought or planning, springing away as the stone turned to slag behind him. Fire followed as the foliage around him burst into flame. He tumbled, flung free the blade to avoid slicing himself open, and gained his feet a heartbeat later.

The monster's tail lashed. Cleod leapt again, somersaulted over the strike, landed rolling, and regained the fallen sword.

The beast took flight. The impact of down-swept air knocked Cleod flat. Gasping, he rolled onto his back, facing the creature as it rose, impossibly rose like the smoke billowing from the mountain top, the Draigon's smolder-scaled bulk blocking out the sun.

"Gods of old! Cleod stop! She'll kill you!" Leiel's voice cut the smoking air. Hoarse desperation tinged her voice, and he recognized the words though they held no logic. "She'll kill you!"

Above them, Shaa folded her wings and dropped with the grace of a falcon striking. Gweld screamed, but the Draigon's intentions were muddled, as though it held a dozen thoughts at once, as though all motion was possible, any outcome.

As though the beast were in Gweld with him.

But that was not possible. No animal could join the trance. He braced himself and prepared to move.

In the last instant before impact, the giant wings snapped wide. Air caught the great expanse, and the smoldering bulk lifted even as the legs struck down and out, shuddering the ridge top. Cleod dropped, rolling. The melting heat swept over him, and as he started to raise his head to mark the Draigon's direction, pain ripped up his back. He tumbled over the rocks, rolled by the claw that had torn the Draigon leather and his flesh.

Unable to hold back a cry as the hot rocks blistered his exposed skin, he scrambled upright and found himself eye to eye with the fiery monster. Green-gold eyes danced with reflections of fire, and its claws exploded stone as it stepped toward him. Beast. Killer. Shaa. *She.* Leiel's words registered like a blow. Still she was screaming. But not at him this time, at the

Draigon. At the monster sent to kill her. And her words held knowledge. His mind stumbled with shock.

He recognized his mistake, his slip in attention, as he made it. The blow swept him off his feet. The smoldering tail cracked across the back of his legs and sent him tumbling. Fire erupted over his body as he crashed through the flaming brush. He fought for consciousness as his skin blistered and his mind spasmed, thrown from the fighting trance and into the reality of a flaming nightmare.

The world was on fire. *He* was on fire. Above him, Shaa's body was awash with sparks. They rained over him until even his hair was smoking. Skin charred under his clothing, the once protective leather now serving only to hold in the ravaging fire. Screaming. His own.

Gweld.

With an act of desperate will, he shifted his mind away from the pain. Though his throat still gave voice to the expanding agony he flung himself back into the fighting trance.

Nothing changed.

His suffering followed him, as though guided by a mind other than his own. He cried out across all the planes of his senses as he realized what he fought, and that the pain was never going to end.

54

Cleod – 23 years – One month after Shaa

"ALL THE GODS PARDON—CLEOD—CAN YOU HEAR ME?"
Through the rubble of pain under which he was buried, Cleod heard the words like water dripping through cracks. They struck his mind, damp and tingling, and he flinched against them, though he could not actually move. Tray? Was it Tray? It seemed it might be. But why was Trayor here in the place of suffering? Why was anyone here? This place was his alone—this place he had made with his failure and his pain.

"Cleod—it—it's Tray. They wouldn't let me see you before this. They said it was too soon, that you needed time to heal."

The watery voice kept seeping through. Then a blunt noise scraped over his senses—a chair moving? Something brushed over his wrist and his entire body jerked as his mind exploded into Gweld.

No control. No precision. His consciousness erupted, pulling in wild colors and glimpses of the places far and near. He saw a man sprawled helpless on a hanging bed, face down, swathed in bandages and slathered in thick ointments. A street rattled with the everyday life of travel and trade. Rain fell in a green garden. The man in the bed thrashed and a black-clothed man seated at his side released his grip on the patient's wrist, a look of horror on his face. A dog and a boy raced up an alleyway to beg sweets from a baker's back door. A mother sang to her baby daughter in a voice laced with tears. The man on the bed screamed and the sound ripped Cleod from trance.

He was shrieking, a high-pitched whimpering that brought more voices into the place where he dwelled. They banged and echoed over his awareness, and he cringed back into the deepest corner of himself.

"Did you touch him?"

"Only lightly—his arm—"

"He felt you—that is good. Part of him knows you are here. We were not certain whether he could truly sense anything outside himself. He has not reacted to any of us, not to words or touch. It is good you have come. You can reach him where we cannot."

"Gods of old—will he live? The burns—"

"There is hope. He survived on the mountain and the trip here. We'll move him to Sibora as soon as it is safe to do so. The Healers there can do much for him if his mind can be salvaged. His body will heal. It's his mind that is in danger."

"Gweld," the voice that might be Trayor said. Where were they, this place where everything was blazing weight and fear?

"Yes," The other voice, female and light. "He slides in and out of it. Those trained can almost hear it happening, so well-honed is his skill. We fear he has lost sense of what is real and what is trance. The Gweld may be an easier place to abide given how painful this body has become to inhabit."

"I saw it," Trayor said. "He slipped just now—into it—but he was not in control of it. I could not follow the vision."

"It is well that you could not. I cannot think it would lead anywhere not fearful," the woman said.

"Cuila—can you use it? Would it ease—?"

"No." The woman again. "The smoke damage to his lungs is too great."

Silence held a moment. "You must do what you can to see him back to himself," a third voice, this one male, echoed through the debris that covered him. Cleod jerked from the brush of it against his mind.

"There! He heard you." Trayor's tone was hopeful and sharp, cutting him like ice could burn a bare hand. Ice—burns—he remembered fire— and a smoke that smothered all rational awareness. Where had that been? Where was he now? Pain crushed him and he shuddered, formed a name on his lips that fled before he could utter it and fell, fell into the darkness under the collapsed wall of his will.

55

Cleod – Two months later

"THE WASTE OF THIS!" SOIBEL SAID.

Cleod looked up at the man through the fading haze of the ercew. Where was he? Back in the bed? Oh yes. A male healer and two other men had dragged him back here from the tavern. He remembered his toes splashing through street slop. He had not felt any pain as they handled him back into the bed.

"We found him drunk in the alehouse down the street. If we leave him alone at all, he finds his way there. With the illness still sweeping the city, we don't have the people to watch him every moment." The female healer's tone was crisp.

"You've tried weaning him from the drink?" Soibel was looking down at him, and the motion of his mouth as he spoke seemed out of sync with the words Cleod was hearing. He smiled up at the Elder Draighil and rolled his head back into the comfort of the pillow.

"The medicines needed for that to work would slow the healing of the burns. He'll never walk upright again if we don't finish the treatments."

Soibel looked to the woman. Cleod followed his gaze and smiled at her as well. She did not look at him. With a snort, he said, "Leave off." The words slopped out of his mouth and neither acknowledged that they had heard him.

"The ercew won't slow the healing process?"

The woman shook her head. "It won't. But I can't promise it won't harm him in other ways. He has a craving for it now. And little interest in anything else."

"Just see to his body. The Ehlewer will take care of the rest in time."

"Won't matter," Cleod said, and this time his words were loud enough that they both looked at him. The frown that bent Soibel's brows reminded Cleod of the squirrels he had watched in the woods as a boy—twitchy and easily irritated. "Chttttt," he said.

"What won't matter, Cleod Ehlewer?"

"No," Cleod said. "Not him. Not Ehlewer. None of it matters. You can't win. They're not beasts. They're wild, wild minds." He laughed, and the sound choked him until he closed his eyes again. "I'm killed," he said. "I'm a killer."

"What is he saying?" Soibel asked.

"Nothing that makes sense," the male healer said. "He's been ranting for weeks. I am not sure his mind isn't already broken, Elder. This damage reached beyond his body."

"We're *killers!*" Cleod shouted. He cracked his eyes in time to see Soibel start back. "Draighil are murderers. The Councils are murderers. All the priests and healers and teachers are *murderers!*"

"*Quiet* him," Soibel said. "Drug him. Gag him. Tie him down if you must."

"Quiet. Quiet," Cleod said. "*Abdication.* I renounce loyalty to you, Elder of the Ehlewer. I renounce *my place* among you. Quiet you go, now. Quiet we all go." He sucked in air and exhaled it as a sob, turning his face into the pillow as his body shook.

"There's nothing to be done, if his mind does not shift. If his courage has fled, he has no place left in the Enclaves." The male healer did not even try to bury his words in a whisper.

"Not this one." Soibel's voice was firm. "Courage is never something he'll lack. It's his loyalty that must be measured. It might be a mercy to kill him now. Those wounds—will he ever be whole?"

"In time." The woman's words held the same tightness as both the others. Her voice pitched higher into Cleod's awareness, and he focused on her.

"Kill me?" he asked, but no one replied. Had he spoken at all? Did it matter if he had?

Soibel was talking again. "His mind will be ours to repair. We know what belongs in it."

"There are months ahead before that even matters, Elder."

"Heal him as well as you can. I will send you his sword. Having it close may help him recall his purpose." Soibel's words were distant, fading echoes in Cleod's mind. "I'll speak to the others about what is to be done with him."

Somewhere a door closed, and he was alone again in the rising pain as the ercew's warmth faded.

56

Cleod – Midwinter, 1180

"**N**o."

It was the first word he had managed in days that wasn't slurred, but it was the first one he had cared about, so that was appropriate. He sat on the edge of the bed and tried his best to stay upright as pain lanced through his hips and back. He gripped the edge of the frame. It was splintery beneath his hands, not the polished lumber of the healer's rooms, this bed in the dark corner above the tavern. He preferred it, as he preferred his drink and his solitude.

Soibel stood over him, chin down at a severe angle, pale eyes sharp and unblinking. "You speak as though you have a choice. You're Draighil, Cleod, no matter the problems you have at the moment. You'll return to the Enclave. It is only there that we can truly give you the care you deserve."

Cleod matched the stare, though his head swayed a little on his neck. "No," he said again. "Ehlewer healers aren't half as talented as those priests you left me with. There's some skill here."

"We have what is needed to take care of you."

"You have my death."

"Cleod—"

"You think I don't know?" Cleod's fingers bit into the wood at the edge of the mattress until his forearms burned with tension. "You want me hidden away. You want me gone. Banished by a broken oath. Banished under the ground if necessary. Down in the dirt."

"We want to help you."

"You want to help yourself. I won't go. I'm finished with you—all of you—and your half-truths. Go back. You can't make me."

Soibel's eyes narrowed. "I can. Your boldness is of no consequence in this, Cleod Draighil. Once in the back of a wagon, you'll have no choice in the matter."

"You think?" An act of pure will, dredged from the pit of his roiling stomach, dragged him upright. He gained his feet, swaying, but determined, and standing a half-head above the Elder. "And just who will force me into a wagon?" He took a step closer to Soibel. "You? These priests? Did you bring Tray? Will you risk his health to contain me?"

"Be reasonable. We are your people. We will take care of you."

"You'll see me dead rather than let me go."

"We would have you back among us, whole. And if not—"

"I won't return." A slur Cleod could not control marred his words. His vision tilted, but a spark of clarity pierced the fog of pain and drink that had bent him senseless for so many weeks. He wanted a drink. Needed a drink. But he needed this moment more—to make certain there was no mistake. He would not go back. No matter what it cost him, he was no longer of the Ehlewer. "You'll have to kill me here. Even in this state, I can kill half the Enclave, old man. I'm your best. Your legend in the making. I'm the first real Draighil in four generations. I survived meeting Shaa, Elder Soibel. If you want me dead, you'll have to do it here in public and where I will shout your secrets to the world as you gut me."

Soibel looked back at him, no surprise in his expression. "You leave me little choice but for me to count you as an enemy." His words were steady, but some of the color had left his cheeks.

"Do that." Cleod heard the rolling in his words, wished for a moment he could hold it back, then smiled. No. It was as much a part of him now as the burn scars branded over his hips—the drink. The drink and the knowledge too harsh to bear without it. Leiel was dead. Killed by the monster he had not been half-prepared to battle. A monster that was so much more than a simple beast ruled by hunger. The Ehlewer had to know. All the years and generations of Draighil—some successful, most dead—the Enclaves had to know there was more to the Draigon than just senseless destruction. And yet they had kept it from him—from all the candidates. Boys came to the Enclaves, claimed their place as Draigre and slaved and hoped and suffered for the title of Draighil; but the prize they sought was based on a lie. The Draigon were humanly intelligent. How many Draighil had died because that knowledge was not shared? How many women had fallen to the monsters because the Enclaves were stingy with their knowledge? "They have minds like ours," Cleod said. "Why was this never shared?"

"Who would believe it?" Soibel turned away. "You?" He demanded over his shoulder. "With your mixed loyalties and your need to face the beasts? What good would it have done to tell you the enemy you sought was as clever as you?"

Like the Draigon heat that had burned Cleod, rage erupted through him, shaking his body and slamming his heart within the walls of his chest. His mind was hot, pressing the edges of his skull, heavy and thunderous. "Had I known—I could have saved her!" Cleod shouted. "I will kill you where you stand before I let you try to force me back."

"You would ruin us all rather than return." Soibel said without facing him.

"You'll not have my name to use as lure for some other fool. Try to take me—or kill me—and I'll give you a spectacle to rival the selection of a Sacrifice. I'll bring down the legend of the Enclaves and leave your vaunted pride in shreds." The last words blurred over his tongue, but he knew they were warning enough. Broken though he was, he was strong enough to make good the threat.

Soibel looked at him then, just a glance over his shoulder, and Cleod read the measurement in it. Yes. There was no need for the Enclave to fear. He would be dead soon enough, drinking himself to death before the Elders ever needed to worry about him again.

Cleod spoke, his voice raw and brittle. "Go away, old man. I am only a threat if you make me one."

The Elder turned away without another word and pulled open the door. It closed with a click behind him. Cleod stood for just a moment more before allowing himself to slump to the floor beside the bed.

He was free. At least for now. He could do just what he wanted—crawl into a mug of ercew and drown out the sound of Leiel's screams and the triumphant roar of the victorious Draigon.

57

Cleod – 38 years

Cleod rode up beside Kilras as the caravan rocked and clattered its way into the new camp south of Melbis. The dust was lessened some by the hard-packed nature of the more frequently used road. He still pulled down his brekko so Kilras could read his lips over the din.

"Market Rules? Or Resting Rules?" Cleod asked.

Kilras also lowered his brekko, took a moment to shove back his hair as it flew wild around his face in the silty wind. "Market. Take Jordin and Nae and settle yourself with a bath and food. Find rest as needed—or whatever it is Jordin prefers these months. The rest of us'll set the camp and the market wagons on the fairgrounds. You three'll have perimeter watch tonight, so don't consider this a favor."

Jordin and Nae—not the two Cleod would have chosen to spend night duty with. The former was prone to distraction, even known to create it for himself through foolish liaisons while on watch. Nae, his worn joints more painful with every year, had simply lost all sense of urgency in his work. It was Kilras's generous nature that kept both of them on—the same nature that had taken Cleod in at his worst and trained him in the arts of protection, despite his wounds and failure at his once chosen profession. Like the lost man Cleod had once been, Jordin and Nae had nowhere else to go.

Cleod grunted and shook his head. "They will be thrilled to hear they at least get first rides in the brothels. I'll be the only sober man on watch."

"Live with the responsibility. You know I'm never sad to know you're sober."

"You're not expecting any trouble, clearly."

"In Melbis? Two weeks early for the Festival?" Kilras shook his head and grinned. "The only worry is that the city'll lack the supplies to keep us for an extended stay. Tonight, I expect you could all fall asleep on watch and we'd not need even worry about a rabbit crossing in."

Cleod grunted. "You best hope a rabbit is all that's bound to cause trouble tonight with this hand-picked batch on the line." Cleod pulled his brekko back into place and reined the grey gelding around to seek the other chosen watchmen.

Nae's response to Cleod's news of their assignment was a predictable snort of disgust, and Cleod grinned as he left him. Jordin's excitement was almost pitiful. He was already planning assignations with the town's ladies for hire.

The packed-dirt streets were not busy as Cleod made his way to the livery. Kilras was correct—they were far too early to have to worry about the usual harvest-season crowds. Melbis was a waypoint for most of the year, a stopover for traders on their way to more prosperous cities of the middle mountain wine region, or the southern ports. Only during harvest, when the mountain herbalists and the horse traders made their rare trip into the town, did the place become lively with visitors.

The liveryman came out to greet Cleod as he swung down off Kicce. A few moments of negotiation arranged the gelding's keeping, and after currying the big grey and assuring he received a ration of grain, Cleod collected his saddle bags and headed for the two-story hostel in the center of town.

The Nest was one of the oldest buildings in town, and one of the few made of stone. Built from rugged Spur granite, with real glass windows, it had a wide porch not connected to the boardwalks of the buildings on either side of it. It was one of the few places that, for all the pain associated with such things, reminded Cleod of home. Even the smell was right, cold stone and old wood. The inn keeper nodded in recognition and turned the register book for him to sign.

"The room farthest from the staircase?"

Cleod smiled and nodded. "Yes, Lorrel. Thank you. And have you heard anything about the Seebo Ferryman and his family? There was damage—"

"Semmio? Yes, he and his wife came through several weeks ago. They said there had been a fire. They were traveling toward the coast."

A small knot that had lodged in Cleod's chest since he had seen the destruction at the river eased at that news.

The innkeeper passed Cleod a key on a leather tab and tipped his head down the hallway. "I'll have a fire lit in the stove in the poit room. We just scrubbed it down. Your timing is right."

"That's all I could wish for," Cleod said as he slung his bags over his shoulder. As he turned, a flash of green through the window caught his eye. A woman, with worn skirts, and a tattered pack marked with a stripe of emerald brocade down the center, was crossing the street away from him. She stopped and turned her head to watch a wagon pass in front of her, and Cleod's heart jumped in his chest. Brown hair pinned high, strong cheekbones and a sloping nose in face, not beautiful, but rugged and hardy.

Tendrils of her hair caught in the light breeze and twisted around her head. She was seated on the bench built beneath the open window, her gaze on the crowd that thronged the square below. She tipped her head. She had heard the sound of his approach. Her gaze met his across her shoulder.

"I used to wonder, when I was a child, what this place was for," she said before he could speak. "I never understood until that day the Council called my mother's name. All these years, coming here for Fourth Market... Always, this place was waiting for me." She turned back to the crowd raising their voices in the plaza. "You should not have come."

"Leiel?" Cleod whispered. He stood frozen at the window of the old inn as the woman started across the street, her back once again fully to him. A wagon passed between her and the building in which he stood. He spun for the door. By the time he burst onto the porch, hurtling into the street, she was nowhere in sight. He stood in the suddenly too bright street for a few seconds, then followed the way the stranger had been walking. As he crossed to the row of buildings on the opposite side, his gaze skipped over every person he saw, but none was the woman he sought. The businesses before him were nondescript. Two general supply shops, a hotel. An alley, then a blacksmith shop and the livery.

Undecided, he hesitated, then entered the hotel. A quick question to the deskman did not give him the answer he sought. He stepped back outside, walked to the next building, a supply shop. The couple who owned it had not seen a woman like the one he described. Where had she gone? Had he seen her at all? The weather and the Draigon sign had brought her close to his mind. After all these years, it still took so little to bring her to mind. A ripple on a pond. The sassy laugh of a bar maid. An old book. Was it any wonder, after what had happened at the river crossing that he should see her in every young woman who crossed his path?

It's this time of year, he thought. The way The Nest reminds you of the Spur Country. The heat and dust of the day. Draigon Weather. That was not Leiel. You lost her long ago. She's dead, Cleod.

Need choked him. A drink. A different life. The correct promise made and kept. Any of those would do. Too late for any but the drink, and that he would not allow himself, no matter the weather or the ghosts that stalked him in the heat.

58

Cleod

THE DRY WARMTH OF THE POIT ROOM PENETRATED CLEOD'S BATTERED MUSCLES as he eased back on the wooden bench and closed his eyes. Naked in the small, dark space, he tried to relax. He was glad for the familiar comfort of the poit. In the Spur, though water was usually plentiful, most homes did not have water baths. Instead, the tradition was to build thick-walled sheds with bench seats and cast iron wood stoves. High, dry heat was used to sweat the dirt from their bodies. Water was only for rinsing off. The advantage over tubs were many. The heat of the poit room soaked all the way through to the bones. Even on the coldest days, the comfort lingered. Sore muscles and old aches were eased, illnesses burned away. And sweet wood burned in the stoves brought to life memories of younger, simpler times. Poit sheds were the thing he missed most since leaving the Spur.

The fact that The Nest had one right off the back of the building, in the Inn's fenced garden, would have caused him to spend all his wages to stay even a single night in the place. But Lorrel and the inn staff took a quiet pride in having such a space to offer weary visitors. They never charged a huge fee for use of the poit. Since he had discovered The Nest nearly a decade before, it had always been his only choice for lodging in Melbis. The staff had come to know him well and so the little-used shed was always ready for him.

Savoring the heat as sweat began to bead over his body, he was glad for more than just himself that the Nest had a poit. If the drought continued, soon it would be the only way for any traveler in Melbis to get clean.

The ache in his hips and back began to ease, and he pressed his hand hard over the rippling scar that marred his right flank. The pressure shifted something deep inside, and he let out a sigh of relief as the muscles around the old wounds slowly released. One visit to the poit would see him clean. But it would take several more before he found true respite from the chronic discomfort of the old injuries.

The woman in the street. It was not possible that she could be Leiel, no matter how much she had reminded him of her. She had looked like Leiel—even walked like Leiel—but the Leiel of fifteen years ago. And that is how he knew what he had seen was not real. Between what had happened at the Seebo and how much The Nest reminded him of the Spur country, his mind had twisted a glimpse of a young woman who looked a little like Leiel into a vision of the person he wished most to see again. If Leiel was alive...no. He was younger than her by nearly a year, and the woman he had seen was not far past twenty. Whoever he had seen, he wished her well, and a better fate than the one that had befallen the woman she so resembled.

Old words, long pushed into the darkest part of memory rose up—Leiel's voice. Leiel's attempt to reach him... *You made a promise to slay Draigon, Cleod, and you are going to keep it. But there is no room, in doing that, for the little girl you made that promise to...*

The moisture running down his cheeks was more than sweat. They had been so young. And so much he thought he knew was wrong. There was more to the Ehlewer's secrecy than he had then suspected. And more he did not know about Leiel and her choice not to fight the Council's decision. Not to try to run. Not to help him save her.

And she had been right. He had chosen the wrong promise, all those years ago, and it cost him everything he had ever thought he wanted. And, in the end, he had failed to keep either one.

He rubbed his palms over his face, dragged them back through his wet hair, scrubbing away dirt and tears. *Shaa* was back. He knew it. Perhaps now it was time to at least keep one promise—for himself this time, and no one else. Just the thought of the Draigon still churned his gut. He was no longer Draighil in title, but he still had the knowledge. And he was wiser now, he hoped. Draigon Weather meant that, somewhere in Arnan, a Council would be meeting again. A woman's name would be presented—a young woman, strong and clever, as they always were. Another horror was about to be committed, another abomination of sacrifice that would end in the useless waste of a vital life. If he was not the man he had been, that was not at all a bad thing, not a disadvantage. Shaa was back. And, this time, he was not desperate. This time he had nothing to prove to anyone but himself. This time he had nothing to lose.

Fool. You are fifteen years the elder of the arrogant boy who faced the Red Draigon. You are broken. You are scarred, and you know the Draigon are more than simple beasts. What had she said to him all those years ago? *"This is not a children's tale, Cleod. You cannot stop what is going to happen, because you are not the writer of this story."*

"Leiel," he said aloud, and was surprised by his own voice. But he spoke again, quiet and unsteady in the dark safety of the poit. "Leiel, I am sorry. If you can hear me, forgive me. I was too much a man, as I knew then what a man was, to listen to you when it mattered."

Would he have done anything differently? Could he have? The truth whispered hard through him. No. But perhaps there was something he could do now, some way he could finish what he had failed. At least then, it might mean something.

59

Cleod

CLEOD CAME OUT OF MASHARUH TAVERN AND STOOD SCANNING THE STREET IN the late afternoon light. Fewer people were about now as the citizens of Melbis headed home for the day. Travelers still wandered between the taverns and inns, and a few carts clattered through the low angle light, but the town was quieting, enjoying one of the last calm nights before the arrival of the rest of the caravans and trade bands.

The public house at his back was the third one he had visited, and still no sign of Nae or Jordin. Every time Cleod entered one of the smoky establishments, the thick air and hoppy scent of the brews drew a line of pure longing from his gut to his throat. But he stayed away from the bar, avoided catching the eyes of the servers. Dangerous as it was for him to enter such places, it was in one of the drinking establishments or brothels where he would find the scouts. Nae wasn't a worry. He would stumble back to camp and climb grumbling onto his horse and ride sentry duty, cursing through the night. He was grouchy, but reliable.

Jordin, however...

"You! Ruhelrn! Swordsman. Cleod Ruhelrn."

Cleod closed his eyes and suppressed a groan. The voice was too familiar. With a sigh, he shook his head and turned to face the thin man striding toward him. "Wern Glassman. What are you doing away from Camp? Kilras has not authorized merchant travel into the city yet."

The man waved a dismissive hand through the air between them. It was unusual that Cleod met anyone with his height, but when the trader stopped short, his nose just inches from Cleod's, they were eye to eye. "Whatever he thinks his rules are on the trail, I am now arrived at my destination. My time is my own. What is the point in waiting around for the morning to enter the city? I am in need of a meal not made from rat-tled-about beans. You appear to have enjoyed such. Why should I, who pay your salary, not have the same privilege?"

The muscles along Cleod's jaw tightened, but he managed a smile de-spite the colorful series of retorts that rolled through his mind. The shock would be Wern's when the glass trader returned to the caravan camp and found his wagon, and all its goods, parked outside the perimeter. If Wern was foolish enough to have declared himself above Kilras's rules, he would be surprised, as well, to find that he had accidentally declared himself no longer in need of the Dorn's protection.

"Are you in need of something?" Cleod asked. He was tempted to take the half step that would bring his nose in contact with the glassman's.

"Did I not call your name?"

Cleod waited.

"Clearly, I am in need of assistance."

With effort, Cleod stopped the smirk that begged to twitch across his lips. "Clearly."

"Where is the Trademaster's Office?"

The Trademaster? At this hour? How in the name of the old gods had Wern managed to become as successful as his reputation said he was? He must have skilled accountants, and his usual caravan runners must be smooth and personable, because Wern was as charismatic as a lump of dung.

A memory flickered, and for an instant, he had an image of a fluffed tail sprouting from the tall merchant's backside. Leiel. The woman in the street had brought her close in his mind, both the hard memories and the best ones. She would have laughed in the face of this man's indignant de-mands.

"That office is on the street behind this one. To the north. It's the white-washed building beside the jailhouse. Though there's likely no one there at this hour."

Wern snorted and stepped back as though offended. "What kind of city is this? By the jail? What tradesman wants to conduct his business in the midst of a horde of criminals?" He paused. "No one there?"

"Unlikely to be."

"They call this a trading city? What respectable trade office closes before moonrise? I'll have words for the lout who runs such a lax station."

"You would be wise to remember where you *aren't*, Glassman," Cleod said with a shake of his head. "Kittown is weeks behind you. Melbis has its own laws. Some aren't even written. But *don't insult the locals* would be at the top."

"Pffha!" The sound that escaped the trader held more scorn than Cleod would have thought possible. "When the locals need lessons in proper deportment of business, I'll insult them as needed. If you will, Ruhelrn, I must see to this matter. I will do them the honor of letting them correct their errors."

Stepping aside to avoid being walked over, Cleod watched the merchant stalk away, his long legs carrying him crisply down the boardwalk, the wood clacking under his boots.

Honor was it? What did Wern Glassman know of that?

"Least he didn't ask you along with him," a voice said at his back.

Cleod glanced over his shoulder at Nae where the old man stood in the tavern's doorway. "How long have you been lurking there?"

"Wasn't lurking," the old man said, then yawned as he peeled himself out of the doorway and came to join Cleod. "Was taking care to not be found by that one."

"Nae, you have moments of wisdom." Cleod shook his head. "I'd rather face another Draigon than work with that man after this trip."

"This weather holds, you'll get your chance at that."

Cleod smiled, but something prickled his spine. He might. Had that very thought not wound through him earlier? It had been flitting across his mind since he had seen the tracks at the Seebo. "I might at that." He realized the words had been spoken aloud. "Where's Jordin?"

Nae shrugged. "Dorein's place. Found him a runaway Farlan girl. Seems she thinks she's having an adventure working that place. Pasty thing. But Jordin's not picky."

"Go back. I'll bring him."

Nae sighed.

"Draigon-damned guard duty," he mumbled as he turned toward the livery.

Cleod watched him go, then shook his head. Kilras's team was a source of both frustration and fascination, even after all these years. And Jordin had chosen Dorein's for his assignation. Well, the man had taste, for all his failings. Dorein's women were smart, and clean, and well trained in their profession. There was, however, a minimum charge that far exceeded that of other establishments. Jordin would be unhappy to be reminded of his duties if he had not yet satisfied himself in line with that financial outlay. Cleod laughed a little. That was the price of having more lust than sense.

He stepped down into the street and started for the row of bordellos that lined three streets to the east. He had not taken a dozen steps when he felt it again, the rising tingle over his shoulder blades that had haunted his senses since they had ridden away from the Seebo. He didn't break stride, but a flicker deep in his mind warned that his awareness sought to take flight, seek the strange presence. With effort, he fought it down. Gweld here in the street was an impossible prospect—too dangerous for him and everyone around him.

A curse slid out under his breath. Glancing over his shoulder, he flashed his gaze across the upper windows of the buildings behind him. No sign of anyone. There wouldn't be. Anyone who could hide on the open plains, could certainly avoid detection in a city.

It came again, the feeling that what surveilled him was not unfamiliar, and he stopped at the edge of the street, closed his eyes. His breath pressed in and out, forcing back the need to *know*. He held still, and will prevailed. When he opened his eyes, the sense of being watched was gone.

His shoulders relaxed from a tension he had not realized had knotted them. "Stay gone," he said into the dimming light. "I have neither the patience nor the desire to play your games."

The expected sounds of the town settling in for the night were his only reply—a bark of laughter from the tavern behind him, the creak of cart wheels and the rattle of tack, footsteps on the boardwalk of the main street, the low chatter of patrons and citizens making their way through the streets. He stood a moment longer, listening, then continued toward Dorein's. Jordin had better have his pants handy or Cleod would haul him back to camp naked.

60

Cleod

Jordin's curses had faded to unintelligible mumbling by the time Cleod rode into the camp leading the scout's mare, her rider not in his usual place, but trussed and slung over her saddle like a sack of grain.

Kilras yanked the last tarp tie-down across the wagon and eyed the scouts' arrival across the back of the cart. His expression held no surprise. "Nae said you might be a bit late getting back."

A grunt was Cleod's reply as he swung down from Kicce. "As you well knew."

Kilras grinned. "Where was this one?"

"Dorein's."

"Ahh. I'm surprised you didn't need to use more rope."

Cleod shook his head. "If I had, it would have been to drag him behind that horse instead of letting her carry him."

Kilras folded his arms across the top of the wagon cargo and looked at Cleod, his eyes narrowing a little. "Something's brought you back in a foul mood. The poit wasn't hot enough?"

Flipping Kicce's reins over the top board of the wagon back, Cleod sighed. "Whoever has been watching us is in Melbis."

Kilras straightened. "You saw someone?"

"No. Felt it. The same as on the trail."

"When?"

"After I sent Nae back."

"You're sure it wasn't Wern's icy stare?" Kilras asked.

Cleod let out a short laugh. Of course, Nae would have recounted that encounter as well. Despite the dark mood that had settled over him since he had felt the strange presence in town, a smile twitched his lips as well.

"Not completely."

Kilras chuckled.

"You plan to leave his goods back there?" Cleod tipped his head toward the dusty wagon standing by itself a few hundred paces beyond the perimeter.

"I am," Kilras said, his tone thoughtful. "The man can pay to store it, and his goods, in the city warehouses for the rest of the festival. I've collected payment, so he's free to find his own way from here as he chooses."

Cleod's smiled flashed to its full brilliance. "I am certain he'll come to appreciate that freedom."

Kilras nodded, his gaze still on Cleod. "What else?"

Cleod sighed. What to say to that? That he had seen a ghost? That a glimpse of a stranger in the street had spiraled his thoughts into darkness? That the stone walls of The Nest and the warmth of the poit had only deepened the memories that gnawed at his mind like woodchits? "A woman," he said at last.

"At Dorein's?"

That brought a brief smile, but Cleod shook his head. "No. In the street. When I was signing in at The Nest. I would have believed she was Leiel Sower, if believing such were not an indication of insanity."

"Looked that much like her?" Kilras came around the wagon and leaned back against it beside Cleod.

"Like the girl I knew. Like she looked when—like the last time I saw her."

"Did you speak to her?"

Cleod shook his head. "She disappeared in the crowd on the street."

Kilras was silent a moment. "That woman is part of you, Cleod. After the Seebo—it's not surprising she's on your mind. A young woman who looks like her—not impossible here in Melbis. Travelers from half of Arnan are arriving here. Someone from the Spur—similar clothes—this weather—suddenly your ghost walks."

"All true." Cleod met Kilras's gaze. "But I don't feel better for all that."

A groan came from the man draped across the mare behind Kicce. It was followed by a loud volley of colorful phrases that knocked the tension from the air with their creativity.

Cleod laughed, and Kilras snorted in amusement beside him. "Might be time to untie him."

"You want the honors?" Cleod asked. He ducked beneath Kicce's neck to catch the bridle of Jordin's skittish mare as she sidestepped under the squirming weight of her trussed up burden.

"All yours," Kilras said. "Get him upright and on patrol. Rimm, Sehina, and I will relieve you at moonset."

"Much appreciated," Cleod scoffed as he tugged loose the knot that held Jordin to the saddle. A shove sent the other man flopping over the side of the mare with a startled shout. He yelped as he hit the ground.

"Contain your grumbling," Cleod said. "Puke somewhere and get to work. There's a watch to be kept."

A fading laugh in the darkness marked Kilras's approval as the Dorn left them. Cleod shook his head at Jordin's fumbling attempts to right himself, but did not assist. If the man could not find his feet, he would not be trusted with the watch. And if that was the case, this day would count as the only round of pleasure Jordin would experience this trip to Melbis. It seemed the scout remembered that, too, because he finally swayed upright, glaring at Cleod.

"Rules and duty," he said with a snarl and leaned his shoulder hard into his mare. She snorted in indignation and tossed her head.

"Be glad I bothered to drag you back." Cleod gathered Kicce's reins and swung onto the big grey. "You've ten minutes to gather your gear. I'll meet you at the cook wagon." He turned the gelding and left Jordin trying to figure out how to get a foot into his stirrup.

Around Cleod, the low noise of the caravan camp was comfortingly familiar. Normal. Homey. The life he had built within the pattern of the sounds was satisfying and secure. The memories and gut instincts that had tugged at him through these last weeks threatened to disrupt that. He could not have that. He would not. The cost was too great.

Hot and brittle, night stretched over the plains, and if the watch ahead loomed longer than usual, that was not a bad thing. It was time to think. Time to settle. Time to breathe.

Still, as Kicce carried him through the deepening twilight, the dry air held the memory of hot wind pushed by Draigon wings, and the roaring of a world on fire. Something was out there. And something stirred, no longer quiet within him.

He drew a deep breath, let it out, and for a moment let himself believe he was ready for whatever was coming.

Thanks for reading *Draigon Weather*. It was an adventure to write, and hopefully to read. If you have come to care about Leiel and Cleod, have no fear, the story will continue. See you in the next volume!

The Adventure Continues...

Book Two of **The Legacies of Arnan**

Coming Soon from PROSPECTIVE PRESS

GLOSSARY

Term	Definition
Adfen	The major city of the Spur region.
Afonaedor	Land of the snaking river.
Annaluft Rayyat	The Great Desert in southwest Arnan.
Ardrows Dur	Western Ocean, also called Across Water.
Bajor	The major trading port on the west coast of Arnan. Western end of the trade roads. Largest city in Ceardedur.
Blayth Hound	Wild dogs not native to Spur region, trained for guard dogs/attack dogs.
Brekko	Face cover made by the desert traders designed to keep out dust and debris in desert wind.
Brenenti	Central region of Arnan, where the capitol city, Sibora, is located.
Bynkrol	Draighil Enclave located near Bajor. One of two remaining, fully active, Draighil training sites.
Ceardedur	Western region north of Annaluft Rayyat and south of Gwinlad. Know among traders as "The long walk to water."
Cefreid	Farlan term for someone not of Farlan descent.
Clumnis	Small island near shore of southwest coast.
Clyfsirth	Coastal town at the western end of the southern trade road.
Crosswell	Town on far southern trade road, located at river crossing.
Crubanis	Island east of Hernis, known as Turtle Island.
Cruwigros	Land of low, wet walking. Marshland region in northeast Arnan.
Cuila	Vision herb that allows Gweld state to be managed. Used early in Draighil training.
Dehir Dur	South ocean, also called Long South Water.
Dinist	Draighil Enclave located between Inris and Giddor, destroyed, and no longer active.

Diflan	Draighil Enclave north of Oryok, abandoned, and no longer active.
Dolencul Dur	Southern strait known for dangerous tides and currents.
Dorn	The trail lead of a merchant caravan.
Draigfen	Draigon Touched Woman. A woman who has been influenced by a Draigon.
Draighil	Draigon slayer trained by the Enclaves.
Draigon	Gigantic flying creature to which the Farlan Sacrifice women to counteract Draigon Weather.
Draigon Weather	Extreme drought conditions caused by the presence of Draigon.
Draigre	Candidate for the position of Draighil.
Drearloc	Carnivorous insects that travel in large groups underground, and emerge to devours any animals above ground. Travel in large groups.
Ehlewer	Draighil Enclave located in The Spur—One of the two remaining, fully active Enclaves in charge of training Draighil.
Enclave	Farlan organizations in charge of training Draighil.
Eroganke	One of the two gods worshiped by the Sanctuary priests—"The God of Belief."
Ercew	Strong alcoholic beverage that is highly addictive.
Farlan	Descendant of the Far Landers.
Fen	Fennar word for woman.
Fennar	The language of the old people of Arnan .
Gernis	Island east of Giddor, very near the coast.
Giddor	Port city on the South-Southeast Coast, major city of Plynduirn region.
Glasvetal	Central grasslands.
Gweld	Trance state allowing expansion of senses, and hyper-natural physical and mental response. Also, allows limited connection of multiple consciousnesses and projection of illusions.

Gwindor	The major city of the Gwinlad region. Accessed mostly by water.
Gwinlad	Wine region.
Hernis	Long island south of Giddor and Gernis.
Hlewlion	Mountain cat, cunning and very dangerous.
Ilris	Southern city south of Melbis.
Kee's Ferry	Ferry crossing and riverport.
Kittown	Town located in Ceardedur. Known for its glass artisans.
Lesuthcwithnis	Large island off southwest coast of Arnan. Sometimes called Left Boot Isle.
Longshore	Fishing village on the south shore of Hernis.
Nearshore	Fishing village on north shore if Gernis.
Northship	Small shipping port and fishing town north of Bajor. Established by the Farlan.
Nys	Draighil Enclave located on Tahnis. Abandoned due to volcanic activity, no longer active.
Orlis	Large town in far northeastern Arnan, the Cruwigros region.
Oryok	A major east coast trade city located in Afonaedor. Eastern end of the trade roads.
Overlash	The physical and psychological backlash that comes as the aftermath of using the Gweld state.
Plynduirn	Eastern plains region.
Poit	Steam-based bathing chamber similar to a wood-fired, dry sauna.
Ruhelrn	The Lead Sword of a Caravan.
Seebo Ferry	Ferry crossing of the Seebo River, located on the trade road west of Melbis.
Sibora	Capital of the Land of Arnan in the Brenenti region. Location of the Palace of the King. Central City known for arts and wine and fine food and drink. The largest city in Arnan. Known also for fine Inns, spas, and Memorial Garden.

Sowd	Fishing village on the east shore of Lesuthcwithnis.
Tahnis	Island of southwest coast. Known as the Fire Isle for its active volcano. No longer inhabited.
Trachwant	One of the two gods worshiped by the Sanctuary priests—"The God of Desires."
Waymete	Crossroads town on the far southern trade road.
Wedill	Draighil Enclave located in the mountains near Orlis. Only a few Draighil trainers remain. Mostly used as an archive site.
Wyntoc Dur	Eastern ocean, known for strong, gusting winds near shore.

About the Author

Raised in Maine, Paige L. Christie became obsessed with books after falling in love with the movie, *The Black Stallion*. When her mother presented her with a copy of the book the movie was based on, worlds opened up. It had never occurred to Paige that there was more to a story than what a movie showed. Imagine her joy at learning that novels had more to say than movies.

What followed was a revelation that stories could not only be read, but *written*. This led to decades filling notebooks with stories.

Two random Degrees later (in English and in Web Technology), the gentle prodding of a friend urged Paige into an experiment that broke loose Paige's writing in completed-novel-form for the first time. (No she was not bitten by a radioactive anything.)

Along the road to authorship, Paige had adventures in everything from weatherstick making to cross-country ski racing, white water raft guiding, wedding photography, website design, and the dreaded 'retail'. (Lots and lots and lots of retail.)

Her current obsessions include the study of Middle Eastern and North African folk dances, costume design, and dreaming up new ways to torture...err...*explore* her characters.

Paige resides in the mountains of North Carolina where she runs a small art gallery and wine shop. She spends her evenings writing speculative fiction, walking her dog, and being ignored by her herd of 3-legged cats.

A believer in the power of words, Paige tries to tell stories that are both entertaining and thoughtful. She enjoys stories with intense impact, and strives in her writing to evoke an emotional response in her readers. Especially of interest are tales that speak to women, and open a space where adventure and fantasy are not all about romance and happy endings.

CPSIA information can be obtained
at www.ICGtesting.com
Printed in the USA
BVOW04*2250150517
483691BV00003B/3/P